Mary

PIPER

by

John E. Keegan

For Mary, I remember signing your HN yearbook — in a circle. We've been friends so long. Love, John

THE PERMANENT PRESS
SAG HARBOR, NY 11963

Library of Congress Cataloging-in-Publication Data

Keegan, John E.
　　Piper: a novel / by John E Keegan.
　　　　p.　cm.
　　ISBN　1-57962-029-9
　　1. Teenage girls--Fiction. 2. Fathers and daughters--Fiction.
　　3. Loss (Psychology)--Fiction I.4. Mothers--Death. 5.
　　Grandfathers--Fiction.　Title.

　　PS3561.E3374P562001
　　813'.54--dc21　　　　　　　　　　　　　　00-064248
　　　　　　　　　　　　　　　　　　　　　　　　CIP

THE PERMANENT PRESS
4170 Noyac Road
Sag Harbor, NY 11963

For you, Macaela and Shanti.

———————

In memory of a writer and a gentle man,
Jack Landwehr, 1929-1999.

I thank the people who helped me write and publish this story, especially Carla Carlstrom, David, Mike, Pat, and Mark Keegan, Sharon "Moxie" Langus, Neil McCluskey, Judith and Marty Shepard, Julie Weston, and Bruce Wexler.

ALSO BY JOHN E. KEEGAN

Clearwater Summer

So this is what I set out to do, to adopt all of you. Because Baudelaire told me a long time ago that in each one of us there is a man, a woman, and a child — and the child is always in trouble.

Anais Nin

1

THE NIGHT OF MY first period I remembered sitting with Mom on the back porch steps. The sun was flaming out behind the garage and we were admiring the bamboo teepees of snap beans and the pink-veined patches of rhubarb in her garden. Her hands were caked with dirt from weeding the beds and I could smell the guano. I was waiting for the big sex talk, but instead she told me about the journey.

"You're just starting it, Piper." She took my hands between hers and I could feel the crust of the loam crumbling between our fingers as she pressed me. "You're going to sprout wings and dazzle some man with your wizardry." There was a glisten of tears in her eyes and the prospect of it all frankly overwhelmed me, but she laughed. "Don't worry. You'll be bathed in light like Aphrodite."

At the time, I didn't have the presence of mind to ask her the details of her own journey. She'd told me about meeting Dad and how he'd fawned over her and coddled her back to health in Chicago when he was at Loyola and she was in art school. They eventually married and moved to Stampede, a small town north of Seattle where Dad ran the newspaper owned by John Carlisle. Mom mainly did her art, but she probably kept up with as much of the goings on in Stampede as Dad did cooped up in the offices of the *Herald*.

I couldn't tell if she disliked Stampede or it just amused her. "The Cold War's over and people here are still building air raid shelters," she told me once. "We're in a time warp, honey."

She wasn't just my mom, she was my sail, the source of my energy. She pushed me as I slouched through the awkwardness of high school. Then the summer before my senior year her hair became enmeshed in the drain of the Jacuzzi at John Carlisle's house and held her under until she'd drowned.

I was devastated. I wished I'd never been born. The bottom had fallen out of all those mother and daughter intimacies. But I refused to believe what everyone else was thinking about her.

I was home alone when the call came from the hospital. The fact it wasn't Dad who'd called should have been a warning. I'd just seen her that morning dancing around barefoot in one of his old dress shirts, watering the house plants with the pink plastic can while I ate my granola. She often danced with herself. Sometimes she'd put on a flowing skirt just to feel it swish and move with her to the salsa and tango music on the CD player.

Dad was in a small crowd outside the double doors that led to the emergency room. Father Tombari, our pastor, was propping him up on one side and John Carlisle paced the floor nearby in a sport jacket and red vest chewing his fingernails.

"What happened?" I asked.

John Carlisle put his hand on my shoulder, and I was glad for his company. He was the closest thing Stampede had to a redeemer. His family had always been generous with its money. I knew the doctors wouldn't screw up if a Carlisle was watching. People in green gowns were going in and out of the swinging doors and each time the doors opened I tried to see inside.

Dad's thick eyelashes were matted with tears. When he tried to say something, his face contorted in the shapes of sounds, nothing coming out. I tried to wrap my arms around him, but touching him only made it worse as he shuddered and hid his face. I was petrified. I'd never seen him so inconsolable. A dull roar was building from somewhere deep inside my head and my eyes were going blurry.

When I started for the double doors, Carlisle grabbed me. "You can't go in!"

I fought to pull my arms free and became entangled in his pukka shell necklace, which broke and fell to the floor. His stomach was soft and his breath potatoish. I was standing on the toes of his boots, trying to gain some leverage. At the time, I didn't even know it had happened at his house.

Dad finally pulled me off. "She's gone, Piper."

The fact he didn't say *dead* left room for hope, but my body must have known otherwise because it went limp. I was empty. I wanted to gorge myself on all the things I still didn't know about her. She'd never refused me anything, but it never felt as if she needed me the way I needed her. I'd always tried to impress her by being as self-sufficient and engaged as she was, hoping she'd invite me along to share more, but because I was adopted I'd never felt qualified to press her. She told me when I was five, before I started school and someone else did. "Don't worry," she said. "Lots of famous people are adopted."

From then on, I'd imagined myself as an orphaned piece of driftwood that looked intriguing on the beach, but never quite fit in with anything at home. And part of me was afraid to find out more about Mom. There was a veil over part of her life, the mystery that gave her strength.

The days that followed were a blur, interrupted by the jangle in my memory of John Carlisle in his red vest and the Frye boots with the Carlisle medallion, hovering beside us like some mockery of the Grim Reaper. People came by the house to mumble their respects — staff from the newspaper, merchants, members of the city council, teachers, policemen, service station attendants in their uniforms. Grandpa Willard, Mom's father, joined us in the living room where we sat around and talked about everything except how it had happened. They scrupulously avoided the details in my presence. It was some kind of *accident*.

"Don't upset your dad by asking about it," they said.

While I was in the bathroom off the kitchen, I heard someone say, "At least Kathryn wasn't her real mother," as if that somehow made it easier.

I had to read the Friday *Herald Stampede* to find out what had really happened, a front-page story under my dad's byline with the understated headline "Citizens Mourn Death of Local." I fell into our sagging sofa, shaking my head in disbelief. Dad had published in ten-pitch font what nobody could tell me in person. He must have written it the day after she died and I was dumbfounded at how he could have managed the equilibrium, the dispassion, the sanity to organize this catastrophe into grammatically correct paragraphs.

"Her hobbies included popular music and art," the article said, not mentioning the fact that one of her paintings had hung in a Santa Fe gallery next to Georgia O'Keeffe's. I couldn't help but think Mom would have been disappointed. How many people got up at dawn to paint the four seasons of the sunrise or stopped strangers on the street to snap close-up photos of their faces or dragged portable generators into construction sites and abandoned buildings at night to run strobe lights for photos that she could paint from and called it a hobby? Dad had sublimated his anger into an indictment of the recreational tub industry, railing against their failure to require double drains and automatic shutoffs. He'd obviously done his research.

There was only one paragraph in the story that cut through all the formalities:

> Kathryn Scanlon drowned when her hair became enmeshed in the drain of the Jacuzzi at the residence of John Carlisle. The force was powerful enough to hold her in place until it had picked her body of its last breath. "Pulled an eyeball right out of its socket," the sheriff's report said. "Judging from the patches of hair ripped out by the roots, she didn't give up without a struggle."

Each time I read it I found myself holding my breath and I had to close my eyes and turn away from the article to breathe again.

There was no indication of who was present and no quote from John Carlisle. The answers were hidden by the veil.

Dad retreated into his journalistic tent after her death, spending inordinately long hours at the paper, but I couldn't really blame him. After all, he was the one who had to be most hurt and double-crossed by the whole thing. While John Carlisle was off studying dance at the Sorbonne, Dad had nursemaided the *Herald* into one of the best small town papers on the west coast.

I remembered how Dad and Mom used to write notes for each other, his words, her sketches, in a hardbound journal with a cord marker they left on the kitchen counter. Dad's notes were sometimes accompanied by a single tulip. Although the frequency of the notes eventually tailed off, Dad had taken her to Seattle for a Rolling Stones concert only last year, and they stayed overnight at the Sorrento Hotel and Mom said they breakfasted in bed even though it was the day before printing.

I suppose I should have blamed Mom as much as John Carlisle for what had happened. They were both adults. She didn't have to be there. But I couldn't blame her any more than I could blame Dad, which left Carlisle.

I grew increasingly angry and wanted Dad to get mad with me, to tear apart that pretentious, nebbish of a man, but Dad never publicly uttered a harsh word against him. I suspected he was holding back because John Carlisle was his boss and, as sorry as I was to admit it, Dad's image as the scrappy, incorrigible editor of the town's paper suffered in my heart as a result.

I knew the very room in which it had happened, the greenhouse where John Carlisle's mother used to grow orchids and tropical plants. He had converted it into a spa or bagnio or whatever else it was he called it the night our family had dinner with him to celebrate his fortieth birthday.

"I'm afraid we didn't bring suits," Dad said when Carlisle asked us to take a tub with him, and I cheered Dad under my breath.

"No problem," Carlisle said, and he walked over to an antique wardrobe and snapped open the doors. On hooks like tie racks there was a selection of men's and women's bathing suits: Speedos, boxers, bikinis, one-piecers.

"Come on, Tom, it'll be good for you," Mom said. "Piper, you too."

Much to Mom's dismay, I left the room while the three of them had their tub. It wasn't out of any forethought of the impending doom or even to scrag John Carlisle. I just didn't want anyone to see me in a bathing suit.

Mom was such a believer in the peaceful resolution of conflict that it wasn't fair she'd be confronted in the end with a violent adversary. It was more probable that her death would have come from a poisonous mushroom she'd picked on one of her painting jaunts, overexposure to the sun, or sheer grief at the indifference of the world to true, unmanufactured beauty.

I had to admit I was proud she'd fought back when the Jacuzzi was trying to pull her through the drain. And I could only hope that somewhere in the pandemonium she realized how much I wanted her to survive.

Mom's father, Willard Cooper, was part of the reason Mom had stood out. Everyone in Stampede knew Willard. And why not? He'd probably once or twice put up their storm windows, climbed a ladder and cleaned the pine needles out of their rain gutters, or slid under their cars to drain oil from the pan. He was a fixer. Widowed for more than a decade, Willard just wanted something to take care of. If there was a bad storm, he was the one who'd show up on your porch with candles and a flashlight. Near Veterans Day, he'd never turn down an invitation to visit the grade schools in a sailor suit that still fit and tell about the war in the Pacific. Inevitably, his war stories would snowball into stories about his cutting asparagus and picking peas in the Yakima Valley and the knife fights over whose turn it was to drive the truck instead of hump the crates.

It seemed as if everything Grandpa Willard attempted turned into a hullabaloo, including the burial of his only child. Dad and I stood with him between us that day next to

Mom's casket, which was suspended over the hole by a series of green web straps. Willard sobbed uncontrollably while Father Tombari walked around the hole rocking the incense burner on its chain. Dad had pulled some strings to make sure Mom received a Catholic burial, even though the baptism in the emergency room was technically too late. She was a Cooper and the Coopers were Protestant, bordering on agnostic. Willard never went to church, wore whatever he wanted to wear, and voted for any Libertarian who made it on the ballot. I pushed in against Willard to support him and I could feel Dad pushing back from the other side. It was a warm day and a few people brought along umbrellas, some wore sunglasses, and older ladies fanned themselves with programs from the church services. The combination of death and heat must have been too much for Willard because when people walked over and dropped their boutonnieres and rosaries on top of the casket, he bent over to kiss the casket right about where Mom's lips would have been, slipped on the plastic ground cover, and rolled down into the hole like an out of control window shade.

People screamed. The casket rocked on its webbing, and I thought it was going to plummet down on top of him. Father Tombari, who was so self-assured reciting his prayers, became helpless and gathered his vestments around his legs. Dad and I bent over and peered down into the hole, but it was so bright above ground that my pupils couldn't dilate wide enough to see anything.

I knew this was going to turn out to be another Willard story. People still talked about the time he'd broken up Grandma Carol's marriage to another man by firing a shotgun into the ceiling of a Lutheran Church over in the Okanogan Valley. The strategy worked because they locked up Willard, and Grandma Carol broke off the engagement and later married him. When she was in the hospital dying of emphysema he snuck in at night and got into bed with her under the oxygen tent. Willard had trouble with wrong endings.

The Coopers moved to Stampede after World War II, and Willard took over the Phillips 66 station that was later razed and never rebuilt. To Willard's regret, the site was now packed with rows of scrap metal, used rain gutters, towing chains, steel rods, rowboat bottoms, all inside a fence with a hand-painted sign that said "NX + MFT = LSD." Whoever ran it was never there.

"I don't know whether it's an outdoor hardware store or an indoor wrecking yard," Willard said.

It wasn't the big things as much as the little things that drew attention to Willard. He once showed up for a musical tribute to Rodgers and Hammerstein at school in a Scottish plaid sportcoat and a pair of Vaudevillian blue-and-white striped pants with a big safety pin to hold the fly shut. Mom said his dress had deteriorated after Grandma Carol's death when he started buying his clothes at garage sales. Stampede was small enough that people recognized the clothes on Willard by their former owners.

The funeral director and the maintenance man at the cemetery finally had to take Mom's casket off the webbing and slide the support apparatus out from over the hole. With the help of a stepladder they managed to rescue diminutive Willard. There was a knob on his forehead, his tongue was cut where his teeth had clamped together when the chrome caught his chin, and the baggy navy blue suit that used to belong to the president of the local savings bank was dabbed with mud. But Willard was conscious and climbed the ladder on his own, mumbling something about the darn flowers.

Dad was the first person to him, grabbing him by one of his padded shoulders. "You stay right here with me," he said, and I thought I heard him add, "you old coot."

Willard just stood there at parade rest, licking his wounds for the remainder of the ceremony, while Father Tombari re-blessed the casket.

She died on August twenty-seventh, so I had about a week to decide whether to run away or go back to school. I dreaded going to school. There had always been this under-current of curiosity about my mother because she painted nudes and played billiards at the Comet and didn't make layer cakes for the bake sales. I had to admit she'd been a source of anxiety growing up, like when I found out she'd raised her hand at parents' night to ask whether the school was going to make condoms available for the students. But she always defended me. When I refused to wear gym shorts for PE and the school sent a note home, she called the principal and interrupted his dinner.

"Are you running a school or a chorus line?" she said. "You tell them to practice abstinence, then you make them run around half naked in PE. My daughter will undress when and for whom she chooses."

I never knew what she'd say or what she wouldn't do that would put me out of synch with everyone else. And in Stampede, kids were held responsible for the behavior of their parents.

The first night Dad worked late at the paper after the funeral I dug the barber set out of the linen closet and stationed myself in front of Mom's dresser mirror. I'd once let my hair grow to the bottom of my shoulder blades like Mom's, but unlike hers, mine was dry and without sheen. I plugged in the clippers, stripped off the comb attachment, and tested it on my forearm. The vibration warmed my skin as I skidded it from wrist to elbow, the teeth of the blades accumulating curlicues of fuzz that fell into my lap. I pressed harder on the second swipe, creating a furless rectangle. I held the clippers against my cheek and just let it run. The buzz made me drowsy. Then I turned it around so that the blades were pointing straight at me and put it on the center of my forehead. *One thousand, two thousand, three thousand . . . .*

With my eyes closed, I mowed the clippers over the top of my skull and listened to the motor as it dumped the first strip down the back of my neck. My hair was kinky if I didn't wash it and it felt good to see it fall in clumps onto the floor around me. Separated from my head the hair looked lighter, almost blonde instead of walrus brown. I felt the places I'd missed with my hand and kept buzzing my scalp until the clippers were too hot to hold. Then I went into the upstairs bathroom and found one of Mom's plastic razors in the soapdish next to the tub, lathered my head with suds, and scraped myself with the razor until I was as smooth as a wet peach.

When I had wiped off with a bath towel, I stood in front of the mirror again. The skin where hair used to be was pale, with a tinge of green. My forehead was a huge expanse of wasted space that made the scrunching together of my eyes, nose, and mouth seem like bad planning. There were blue veins over my eyebrows with pathways that ran up the skull that I noticed for the first time. When I opened and closed my mouth, the jawbones moved enormous muscles underneath the temples. I looked like a monkey, but I couldn't just do nothing. I had to offer some protest. Besides, I'd become obsessed with the idea that I was also going to die by my hair, catch it on fire, entangle it in the press at the paper, or somebody was going to just tie a hank of it to their bumper and drag me around until they wore the skin off me. Almost as if I was afraid of what I'd done, I swept up the hair on the floor with the sides of my hands as best I could, stuffed it into a leftover lunch sack, and hid it in my dresser.

"You look like a skinhead," Dad told me next morning, which I knew from his moral compass was the wrong direction to go. That night, he called me downstairs and I could tell by the narrow set of his eyes that something was wrong. "I'm taking you to see Father Tombari," he said.

"I'm fine, Dad. Some people are doing tattoos and rings in their lips. It's just a kid thing."

For the next several nights, I could hear his footsteps on the stairs and see his shoes darken the crack under my door as he checked up on me, which I obliged by taking long audible breaths until the full length of the crack lit up again.

Dad was the one we had to worry about. Besides his longer hours at the paper, he'd taken to fixing himself a drink when he came home — gin, vermouth, and marinated onions. He didn't even measure the ingredients, just glugged them into a glass, and swigged them down. Nor was his drinking confined to the house. One night a police car pulled up and two policemen practically had to drag him up the sidewalk to the front door. Next day I found out he'd gotten into a fistfight at the Comet Tavern when someone asked him if it was easier to keep track of his wife's whereabouts now.

Some days he seemed to revere her memory, like the night I heard rustling in the attic and found him sitting on the floor in his underpants and socks surrounded by rows of family photos. One morning I came down for breakfast and he was out back stoking a fire in the barbecue grill that turned out to be Mom's brushes and oils. Later, I noticed he'd hauled one of her unfinished canvasses out of the attic and hung it in their bedroom. He put paintings up and took them down, sometimes both on the same day.

I couldn't blame him for wanting to stay away from the house. Every room was marked by her absence — the candle chandelier over the dining room table, the bean bag chairs in the living room she'd saved from college, the unframed canvas over my bed of the wobbly fawn in the long corridor I'd chosen as my own while she was still alive. Dozens more unsold paintings leaned like dominoes against available walls throughout the house.

I didn't know if it would help more to talk with Dad about her or to totally ignore the subject. I thought we should be making visits to her gravesite, kneeling and wailing together on her stone, but as far as I knew Dad hadn't gone out there since we buried her. He certainly hadn't volunteered her name in a conversation, which was unnatural because it was obvious she was the main thing on his mind.

Through notes I'd left on his bathroom sink, I tried to plan meals together and then he'd come home late and I'd eat alone anyway. He was always at the newspaper or a city council meeting or school board and I was usually in my room reading. "The best stories never break on day shift," he told me. I wanted to scream at him for acting as if nothing had happened, but what was the use? We were practically strangers to each other and, without Mom, we'd lost our broker.

You'd have thought I had bird shit on my head the way everyone stared at me the first day back at school. I wanted to interpret their silence as respect for the dead, thinking they couldn't criticize me without criticizing her. Even though Dad's newspaper article had finessed around the deeper implications of the story, the sheer horror of how she'd died had rocked everyone back on their heels. For some, the drowning had made her a martyr. The grace period at school, however, was short-lived. Behind locker doors and in the cafeteria line the grapevine bristled with thorns.

"She had hinges on her heels," someone said.

Condon Bagmore at least had the temerity to speak to my face. He was the kid who'd lost an older brother when his chute didn't open while skydiving at Harvey Field. He was one of the people I'd thought of when Mom died. I couldn't ever look at Condon Bagmore without thinking of how his brother had died, but rather than soften him the loss had made him bitter. I'd always been attracted to Condon in grade school, and not just because of the wavy Adonis locks that slipped over his forehead like honeysuckle. He had a rawness that refused to be haltered.

I was on my way to sociology class and the crowd around Bagmore was blocking my path. There was always a crowd around him, the kids whose lot in life was to inherit his cliches and hand-me-down girlfriends.

"Hey, Scanlon, come here," he said, leaning against the lockers, glancing behind as if pretending to make sure no one would hear him. He looked down at his crotch and my eyes couldn't help but follow his. There was a noticeable bulge in his pants that I figured had to be ping-pong balls to enhance what nature had probably cheated him of. He cupped himself to adjust things. "The hair's gotta come back, kid." His boys tittered.

"Why's that, Bagmore?"

He looked around again to make sure everyone was listening. "'Cause swear to God, it's the only way anyone's gonna know you're a dame."

You, nonstarter, I thought. He put his fists against his chest where a woman's breasts would be, and his boys tittered again. I couldn't help myself. I kneed him in the ping-pong balls and watched him buckle over in disbelief. I knew I wasn't really being fair because even Bagmore wasn't going to hit a girl in public, but I couldn't have cared less. As I walked away, I asked myself what Mom would have done and, of course, the question was ridiculous from the get-go because nobody would have questioned her sexuality. Me, I was gangly, undernourished, over-read, cheeky, now bald, and pissed off at the whole world.

2

WHEN I WAS STILL small enough to sleep in the sleigh bed Mom had used as a child, she would climb under the covers and tell me bedtime stories about her and Grandpa Willard when she was young.

"When the circus unloaded from the train in Everett, Daddy and I would be there, watching the elephants parade and poop down the street."

"Did Grandma Carol go?"

"Crowds gave her heartburn." That was something I could understand, even as a child. After all, the most frightening part of the world was the other people. "We'd get in these tug of wars where she didn't want me riding horses because of what happened to someone she knew as a child. My mother always had a doom and gloom story to go with everything. People choking on fishbones, ladder rungs collapsing. And Daddy would nod his head and tisk tisk along with her. Then the first lonely cow we'd see in a pasture, he'd stop the car and climb through the barbed wire to pet it."

"No way."

She stroked my arm. "Don't act so surprised. You're just like him."

Grandpa Willard covered for her when she had a boyfriend by saying she was over at a girlfriend's doing homework. "'Kitty,' he liked to call me Kitty, 'I know the boy's father and I'll beat the stuffing out of him if that kid so much as touches you.' Not that I was going to tell him." She laughed and I wondered even as she was telling me these stories whether this was good parenting. Wasn't she worried I'd take these indiscretions and coverups as invitations to try the same thing on her? But Mom seemed to glory in making me feel I was missing out on my youth by not fooling around more. The picture of her childhood that emerged was a conspiracy between her and Grandpa Willard against her stick-in-the-mud mother. It seemed

20

strange to me at the time that a young girl would buddy up to an old man when she could have had her mother, but the idea of a co-conspirator of any sex had obvious appeal.

When I turned ten Mom took me downtown to Marge's Cafe for a club sandwich with a toothpick and a flag in it. I blushed when Marge brought over a wedge of peach pie with candles blazing on top. Mom started singing happy birthday and everyone else in the restaurant joined in. As we were coming out, somebody hit a putty gray VW bug at the only signal in Stampede and spun it around right before our eyes. Shards of glass sprayed across the asphalt and the front of the VW ended up wedged under the elevated boardwalk. If it had careened in the other direction, it would have decapitated the landmark drinking fountain with the brass foot pedal that said "Brock Manufacturing, Cincinnati, Ohio" on the lever.

The driver, a black man with dreadlocks, was slumped over the wheel. His passenger, a white woman who'd been thrown from the car, kept standing up and falling back down on the pavement. Although lots of people ran out of their shops and stopped their cars to gawk, everyone but Mom seemed to be in a daze.

"You watch her and I'll see about him," she shouted. "Just keep her on the ground." The woman's face was scratched and there was a raspberry on her elbow, but otherwise she seemed okay except for her insistence on getting back in the car. I hooked two fingers inside one of the belt loops on her jeans and pulled down hard, trying to mimic the law of gravity. Her arms were tattooed with flowers and swans and a vine-draped heart that said "Cecil." She was wearing a T-shirt with no bra and her thick nipples were erect, probably from shock.

It was like Mom and I were in the circus, her in one ring and me in another, and everyone else was just watching our act. Mom didn't disappoint. She stripped off her blouse (fortunately, *she* was wearing a bra), folded it into a bandanna, and wrapped it around the gash on the man's forehead, making no attempt to cover herself with her arms or cower behind the wing of the door she'd managed to push open. She just paced back and forth in the street between me and the man in the car until the ambulance arrived and the driver offered her a sheet to cover herself, which she refused. Afterwards, when people talked about what had happened, nobody mentioned the fact that it was Jesse Little's dead-drunk dad who had run the red light and rammed the VW. What they remembered was Mom stripping off her blouse.

"What was I supposed to do," she told me afterwards, "wait for Jesse Little to sew stitches?" Sometimes I thought she didn't give two spits what people thought of her.

Another time she created a public stir when we were in line at the pharmacy behind Carmela, the Mexican woman who later rented Grandpa Willard's house over on Socket Street. Carmela, a beautiful woman with luscious black hair, was struggling to make herself understood to the pharmacist. He was a bald man whose only body hairs were nose whiskers and he kept looking over at his assistant in her matching starched smock for help.

"For God's sake, Fred," Mom finally said, "she wants something for her husband's hemorrhoids. Piles! Is that so difficult?"

It was hard to tell by Carmela's cinnamon skin whether she was blushing, but she turned to Mom with a kind smile and they hugged right there in front of the vitamins.

In a small town people talked, Mom too. "There's only one thing worse than being talked about," she used to joke, "and that's not being talked about." Still, she had her limits, like the time we attended the ecumenical dialogue Father Tombari arranged with the Presbyterians.

"Is it mandatory?" I wanted to know. I was already having trouble maintaining my enthusiasm for church. In most things we had a democratic household and everyone did what they wanted with their time, especially Mom.

"Till you're eighteen or living on your own, you'll go," Dad told me. I suspected the whole thing had been cooked up between Dad and Father Tombari as a way to show Mom how close their two religions were. Even though Mom had never converted to Catholicism, she let Dad have free rein over me in that department.

The ecumenical mass included a hand-holding episode, where Father Tombari made every Catholic grip a Presbyterian and vice versa while we sang "Amazing Grace." Afterward there was a reception in the church basement with sugar cookies, purple punch, and coffee in silver urns as big as garbage cans. Mom and I were cornered by Twyla Morrison, the minister's wife, who was wearing a brown felt hat with a cluster of baby's breath on the brim. Twyla made the mistake of talking about John Carlisle's younger sister, Ashley, who as far as I knew had never set foot in Stampede since we'd been there. The rumor was she'd run away and become a street person back east.

"I wonder how they ever put up with that little slut," Twyla said.

Mom exploded with a slap so hard across Twyla Morrison's cheek that it knocked her felt hat with the baby's breath sideways. "You're in no position to judge that woman!"

I'd been taught that if you struck a priest or even a nun your chances of living for eternity at the right hand of God were about as remote as the odds of winning the Irish Sweepstakes. Watching Mom's lower lip quiver, I could only pray that a Presbyterian minister's wife wasn't so sacred. I was completely taken aback at the intensity of Mom's reaction. Why defend someone like Ashley Carlisle?

"It just burns me," Mom said afterwards, "the way nobody's willing to spend two seconds in someone else's skin around here. Being rich doesn't mean you're not human. Every step those Carlisle kids took, it was never good enough."

That didn't exactly explain why Ashley ran away, but the vehemence of Mom's reaction left no question on whose side she stood.

When I begged her, Mom took me on her sorties into Seattle for art supplies. For unusual merchandise, Seattle was where everyone went. From hints she'd dropped, I figured that's where they'd gotten me. Mom was always in such a good mood at Daniel Smith's, fingering the rag hemp, mulberry bark, banana stalk, and grass paper the way I'd seen other women stroke lingerie. The trays of pastels were precious gems. She drooled over the Senneliers, a pastel made by a third generation family company in France. A single stick cost as much as a paperback book. She tested out the brushes on the veiny part of her wrist and then painted circles on her cheeks with her eyes closed. Sometimes, she'd bring her paints along and take a class there or she'd teach one and I'd sit in the aisle doing home-work or reading a novel, listening to the laughter she always managed to squeeze out of the student artists who surrounded her with their sailcloths like so many sloops.

After Daniel Smith's, we sometimes went to the Pike Place Market and wove our way through the produce and fish stands, then up the metal stairs on the outside of a trian-gular shaped building to the deck of the Copacabana, where we could look out over the flower boxes on the main Market building and watch the throngs of people on the brick street below us. Mom introduced me to foods I'd never heard of — saltenas, shrimp soup, and paella. If she'd taught a class, Mom would order a glass of Bolivian wine and I'd toast my ice water with her.

"Someday, both of us will be doing art," she said, and I had this lump of regret that she was so good at something I had absolutely no aptitude for.

When it was sunny, men in dark glasses with extra rings on their fingers, gold chains around their necks, and studs in their ears came by the table and asked if they could join us. I felt that it was my job to mention Dad somewhere in the conversation just to make sure they didn't get the wrong idea. Mom always wore her Irish claddagh ring with the hands holding a crowned heart that the men must have mistaken for something besides a wedding ring because they often lingered at our table and asked her where we were staying. Mom seemed to enjoy the challenge, never telling them to beat it, but never asking them to stay either. I'd watch for drug deals down on the street with one eye, enjoying the hubbub and anonymity that was impossible in Stampede, and watch Mom with the other, ready to beat the stuffing out of anyone who touched her. While I always envied her easy sexuality, I was also scared of it.

Where Mom was my sail, Dad was the anchor.

When he handed me a paperback copy of *A Portrait of the Artist as a Young Man*, he said "You're almost finished with high school. Time to discover the Irish version of a hero."

We kept the book on top of the toilet in the downstairs bathroom, so that we could both read it, him for the third time. When his marker passed mine, I told him he was spending too much time in the toilet and he laughed. Dad treated the bathroom like a sacred chamber, always locking the door to do his business, rolling the toilet paper back so that you couldn't tell where the last square ended, and spraying potpourri from the can in the medicine cabinet before emerging.

I loved it when nobody was home and I could leave the bathroom door wide open, something I found deliciously liberating, then crank up Janis Joplin on the stereo. Sometimes I'd read the erotic Anais Nin diaries that Mom kept under the magazines in the wicker basket next to their bed. Much better than *Portrait*. The diaries started out as a letter to the father who had deserted her and ended up as thirty-five thousand handwritten pages describing her most intimate thoughts over a lifetime.

Dad was fiercely proud of his Irishness, even though he had none of the swagger and brashness I associated with the Irish. He seemed too cerebral, too disciplined, too even-tempered. But say the wrong thing and I'd seen him ready to come to blows, like after another one of those exposés on the Kennedys came out and I overheard the guy at the service station who was running Dad's charge card through the register. "That Kennedy couldn't keep his pecker in his pants, could he?"

Dad clenched his fist and bristled. "Leave the man alone. Don't you think one assassination is enough?" It shouldn't have surprised me; they had to pull him out of a fight at the Comet Tavern over Mom.

When Dad came to the Pike Place Market with us, we went down an alley to Kells instead of the Copacabana. Kells was an Irish pub that served soda bread and thick, chewy clam chowder that Mom and Dad washed down with Guinness. On these visits, nobody came up to our table and asked us where we were staying.

On the car ride home from Seattle once, when it was just Mom and me and she was a little tipsy — I must have been fourteen at the time — she told me about meeting Dad when he was at Loyola of Chicago and she was at Northwestern. "I was still coming off Lloyd then," she said. Lloyd was the vague title given to that period in Mom's life when she was into rock singers, motorbikes, and recreational drugs, something I knew she'd told me not as encouragement but as parable. I remembered praying then to Saint Anthony, the patron saint of the lost and found, hoping she'd not damaged too many brain cells from the drugs.

"Your dad courted me with herbal teas and protein," Mom said. "He'd go to the store and stock the refrigerator in my apartment with chocolate milk, Swiss cheese, and yogurt. If I hadn't eaten enough protein by the time I saw him again, I'd pour a little down the sink or flush it in the toilet so he wouldn't be disappointed. He'd do the laundry and give me massages even before we were sleeping together. Best of all, he read to me. Every word of *Crime and Punishment*, half of *Anna Karenina*" — she smiled when she said this — "that's when we, well, you know, ended the abstinence."

Dad had invited his brothers to Mom's funeral. I was standing next to him when he called Seamus, his younger brother in New York, and he let me listen to the answering machine message, which said he was off sailing with a woman friend in Nova Scotia. At least with Seamus you didn't get misdirection. Dad's older brother Colin, a doctor in Minneapolis, was too tied up at the hospital to get away for the funeral and sent a huge wreath in the shape of a horseshoe. It seemed as if Dad and his brothers were victims of mobility, the way they'd scattered to different parts of the continent to make families with strangers. Now, they were as much absent from each other's lives as Ashley Carlisle had been from her brother's.

Most of what I knew about Dad I'd learned from someone else, including Seamus, who stayed with us one night on his way to Alaska to work on a fishing boat when I was in eighth grade at Saint Augustine and I sat on the floor of my bedroom pumping him with questions. Seamus was good-looking like Dad, with a fetching Rugby jaw and unruly hair, but most important he treated me like an adult. He had those thick Scanlon eyebrows and devil's bumps on the tops of his ears that he said were a sign of intelligence.

"Your dad didn't have brain one when he was your age," he told me. The way he said it, of course, I knew he meant just the opposite. "Our mom was always getting up and going to six o'clock mass so we'd grow up to be good boys. She wanted Tom to be a priest so bad she could taste it."

"Why Dad?"

Seamus rolled his eyes and hoisted his eyebrows. "Tom always made the nicest doilies for Mother's Day, I guess, all put together so the paste didn't show." We both laughed. "And he composed little prayers that he'd read at holiday dinners. Tom always had a freaky mysticism about him."

"What do you mean, mysticism?"

"You know, contact with deeper truths." Seamus shook his head as if disbelieving my dad could really be his brother. "Tom liked words. Me, I'd rather squeeze it between my fingers or suck on it, but Tom wanted to write about it. Mom had an old Royal typewriter, one of those black jobbies that weighed fifty pounds, and he typed his prayers on the back of handbills and crammed them into a brown expando. Like some junior Gutenberg in cutoffs. Course, Mom didn't know he was pounding out adolescent erotica in between his dinner prayers. Colin folded one into her missal once, but she refused to believe it was Tom's."

Seamus paused and looked around my room at the bulletin board with my Blessed Virgin bookmarks and ribbons from spelling bees, and I thought he'd remember he was talking to a child and cut me off. I probably should have stopped him, knowing that it wasn't fair to hear these stories without getting Dad's version, but Seamus mesmerized me. This was real life and I hungered for it. Finally, he took a deep breath, ruffled his hair, and plunged ahead again.

"We had this pimply babysitter named Judy who used to come over on Saturdays when Tom was working as a box boy and Tom would sneak home on his lunch hours and neck with her on the couch."

"My dad?"

"He'd get his hair all mussed up and have to reattach his little black clip-on bowtie before going back to work."

"Did you ever tell your mom about it?"

"No. I kinda liked the idea that Tom was aiming away from the priesthood."

"Was your mom disappointed he didn't become a priest?"

"Sure, then she thought he'd be a lawyer. Everyone did."

"What happened?"

"He took a part-time job in college as a cub reporter for a local daily and fell in love with the newspaper business. 'Why would I want to be someone else's mouthpiece?' he told me. 'I want to write what they don't want anyone to hear.'"

It was no surprise the Scanlon brothers had drifted apart. They'd lost the glue when their mom died. Although she never smoked, she passed away from lung cancer that the doctors attributed to their dad's chain-smoking. Then their dad married his former secretary, a woman who wanted nothing to do with the boys, which put Mr. Scanlon to a choice between the new wife and his three sons. I remembered Mom telling me how Mr. Scanlon was unable to make it to their wedding because of the reservations his new wife had booked on a cruise ship through the Panama Canal. So much for the family that prays together stays together.

Most things involved in my rearing were Mom's responsibilities. Dad was the master of the handoff as in, "Can you help your daughter with her homework?" And he could have added, *with her manners, social skills, inferiority complexes, and delusions of grandeur.*

But Dad handled the allowance, for which I had to prepare an itemized budget on a sheet of unlined, pulpy, grammar school drawing paper. "If you want an increase, you've got to have a base to work from," he said. My budgets included the kinds of things he'd go for like school supplies, family presents, donations to the Poor Box, and bike reflectors. Of course, once I had the money, I figured I could spend it on whatever I wanted. As I got older, the allowance increased but so did the things I became responsible for, like clothes. Because I grew about ten inches between ages twelve and fifteen, Dad's laying off of the clothes onto my budget turned out to be a shrewd business decision for him. I couldn't keep up, but so what if I had a few pairs of high-waters?

For better or worse, Dad was the one who got me into reading, which I realized later also served as a surrogate for those otherwise awkward parent-child conversations. When he found out I still hadn't taken biology by the end of my sophomore year, he put a textbook outside my door with masking tape all over the binding. The letters on the cover had been filled in with blue ink and changed from *BIOLOGY* to *APOLOGY*. On the inside, the last name not crossed out was "Tom Scanlon." It was Dad's contribution to my sex education.

I started taking books with me when Mom and I went on painting expeditions into the country. She'd station herself in front of the root ball of a fallen pine tree or next to a lopsided barn and I'd read the books from Dad's bookshelf. At first, the reading was a shield to make me seem engaged while all those silent hours passed without her saying anything as she slipped deeper into her work. Then I realized that reading satisfied the same appetite I had for Seamus's stories. It allowed me into the parlors and bedrooms of real people with chinks in their hearts. I became two people: the reader who was the voyeur, the person who knew the meaning of words she'd never even said out loud; then there was the self-conscious Scanlon girl everyone else knew.

It wasn't as if Mom or Dad didn't care what I was thinking. I remembered listening to them one night from the crawl space where we kept old hoses and trellises. I had one hand on the cold water pipe and I could feel the water rush through the grip of my fist. The other hand I pushed up inside the stuffing on the hot water pipe where the squirrels had picked away the insulation and squeezed it like someone's esophagus. They were arguing over whether I should stay at Saint Augustine's for seventh grade or switch to public school.

"For heaven's sake, Tom, let her get immunized to the real world and away from all those Bible-bangers."

"Catholics aren't Bible-bangers, Kate. How can you say that?"

"Knee-benders then."

Instead of Mom, Dad came to my room that night. He looked awkward and, out of respect for my privacy, diverted his eyes from the dirty underwear strewn around the room. He didn't tuck in the covers and there were no stories and no goodnight kisses. He just gazed at me with those earnest Irish eyes. "You know you can be anything you set your mind to, Piper."

It was a reassuring statement and one that I treasured in the days and months that followed, despite the fact I stayed one more year with the nuns at Saint Augustine's. But Dad never repeated it, and I later wondered if he'd really come into my room that night at all.

---3---

SEVERAL WEEKS AFTER I'D shaved my head, Dad brought
Grandpa Willard home with him.

"I have some good news," Dad said, which right away
made me suspicious because I knew that good news was the
bane of the newspaper business. People wanted scandals
and roadkill. "Your grandpa's going to live with us."

What was I going to say? Willard was standing right
next to me in the hallway, hatless, fingering the brim of an
old buttoned-down-at-the-peak chauffeur's cap he held at
his waist. I'd called him Willard for as long as I could
remember. It was his idea. *All my friends call me Willard*,
he'd said. He hated Will, because people assumed it was
short for William and he was a Willard. He was looking up
at me with those hard brown eyes that rolled around in the
sockets like marbles in the palm of a sweaty hand. Willard
always looked as if he'd just been caught at something the
way he shifted his weight back and forth on his scuffed
wingtips. He had nothing to feel guilty about. This was his
house until Grandma Cooper died and he'd moved into a
smaller place over on Socket Street that was walking
distance to the drugstore where he bought his cigars. Dad
had decided it wasn't safe for him to drive, so his car was
stored in the garage at the Socket Street house with a tarp
over it.

"How's business?" Willard said.

I faked a smile, trying to be polite.

He chuckled and crushed his motorman's cap in his
hand. The subject of money always fascinated my grandpa.
He grew up without much of it in Yakima, where he got up
at four a.m. to cut asparagus with the migrants, then went to
school with them at night until he dropped out and pumped
gas. Somehow he'd saved enough to invest in penny mining
stocks because that was the first section of the paper he
turned to.

"I thought it would be kind of nice to have your grandpa

31

here." Dad's "Paperback Writer" tie with the impression-istic manuscript pages flying up and down the front had been pulled loose around his neck and there were tell-tale beads of perspiration on his forehead. It was three-thirty on a Thursday and I knew he was probably frantic to get back to the shop to meet his printing deadline. "Willard, you're going to help Piper cook and take care of the house, right?" Dad raised his voice when he spoke to Willard even though as far as I knew he could hear as well as the rest of us.

"Whatever you say, Tom," Willard said, with a you betcha' nod of his head.

Groan. I didn't like the direction this was heading. Willard had begun acting strange lately even by Willard's standards. Earlier in the summer they'd found him walking out on the Horse Heaven Highway with his lunch bucket under a full moon, puffing on a rum-soaked cigar. He said he was on his way to Bonnie Holliday's to adjust the carbu-retor in her Studebaker, which was a disturbing explanation. Bonnie was a spinster who everyone thought had her eyes on Willard long before Grandma Carol's passing. Furthermore, she was deceased. But Willard wasn't totally daffy. Even before Mom died he'd figured out that when it came to the big decisions, like whether he would drive his car, Dad was going to play a major role.

I pulled at Dad's sleeve to get him over by the bannister. Over Dad's shoulder I watched Willard, who was still standing alone on the oval rug in the entry way surrounded by a hard suitcase with broken hinges that was wrapped with a bungee cord and two cardboard boxes criss-crossed with gray duct tape. He was working his cap through his fist like he was milking an udder. It was unusual to see Willard upright. Me and everyone else in Stampede were used to just seeing his legs, crossed at the ankles and sticking out from under a neighbor's broken-down car, his fingers feeling out onto the curb for end wrenches.

"I don't need a babysitter, Dad," I whispered.

"I thought you'd like the idea. The house is too big for just two of us." I knew what was going on and it had nothing to do with the size of the house. Dad was still freaked out that, left to my own devices, I was going to do something self-destructive. Willard was the suicide watch. But I wasn't going to make it that easy for our detractors. Anyone who wanted to take a swipe at Mom was going to have to come through me first. "It's what your mom would have wanted."

"You don't know that," I said, but I knew he was right. It was hard to argue against Mom when it came to Willard. I'd heard Dad try when they talked about putting him away in Mount Vernon. "There's no way I'm going to let him be cooped up and shot full of tranquilizers," Mom said. "You might as well shoot him." I'd been to one of those places, to visit Willard's older brother, before he died in the midst of the incontinence and gaping stares they called a nursing home. No wonder Willard trembled when they talked about it.

"So do we have consensus?" Dad said.

"I'm thinking." Willard winked when he noticed me looking at him. There was no mistaking he was Mom's father: same hook in the nose, the cowlick on the backside of the crown, and a twinkle in the eyes. They weren't spectators, they were doers. And they were damned if they were going to just do what everyone else was doing. A fire burned in the Coopers and, without Mom, maybe the only way I was going to get any of it was to be near her father.

"Help the old man get settled in the basement," Dad said, patting me reassuringly on the shoulder. "I told him he could keep his dog."

The debate was over.

The spare bedroom in the basement was full of bundled newspapers, back issues of the *Herald*, and empty Mason jars that had been there since Willard lived in the house, the flotsam and jetsam I associated with older people. Mom had used the jars to clean her brushes, but I'd never seen her put fruit in them. Willard and I hauled the newspapers and boxes of jars into the furnace room and stacked them against the walls. The edges of the bundles were shredded where mice had nibbled off nesting material and the papers on the top of the stacks had miniature piles of rodent dung that rattled onto the floor as I picked them up.

"At least they're paper-trained," Willard joked. I knew from Mom's stories that Willard loved animals of any species and I doubted he'd ever set a mousetrap in his life. One of Dad's worries was that a solicitor was going to come to Willard's door asking for a donation to the Audubon Society or Greenpeace and he'd write a check big enough to wipe out his bank account. Willard was one of those people who would handcuff himself to the winch of a factory trawler to prevent it from killing the dolphins.

"I can't believe you're going to actually sleep down here," I said. "It stinks."

He pushed up the bill of his cap. "The aroma of life."

With a broom, I whisked the cobwebs out of the corners of the room and off the windows that peered into concrete wells outside. It occurred to me as I was sweeping the dung off the mattress that maybe Dad didn't really want Willard to live with us after all and this was a way to make him accept the idea of the nursing home. After a night in this god-forsaken space, he'd be begging for a ride to Mount Vernon. When I brought in the vacuum cleaner though, you would have thought I was the maid at the Hilton.

"This is gonna be dandy," he said, "real dandy."

I went up to the linen closet and picked out a serviceable but never used set of lime-green contour sheets and the Mexican blankets Mom had bought from a roadside stand on our way back from the Tulip Festival one Sunday. Dad kept trying to tell her, "Bargain, Kate, they're not fixed prices," but she wouldn't and when she explained after-wards in the car how the man was sending the money back to his family in Chihuahua Dad let the subject drop. I left the sheets and blankets on Willard's mattress and went back up to find a couple of couch pillows. When I returned, Willard was on his hands and knees on the floor smoothing out the sheets over the top of the blankets.

"What are you doing?"

"Making a dog bed," he said, without the least bit of apology.

Jesus. It was as good of a time as any to set some rules, I thought. He was seventy-seven years old, he'd lived through the Great Depression, fought the Japanese in the South Pacific, and volunteered for Vietnam, but if I was going to have a life I had to contain the situation. "Willard, listen. Let's get a few things straight." I motioned for him to take a seat on the bed, but he crossed his legs and sat on the floor instead. "I'm seventeen years old. I don't need a care-taker. Dad didn't do this for me. He did it for you." Willard stroked his knuckles but paid me full attention. "You remember the Monroe Doctrine?"

"'Fraid that was before my time." There was a smirk on his face and I had the eerie feeling Willard was as lucid as any of us, that he was just play-acting.

"I'm not kidding. We're making a bargain. The base-ment is yours, the upstairs is mine, we share the main floor." He raised his hand to interrupt and I cut him off. "Outside the house, we travel separately. I don't mess with your extracurriculars and you don't mess with mine. Okay?"

He was nodding his head up and down, all serious and contrite. No wonder Mom couldn't stomach the idea of sending him off. "Makes sense to me," he said.

"I'm working through a lot of crap these days and it's nothing you'd be interested in." I deliberately spoke a little coarsely, to cut off any inquiry.

After dark, Willard said he had to walk back over to the house on Socket Street and get his dog. It was about twelve blocks, but that was nothing for him. He'd tramped half the county since Dad had de-keyed him. He knew which side-walks were tilted, which ones were cracked and which ones were overgrown with blackberries. He'd marked his paths like a bloodhound, sometimes with his own urine when he couldn't wait to get home. I wasn't worried about Willard getting lost. Blowing town maybe, but he wasn't going to get lost in Stampede.

I was reading in bed when I heard the screen to the basement door slam. After my little talk with Willard, I'd decided I might have been too harsh with him and went downstairs to welcome him home for his first night.

When I opened the door to his room, the bed was full of wagging dogs! I counted five of them: a black and white border collie, an Irish terrier with wheat red fur, a smooth off-white mongrel with lemon markings, a black and tan hound with bloodshot eyes and droopy ears, and a pug with a tiny body, massive head, smashed in nose, and wrinkles in his face like elephant hide. Willard was propped against the headboard, feeding them kibbles out of his hand.

"Jesus, Willard, Dad's gonna call that nursing home so fast! Whose are these?"

He bowed his head. "They're from dead bowling pals. Except for Freeway here." The border collie brightened at Willard's touch. "Police found him in a plastic bag out on the highway. I could hardly turn down the law, could I?"

"There's no way you can hide this many dogs down here." Besides the dishonesty, I knew Dad wasn't that fond of dogs. Mom told me how when he delivered newspapers as a kid, he'd slammed a double-folded paper into someone's door and a German shepherd bounded through a bay window and tore a hole the size of a crabapple out of the fleshy part of his calf. There was still a dent there.

I thought I'd succeeded in intimidating Willard, but a big grin spread across his face, revealing a set of tobacco-stained dentures that were his only perfect feature. "Say, what was the name of that doctrine again?" he teased. A boil of spit worked its way to the edge of his mouth and he just left it there the way a dog would.

Since Mom's death, I'd developed a passion to touch everything she owned, to run my fingers over her canvasses, to put her patchouli behind my ears, even to use her pillow and slip under the sheets on her side of the bed when Dad wasn't home. It was all there was left of her.

As I stood on the chair at the foot of my bed and studied

myself in the mirror, it was obvious I bore no resemblance to her. My left rib stuck out like there was an elbow inside. My fingernails were bitten off, my skin pale and bloodless, and my face a combination of flat planes. I hoisted up her belly-dancing skirt, tucked it into the sash, and gathered the extra material at the waist and wadded it into a ball that I stuffed into the back of my underpants. Even though she always thought she was too short, Mom had a perfect figure. I tried to sashay my hips and make the dress swish, but I had no sideways motion. I was the tin woman who only moved forward and backward. When Mom came into a room, she was a study in gyrating circles. It was no wonder that men looked at her and had to reach out and touch her on the arm or rest their hand in the small of her back when she came to rest.

She took me once to an astrologist named Gemini who lived in a decrepit Victorian house with chrome and vinyl kitchen chairs and a warped card table on the front porch. We passed through the kitchen, which had dirty dishes and corn flakes spilling across the counter and a plastic cat litter tub with pieces of poop sticking out of the sand like Almond Roca candy. Gemini was obese and I could smell her perspiration in the cramped, curtained room she called the chambers, but she had dark, possessive eyes. Mom treated it as a rite of passage, my introduction to the world of the supernatural. I thought Gemini was as phoney as the rhinestones on her fingers, but I went along with the gag for Mom's sake. When it was done, the only thing I remembered the astrologist telling me was that I was too skinny. "There's no milk in your breasts," she said. Mom defended me. "I was a late bloomer myself," she said, neglecting to add that I was adopted and, therefore, not even traveling in the same genetic constellation. Mom later developed another theory. "Girls with small breasts have more testosterone," she told me. "Your sexual prowess will be centered in the genitals."

Dirk Thurgood came by later and flung a pebble against my window, and I yelled at him to come up. If I were normal I probably wouldn't have let a guy come into my room while I was trying on clothes and strutting in front of the mirror to ripen my breasts. But Dirk often came over after school to get away from all the "Yes, sirs" and "No, sirs" at his house. His dad was retired Army and Dirk had to keep his bed made and stand for inspection on Saturday mornings. If his socks weren't rolled and rowed just right or there were dirty clothes under the bed, he'd have to drop for push-ups or be confined to his room. I'd seen bruises on Dirk's forearms that I knew were from his dad. The guys his dad played handball with at the YMCA in Everett and drank beer with afterward at the Comet Tavern called him "Colonel," even though Dirk told me his dad didn't get past Master Sergeant.

Dirk was puffing when he reached my room. "What're you doing?"

"Just fiddling around."

Not a minute later the door downstairs slammed and I knew it had to be Dad because Willard always used the basement entrance.

Dirk looked startled. "I thought you said he didn't come home this early."

"You're fine. Relax." Dirk had become particularly jumpy since Mom's drowning, like he didn't know what to say or do that wouldn't remind me of her. When kids at school teased me about what Mom might have been doing at Carlisle's that day, Dirk told me to blow it off. "They're just making up shit to entertain each other." Basically, we didn't talk about the drowning. If I brought it up, Dirk changed the subject, which was unlike him. Normally, he reveled in the weird, although he didn't like my shaved head. "You look like a convict," he told me.

"Piper! Come on down, we've got company."

Dirk backed into the walk-in closet and hid behind the hanging clothes Mom had stored there. "Don't tell him I'm here," he whispered from between a leather jacket with fringed sleeves and a parcel post colored smock dabbed with paint. Of course, his legs showed from the knees down.

The cuffs of his jeans broke across a pair of scuffed Nikes that were pointed away from each other as the result of a lifetime of duck-walking.

"He won't come up," I told Dirk, picturing exactly where Dad was standing, with one foot on the black rubber runner he'd tacked on the stairs to save the threadbare carpet from total destruction. He'd put the runner down the weekend before Mom died and I could still smell the rubber each time I went to my room.

"Just for a minute," Dad called again, and I could imagine his arms around the banister post that teetered in its socket like a loose tooth.

"How about later?" I yelled.

There was no reply.

"How do you know he won't come up?" Dirk said. If I didn't know better, I would have thought Dirk was scared of my dad.

"'Cause I know." Dad hadn't set foot in my room since Mom made me start wearing a bra, which was a non-event. To please Mom, I had started putting olive oil on my salads and processed cheese spreads on my toast the way the astrologist had suggested, but my breasts were still dollar pancakes. Dirk had better breasts than I did.

When I didn't hear anything more from Dad, I went back to trying on Mom's clothes and Dirk parted the hangers. His face was red and there was a bush of hair sticking up in the front like a miniature whisk broom. Although Dirk was a little pudgy, he wasn't a bad looking guy. With his lazy eyes and broad face, Mom thought he was a dead ringer for Jackie Gleason. He was sensitive about his weight though and made jokes to deflect attention away from it. If he'd jogged or ridden a bicycle or done anything physical, he'd have been fine as far as his physique was concerned, but Dirk was more into sedentary adventures. He'd recorded over a thousand movies on the VCR in his room, stacking them alphabetically in his dresser drawers and on his bookshelves. Whenever I went to his house, he'd insist on running one. If I seemed bored, he'd fast forward to the good parts. What he said were the good ones, like *Top Gun*, he watched over and over until he could lip-synch the lines. He'd never even seen all of those he'd recorded in the middle of the night or while he was at school. I didn't know exactly why we'd befriended each other. I'd rather have read a book than watch his videos. Where Dirk loved the familiarity of contemporary America, I preferred reading about people and places I'd never been and never would be. Nevertheless, the videos stuck on my brain like chewed gum.

I tied the tails of Mom's blouse together to show some stomach skin.

"Bitching, Piper. You look like a stripper."

I *could* have stripped right there in front of him without so much as getting a goosebump. Dirk was safe. Dirk was a buddy. Most everyone else thought Dirk was a dork. It wasn't as if we didn't talk about sex; in fact, it had become one of his main topics. We'd had a scattered history of our own failed attempts at intimacy. Watching videos in the dark in his room, his hand had wandered over to my chest a few times. Once, when we slow danced to *Stand By Me*, I could feel his hard-on against my leg, but it did nothing for me. I thought it was just Dirk, because I still had fantasies about other guys then, even Condon Bagmore. At seventeen, without ever having to go through the messy business of fighting off temptation, Dirk and I had reached a kind of Platonic love that freed us to talk about his other sexual interests.

We'd become best friends by default, for lack of other offers. Apparently, I was the only one who saw potential in a kid who could name every movie made by W.C. Fields, but couldn't tell you who played in the last Superbowl. And I'd become his sexual pathfinder. "You're a girl," he told me. "You know what makes 'em tick."

"Piper!" Dad was in the hallway and knocking on my door. Dirk's hand froze in mid-reach to my belly button. I motioned him into the closet and his shoes squeaked as he backed across the hardwood floor on his tiptoes. "John Carlisle wants to talk to you."

"Tell Carlisle to write it on a brick and shove it up his ass," Dirk whispered. This was where it helped to have a co-conspirator. For as long as I could remember, Dirk had curried John Carlisle's favor, mowed and watered his lawn, washed his windows, accepted rides from him any chance he got. I was heartened when I found out that Dirk had quit as John Carlisle's errand boy after the drowning.

"Tell him I'm starting my period," I told Dad.

Dirk poked his head out of the closet. There was silence on the other side of the door and I felt guilty for lying. Dad wasn't good with female stuff, which was surprising because he was so bold in other ways.

The door knob to my bedroom turned, like he was checking to see if it was locked, and I stiffened. "You can't live in your room, you know." There was a long pause while I thought sure he was going to burst in. "How 'bout you and me going to a baseball game or something this weekend? We can sit outside and watch the Aquasox."

"Maybe some other time, Dad." I was sure he was going to call my bluff and Dirk would see what a poor judge of human behavior I really was. There was a shuffling of shoes, then I could hear him sifting change through the keys in his pocket. The truth was I hated to see him disappointed.

"We're going over to Marge's to grab a bite to eat. Join us if you change your mind."

His footsteps padded down the rubber runner and Dirk emerged from the closet. "You should have told me you were having your period."

"What for?"

"Well . . ."

"It's not as if I have to be sedated or something."

"I just thought, you know, you'd want to be alone."

"Have you ever been constipated?"

"Yeah."

"That's all it is."

He shrugged his shoulders and pulled up on his belt. His cheeks were still pink from hiding in the walk-in. "You sure know how to handle your dad. The Colonel would slap me if I talked to him that way."

We always had this debate about our fathers. Even though there's no way I would have traded for Dirk's dad, I found myself trying to convince Dirk that his dad wasn't so bad. The Colonel worked for a linoleum shop when I was little and I remembered him installing the speckled linoleum that was still in our kitchen. He wore one of those men's undershirts with shoulder straps, snubbed out his cigarettes in the kitchen sink, cussed every time he had to cut for the outlets sticking out from the baseboards, and sweated profusely in a way I'd never seen my dad do. The Colonel kept a good yard, kept himself in excellent physical condition, and had an extensive gun collection in his basement under lock and key with a cardboard sign you could buy in any hardware store that said, "Keep Out." There were rifles, pistols, swords, whips, bayonets, Billy clubs, an iron collar Dirk told me was a garrote, and even a set of brass knuckles. The Colonel collected weapons the way Dirk collected videos. Although his dad was tough, he and Dirk at least had the same agenda: Dirk's manhood. Since Mom's death, I'd come to appreciate one other thing about the Colonel. He looked down on John Carlisle for not following his father's footsteps into the military service.

Of course, Dirk didn't know I was adopted, which lent an air of make-believe to these debates. Dirk's family had moved to Stampede when the Colonel retired from the service and, even though the Thurgoods weren't Catholic, they put Dirk in St. Augustine because of the discipline. That's where we met, in second grade.

Dirk sat down on the floor, untied his Nikes, and began restringing them to get the laces even. He stuck his little finger in his ear and ratcheted it back and forth, then studied the wax on the tip of it before wiping it on the back of his pants. "If *my* mom ever kicked the bucket, I'd be outta there."

"That's different."

He licked the frayed end of the lace and twisted it into a point. "You're not shittin' it's different. Your dad's human."

"He leaves me alone," I said, as if that were an asset. In fact, I would have welcomed a little meddling. I'd rationalized Dad's aloofness since Mom's death by reminding myself that he wasn't my real father. In my theory of creation, there was no such thing as genetics anyway; everyone was free-floating, ad hoc. Heaven was filled with amateur artists and each soul was a new canvas. God handed out paint brushes and said, see what you can do with them. They'd painted Dad with a Roman collar, Mom with a great body, and me with no breasts and a giraffe's neck.

When Dirk finished tying his shoes and tucked in his shirt, I opened the window over the porch roof to let him out, head first. I had to slide his socks down and hold onto his ankles, which were smooth and hairless, until his hands reached the asphalt shingles. From there, I knew he could shinny his way down the maple tree that had worked its way into the eaves because I'd done it plenty of times myself.

As I watched him tip-toe toward the alley between the dead corn stalks and barren tomato vines, I remembered one of the big dinners at our house for the newspaper staff when Mom had adorned the house with vases of wildflowers and mustard weeds. Through the rails of the banister, I watched them after dessert begging Dad to do a poem, and he waved them off until Mom dragged a kitchen chair into the middle of the living room and led Dad over to it with her little finger. "He just needs a stage," she said.

Dad stood up on the chair, cleared his throat, and recited Yeats' "Innisfree" by heart. There was an Irish lilt in his voice and the air in the room seemed strewn with stardust as he spoke. Maybe this was the mysticism Seamus had spoken of. When he was done, Dad pushed the chair back to restore noise to the room and seemed almost embarrassed by the respect they'd paid him with their gaping silence.

As I stared out the back window, I also thought of running away. It was probably the honorable thing to do in the circumstances. But then I remembered how people had bad-mouthed my mother and I felt like a traitor for even entertaining the notion.

I was needed here in Stampede to make sure no one trampled on her grave.

———*4*———

WHILE I WAS WAITING for Dad to show up for dinner, Marge brought me a piece of chocolate pie with whipping cream around the perimeter that had been squeezed through a pastry nozzle in a star pattern. The mustard stain on her uniform was at eye level.

"It's the first wedge of the pie," she said, "the one your dad always gets." For Marge, food was love. She was pleasantly plump and invited others to join in her quest. *Love thy neighbor as thyself.* I knew what was going on though: Marge was trying to restore normalcy.

"No thanks, maybe later," I said, shoving the plate with my thumb to the center of the table. I used to love to come into Marge's and sit on my legs on one of the stools and joke with her until she gave me someone's leftover french fries or the part of the milkshake in the steel mixing canister that didn't fit into the customer's soda glass, but that was then. Now I wanted change.

"Shame on you, honey. I can practically see your ribs. Your father must be starving you." What she really wanted to know was how things were going at home without Mom. She clicked her tongue against the back of her teeth. She must have been a knockout when she was young: high cheekbones, good eyes, full figure. She seemed oblivious to the transformation that time had accomplished on her and she always flirted playfully with my dad.

"Really, Marge, I'm eating fine," I said.

"Got to be well-rounded, honey," and she put her hands under her breasts and clucked out the side of her mouth, all the time looking straight at my chest. Why did everyone have to have milk jugs for tits?

"Did my dad leave a message?"

"You know better than that. Why do you Scanlons always have to be so busy anyway?" She picked up the pie plate and carried it with both hands back to the counter like it was a religious offering and put it into the refrigerated

44

rack next to the coffee makers. I knew it wasn't the last time I'd see that piece of pie.

Marge's was Stampede's meeting place. It was where the police took their coffee and donut breaks, where salesmen met clients to sell life insurance policies or recruit Amway dealers. It was also where you met your dad to talk about your report card or explain how things were going with a grandpa at home instead of a mother. At least I figured that's why he'd asked me to meet him. There was nothing fancy about Marge's. The pictures on the walls were prints of cattle drives and whiskered cowboys sitting on their haunches around a campfire that probably reminded Marge of Mussellshell, Montana where she'd grown up. The cafe was designed in an L-shape with padded red booths along the windows and matching swivel chairs mounted on pedestals at the counter. No matter the time of day, Marge served breakfast, her two eggs any way you wanted them, little pig sausages, hash browns fried in the sausage juice, and a choice of white and dark toast or homemade biscuits. The smell of grease that had seeped into the foam rubber cushions pretty well dominated the cafe, except for those times when she was baking biscuits. Tonight it was biscuits and there was a sweetness in the air thick enough to chew.

As I sat in the booth, tracing the lines in my palm the astrologist had read, the bells on the back of the door jingled and John Carlisle walked in. I slid over next to the window, turned my head, and watched the vapor wafting out of the exhaust pipe on his refurbished Mercedes. Carlisle collected old cars and fixed them up to look like new. People from all over Puget Sound came to the Stampede Antique Car Festival and drove down Main Street in the annual parade. Mom told me he started it as a way to bridge the distance people put between themselves and the Carlisles, which I thought was a strange choice of activities since John Carlisle and Harry Hosey, the retired banker, were the only people in Stampede with antiques that still ran on their own power. Behind me, I could hear Marge greeting him with the same motherly enthusiasm she'd used with me. I didn't care, as long as she kept him busy. I didn't have a thing to say to that man for the rest of my life.

There was a time when I thought our family had to be the luckiest in town because of how close we were to the Carlisles. The Carlisles were royalty. John Carlisle's father, Stewart, had died in the Vietnam War and there was a natural gas torch permanently lit for him in Klah Hah Ya Park. Stewart Carlisle's heroism in dragging his commanding officer to safety after a firefight in Dak To was better known in Stampede than John F. Kennedy's adventures on the PT 109. In fact people talked like the Carlisles knew the Kennedys. John Carlisle attended school at the Sorbonne, where he studied fine arts, French, and dance, not exactly world-beating skills in a town like Stampede. Mom said he never actually received a degree because of some kind of trouble. "There were letters back and forth with French stamps on them," is all she said. Instead of medals of honor, John shocked his mother by bringing home women friends like Monique who smoked cigarillos and spit on the sidewalk. The Sorbonne was part of the reason people said John Carlisle was spoiled. The bloodline had run thin. There was never a question about his returning to Stampede, however. Mom said his mother would have disinherited him if he hadn't.

I remembered the time one summer John Carlisle came by the house in a fire engine red jeep and honked in front of our house. He'd been cut by a dance company in New York, moved into the family mansion up on the hill with his invalid mother, and taken over the newspaper even though he was ten years younger than Dad and without a shred of journalism training. He had the window of the jeep rolled down and his green beret was set at a jaunty angle. Me being on the verge of seventh grade, he was what I imagined the playboy of the western world would be.

"Let's go up the Stillaguamish and have a picnic," he said, revving the engine. "Kate can do some painting."

I remembered Dad massaging his whiskers and looking

at the tires. "I gotta finish a story. Why don't you guys go without me?" This always happened. Dad was the work boy of the western world.

We headed north to Machias with the top down, Mom in the frontseat and me in back, leaning forward far enough to let the strands of her hair tickle my face. I measured the length of my hair against Mom's by feeling how far in back of me it was blowing. When I looked up, there was a propeller plane leaving a tube of white smoke that thickened and rolled away like a snake shedding its skin. The rush of the air was so loud we had to put our heads together to say anything.

At Granite Falls, we turned onto a two-lane road that pointed us toward the Cascades and I could see snow-marbled peaks off in the distance. Each time we passed through a shady section of the road, it cooled down like an air conditioner and the smell of pine rushed up my nostrils the way chlorinated water did when you jumped into the pool without plugging your nose. We stopped at Monte Cristo, a one-time mining town with remnants of old buildings, railway turntables, and mining machinery that Mom wanted to sketch. We made her settle for photographs she could paint from later. She shot an entire roll, taking pains to compose each picture from the perfect angle, close-ups that would turn out to be the slice of a building or have a weird shadow effect. Carlisle sat next to me, on the trunk of a fallen tree, watching her.

"This is a real treat for me," he said, "to take you and your mom up here."

"It's okay," I said.

"Takes a lot to turn your head, doesn't it?"

"No, it's great. Really."

"Look at her. She's in heaven."

For our lunch, we hiked up a trail with switchbacks. Carlisle and I took turns carrying the wicker basket, and Mom carried her easel and paints in a brown metal toolbox with drawers that fanned open in tiers. We weren't exactly Lewis and Clark. Carlisle, in his Birkenstocks, wanted to stop at every vista to wipe the sweat off his face with a hanky. I thought Mom would complain, but she seemed energized by the increase in elevation.

"Why did we wait so long to come up here?" she said.

"There is no *here*," Carlisle said. "The three of us could divide up and hike these mountains every weekend for the rest of our lives and never bump into each other."

I never forgot Mom's response, which probably explained why she'd taken to Carlisle in the first place. "I couldn't stand to be that alone," she said.

"It's hyperbole, Mom."

She smiled and wrapped her arm around me. "See? I told you she's smart." Her fear of isolation might have also explained our own bond. There was no place she could go, no endeavor so boring, that I didn't want to be with her. I was unconditional company.

Carlisle spread our lunch out on a red and white checkered tablecloth in a heather meadow: artichoke hearts, marinated onions, feta cheese on rye crackers, spiral pasta salad with pesto, a choice of Italian sodas that we iced down with cubes from the tupperware, kiwi and strawberry slices for desert. The champagne was French, of course, and pink. When Carlisle shot the stopper into the lupine and devil's club surrounding us, the champagne fizzed all over the tablecloth before Mom could get her glass under it. I thought it was all a bit dainty and not the fare of pressed ham and pre-sliced cheese that Dad would have chosen, but Mom savored every bite, dunking her strawberries into her champagne and practically kissing the kiwi into her mouth.

After dessert, she set up her easel and tied a scarf around her head to keep the hair out of her eyes. Barefoot and in shorts, I could see the muscles in her legs work as she leaned into her board to sketch the face of the mountain reflected in the stillness of the pond next to us. Carlisle sat on the ground, loosened his belt buckle, and opened up the case I thought contained a telescope. But it was a black piccolo with silver finger buttons that glistened when he played something that sounded like butterflies fluttering over a field of buttercups. Mom put her arms around her middle, closed her eyes, and listened, while a stick of charcoal dangled from between her fingers. John Carlisle's cheeks puffed in and out, the skin stretched beyond normal size. As I watched him pointing his piccolo toward the easel, it was almost as if he was trying to will the picture up out of the paper. I remembered feeling sorry that his family had left him with a newspaper instead of an orchestra or a dance troupe. I didn't know anyone else in Stampede who even listened to classical music much less played an instrument. John Carlisle was a soloist by default.

In those days I was glad Mom had someone like Carlisle, someone besides the typical Stampeder who stopped by wherever she set up her easel and said, "Hey, Van Gogh, why don't you just snap a picture?" As time wore on and the kiddish mucous cleared from my eyes, I began to see him differently. I began to worry about the amount of time she spent with him, at his house, on rides in the country, on the telephone. It started to irritate me the way he bowed and kissed her hand, escorted her by the touch of his fingers into a car, and patted the curve of her waist.

"It's too bad your dad doesn't care for the outdoors," Carlisle said when we got back to the jeep. He probably meant it as a joke, but my eyes burned tunnels into the back of his head on the way home.

At breakfast the next morning with Mom, I mentioned how I was getting kind of tired of all the Carlisle mystique, and she jumped me.

"He doesn't go for all that town founder stuff either," she said. "Frankly, I think it's a big pain in the ass for him. He'd trade it all to have Ashley back."

If it was such a pain in the ass, I thought, why didn't he go over to the park and shut off the gas flame or etch onto the stone the names of the rest of the Stampede citizens who'd died in wars? Or take the Carlisle name off the bridge? Or convert his monstrosity of a house into a soup kitchen and move off the top of the hill so he could be down with everyone else? Or just leave my mom alone? If I'd spoken up and stuck to my intuition, maybe Mom wouldn't have drowned in his Jacuzzi.

When I glanced back over at Marge's counter again, John Carlisle caught my eye and I started muttering long-abandoned invocations to myself. *Jesus, Mary, and Joseph, have mercy on us. Jesus, Mary, and Joseph have mercy on us.* God, as was his wont these days, ignored me. John Carlisle, with the chocolate cream pie in one hand and a mug of coffee in the other, slid into the booth opposite me.

"Mind if I join you?" It was a rhetorical question because he sat down before I could say anything.

I fixed my stare on his veinless, pasty hands. The finger-nails were nicely manicured and his hands were clean like he'd just washed dishes. Flesh was the word that came to my mind when I looked at him. Loose, tender flesh. He wore his hair long like a concert pianist and patted it down gently above the ears. Dirk said he looked like the pictures of Liberace on his mom's long play records. "As a matter of fact," I said, looking at the clock behind the counter, "I'm expecting someone."

He reached a hand across the table to put it over mine and I dropped my hands into my lap. "Oh, come on, Piper, this is feeling like a cold shoulder. We're practically family." He took a bite of pie and gummed the pudding, smacking his lips. Even through the masticating, he managed to clip his words in a way that sounded British and prissy. It was the voice of a man who had never been stooped over in labor, whose pituitary gland was as super-fluous as tonsils. "Your mother wouldn't have wanted it this way, you know." He paused to gum another bite. "She was the most open person I've ever known. No fear of her own heart. I told her she was going to be another Frida Kahlo." He was babbling, trying to make something stick. My lips were trembling, but I didn't want to touch them and call attention to it. "There's no reason we can't at least be friends."

I put my hands back on the table, fingernail grime and all. "Except for what you did to my mother."

He drew back like I'd spit at him. "What kind of bunkum is that?"

"It was *your* Jacuzzi." This was why I didn't want to talk to him. I knew I'd end up spouting off with nothing to back me up.

"Please, Piper, don't . . ." He bit his lip like he was going to cry on me. I was Tom's little girl and he thought he could say anything he wanted to me. Everyone in town was scared to lay a glove on him after what his family had done for the community. John Carlisle's personal charity was the Boys' Camp at Lake Spigot. When the day lodge was completed, the paper ran a picture of him in short pants and a Safari hat surrounded by all those cute little boys in scout uniforms and kerchiefs. In a way, we were all Carlisle's charities. The assumption in every conversation and encounter was that he was better, smarter, and richer than the rest of us poor heathens who'd never touched down in the Sorbonne.

"Do you still use it?" I asked him.

"Yes, and every time . . ."

"Save it."

"You may not have all the answers, Piper."

"I gotta go."

"We weren't alone, you know." His face seemed wide and squishy like a jellyfish pressed against the side of an aquarium and I wished I could have believed him because the thought of him being the last person on earth Mom saw was almost more than I could stand.

I gripped the edge of the table and pulled myself out of the booth. I was going to ask Marge to say something to Dad if he showed up, but she was talking to someone in an old Stampede High letterman's jacket at the counter. I ducked out the door and turned left, even though it was the wrong way home, so I wouldn't have to pass in front of John Carlisle's window and subject myself to his false pity.

We'd had a September of sunny days and cold nights, the kind Mom said made the leaves go crazy, turning them into the colors from her tubes — Indian yellows, cadmium oranges and swatches of intoxicating Bordeauxs and bloody scarlets. Last September we'd hiked down to the river with our Igloo ice chest, the portable easel, and a tool box full of oils and brushes.

"Leaves are like people," she said. "Sometimes you don't know their true colors until they die."

She dabbed blobs onto her palette and became lost in her canvas while I lay in the weeds at her feet reading. When I sat up to look at her painting it was nothing like the landscape in front of us. She'd taken a bird's nest in the denuded tree on the bank and magnified it into a fortress with the heads of hungry children peeping over the sticks and straw.

"Reality's just a platform," she said. "My job is to rearrange things in a way that provokes people."

The paintings I liked most were the unfinished ones, and there were plenty of those in the attic. She sometimes painted there, under a skylight Dad had installed for her. When she fell asleep up there at night, I'd go up and say good morning before leaving for school. You could tell by the brightness of the palette what kind of mood she was in, saving the darker colors for when she was in a good mood and "could handle it." The finished pictures seemed more obvious. The unfinished canvasses, with dismembered torsos and misshapen faces, showed the struggle.

I must have been a disappointment to her because I was so plain. When I had hair, I abused it, washing it with hand soap, too much in a hurry to use conditioners, never bothering with face creams and coverups. My wardrobe consisted of jeans and plaid shirts, dark socks, and ankle-high boots with hooks for the laces. I didn't want anyone to mistakenly think I'd entered the competition for the boys on the playground. Of course, my strategy worked because they didn't notice me either. It was probably better Mom hadn't seen how I was turning out. It would have crushed her.

Since he'd come to live with us, Willard and I had more or less avoided each other in public. Once I found him loitering around school behind the cyclone fence in an old overcoat with one of the dogs. He looked like some pervert waiting to expose himself, and I told him to scram before someone called the police. We'd gotten into the habit of eating dinner together though. I never invited him; he just seemed to show up whenever I pulled the stove drawer open or closed the refrigerator too hard.

One night he showed up in an orange bib someone from a road construction crew had given him. Visiting job sites was one of his hobbies. "What's cookin', Piper?"

"Matar Panir." Mom had shown me how to make it.

He wrinkled his nose, opened the refrigerator, and studied the alternatives as if this was the night he'd go gourmet, but it was always the same thing: a fried egg and the canned Spam he kept covered with a sandwich bag. "Aren't you gonna ask where we went today?" *We* meant him and one of his dogs. He never took more than one at a time in daylight for fear of being seen by Dad.

While I stirred the sauce, I was reading *Lolita* through the plastic cookbook holder, spying on her through Humbert Humbert's eyes, listening to Willard with half an ear. "I could never guess."

"You know that project over by the Caterpillar place?" I could hear the Spam glucking out of the can and onto the breadboard. I didn't have to answer every question, because Willard's verbal momentum usually carried the conversation without me. "They're making a mess out of the street. Putting in sewer pipes." In my peripheral vision, I saw his hand reach for a paring knife from the wooden rack next to me. "The old ones were cast iron and rusted out."

"Uhm."

"Now they're using some polyprobable stuff that lasts forever. I asked if they needed a hand." There was something about subjects with five or more syllables that brought out the pedant in him. He poked me in the rib that stuck out. "You with me?"

"Huh?"

"I'm trying to tell you about the real world and you're reading make-believe."

"What do you mean? Polypropylene's synthetic." I sometimes surprised myself at my inadvertent retention of minutiae.

He'd speared a cadaver of pink Spam on his knife and there was gel all over his fingers. "I meant the job."

"What job?"

"I'm trying to get hired on."

"You're on Social Security, why would you want a job?"

He lowered a slice of meat into the small frying pan with the dent in it where Dad had driven a stake for my tent in the backyard. "I thought I could save up for a camper or something. One of them aluminum airstream jobbies with the steps that fold out. That'd be slick, huh?" His flights of fancy resembled the ones Mom painted, but his chances of ever pulling off such a ludicrous scheme were about as good as the chance those kids in her birdnest would wake up some morning and fly.

His meat was sizzling. "You're not eating your food groups," I said. "That stuff is pure cholesterol."

"I'm having an egg with it."

"That's what I mean. You need vegetables. You know, those pesky green and orange things that grow in the ground."

"Where's Tom?" We went through this every night. It was as if he forgot Dad worked at the newspaper. "Why doesn't he take you fishing or bowling?"

"I don't like to fish. It's boring."

"Sittin' in your room is boring. Believe me, that's why I have my dogs."

"That's why I have this," I said, pointing to *Lolita*. My finger left a smudge on the plastic holder and I tried to wipe it off with the side of my hand, which made it worse. *Damn.* Willard wouldn't let me read and now I couldn't see the print. "Besides, Dad's swamped at the paper."

"No man on his deathbed's gonna cry 'cause he didn't put in enough hours at the job." He flipped the Spam with the point of his knife and the pan attacked the virgin flesh with a crescendo of voracious sizzles. The black scab on the top side made it resemble real meat. "What's he do down there anyway?"

I didn't want to tell Willard what I suspected was really going on, but I'd overheard Dad say the paper was hurting. Everyone was getting as much news as they wanted on TV. "Print media is a dinosaur," he'd told me, but that hadn't stopped him. The *Herald Stampede* was the only paper in the country that had run a six-part series on "The Decline of Excellence in American Arts and Letters" under Tom Scanlon's byline. He must have felt sometimes as if he were howling into the wind. Seven years ago, somebody had listened to him though because he was nominated for a Pulitzer prize in beat reporting for his series that led to the County Executive's indictment for taking kickbacks on the construction of a sanitary landfill that never opened. The big papers had missed it.

Business at the *Herald* was punk enough that they'd laid off several staff, and started using the press for printing junk mail, greeting cards, and school workbooks on the side. Although we never had much money, Mom always made sure we ate well, buying the best cuts of meat and organic fruits and vegetables. Now we were eating canned vegetables and ice milk instead of ice cream.

"Carlisle wants to turn the paper into more of a high society thing," I told Willard, saving him the messy details.

"A what?"

"You know, personal interest stories about people who are loaded. Who just got back from Italy and who's going next."

Willard had a puzzled look on his face.

"It's a joke, Willard. There *is* no high society in Stampede." My rice was done and I flipped off the back burner and slid the pan onto a newspaper. "Dad could have been a Pulitzer prize winner at the *Washington Post* and

Carlisle's got him babysitting a glorified handbill for the local merchants, running pictures of widows with wrinkled necks in costume jewelry." I picked up the lid on the rice pan, forgetting to use a pot holder, and dropped it to the floor. "Ouch!"

Startled, Willard's egg went half into the Spam pan and half out as he cracked it. He licked the egg white off his fingers. "Them Carlisles could buy the *Post*."

"That would take class and John Carlisle doesn't have enough of that to shine his shoes." I licked the burn on my thumb and waved it in the air.

"They say never argue with someone who buys ink by the gallon."

I couldn't help but laugh. Sometime I would have to find out what he really thought of the Carlisles. He'd been around long enough to have seen the full cycle, from the homesteaders to the freeloader.

I sat at the table in the nook to eat, not bothering with my book. Willard ate his fried egg sandwich standing up, as if he was in a hurry to get back down with the dogs. The catsup that he'd added to expand his food groups dripped onto his Scott towel. As he paced the floor and rattled on, I looked at his right ear, the cauliflower one that had been bitten off in a fight in the asparagus fields. Willard wasn't that shy about sticking up for himself. Mom told me that when Willard lost his ear the doctor had to attach it to his groin so it would heal before they sewed it back on his head. I wished sometimes Dad had some of that spunk. The Irish were supposed to be the ones with the hair-trigger tempers, but Dad was always the consummate gentleman.

"My Carol was high society," Willard said. "Almost didn't marry me, you know." He wobbled his head, pulling up his recollections slowly like a bucket from the bottom of a deep well. I thought he was going to tell me again about the wedding in the Okanogan Valley when he fired his rifle into the church ceiling. Willard had trouble remembering where Dad worked, but his memories of Grandma Carol were always resplendent in their detail. "I fixed a

Valentine's Day dinner at her house once when the parents were away. Chicken fricassee and rice. Put a cup of them candy hearts next to her plate for dessert and she held it under the light, stirring it with her little finger. When I asked her what she was doing, she said she was looking for the jewelry. Can you beat that? I couldn't afford bus fare and she was looking for diamonds." Tears of lost joy welled in the corners of his eyes, but I was stung by the insensitivity of the woman who'd turned out to be the love of his life.

"I never really knew Grandma Carol."

"She was a real fussbudget. But I finally came through. Proposed to her in a hot springs under the moonlight and you know what her first question was?"

I shook my head.

"Where's the ring?"

Now tears were welling in my eyes. Willard was obviously blinded by his love for this woman. Rather than turn bitter though, he'd taken her uppityness as a challenge, proof of her good breeding.

———5———

I WAS THE FIRST one to arrive at the double-sided billboard on Horse Heaven Highway. Nothing of importance in Stampede was beyond walking distance, even though most people drove everywhere as a matter of course. While waiting for Dirk, I checked out the latest advertisements, which were illuminated by spotlights. One side featured a larger-than-life blonde in high heels on an ottoman with a bent knee cupped between her hands, revealing two perfect legs in pantyhose. The board that faced motorists on their way into town had an inscription in a formation of cumulus clouds that read: "If there's a heaven, you've just found it!" It was signed by the Greater Stampede Chamber of Commerce.

Mom used to say Stampede was a time capsule people had buried under a corner of the state. "Civil rights is still a debatable issue here," she said. "And they haven't dared crack the lid on women's issues." Even though I knew what she said might be true, it always hurt because I knew that, like it or not, Stampede was always going to be part of me. If Stampede was impaired, I was impaired.

I hitched myself up between the braces to the running boards and looked back down towards the highway. The billboards were about fifty yards beyond the four-way stop that represented the city limits. Dirk and I had discovered years ago that the police turned their cars around at the intersection and, unless they went beyond the city limits and shone their spotlights directly into the crossbeams, there was no way they could see us. Dirk used to fill his pockets with pea gravel and fire his slingshot at passing trucks. There was little risk of injury. He had trouble hitting the ones standing still at the truck stop.

The billboards were a perch from which we could play God — hand the stone tablets to Moses, or make soldiers in the plaza march goose steps. I used the billboards to prac- tice my Mark Antony speech before the freshmen elocution contest and the enclosure did for my oratory what the shower did for my Janis Joplin. Of course, when the real thing came, the gymnasium soaked up the drama in my voice like a thirsty desert.

"Hey, give me a hand." It was Dirk, with one foot braced against the diagonal below me.

"Where you been?"

He was puffing and reaching up for me. "I had to . . . do the beds."

"The beds?"

His hand was sweaty and I slid mine down so I had him by the wrist. "You know . . . Thursdays . . . change the sheets . . . ouch, you're pinching me!"

The slingshots and Cokes Dirk used to cop from the cooler at Ned's and stick in the pockets of his Army fatigues eventually gave way to filter cigarettes we'd sneak out of our parents' packs, one at a time so they wouldn't be missed. I hadn't felt that good about stealing Mom's cigarettes, but I figured she'd live longer if we smoked some for her. She later gave up on her own when she started doing yoga. Dirk was the first one to bring a "brewskie," a Lucky Lager that tasted like elk urine. We were hunters and gatherers then, venturing into the world to see what contraband we had the courage to snag, bring back to the billboards, and ingest. Dirk brought wine cooler in a Gatorade jar once and I outdid him with a couple of jiggers of Gilbey's in a jelly jar that he spit all over the front of his Chicago Bulls sweatshirt. We smoked our first pot from one of his dad's pipes that was all mossy and chewed up on the mouthpiece. Holding the smoke in his lungs the way he'd seen Peter Fonda do in *Easy Rider*, Dirk put his arm over my shoulder and let his hand dangle against my chest. Even with the dope there was no sexual chemistry, but I let him do it for practice. His and mine.

Dirk settled himself onto the plank with his legs hanging into the void next to mine. We had to remember to place rather than slide our hands on the boards in order to avoid slivers. Once when he was wearing cutoffs, Dirk took a sliver as long as a pencil into the back of his thigh that pinned him to the board, and I had to drag his butt the opposite direction to free him. Now, he reached into the inside pocket of his jacket, took out a pack of unfiltered Camels, and tamped one out for me, which I refused. It wasn't anything highly principled on my part. I still enjoyed a smoke once in a while, particularly with a beer, but I didn't want to immunize myself against the few pleasures life had to offer by indulging when I could give a damn.

He took a first, rabid drag with his eyes closed, leaving the cigarette in the corner of his mouth on the exhale. Smoking was a way for Dirk to prove his manhood without having to work up a sweat or risk physical harm. Each time a car went by, the lights washed the insides of our perch, a space that resembled a medieval gallows. I was enjoying the smell of Dirk's Camel, but then I had always been drawn to toxic aromas. The fumes at the gas pump reminded me of the times our family had gone to the outdoor movies. The fireplace smoke that billowed into the living room when Dad forgot to open the vent was Christmas dinner. Dirk's cigarette reminded me of those bygone days when I thought I was as normal as everyone else.

"That dork'll make someone a wonderful wife," Dirk said, when I told him about my meeting with Carlisle at Marge's.

There were plenty of theories as to why John Carlisle had never married. Some said it was because he was so well-educated he'd priced himself out of the local market so to speak. Others who were less charitable said it was because he was still whoring around. At a time when the town was losing everyone who made it past high school to higher paying jobs in Seattle, however, most people were just grateful he'd chosen Stampede as his home. Of course, John Carlisle didn't need a job, and he had the most imposing home in Stampede, a chalky yellow Queen Anne at the top of the hill with steeply-pitched gable roofs, turrets, and a porch with turned posts and a balustrade. His house was the main attraction on the Historical Society's

Christmas walking tour of the town's Victorian homes. Last year, there was a ribbon on the master bedroom doorknob with a sign that said no visitors allowed, but Condon Bagmore snuck in anyway and said he found a box of Trojans in the drawer of the nightstand. Considering the source, I didn't put much stock in it. I just hoped this year the Jacuzzi would be blocked off.

Dirk picked a piece of tobacco off the tip of his tongue. "The guy's helpless. I guess that's why I was his yard boy. I hoped somebody would kidnap me and they'd make Carlisle pay the ransom." Dirk had always craved the idea of instant fame and complained about the guys who'd taken shots at the President or mailed pipe bombs around the country and became household names overnight. He was always dreaming of a shortcut.

I kicked him on the ankle bone with the side of my shoe. "Thanks for the support, Dirk."

"You'd do the same for me."

"Hey, you didn't ask me up here to talk about John Carlisle."

He snuffed out his cigarette against the wall and flicked it out over the top of the billboard. Then he pulled out his pack and tamped out a fresh one, his fingers tense in the flare of his match. He took the first big drag, the one that carried all the sweetness the way the first chew on a stick of gum did. "I'm pussy-whipped, Piper." Nobody but Dirk talked this way. He seemed burdened with the historical jargon of teenage angst.

"Who is it this time?"

"Rozene Raymond."

My brain seized at the mention of her name. Rozene Raymond was the Makah Indian girl in our class with the mermaid chest and Mona Lisa smile. Even I got goose bumps around Rozene. "You haven't gone out with her. How could you be pussy-whipped?"

"I've stopped studying. I've memorized her class schedule and walk out of my way just to run into her at breaks. She's the last thing I think of when I fall asleep."

I looked over at him to make sure he wasn't putting me on. "And she doesn't even know you exist."

"I'm just a beefy white kid with a mild case of acne who's got the hots for her."

I probably had no business prying into this, but I couldn't help myself. "What's so special about her?"

He sputtered and coughed from the smoke, his voice strained as he tried to catch his breath. "Shit . . . where do I start? Those burning black eyes, her lips, the taper of her ankles." He reached up and held onto the overhead brace. "I could die and go to heaven if she'd just look me in the eye once and whisper my name like it meant something to her."

"You're wasted, Dirk. Take up the marathon."

"Come on, don't do that. How can I turn her on to me?"

This was the blind leading the blind. I'd never seduced anyone or been seduced. Dirk was my friend, my only friend, but I wasn't sure I really wanted him to get to where he was heading. This would have been the right time to say something about the strange mixture of passion and panic swirling inside me, but I couldn't. I answered instead. "Mom told me women like vulnerability."

"Hey, perfect. I'm a basket case."

"I think you're missing the point." I remembered a line from Yeats Dad had recited — *Do not love too long, or you will grow out of fashion like an old song* — but I couldn't figure out how to use it. "Show her who you are and the rest will follow."

"You sound like a fortune cookie."

"Bite your ass. I'm trying to help."

What I liked about Dirk probably bore no resemblance to what Rozene Raymond wanted from someone. There was a profound sense of confusion, even duplicity, in Dirk that I trusted. One of my fondest memories of him was the time he played the lion in the *Wizard of Oz* in grade school. You couldn't have recognized Dirk through the costume, but as much as he hated his Gestapo father he dearly wanted him to see that play. His dad didn't show for the performance and Dirk cried afterwards out by the girls' kickball backstop, a scene more moving than anything he'd done on stage. It wasn't as if Dirk was an innocent. I was still mad at him for the time he copped one of my mom's cotton candy brassieres and I found it in a drawer in his room when I was looking for a cigarette. He said he took it because he liked her.

As we climbed down the billboards and headed back toward town, we passed the power transformer next to the highway and it was humming and buzzing. In summer, you could always hear crickets chirping from the alfalfa fields below the billboard, but as the temperatures dipped in the fall they disappeared and took their show somewhere else. A semi braked for the four-way stop sign and its hydraulic brakes hissed at us as we crossed the street.

"Let me ask you something, Piper. Am I sexy?"

I knew this wasn't the time to scrutinize the evidence. I looked him up and down, searching for the right words. "You've got warm eyes."

"That's all, warm eyes?"

"And presence . . . and a sense of humor" — from the slouch of his eyes, I could tell I wasn't convincing — "and a sexy voice." I reeled every video I could think of through my brain. "You remind me of Alec Baldwin."

His face brightened. "Really?"

"Sure."

He socked me on the shoulder and I knew I'd said the right thing.

After we said goodbye in front of the Eagles Lodge, I sat down on the sidewalk and leaned against the building, watching Dirk head home. I tried to picture Rozene Raymond and Dirk together. Why not? She'd never lack for attention, or would she? I remembered Mom telling me how Dad had written sonnets to her and picked roses from people's yards when they were courting. "Your dad would pose for me while I sketched him," she told me. "He said he'd follow me wherever we had to go for my art career."

She didn't have to tell me the rest of it because I knew what came next: Dad disappeared into his journalism and Mom had to paint her own flowers.

Frankly, I couldn't be sure Rozene would be able to hold her own against Dirk's video collection if the truth were told, but maybe my cynicism was born of my own attraction for Rozene. An attraction that scared me. When Mom was alive we'd never talked about that possibility and I wasn't sure for all her sexual savvy how she would have accepted it.

At the last Christmas party for the newspaper staff in the Eagles Lodge, when Rozene's mother still worked for the newspaper, Rozene was there in a burgundy jumper and pumps that made her look like a model. I found myself standing at the edges watching her chat with people, exuding an unconditional warmth she withheld from no one. She was naturally shy, a straight-A student, but because she was part Makah Indian she'd never penetrated the cliques at school. The nerds as well as the turds teased her. She seemed oblivious to it though, busying herself with school work, trying out for girls intramural basketball, always carrying her head high, sitting wherever she wanted in the lunchroom. There was an amazing stillness about her that I thought had to be wearing. I could only hope she stuck needles in voodoo dolls in the privacy of her own bedroom at night. Secretly, I hoped her heart was as dark and twisted as mine.

Living alone with her mother in a double-wide at the Cedars Trailer Park, I imagined they had to be close. Her mother must have been proud to have raised someone as accomplished and beautiful as Rozene. But then there was the Great Equalizer in the sky. Whenever someone got too far ahead in one department, he'd clobber you in another. That's probably why Mrs. Raymond had lost her job at the paper, and Dad had lost his wife.

As I watched Dirk pass the facades of the shops on Commercial Street, I wondered if the Great Equalizer worked in reverse, when someone got too far behind. If so, maybe there was a windfall in Dirk's future, something to counterbalance all the crap he'd taken from his dad. It was just a matter of how sweet the payoff was going to be.

Everyone was tittering when I came into home room next morning. At first I thought it had to have something to do with me — my bald head, or blood that had soaked through my crotch. I took my usual seat on the aisle closest to the windows, trying to ignore the sophomorics. God, I could hardly wait to get out of high school and not have to worry about what I looked like every time I walked into a room. But my self-consciousness was wasted because nobody was looking at me. Secured with torn strips of masking tape to the blackboard was one of those blown-up posters the copy shop could make from an ordinary photograph. It was a picture looking down at a kid in a toilet stall who was masturbating. The photographer must have yelled something as he snapped the picture because the kid's mouth was agape. At the bottom of the poster, someone had printed in big letters: "Dirky Jerky."

I looked around trying to size up the situation. Dirk must have still been prowling the halls to catch a glimpse of Rozene, but she was one of those at the poster. I had to do something before he saw this. The bell rang and Mr. Wendall breezed through the door with a stack of papers coming loose from under his arm and a pencil over his ear. He stopped to take in the bedlam.

"Everyone take their seats and pipe down."

While the bell was still ringing and before the door closed, Dirk sliced his arm through. Averting his eyes from Mr. Wendall, he missed the poster. He was breathing hard and his shirt flap was hanging outside of his pants as he trudged back to his seat at the back of the middle row. Dirk was so intent on not being the last one to sit down that he didn't seem to notice the people staring at him. I wanted to yell, *Run for it, Dirk*, but what good would it do? Everyone had already seen the picture. The class quieted to a dull roar and Mr. Wendall dropped his papers onto the desk with a bang to signal his irritation.

"Tweezer dick," someone said in a deep monotone like a bullfrog. I snapped around to see Condon Bagmore drop his cupped hands away from the shitkicker grin on his face.

"Tweezerdick." It was someone else from the other side of the room.

"Tweezerdick." There was nervous laughter after each intonation of the mantra.

"The next one of you who mouths off is facing detention." Mr. Wendall was oblivious to the reason for the excitement. He pinched at the hair in the neck of his shirt, something he always did when a pretty girl approached his desk or he was on the verge of losing control of his class. Due to his mannequin good looks some people called him "Ken Doll," and he always had a large turnout for his girls' volleyball team.

Rozene Raymond sat two rows over and three desks ahead of me and I tried to see if she was joining in the laughter, but she was looking straight ahead at Mr. Wendall and I couldn't get a reading. Dirk was slumped in his seat, looking in the general direction of Rozene through bars formed by the fingers over his eyes.

I could wait no longer and marched up to the front of the class. Mr. Wendall had on a cologne like over-ripe peaches and I could vaguely feel his hands reaching out to stop me, which he probably would have done except for the fact he'd already been disciplined for touching female students. As I walked over to the poster, I could hear the jeers.

"Lick it, Piper!"

There was an uproar as I grabbed the top corners of the poster and ripped it down.

"What's that?" Mr. Wendall said. "Give it to me."

When I turned to face the class, Dirk was running up the aisle, his face a mushy dike on the verge of bursting.

Mr. Wendall made a pathetic effort to block him. "Where are *you* going, Mister?"

Dirk raised his elbow to protect his face from Mr. Wendall the way he'd probably done with his dad when his sheets weren't turned down just right, but Mr. Wendall wasn't his problem. It was Condon Bagmore and his band of sickos. For them, the rest of us were white mice they could inject, prod, and electrocute. Dirk pushed out the door and was gone.

"Take control of your goons," I said to Mr. Wendall, rolling the poster under my arm.

"I don't want any lip out of you, Ms. Scanlon. Now give me that."

I took a step back. There were catcalls and more laughter. "Not a chance," I said. If he reached for the poster, I was going to kick him. Nobody else was going to see that poster.

Someone in the back of class yelled out, "Scanlon sucks dick!" Laughter again.

I could feel the blur of Mr. Wendall coming towards me from the right. Somehow I had become the plug he needed to pull in order to drain this whole sorry mess from his classroom and I wasn't going to let him touch me. "Bugger you, Bagmore!" I yelled.

Someone in the front row said, "Ooh, she bites."

"And bugger any of the rest of you who think this is funny!" I gave Bagmore a left-handed finger, trying to make it as stiff as I could, and then I fanned it back and forth in front of the class like a shaman trying to exorcize the vermin from the room. The last pair of eyes I caught before jerking my shirt out of Mr. Wendall's fingers were Rozene's. They were riveted, unblinking, and, I wanted to believe, full of compassion.

I bolted for the door and would have slammed it but for the mechanical closer which allowed only a gradual muting of the racket as I ran toward my locker, looking up and down the hall for signs of Dirk. I couldn't stuff the poster into one of the waste cans for fear someone would dig it out and start the horror all over again. My locker was the only safe place. Except for the janitor's end of the year clean out, nobody messed with your lockers. Kids left pot and whiskey in them. When I reached my locker though, I didn't stop. Instead, I slowed to a fast march, then a stroll, and kept right on walking out the double-doors at the end of the hallway.

The outdoors was cool and cloudy, but it was devoid of voices and, for that reason, it was heaven. My skin was sweaty and I fluttered the front of my shirt to dry out. As I passed Marge's Cafe, I didn't do so much as an eyes right. My heartbeat had slowed and my wits were back in their pockets. If anyone asked, I was going home to get the project I'd forgotten for sixth period biology.

I thought of last night at the billboards with Dirk, how he'd scooted in close to me to keep warm, how he'd declared his infatuation with Rozene Raymond and his hopelessness. I wondered, on the ladder of human misery, what came below hopeless.

——6——

FOR DAYS, I DIDN'T touch the poster. I'd stuffed it into the shopping bag with the wrapping paper at the back of the closet, but I couldn't say I didn't think about it. In fact, the mere thought of it was making me itch.

In all the time we'd spent together — making kites to fly from the island in the middle of the river, sneaking into Carmichael's pasture and riding bareback on their old mare, or changing oil in the Thurgood's pickup — I'd never really thought of Dirk as someone with a sex drive. Mostly, we talked about sex as observers: his movies, my books. I'd never imagined that the same hands through which the kite string slipped during the day would be wrapped around his apparatus at night. Somehow, I felt cheated that he'd tranquilized me with his Tom Cruise video collection, yet had never gotten around to mentioning this. For all of our vows of fidelity, he hadn't trusted me with the real stuff. Nor had I him.

My formal sex education consisted of three visits by Father O'Malley at Saint Augustine's grade school (Stampede didn't have a Catholic high school or Dad probably would have made me attend it). The first two visits were devoted to the papal encyclicals on marriage. I only remembered the third visit, which the class ahead of us had promised got into the good stuff. Father O'Malley stood up in the front of the class while Sister Graziana sat at an empty desk in the back saying her rosary. He was a stooped over man with sagging jowls and perspiration that he sponged off with the handkerchief wadded up inside the sleeve of his black jacket.

"It's called self-abuse," he told us. That was no surprise, I thought. For Catholics, most things starting with "self" were troublesome. I never questioned the characterization. It was one of those terms you grew up with, like "adultery" and "fornication." "Your penises are for procreation," he said, the phlegm in his voice rattling like loose gravel across the bed of a pickup. I waited anxiously in row four, seat three, for him to say something about vaginas, but he never even uttered the word. Apparently, all of us St. Augustinettes were merely foils whose role in the great sexual escapade was to push eager hands away from our breasts and thighs. "If you're tempted with impure thoughts, boys, read *The Confessions of St. Augustine.*"

Father O'Malley's talks were no help. The stories of Onan spilling his seed became confused in my mind with Sodom and Gomorrah. If God or your dad caught you at it, he'd turn you into a pillar of salt. Whatever the theological implications, I was pretty certain based upon what Father O'Malley had said that self-abuse was a male thing. The act itself had been named after the master, not the mistress. Until reading Anais Nin, I'd never heard of a woman doing it and I still hadn't found anyone who did it as often as I did.

Ironically, it was something I later used as evidence to convince myself I was normal. My fantasies included men in tight jeans, male body parts, guys on road crews. It wasn't until later that the images changed.

Of Dirk's poster I could say in all candor, "There but for the grace of God go I."

At lunch hour, I started leaving the school grounds and walking along the river for a smoke to get away from everyone, hoping I'd run into Dirk, who still hadn't returned to school. It was against the rules to leave the grounds, but nobody enforced them unless you were late for class.

Instead of doing the river, I decided to stroll through Kla Hah Ya Park. I knew Dirk couldn't be home or his dad would know he was skipping. In the field where kids played Ultimate Frisbee, I noticed a man in knee pads with a pair of earphones, traversing the grass, moving an apparatus that looked like a weedeater back and forth in front of him. I walked over to see what was going on. His back was to me and there was a collie following him. Suddenly the man stopped, dropped to his knees, and took a trowel out of his back pocket. With both hands, he leaned on his trowel and pushed the blade into the earth again and again until he was able to rip out a rectangle of sod about the size of a squirrel grave. When I leaned over to see what was underneath the sod, he must have noticed me because he turned around.

"You scared me."

"Willard? What are you doing?"

"Treasure hunting." He reached into the pocket of his tattered sportcoat with the leather elbows and pulled out an assortment of bottle caps, rusty screws, coins, and a needle valve. "Here, lookee." Freeway looked up at me appreciatively, panting.

"It's junk."

Wheezing with delight, he reached into his other pocket. "Junk? This is junk?" Between his thumb and index finger he held what could have been a diamond ring that still had mud encrusted in the setting.

"You can't keep that, you know."

He pushed the ring against my sternum. "Finders keepers, losers weepers."

"Nice try, Willard. Someone's probably looking for it. They'll nab you when you try to fence it."

"In Wapato?"

"What are you talking about?"

"I have a second cousin there."

"Is he alive?"

He cackled, cracked open his jacket pocket, and dropped the ring back in.

"Have you seen Dirk?"

He started shifting his weight from one foot to the other, his eyes alternating between me and the hole in the grass. "The Army officer's boy?"

Yeah, sure, Willard, as if you didn't know. Something didn't fit.

After dinner, I wasn't in the mood to read and found myself following Willard downstairs. Before he came to live with us, I never went to the basement unless it was to flip the breaker switches when one of the circuits went out. He stopped at the bottom of the stairs and turned around, obviously trying to block me. His eyes were doing that flitting around thing, like he was tracking fireflies.

"You looking for somethin' in particular," he said.

"I'm bored." With Dad gone all the time and Willard in the basement, the house's center of gravity had been lowered. When there was nothing else to do, I headed down instead of up these days.

"This visit is off the record?"

"You have another mutt downstairs, don't you?"

He snorted and shuffled, tapping his toes against the baseboard, his eyes still flitting. "They're not mutts. They're disciples."

"Whatever. The point is you're over the limit." I side-stepped Willard and proceeded towards his room.

"Remember our deal . . .?" He walked backwards next to me as he talked, a pretty nimble feat for an old man who said he was a disappointment to his wife as a dancer even in his prime. Of course, Grandma Cooper had the benefit of toe dancing lessons on those days when Willard was out cutting asparagus spears.

The door to Willard's room had a wooden dowel handle like the latch for a barn. I could hear the anticipatory squeals and wags of Willard's disciples coming alive inside, wondering what else their master had pinched from the refrigerator. As soon as the door opened, they flowed past me in waves to get to Willard, their tails beating against my pantlegs. The silver pug with the black mask was the lowest to the ground and the last one to reach him. Willard sprouted extra hands as he cupped each one of their heads, tugged at their ears, and itched the hindquarters of those who turned their butts to him. I counted five, which was right. Mrs. Churchill, the black and tan beagle with the droopy ears and pendent lips whom Willard said was more of a coonhound, circled back inside the room after getting her touches and stood in front of the closet, with her tail wagging.

"Are you satisfied?" he said, shoving his hands into his front pockets.

I sprung the closet door. "Jesus!" On the floor, in a half-lotus position, a pair of dirty jeans, unlaced Nikes, and no socks, was Dirk Thurgood. His eyes were bloodshot and hollow, like someone who'd just fought a forest fire.

"Your grandpa said I could stay here."

"You could have asked me."

"Leave him be," Willard said, patting me on the arm.

"Did you tell Willard why you're here?"

"Not exactly . . ."

"It's only shameful, you know, if you make it that way."

"Tell that to my dad . . ."

"Screw your dad! Hasn't he ever played with himself?"

"He found out about it."

"It's not like you robbed a bank, or forgot to salute. You've got to unfasten his grip on you."

"Yeah, how?"

"Give him something he can really cry over."

"Like what?"

"I don't know. Something."

Freeway, the twelve-year old greybeard with arthritis, edged his paws into the closet and methodically licked the dirt off Dirk's bare ankle. I could see why Dirk liked to hang out down here. Acceptance by his peers was instantaneous. Willard brought him food and water, newspapers, whatever he needed. The only essential he lacked was his VCR.

It was late by the time I convinced Dirk he had to go home and take control of his life again. We made him shower and clip his fingernails. Willard lent him a pair of clean under-wear and socks. We figured the cleanliness would neutralize his dad. Although Dirk protested each step of the way, the attention seemed to get his blood circulating again.

"You guys are nuts," he said.

Willard and I walked him home with the dogs, taking the back streets so we wouldn't run into my dad. As we got closer to Dirk's, I watched his shoulders collapse and his head droop. His gait changed to a shuffle, his shoes scuffed against the sidewalk, and his words turned to a mumble.

"Thas enuf," he said when we were about to cross the street onto his block.

His house was the one with the well-squared hedgerow and the lattice arbor that arched over the entrance to the walkway. The only lights on were those upstairs. "We'll wait here," I said.

The dogs started to follow him and Freeway herded them back to the sidewalk where they waited as Dirk slouched across the intersection under the glow of the streetlight. When he reached the opposite curb, he stopped to hitch his pants and tuck in his shirt. It was a gesture of readiness and I nudged Willard. "See?"

Willard turned to go home, the dogs rustled, and I grabbed his arm to detain him. I wanted to see the front door crack and Dirk go into the house. He looked back at us just before crossing under the arbor. I could hear the door unstick and thump shut again. I waited to hear voices, but none were decipherable over the faint buzz of the street-light. Freeway seemed to know something was going on because his ears perked up and he stared dead-straight towards the lattice arbor.

On the way back, Willard seemed preoccupied and I finally asked him what the matter was.

"You didn't need to get so mad at him," he said.

"I'm not mad. We're friends."

"Looks like you're more'n friends."

"What do you mean by that?"

He picked up a rock from the sidewalk and dropped it into the fenced circle at the base of a sapling. "I seen him coming out of your bedroom."

"Oh, come on, Willard." I bumped my shoulder into his. "He's just a neighbor."

The light was on in Dad's bedroom, so Willard and I separated in the driveway. He headed for the basement entrance and I went to the front door, timing my opening to cover the racket of Willard and the dogs entering from below.

Dad's door was shut, and I stood in the hall deciding whether to say anything. Their bedroom had always been private space and I only went in there when they weren't home. It had a smell like air trapped between the sheets. Maybe he was reading the national periodicals that had been piling up in a heap under the mail slot. Maybe he was falling asleep in his clothes again. Earlier in the week, I'd seen him wear the same clothes two days in a row, and his pin-striped dress shirt looked like he'd wadded it up and sat on it.

"It's me, Dad. Goodnight."

I heard ice cubes fall against the bottom of a glass and I thought I could smell a trace of dope eking out from under the door. I knew Mom had experimented when she was young, so had I, but the thought of Dad having a toke startled me. "You shouldn't stay up so late on a school night," he said. Some people got frivolous when they smoked; Dad was probably the kind who became paranoid. If he asked me where I'd been, I was going to tell him I was watching a video with Dirk. Although Dad didn't particularly care for Colonel Thurgood, he knew the Colonel was strict and, therefore, safe. "Sorry I stayed so late at work." He always said that and I think he meant it, but he couldn't help working any more than I could stop thinking about Mom in the bottom of the Jacuzzi.

My toes were cold and I put on a pair of socks to wear under the sheets while I read. Lately, it seemed as if I had to read to sleep, but I also had to read to stay awake. I kept thinking of Dad smoking dope by himself in the melancholy of his room. I hooked my toes into the back of my socks, pulled them off and stuffed them into the foot of the bed along with the others. I doused the light and tried to follow the exhalations out of my body, something Mom had taught me. *Pranayama,* part of her Hatha Yoga practice.

My mind drifted to Dirk and the hangdog attitude that had enveloped him since the poster thing and it made me mad that he could be reduced to such a pathetic condition for doing nothing wrong. I tried to think of the good times when his back was straight and his humor was cutting and we thought we were two of the smartest people Stampede had ever begot. But the only place I could picture him was in the lavatory stall with his pants down around his ankles.

I flipped on the goose neck light next to my bed and found the wrapping paper bag in the closet. I just wanted to take a quick look and see what all the fuss was about, get it out of my system so I could relate to Dirk again the way we always had. I propped my pillows against the wall and slid back under the covers. Pieces of masking tape were still stuck to the poster and I had to unroll it carefully so the tape didn't rip the picture. I flattened the edges against the bedspread to keep it from curling back on itself. Someone must have had his finger over the lens because the top corner of the poster was dark. The rest of it was unmercifully clear. Dirk was leaning back against the toilet tank, his butt on the edge of the seat, and his legs wrapped around the toilet bowl. His left hand was holding the shirt out of the way, and his right hand was doing the business. It was hard to imagine a more vulnerable position.

I covered the center of the poster with my hand, uncertain whether the nausea I felt was the result of bitterness over what Bagmore had done or something else. I'd seen pictures of male organs before, but there was something disappointing about it that had nothing to do with Dirk. In fact, I didn't really believe that the thing in Dirk's hand had anything to do with Dirk. It was a piece of meat, and it confirmed what I'd always suspected. The aesthetics of the imagination were superior to the real thing.

I licked my lips; they were dry. I rubbed the insides of my thighs; they were numb. Instead of titillation, I was feeling the early stages of rigor mortis. I shook my head and couldn't help but chuckle at what a perverse joke the culture had played on all of us. All the hype, the shows I wasn't supposed to see, the magazines I wasn't supposed to read, the eternal anticipation of that magic moment when penis meets woman. Instead of dancing around it, Father

O'Malley should have just shown us his and ended all temptation.

Mom had bandaged the boy in the accident and all anyone remembered was the fact she'd stripped down to her bra. Dirk was crazy about Rozene Raymond and all she'd probably remember about him was this damn poster.

---7---

THE FIRST DAY DIRK came back to school he slunk around with his chin on his neck and his hands in his pockets. The hunchback of Notre Dame had better posture. People ribbed him, but he'd never had more girls looking at him in the hallways. At lunch hour, I took him out to the pole vault pit so we could have some privacy. I had to practically yell at him, but he finally told me what had happened with his dad.

"He got out the camcorder and made me strip."

"He filmed you?"

"'Come on, cowboy,' he kept saying, 'beat the hog. I want to see cum. Where's your cum?'" This had to be worse than the taunts of his classmates when he ran home, because this time there was no place to run. He *was* home. The Colonel had used Dirk's video recorder to magnify the shame. Nothing was beyond the reach of the Colonel. "I've never felt so small," Dirk said. "I wanted to make something happen just to get it over with." He bulldozed the weathered wood chips in the pit with his shoe. "I figured I could burn the film later . . . but I couldn't do sickum."

It was cold. I was wearing a short-sleeve shirt. That might have been the reason I was trembling. "You gotta get back at him."

"Don't worry, I've got something in mind." There was grit in his voice, the leftovers from the rock in his jaw he must have chewed to pieces.

When some guys appeared doing chin-ups on the goal-post, I nudged Dirk to finish this somewhere else. We walked across the running lanes on the rubberized asphalt track, ducked under the railing, and into the grandstands. Neither one of us said anything as we passed through the tunnel, which smelled of urine and was littered with candy wrappers and cigarette butts. Kids went in there when it rained to have a smoke. Once we were out in the open again, Dirk drifted apart from me and I couldn't blame him. He was carrying enough baggage at school without taking on the daughter of Mary Magdalene.

"Meet after school?"

He shook his head. "Nah."

"The billboards?"

He shook me off.

Maybe it was a mistake to force out of him what had happened with his dad. He'd been subjected to double jeopardy already and I'd added a third. I'd caught him afraid to stick up to his dad. Whatever it was, our talk in the pole vault pit marked the beginning of an estrangement between us. He started avoiding me in the hallways and made a point of sitting at the opposite end of the cafeteria, even though that meant he usually had to eat alone. When I called his house, his mom answered. "Colonel Thurgood's residence," she'd say in a dutiful voice. I'd hear her call up the stairs, where there was an extension phone in the hallway, and I'd wait for it to click on, but she'd come back and say he didn't feel good or he was studying or he'd call me back, but he never did. Then he stopped showing up at school again.

I bounced back and forth between angry and just plain worried. He'd never done this before, even when I'd accidentally recorded over his copy of *Casablanca* or left his new ten-speed at the park and we found it rusted out under the bridge. I wasn't stupid. This was poison and it had the potential to drag him under, but he obviously didn't want me in on it. All I could do was watch and wait.

Dad surprised me one night with an invitation to go whale watching on the Greenpeace boat that ran out of Anacortes. It wouldn't have been my first choice of things to do, but I knew it had to be important to him because he was going to take off a day of work and let me skip school.

"You always turn me down for baseball," he said. "So I tried to think of something at the other end of the spectrum." Dad had made the obligatory attempts to engage me in sports when I was little, to help Mom break down the sexist stereotypes. He'd stand in the yard throwing me short spirals with the football, but mine wobbled back in return. He always said *Nice throw*, but I could see the pain in his eyes. If there was a vote when I was adopted, I was pretty sure his had been for a boy.

The morning of the excursion I got up at six a.m. so I'd have time to shave my head. Maybe I was arming myself against whatever Dad had on his mind. My baldness would remind him he had to keep his expectations realistic. We stopped at Marge's for breakfast on the way out of town and neither of us said anything for the longest time. I kept my mouth full of pancake, which was crazy because I'd looked forward to doing something with him and there were so many things bubbling inside that it had never occurred to me I'd be so empty-headed. Dad must have had the same problem because whenever I caught his eye, his mouth was full too and he pointed his knife to his cheeks as if to blame it on the chewiness of the rib steak, part of Marge's "Western Breakfast." I wished someone had put a quarter in the jukebox.

Our voices didn't come until we'd boarded the *Pequod*, a made-over fishing trawler with a cabin in the center where you could go for coffee and watch a whale movie. There were about twelve of us, in addition to the skipper and a wildlife biologist with a battery-powered megaphone looped around her neck. Dad and I went to the bow where we could feel the spray off the tops of the whitecaps against our faces. He was wearing a yellow rain slicker with a rip across the chest that had been mended with duct tape and rubber boots that were unbuckled. The hair on his head danced in the wind.

"Beats work," he said, raising his voice above the rumble of the engine and the breaking of the vessel through Rosario Strait.

"I didn't know you liked boats so much."

"It's not the boat. It's the whales." His eyes were squinting into the face of the wind. "Didn't you read my story?" I vaguely remembered skimming an article he'd written about the Makah tribe's petition to resume hunting of the gray whale. Knowing how delicate Rozene was it was hard for me to picture her people harpooning whales.

Maybe it was to settle a score. Although the gray whale was a threatened species, the article said there were more of them left than Makahs. "The whale has the largest brain on the planet," Dad said. "Twenty pounds. A sperm whale can dive a quarter mile down and stay forty minutes."

"Not too smart."

He laughed. "Depends on what's down there, I guess. Moby Dick was a sperm whale."

"I thought Moby Dick was fictional."

"The ones we're going to see are Orcas." Passing through the cabin, I'd seen a picture of an Orca swimming upside down under water with a baby whale riding its stomach. They were sleek, two-toned animals, with an ivory lower jaw and belly and the rest of them rubber black. "The females suckle each other's young," Dad said. He looked wistfully across the water and blinked several times to clear the tears that were building in his eyes. "The families bond for life." He turned away, wrestled his arm under the rain slicker, and fished a handkerchief out of the back pocket of his pants. The words *for life* still weren't something that rolled easily off his tongue. The pod represented what we could no longer have, maybe never had. The bond. The fidelity.

We went inside the cabin with everyone else for hot cocoa. Two tables were secured to the floor by a thick pipe and their tops were nicked with the ravages of time, probably by ordinary folks like us who'd sliced their apples and sandwiches there. In the video that played continuously from the overhead monitor, there was an Orca with its mouth clamped onto a seal struggling for its life. Nature was innocent only in the abstract.

The biologist whose name tag said "Nadine" took the seat across from us. Her rough brown hair was gathered by a rubberband into a ponytail, and the weight of the megaphone pulled a pink cord taut between her breasts. "First time on the *Pequod*?"

Dad looked at me. "Yes, it is," he said. "For both of us. We'd heard about your expeditions."

She chuckled and I noticed that one of her front teeth was chipped. "I'm not sure it's an expedition."

"Trust me," Dad said. "For us, it is." I knew what he meant. We hadn't managed to leave the house together for a common purpose since Mom died. If an expedition was something rare and fraught with uncertainty, this was an expedition.

"They're sure an elegant creature, " I said, pointing to the video, trying to show my allegiance to the cause.

"That's a female," she said proudly. "They're sexually dimorphic." *Oh, God*, I thought, wasn't there anyplace I could escape it? She must have seen my panic because she chuckled, the same way Mom would have. "That just means they're built differently. The males are larger than the females and they have those huge dorsal fins on their back. Sexy, huh?"

I laughed politely.

Dad changed the subject and fell into his journalist's habit of asking questions. She explained how they knew every member of the pod we were searching for. They'd assigned names to them. Some of them were marked for tracking purposes. But Dad couldn't control the direction of her answers anymore than he could control the migratory paths of the Orcas.

"The men leave the pod temporarily to mate outside of their natal group," she said, bending a stick of gum into her mouth. "They form bachelor schools and head to cooler waters. Sound familiar?"

I looked over at Dad and he moved the corners of his mouth upward, but it wasn't a smile.

Nadine made an announcement that we were getting close to them and everyone put their headbands and parkas on and went out on deck. The pilot slowed the engines and we cruised the western shore of San Juan Island. At the slower speed, the smell of the diesel was more pronounced and I thought how presumptuous it was for us to think the whales would trust this hunk of human machinery, no matter who owned it. I leaned over the rail and tried to train my eyes past the glare on the surface and into the depths, but the best I could do was detect a subtle change in the coloring of the water from blue to inky green.

We cruised all the way to English Camp at the north end of the island without a sighting. Dad had warned me on the way up how much of a gamble this was. Nadine had resorted to describing the features of the shoreline. "You can still see the old lime quarries carved into the hillsides. Someday, they'll probably be part of a subdivision."

Dad paced the starboard deck with his gaze forward. "It's all right," I told him on one of his turns. "I've learned something about whales anyway."

"I wanted you to see them. Until you see one in the flesh you won't feel it."

I wandered up to the bow, climbed over the anchor, and leaned into the wind. The front of my jeans was pressed against the insides of the boat and the gunwale hit me at the beltline. I felt like a gargoyle. What had Nadine called it, dimorphic? I was taller than half the boys my age and flat-chested. If I were a whale, maybe I'd have a dorsal fin and swim to cooler waters with the boys in their bachelor schools. And if I didn't play by nature's rules, they'd probably chew me up and spit me out like the hapless seal.

I was near the spot where Dad was standing when he'd wept earlier and I was feeling a strong sense of estrangement. His attempt to patch together a substitute family with me and Willard was valiant, but problematic. We were different generations, different temperaments. Dad and Willard weren't sucklers. I couldn't tell either of them that I didn't want what I was supposed to want, that instead of salvaging Mom's reputation I was going to further shame it.

"Starboard, thirty degrees!" Nadine yelled.

At first I couldn't see anything. The horizon was flat, wet, and unbroken. Then Dad came up behind me. The chocolate on his breath was pleasant and reassuring as I followed the imaginary extension of his index finger out across the water.

"They're like smooth rocks," I said.

"There's six of them."

Then another one surfaced closer to the *Pequod* and snorted water into the air. "My God," I yelled, "look at that dorsal fin!" It stuck up like an erection.

Dad was leaning into me, pressing me harder into the gunwale. "He must be the bull."

"What if he decides to capsize us?"

"Seeing them makes you believe there's a God, doesn't it?"

We locked in on their speed and followed them south, staying about a hundred and fifty yards back. The boat was alive with murmurs and gasps. Nadine, who could recognize them by their flukes, counted nine as they arched and breached and slapped their tails to entertain us. People along the rail ran their video cameras nonstop. One man had a telescopic lens that was so hefty that he had to brace his elbow against his chest to hold it steady. Nadine walked along behind us with a huge smile across her face. No need for the megaphone now. The mammals were speaking for themselves and I was in awe. I could feel the power of that bond. They were fearless, and they were flaunting it. Now I understood why the men who pursued the whales became tribal leaders. The whales were gods.

When we lost them near American Camp, everyone went inside the cabin and finished their sack lunches, played cards, and talked excitedly like they'd always known each other. Dad made the rounds like he'd gone to college with them, laughing easily, talking politics, making jokes. He ended up sitting with Nadine and they became engrossed in a conversation about sperm whales and grays. Dad knew something about everything. "It's a survival skill," he told me once. "What if you're stranded in an elevator with a total stranger?" It was times like these that drove home the reality I wasn't really his daughter, nor Mom's. I had none of their softness with other people, none of that desire to befriend every member of my species. I found a place on the floor in the corner of the cabin where there was a decent light and pulled *Giants of the Sea* off a nearby shelf.

It was dusk when we reached the dock. People shook hands and congratulated each other like we'd circumnavigated the globe together. I was surprised to see Dad give Nadine a kiss on her cheek. When she hugged me, I could feel the full measure of her breasts. They were her softest part and she let go before I did.

Dad had to get back for a meeting, so we ordered dinner from a squawk box in a drive-thru on the way home. I was kind of disappointed. In my fantasy, we were going to continue this expedition into the evening, sit in front of the fireplace and play Scrabble, then go for a walk with Willard. I'd have the courage to tell him what had happened to Dirk and get his advice. And if that went well, maybe we'd talk about how to negotiate my way across the canyon in my chest that had opened when Mom died.

We passed the oil refinery across the bay, every building and tank ornamented with red and white lights like a carnival grounds. A plume of orange flame flared out one of the stacks and, even with the windows closed, I could smell something like creosote. It was a miracle that the same hydrocarbons could smell so deliciously intoxicating when they turned into gasoline fumes at the pump. Dad dimmed his brights for oncoming cars. Click off. Click on. We were whales, communicating through clicks like Morse Code.

"You've become such a loner," Dad said out of the blue. "I'm worried about you."

I'd slouched down in the seat and straightened myself up to respond. "Me? I'm busy, what with senior year and everything." In truth, school had become a bust. I hadn't had homework in months. The teachers had slowed the pace of the classes to match guys like Jesse Little who still stumbled on his multiplication tables. To Dad's consternation, I'd quit yearbook staff. Every yearbook was so canned, the same mug shots of students, pictures of the one play the drama club managed to stage, guys dodging tacklers along the sidelines, and the obligatory hi-jinks shots of boys in dresses and cats drinking out of the water fountains.

"You need to get involved. Make new friends."

"I can barely keep up with the ones I have."

"And go out."

My groan was audible. Mom used to beg me to talk about the guys in my class. If I said anything the least bit complimentary, like he's read *Catcher in the Rye*, she'd seize on it. "Sit with him at lunch," she'd say. "Ask him on a study date." It was that ridiculous and unrelenting. Mom would have done cartwheels if I'd lost my virginity. "Don't make the mistake of waiting until you marry," she said. Fortunately, Dad lacked Mom's follow up.

"How'd you like a job at the paper?" he said. "We could use a good copy editor."

I was stunned. The only job I'd ever aspired to at the *Herald* was driving the delivery truck, which was really an old black hearse with no door on one side. For a lark, Les Showalter used to let me ride with him and fling bundles of papers out the door for the carriers. The paperboys would give me the finger and yell at me if I didn't get the bundles all the way to the sidewalk. He'd even let me empty the money from the metal newsstands and slide the new issues in. "Didn't you just lay off some people?"

"It was a budget-cutting measure." That meant it was John Carlisle's idea. Dad would never lay anyone off. He'd pay them out of his own pocket first.

"I'd work for free?"

He laughed. "Of course not. It's part-time. If it works out, maybe you can even do a little reporting." There was a gleam in his eye, the same gleam when he told me I could become editor-in-chief of the *Hoofprint*, the yearbook.

"You mean sports?"

"If you want."

"Dad, I was kidding."

"Come on, Piper. It'd be a chance to meet people."

I bit my tongue before I said something I'd regret. After all, the paper was who Dad was. It was what he had to give. If I didn't take that, when would there come along something else? "It's a generous offer."

Because he had to pick up some papers at the office, I walked home, taking the street. There was little or no traffic in Stampede once the shops closed and the chance of two cars passing each other at the same time was about as likely as an eclipse. I thought of Dad giving that peck on the cheek to the marine biologist. The stories Seamus had told me about him, how he was so crazy about women when he was young, seemed possible and not particularly offensive in theory, but seeing him kiss someone besides Mom jarred me. Maybe it was some kind of Oedipus complex.

The overweight tabby cat who sat in the window at Monkey Shines Antiques followed me along the boardwalk, probably hoping to be petted. Everyone wanted to be petted. Why not? I waited under the streetlight for the cat to catch up, but as soon as I stopped it stopped. Screw it. I tried.

Willard was flat on his back on top of the bedspread and snoring when I looked in on him. A few of the dogs beat their tails softly against the cement in recognition of my presence. I felt around the foot of the bed for the spare blanket and, trying not to wake him, I opened it and spread it over him. When his snoring hiccupped, I froze, but then he licked his lips and let out a long breath. I waited until the cadence of the snore returned before leaving.

Dad had said make new friends, but I didn't want any new friends. I couldn't effectively handle the one I had, and the only other person out there who interested me was out of bounds. Maybe I was becoming a little daffy myself, but I decided Willard's choice of dogs was brilliant. Who in my universe of people could match Freeway? Dogs overflowed with affection. They forgave readily. And sex wasn't a big issue.

I read until after midnight, but I still wasn't sleepy, so I turned on the radio and doused the light. Sometimes the talk shows lulled me to sleep if I listened to the voices but tuned out the words. It was my headache. That's what was keeping me awake. There must have been MSG on the burgers. Mom used to be able to make my headaches go away by finding the "trigger points" in my neck and shoulders and massaging them until they melted and floated away in the tributaries of my lymph system. I missed the touch of her fingers and the purr of her voice, the way she'd turn the lights down and talk to me in the dark about how it was going to be.

When I heard Dad come in, I leaned over and looked at the clock. He didn't usually work this late. *Come on, Piper. You're not his mother.*

I tiptoed downstairs to get some aspirin out of Dad's medicine cabinet. With no lights, I snapped the plastic top off, poured two into the palm of my hand, and threw them against the back of my throat. Then I cupped a couple of mouthfuls of water from the tap and smeared the last one against my face, massaging my forehead. When I dried my face, I smelled something sweet in the hand towel. Someone's perfume.

I WAS ENGROSSED IN an article from *Hustler* entitled "Dating Younger Women" by a man who told how to "answer the ten inevitable questions without lying or bullshitting." Ned kept the dirty magazines in the regular rack instead of behind the counter like some stores.

"Hey, Piper!"

I hurriedly closed the magazine and shoved it back on the rack, cover facing in. I knew I was blushing when I turned to face Rozene Raymond. "Oh, hi."

Rozene had a gaze that was non-judgmental and built on her natural strengths — prominent eyebrows, a rather broad nose, and full lips, which right then were parted in a kind smile. There was no makeup. The intensity of her eyes was deepened as the result of strong facial bones. She was standing erect, with her shoulders back. I was guarding my chest, hollowing it inward, hiding what wasn't there, while she made no attempt to hide what was. "Find anything interesting?" she said.

I shook my head, tried to slacken my cheeks, and glanced back at the rack. "It's just junk. I was looking for something light, maybe *People*."

The pleasant smell of spearmint gum accompanied her words. "Personally, I'd rather read a skin magazine."

My eyes drifted down her black tights to her running shoes. She had slender ankles, nice calf muscles and, instead of the knotty bulges for knees I had, her legs thickened gracefully above the knees and disappeared under a baggy Sonics sweatshirt that she managed to give shape to. A windbreaker was tied by the arms around her waist. She was holding a box of Super Tampax casually in one hand, and I tried to match her openness. "I wish they didn't airbrush the models though."

"Yeah. Who says an appendix scar isn't sexy?"

We both laughed and then separated. I made sure she noticed me walking away from the magazines. I'd forgotten what I came in for, but quickly made up a list in my head to give my visit a licit purpose. We were always running out of toilet paper and Scotch tape. I didn't want to get anything too expensive, what with her mom being laid off and all. Normally, I would have jettisoned the toilet paper, but the fact she was buying Tampax made it feel as if the toilet paper would link us in some earthy way. As I picked out a four-pack, I looked over the tops of the shelves to see what else she might be getting, but all I could see was the part down the middle of her thick black hair.

"It's raining," she said when we reached the checkout stand at the same time. "Can I give you a lift?" I politely declined and she asked again, looking me up and down. I was wearing jeans and a flannel shirt that seemed fine when I left the house. "It's no trouble, really. I won't feel so guilty about bringing the car if two of us use it." I didn't have my driver's license yet, the result of an anti-technology corner I'd worked myself into to avoid the consumption of non-renewable resources. Now, in Ned's, my stand seemed so transparent.

On the third invitation, I accepted.

The Raymonds' car was immaculate. No thermos and plastic water bottles kicking around loose on the floor like ours. Neither were there maps, tablets, manila folders, pens, coffee mugs, Styrofoam cups, triple-A batteries, and old newspapers littered on the backseat. One of those Christmas tree-shaped pine fresheners hung from the rearview mirror and Rozene snapped it with her finger once she'd turned the engine over.

"My mom's a little bit anal, bless her heart," she said. She must have picked up on my fear of things that were too neat, but the fact that she said it was positive.

"I'll bet she's mad about the whole paper thing." I knew that her mom getting laid off at the paper had to be on her mind so I thought I might as well say it before I got too used to sitting in the same car with her.

"Disappointed would be the better word." We were moving now and she didn't want to take her eyes off the road, but she gave a huff I interpreted to mean *Don't get me started.*

"It wasn't my dad's decision, you know." That was my wish, at least.

"I'll bet nothing happens at the paper your dad doesn't bless," she said.

"You think so?" I was ducking. I really had no idea what had happened.

"What did *he* say?"

"We don't talk about that kind of stuff." I was whipping myself for bringing up her mom. I also had this premonition we'd run into Dirk and he was going to be confused at seeing Rozene and me hanging out together. If we did see him, I was going to yell out the window and tell him the truth. *Don't worry, Dirk. By the time she drops me off, I should have pretty well shit-canned this one.* I seemed to have a death wish when it came to relationships. I didn't talk to people; I stabbed them with reminders of what they didn't want to hear.

"Mom's working again," she said. "The Stamp Box weekdays, and cleaning motels on weekends."

"Bummer."

"She's used to it. That's what got us off the reservation. She'd shine shoes if it meant getting me into college. She spoils me, like with the car."

Rozene remembered where I lived even though I didn't think she'd been to our house since grade school when Dad was still throwing Christmas parties for employees there. As the staff grew, the parties had moved to the Eagles Lodge. The summer picnics were held at Kla Hah Ya Park where there was room to set up a volleyball net, do the egg catch, and organize other children's games. The year I held onto Rozene's smooth brown legs and wheel-barrowed her over the finish line ahead of everyone else might have been the spark. She had on a pair of white shorts and a starched orange blouse that day with kisses of perspiration showing under the arms.

In front of our house, she put the motor in neutral and

rested her arm on top of the seat behind my neck. The awkwardness of how I'd handled her mom's situation was eating at me.

"I'm sorry what I said about the job, Rozene. I wasn't trying to gloss it over."

She tapped me on the shoulder with the tips of her fingers. "Hey, I know that. I saw what you did with the poster." The wipers washed back and forth, a smooth swipe against the wet window followed by a rubber to glass backstroke that shuddered like my insides. I was still looking between my feet at the protective mat on the floorboard, but I could feel her turn and rest one knee on the casing between the bucket seats. The part I remembered about the poster was giving everyone the finger. She must have thought I was unbalanced and she didn't want a repeat performance right there in the frontseat of her mom's Corolla. "I wish *I* had an attitude," she said.

"Attitude?"

"You know. Indians are supposed to be on the warpath for self-determination. I always do what everyone expects of me."

"That's not easy either."

"It is if you want to become a nurse and marry a doctor."

"That's what you want?"

"Mom thinks because I water the plants and turn them to the sun so they'll grow straight I'd be good at nursing."

"Go for it."

"I'd rather rob banks," she said, tapping me on the shoulder. "How's Dirk?"

"Not good." I almost told her about the crush he had on her, but realized that would just be another awkward subject. "It would mean a lot if you said something to him."

"That was such a crappy thing they did."

Caucasian skin was so blah. Hers was tawny, almost bronze, and even through the mottled light from the windshield it looked warm and alive. I wanted to reach out and touch her cheek. Her knee was shiny where the fabric of her tights stretched over the bone and I wanted to cup my hands around it and squeeze. I wanted to say more and I wanted to sit there longer, but I saw Willard coming down the sidewalk with one of the dogs, a newspaper over his head. In a minute the dog would have its paws up against the passenger window. "I better let you go," I said.

She patted me on the shoulder again with her hand. "Hey, I hope you go back for your magazine."

I swatted her on the knee. "No way."

She put her leg down and pumped the gas pedal. I opened the door, pulled the flannel shirt up over my fuzzy head as I stepped out, then leaned down to say goodbye before slamming the door. I walked backwards up the walkway, the rain blowing sideways against my bare midriff, and watched her drive away.

"Who's that?" Willard said when he reached the cover of the porch. Freeway shook himself, in a shudder that progressed from his tail to his ears.

"A friend."

"I didn't know he had a car."

"Different friend."

He looked puzzled and squinted up the street in the direction of the Raymonds' receding tailpipe. Only when I turned to go inside did I remember that I'd left the sack with the toilet paper and toothpaste in her car.

The ride home with Rozene both excited and scared me. I kept thinking of how my throat had thickened in her presence, the pleasure I'd taken from swatting her knee. But I was on the edge of an abyss deeper than mere lust. This was down there with bestiality and Hermaphroditus. And the strange thing was, it was all happening inside my head. Rozene would have given anyone a ride home. She'd probably have laughed if she knew what was going on. So would have Mom. "Every girl goes through stages," she'd have said. "Now fix yourself up and go out there and find a nice guy."

I tried. I really did. For the next week, I wore blouses instead of flannel shirts, put rouge on my cheekbones, and even plucked my eyebrows. In Mom's closet, I found a floppy satin beret to cover up my baldness. I wore brown leather loafers instead of tennis shoes. I practiced walking in front of the full-length mirror on the back of Mom's closet door, cocking my hips, trying to get my buttocks in motion. I was going to beat this thing. I was going to quit straddling the fence. I was practically on the make.

I avoided Rozene in the lunchroom, taking a table as far from her as I could and away from the aisle so she'd have no reason to pass me on the way out. I sat on the edge of groups of guys and, when they talked about something I knew, I joined in. Sometimes I had to fake it and it got me in trouble, like the debate over why they shot horses.

"It's to save them from pain," I said.

Jesse Little, who was across the table licking cold spaghetti sauce off a piece of wax paper, laughed. "You think a bullet in the brain doesn't hurt?"

Everyone else laughed, more at Jesse than with him.

Bagmore joined in to save the debate. "You're saying they do it for euthanasia?"

"Yeah."

"Then what if the winner of the Kentucky Derby slips and falls in his stable after the race and breaks an ankle?"

"They shoot him?"

"Wrong. They fix him up and put him out to stud. Fifty grand a fuck."

Everyone laughed, Jesse Little included. Certain words, when used with panache the way Bagmore could, always brought a laugh. Anyone who didn't join in, the laugh was on her.

There was another twenty minutes before fifth period bell and Bagmore asked me to join him in the tunnel under the grandstands for a smoke. When a couple of his buddies followed, he signaled them to beat it. Bagmore wasn't the target of my campaign — I was aiming for a species rather than any particular person — but the invitation was encouraging nevertheless. It meant that my efforts were paying off, I was putting out the right scent. I figured there'd be a crowd in the tunnel because of the rain, and being seen with Bagmore wouldn't exactly hurt the value of my stock. There were a lot of girls who'd trade their reputations to go out with him, and many of them had. He was one of the local horses who should have been shot, but was put out to stud instead. What the heck, I thought, I had to start somewhere. It wasn't my way to nibble at the edges.

The tunnel was empty.

"It stinks in here," he said. "I know a better place."

We walked down the steps to the running track, turned left, and walked another twenty-five yards. Bagmore jiggled open the door to a storage shed under the stands that I didn't even know existed. There were blocking sleds, hurdles stacked like portable chairs, yard markers, starting blocks, bags of wood chips, and other sports paraphernalia. The smell was pleasant, cut grass and cedar. He left the door open a crack, enough light to see the gleam in his eyes. He pulled a pack of Salems out of the inside of his jacket, jiggled the filters of two cigarettes out, and flicked a flame onto his lighter.

"Here," he said.

"Sure."

"You know what day this is?"

"No. Should I?"

"Evan went down seven years ago."

Evan was his older brother, the one whose chute had failed skydiving over Harvey Field. I remembered the day it happened. There were sirens all over town and I was in the mountain ash tree in the backyard, trying to stop a cat from messing with a bird's nest. The meter reader from the water department was walking down the alley in his short pants and I yelled at him to find out what the sirens were for, figuring that his being part of government he'd have access to that kind of information. He told me they were heading to the air field, and I figured a plane must have gone down. "Sorry about that," I said to Bagmore.

We were leaning against a blocking dummy, shoulder to shoulder. "Hey, you didn't do it. I don't know why I mentioned it."

"I understand."

"Of course. You lost your mom." He put his arm around me and pulled me tight against him. I had to admit it felt nice and stirred up the old attraction I used to feel for him about the age I was when I climbed the mountain ash. Maybe there was nothing peculiar about me after all. I just needed exposure. "We should form a club," he said.

"What do you mean?"

"The survivors." He was massaging my shoulder so hard it was painful.

I dropped my cigarette to the ground and straightened up to grind it out. "We better get back."

He swung around and corralled me against the blocking dummy. "I've been noticing you more lately."

We were about the same height and I could smell the lunch on his breath. I tried to lift one of his arms, but he wasn't budging. "Let's continue this later, huh?"

"There has to be something to continue." Then he pushed into me, grinding his package against my crotch, with his hands on my buttocks. "Come on. Haven't you ever wondered what it'd be like to jump my bones?" My brain said spit, but I couldn't. He put his mouth on mine. "*I've* wondered . . . those legs . . . I love long legs." The grinding continued as I tried to move my mouth to wherever his wasn't. His lips were smearing my cheeks. "You'd be like riding a tiger."

He pushed his tongue between my lips and I clamped my teeth together, but when I gasped for air he locked his teeth into mine and swabbed his tongue around the insides of my gums. One hand squeezed the back of my head, while the other one pushed down inside the front of my pants. I tried to make myself fall to the ground, to put my crotch beyond his reach, but he was strong enough to keep me pinned against the dummy. The flashes and sparks of recrimination exploding inside me only made it worse. How I was so stupid to follow him into this cave. How this could be the way I'd lose my virginity. How I'd practically begged someone to screw me to prove a point.

Then something strange happened. I could feel it rise in me like the flushed water in a toilet bowl. An otherworldly calm. I stopped struggling and concentrated on his breath, which was coming faster and faster, in shorter and shorter strokes. *Pranayama.* Even as it was happening, I realized this had nothing to do with me. Bagmore was snorting and thrusting against me, but I could have been anybody. He was in a zone. If I could have stepped out of the way, he would have just banged away against the pad on the blocking dummy. This wasn't sex. I was bait. This was masturbation with his pants on. It ended in a series of moans as he shot his wad, loosened his grip, and withdrew in a daze.

When I pushed him to the side, he offered no resistance. I should have kneed him in the balls or swatted him around the side of the head. "You're pathetic, Bagmore. And a premature ejaculator."

"Fuck you," he said.

"I doubt it."

The light from the door made a stripe down his body. His shirt was ruffled, the belt buckle unclasped, and there was a wet spot the size of a half dollar on his pants, which was twenty-five cents more than he was worth.

I showered that night until the hot water ran out, then sudsed up my head and shaved. My hands were so shaky I made nicks that I had to dab with toilet paper. So what? There was no way I was going to let myself be the least bit attractive to the likes of Condon Bagmore again.

Bagmore trying to screw me with his pants on in the supply shed convinced me I wanted less to do with school. I told Dad I'd take the job at the newspaper, anything they had. I was steering my dinghy between the rocks and I had to plug my ears with wax to avoid hearing the singing of the Sirens.

They converted a storage room off Dad's office into an after-school work space for me at the paper. Dad was on the phone when I arrived on the first day, so I tiptoed through his office to get to mine, which was stuffed with stacks of

97

xerox paper, old issues of the newspaper, toner cartridges for the copy machine, and extra swivel chairs, boxes and tables that had been nested together. The walls were blank except for nail holes and patches where pictures must have hung and been painted around. At one end there were black steel shelves mounted on uprights. A bare light bulb hung over my desk, which had a water-stained deskmat full of doodles and curled at the edges. On the desk, there were dusty "In" and "Out" trays, a staple puller, metal bookends, and one of those prongs for spearing telephone messages. The typist's chair, a swivel model with five legs and casters, squeaked when I leaned back and popped up when I got out.

"I'm not sure it's such a good idea for the most junior employee to be next to the boss," I told Dad.

"Titles don't mean anything around here," he said. "Besides, you don't have a window and I'm going to make you work harder than everyone else."

"You're the boss," I said, laughing.

"Carlisle's the boss. I'm just a drone. But you working here was his idea too."

"Whatever." I didn't want to get into it about Carlisle on the first day.

"Hey, you're going to fall in love with this place. When you're a newspaper reporter, you can knock on a door and someone else's life plays out before you. All you have to do is shut up and listen."

"But I'm a copy editor, right?"

"For starters. But never forget you're part of something larger." I still wasn't sure if I believed what he was saying, but it sure beat hanging around the athletic field.

The first few days Dad kept sticking his head into my office with tidbits of advice. "It's your job to fly-speck the first run for spelling mistakes, punctuation, capitalization, and bad grammar," he said. "Ignore the content, unless it affects your editing choices."

I worked from the hard copy and when I found a mistake, I put a tent over a new comma, a circle around a missing period, or double lines under a letter that was supposed to be capitalized. Dad rounded up *Strunk and White*, *A Writer's Reference*, a dictionary, and the AP stylebook. "The dirtier the copy is when you pass it on to me the better you've done your job," he said. Dad had final say over which edits were entered into the computer. Copy editing practically ruined my reading for pleasure. I found myself at night looking for typos and syntax and pretty soon I was unable to keep track of the story line altogether.

I usually got to the paper in time for the afternoon break when everyone except Dad drifted into another windowless room they called the "doghouse," where there was hot coffee simmered to the bitterness of castor oil, a refrigerator full of leftover brown bag lunches, and old magazines people brought in and dumped on the coffee table. You could gauge where we were in the cycle of weekly deadlines by the level of energy in the doghouse. I liked the way people called each other by last names. Everyone took me under their wing.

"See that spot on the wall?" Gerry Alexander, the wiry photographer with the cleft lip, said. "That's where Rummage threw his peanut butter and jelly sandwich when they announced the layoff. It stuck for weeks, everyone betting on when it would drop."

There seemed to be no resentment about the editor's daughter getting a cushy job at the paper, mainly because they'd long ago canonized him. Now they were in the legend-telling phase, sharing stories I'd never heard. "You knew he had an offer to go with the *Seattle Times*," Louise Mead said, fiddling with one handle of a can opener, which was a surrogate for the cigarettes she'd given up. "Tom could have had his own column, probably syndicated it. You know how smart your dad is."

All I could do was nod and pretend I had at least an inkling of the glow that shone from his halo. The stories helped me though to understand the ceaseless devotion he'd given to this place, but I wasn't sure he could live up to their heroic expectations. I'd seen him defer too often to John Carlisle.

I was going over the "Nickel Want Ads" when I heard a familiar voice in Dad's office. It was John Carlisle. I was the one who'd insisted on closing the door between our offices, for purposes of independence, but I could still hear Dad when he talked on the phone. Most of the time it was wearisome business stuff — advertisers and suppliers — and I couldn't have cared less what was said.

I tiptoed over to the door.

"It's a chance of a lifetime, Tom. Maddock's the major leagues." I'd never noticed how thin Carlisle's voice was compared to Dad's. It made his sports metaphor ring hollow.

There was some shuffling of papers "I didn't work this hard," Dad said, "so I could cut and paste the *Seattle Times* into bite sizes for our readers." I wished I were a fly on the wall so I could have seen his face. "There are almost twenty thousand people counting on us. Maybe that's not LA or Salt Lake City, but they're ours and I think they deserve their own voice."

I put my ear on the crack between the door and the jamb. "Tom, it doesn't have to mean the end of all that . . ."

"I don't know about you, but I've had enough of media giants telling me what I'm supposed to think. They don't know Stampede. They don't *care* about Stampede. Let's put it to a vote of the staff, what's left of them."

"Tom."

"Why not? United Airlines belongs to its employees. While we're at it, we can hire back some of our people."

"I told you you'll have a position."

"This isn't about me!"

"I know this has been a rough year, Tom. It was just an inquiry. Think about it, okay?" I could imagine Carlisle's fleshy hands reaching out to glom onto Dad. He was one of those touchy-feely people. "Let's talk tomorrow."

"What's wrong with right now?"

I couldn't make out the beginning of John Carlisle's answer, but the end was clear. ". . . I don't want to have to use my prerogative as owner."

"Get out!" Dad yelled. I clenched my fist and shook it. *Yes!* That's what I would have said.

There was foot movement and the sliding of chairs. I backed off the door, picked up *A Writer's Reference*, and sat on the edge of my desk in case one of them came in. The outer door to Dad's office shut hard and then there was silence. I wanted to burst in and congratulate Dad, but I knew he'd be upset for me butting into his business. If we couldn't talk about Mom's death, how did I expect him to tell me about the fate of the newspaper?

I went back to my desk and made up an ad to slip into the proof that I was working on, so he'd see it when he reviewed my work:

Proud, local newspaper with promising future seeks new owner with the guts to put his heart ahead of his wallet. Terms non-negotiable.

But I chickened out and wadded it into the recycle box. I'd think of a way to tell him in person, to break this habit of communication by misdirection.

That same night, after Dad came home, he got a call from the Stampede Police and we rode in the patrol car out to the scene of Willard's accident. The wrecker was already there as well as another police car. Willard was in the frontseat of his Olds, shivering. Freeway was sitting next to him, licking the back of Willard's hand. *Thank God*, I thought, *he hadn't brought the whole stable with him.* Given Dad's mood, Willard couldn't have picked a worse time to go for a joyride. He must have stolen the keys out of Dad's dresser. Willard was basically an honest man, except for his hiding of the dogs, and even that was for a humanitarian purpose, if you could refer to it that way. But he'd gotten sloppy and must have figured that negotiating an Oldsmobile Skylark along the back roads of Cascade County wasn't any harder than shuffling five dogs in and out of the underground railroad which was our basement. He hadn't figured on Buzz

Little backing out into the road from nowhere. Buzz turned out to be drunk, per usual, but that didn't mollify Dad.

"Where'd you think you were going anyway?"

Willard was rocking back and forth, staring straight ahead over the top of the steering wheel.

"Huh? Answer me." I wasn't sure if Willard had even heard him.

"Going to Bonnie's," he finally mumbled.

"What?" Dad had one hand braced on the wheel and the other against Willard's shoulder, like he was going to pry him open.

"It was only a fender bender," I said, tapping Dad on the back, but he ignored me. This temper, twice in one day, was something I hadn't seen.

"Who in Sam Hill is Bonnie?" Dad said. Willard kept up his catatonic rocking, still not looking at Dad. This Bonnie woman must have made some impression on Willard when she was alive, I thought. The pilgrimages to her were becoming a habit. "Look, old man, I don't know what you're talking about or what you're trying to prove, but I'm not going to have you living in my house and sneaking around stealing keys and wrecking cars." He was madder than he was when John Carlisle came into the office. I thought he was going to drag Willard out of there and just shake him till he broke. "You understand?"

"Dad, that's enough. It wasn't even his fault."

Dad swatted his hand back at me. "Watch it or you'll never drive either."

"I don't want to."

"This isn't over, Willard."

The right front fender of the Oldsmobile was pinched against the tire and the radiator had lost its water, making the car undrivable. The police officer put Freeway in the frontseat and Dad put Willard between us in the back. All the way home, Dad kept grumbling at Willard. "You're going to pay for the damage out of your Social Security and this is the end of your privileges." I wondered what privileges he was talking about, unless you counted the roof over

Willard's head and running water. "This isn't the end of it," Dad kept saying and I knew what he meant by that, probably so did Willard, although he didn't utter a protest all the way home. I wished the officer had put Dad in front and Freeway back with me and Willard. It would have been more pleasant all the way around. I knew there was more going on in Dad's mind than the accident on Skylar Road, but it didn't seem fair that Willard had to take the hit for something John Carlisle was trying to pull off.

———9———

MONDAY NIGHT WHEN I came home, there was a sack inside the front door with toilet paper, Scotch tape, toothpaste and a frayed paperback copy of *The Second Sex* by Simone de Beauvoir. Inside the book, there was a folded piece of notepaper with a printed header that said, "From the desk of Rozene Raymond." For some reason, I put the note to my nose and inhaled. It was just paper, but the words were sweet:

> *Thought this would satisfy your curiosity for the mystery of it all.*
>   *Rozene*

Maybe she *had* noticed that insipid article I was reading in *Hustler*. What a nice comeback. I was distracting myself with cosmetics and she was diving into her soul.

I put the note in my pocket and headed downstairs to drop off a spare roll in the basement bathroom. Willard's door was open. Except for Freeway, the dogs were lying on the floor. Since we'd become buddies they knew they didn't have to get up and greet me each time I entered the room, which smelled like dog hair mattresses.

"Hey, how's Crash Corrigan?" I said.

He swung his shoes off the spread and planted them on the oval rug next to the bed. "I was thinkin' of you."

"Good or bad?"

"You're gettin' to be just like your dad."

"How's the head?"

He looked down at his ankle boots. "*I'm* fine. Now it's him." He pointed to Freeway, who was lying on his side next to Willard, his front paws crossed, tail drawn tight between his legs. A grey snotty substance oozed from Freeway's eyes and his breathing was labored and jagged. Willard had covered his midsection with a pair of grungy boxer shorts. Willard rocked back and forth, rubbing his palms against the top of his thighs. "Am I going to jail?"

"Oh, come on. Dad's forgotten all about the wreck. Besides, he's got the paper to worry about." Willard grabbed his pants above the kneecaps and pulled them up, revealing a cuff of boney white shins. "If Carlisle sells it, he'll be out of a job."

"That'd be good for Tom," Willard said.

Except for the fact it'd kill him, I thought.

Later we took a walk with the dogs, except for Freeway who offered no protest when we left without him. There must have been a change in the weather coming because the clouds were racing past the moon in fast forward. The dogs spread out, sniffing the weeds along the sides of the road the same way Willard liked to comb the ground at the park for his treasures. They always seemed to know where Willard was though and never lagged far behind. Mrs. Churchill, the black and tan coonhound, zeroed in on what must have been a randy odor at the base of a telephone pole because several of the dogs joined her.

"Must be one of the town bullies," Willard said.

Mrs. Churchill positioned her back end as close to the pole as she could, squatted, and peed. Then Billy doused it again. Finally, Paddy marched in, cocked his right leg, watered the pole, and pawed the grass, throwing little grass divots in the direction of the bully. Now it was their territory. Nobody messed with Willard's gang.

We ended up at the most spectacular piece of engineering in Stampede, the Carlisle Bridge, which resembled two German barmaids with enormous concrete legs balancing a steel span criss-crossed with vertical and diagonal bracing. At the center of the bridge we stopped and rested our arms on the railing, staring down at Commercial Street. It wasn't a bridge over water; it was a bridge over land. You had to pass under the bridge to enter Stampede's downtown from the west and there was a weathered signboard attached to the girder just below us that read: "Nathaniel S. Carlisle, 1878-1957." He was John's grandfather and considered the founder of Stampede, something else we had to know for the course in Washington State History, at least the version taught in our town. Dad had devised a way of remembering the years. Eighteen seventy-eight was the same year that Joseph Pulitzer bought the bankrupt *St. Louis Dispatch* for $2,500 and nineteen fifty-seven was the year Sputnik orbited the earth. Of course, that's not what the Carlisle Bridge was remembered for by the rest of us. It was an attractive nuisance, a place for kids to drop boulders, old tires, burned out television sets, and once even a Frigidaire, onto the cars below. The Frigidaire missed its target, but the pavement was soft enough from the summer heat that the corner of it penetrated the pavement and left the refrigerator standing upright like a pillar of salt.

"How's my pal, Dirk, doing?" Willard said, letting go of one of the pebbles he'd picked up. Nobody could resist the fascination of gravity.

"Pretty much the same." Of course, that wasn't the whole truth. The "Peter Poster" had etched itself into the collective memories of the student body, including those who'd never even seen it. The oral history of Stampede High would forever include the story of Dirk's hand job in the boys' can. The school district should have just erected a plaque commemorating the event so they wouldn't have to keep painting over the graffiti people were putting on the stall. Colleen Waterston and I snuck in after school and read it ourselves. "What are you looking up here for? The joke's between Dirk's legs." "Get a grip on yourself, Dirk."

One of the pebbles Willard flicked off the bridge hit a galvanized mop bucket near the curb and pinged. A pickup with one headlight approached from the east and, as a precaution, I reached over and covered the hand Willard had filled with pebbles. I didn't want another run-in with the law so soon after the car wreck. He cleared his throat like he was going to launch a big goober instead.

"Don't you even think of it," I said.

He laughed and dropped the goober between the toes of his high-tops. "I may be foolish, but I'm not stupid," he said, and I had to think about that one for a minute. It would have made just as much sense exactly in reverse. Dad would have called it a non-sequitur, but Willard was friendly with non-sequiturs. They were shortcuts through the red tape of otherwise inscrutable problems.

"I'll break you out of that nursing home, but not if you do something patently crazy."

He looked up at me and there was moisture in his eyes. "You'd do that?"

"Of course."

"I have to get a job." He always said that when he was feeling insecure. In his system of values, you didn't put down a horse if it was still able to race.

"I thought you had an offer."

He perked up. "Oh, yeah?"

"The guy doing the street work over by the Caterpillar dealership."

"They called you?"

"Willard! You were the one who told *me*."

There was silence while he rummaged around in his head for a clue as to what he'd told me about them wanting a skilled mechanic. The toe of his shoe pushed a flattened Coca Cola can up against the bridge span and turned it over, but the memory must have evaporated.

The dogs finished their field work and collapsed onto the dusty asphalt next to us. I turned my back to the street below and looked up through the bracing to find the moon again. Someone had slowed down the weather because now the moon was hidden behind a stationary cloud in the shape of an enormous snail. Looking away from Stampede made me think of Rozene's note and riding home in her car. Somehow she'd turned the awkwardness of that day into a private joke. Maybe I'd made a mistake in running from her so fast.

A car I recognized passed under the bridge and pulled off onto the shoulder just past a crumpled-up beer carton. The headlights went off, but the motor was still idling as traces of exhaust chugged out the tailpipe and vaporized into the night. Through the rear window, I could see the outline of two people in the frontseat. The passenger's silhouette moved over and merged with the driver's. The brake light flared momentarily and went dark again. My stomach churned.

"Who's that?"

How could I tell him it was Dad necking under the bridge like some commoner? As much as I wanted Dad to be like me, it unsettled me whenever he was. Maybe it was the disloyalty of his touching another woman so soon. "Nobody," I said.

About a week later Willard knocked on my bedroom door. He never came upstairs. I had to hand it to him; he'd adhered to that part of our pact.

"Something's wrong," he said. He was barefoot, his pants were rolled up, and he looked like an older version of Huckleberry Finn who'd been crying.

All I had on was a T-shirt so I told him to turn around while I got out of bed and pulled a pair of jeans on. He was shaky and wobbled the banister on the way downstairs. When we reached his room, there was blood all over the rocking horse bedspread that I'd used when I was a kid and Freeway lay in the middle of it.

"Jesus, Willard! Have you called the vet?"

Willard grabbed my forearm. There was panic in his eyes. "He hates the vet."

"But he's" — I almost said dying — "sick."

I made Willard stay there while I went upstairs and looked up Payton Miller's number. He was the large animal vet, but I knew I could trust him more than the fancy Dans who worked on the poodles and pussy cats at All the Best for Your Pets downtown. Payton Miller's son, Martin, was in my class, a giant of a kid who resembled one of his dad's patients. Dr. Miller just ahemmed in his deep bull voice as I told him the story over the phone and it was impossible to figure out what he was thinking. Their television was going in the background and I must have apologized at least six times for disturbing him at home.

"That's my job," he said matter of factly, seeming to understand Willard's reluctance to bring his dog into the vet. "Most of my consultations are house calls. With cows, it's just easier."

I waited outside the house by the basement entrance for Dr. Miller to arrive. As I'd asked him to, he parked his four-wheeler in front of the neighbor's, as a precaution in case Dad came home. I watched Dr. Miller get out of his rig, reach back for his cowboy hat, then open the back door for a black leather tote bag. He saw me at the corner of the house, touched the brim of his hat, and cut across the neighbor's lawn. He was wearing a rumpled vest that hung over his frame like an old shoe rag. The sleeves of his shirt were rolled up, revealing the muscled forearms of a Michelangelo sculpture. I guessed you'd have to be strong if some of your patients weighed a thousand pounds.

Dr. Miller had to take off his hat and stoop to miss the header on the way down the basement stairs. Willard was on the bed with his arms wrapped softly around Freeway's middle and at the sight of the vet Willard pulled him in tighter.

"Got a sick one here, do you?" Dr. Miller said, as he unclasped his bag and pulled out a stethoscope.

Pretty much working around Willard, he held the little suction cup in a spot on Freeway's chest, stared off into space, then moved it and stared some more. It was as if he hadn't even noticed the blood. He took out his penlight and checked each eye, holding the lids open with his thumb. I watched Dr. Miller's face for a sign. He was older than his walk, his jowls sagged, and his eyes were baggy like he'd wept a lot, but he looked so determined. I imagined he'd stared death in the face more often than the average man in Stampede. Death was his adversary. With one hand palming the side of Freeway's head, he used his other hand to push up into Freeway's stomach like he was trying to shake hands with the kidneys. Then he sat down on the bed and patted Willard's leg.

"How long's he been coughing up the blood?"

Willard looked over at me for guidance and I shrugged my shoulders.

"He's suffering, Willard."

Willard buried his face against Freeway and Dr. Miller turned to me. "The humane thing is to put him to sleep."

Jesus, Doctor, don't say that to me. I'm never . . . I can't give you permission to do that. I pointed to Willard. "Tell *him.*"

"He knows."

I put my hands over my face, wishing now we hadn't kept the dog thing a secret from Dad. Willard always listened to Dad. How could I convince Willard to put Freeway down? This was the one the police had found in the plastic bag on the highway. His very life was a miracle. "Can't you just let it happen naturally?" I said.

"Everything's come apart inside," the vet said. "He'll die a thousand times this way."

I wanted to run from the room and lose myself in one of my books. Why did Willard have to bring all his dogs over here anyway? Our house had had enough of death.

"Let me take him down to the office."

"No!" Willard said. "He's a home dog."

I looked over at Dr. Miller. "I told you."

Dr. Miller wrapped a blanket around Freeway and carried him up the stairs. Apparently scenting death, the other dogs made no attempt to override Willard's gentle command and stayed in the bedroom. I followed with my hand gripped hard around the shredded handle of the vet's bag. It was heavier than it looked and I wondered how he knew what to bring based upon my frantic description. Willard motioned Dr. Miller to set the dog down on the parking strip when we got outside. Freeway had trouble standing, but he managed to turn his back to us and pee a stream of blood that ran out of the grass and onto the edge of the sidewalk. Willard sobbed and started to crumple. Dr. Miller put his arm around Willard with one hand under the armpit to hold him up. Freeway gazed down the street like he wanted to take off on a venture the way he always had. I remembered Willard telling me, "Dogs live small and dream big." This time, Freeway had to settle for folding up on the grass next to the puddle of blood.

We did it in the backseat of the four-wheeler, with Freeway stretched across our laps, his head on Willard. The white pool of hair on the top of Freeway's head flowed like a waterfall between his eyes, spreading to his nose and chest. He looked up at Willard, blinking, waiting for his next command. His eyes were soft and missing the old intensity that Willard told me he could hypnotize cattle with. Maybe he thought we were going to Ocean Shores to chase tennis balls on the beach, or take a hike up Mount Shuksan. Dogs loved cars. The car represented new frontiers.

Dr. Miller attached a needle to a syringe filled with a purplish liquid, being careful to work from behind the bucket seat so neither Willard nor Freeway could see what was happening. Then he pulled a patterned blue handkerchief out of his pocket and draped it over the syringe before reaching back between the seats. "This won't hurt you, boy."

I felt Willard brace himself and I found the hand closest to me and squeezed it as hard as I could when Dr. Miller inserted the needle into the big vein in Freeway's front leg and slowly pushed the plunger down with his thumb. Dr. Miller bit his lower lip, making the syringe shorter and shorter under the hanky. I could smell something pungent. Willard was trembling so hard it made Freeway vibrate too. I kept thinking of Mom and wishing I'd been there to hold her, to squeeze her hand, to let her know she wasn't alone. Willard shuddered and I realized how shaken he must have been by Mom's death. Mom was his only child, the light of his life. He'd always said how glad he was his "Kitty" had stayed in Stampede. I'd never thought of Willard as sorrowful. He always seemed to be off in his own forgetful world, more worried about changing the oil in someone's car. But Willard was a veteran of death too: his wife from a stroke, his bowling buddies from old age, his daughter, and God knew how many dogs. Instead of becoming calloused to it, each death had just gouged a deeper ditch across his heart.

At the moment I saw Freeway's face go lifeless, it felt like he was all of us.

"He's gone," Dr. Miller said.

At Willard's request, we let Freeway spend one more night in his bed so that he could pet him in all the places he liked to be touched.

After Dad left in the morning, I went out to the garage and found the shovel with the black electrician's tape wrapped around the split handle and dug a grave in Mom's tangled and abandoned garden. Dr. Miller said it was against the law to bury carcasses in town, but he agreed it was the best option under the circumstances. There was no way this dog was going to the rendering plant. Just below the topsoil I encountered rocks and had to use the pick, but I managed to make a pit about three feet deep. On his side and without a casket I thought he'd be down far enough.

Willard and I carried Freeway up from the basement on one of the contoured sheets from my bed. The other dogs followed in a bedraggled funeral procession — the terrier, the pug, the mongrel, and the coonhound. Willard had suggested we put him on the bedspread that was already bloodied, but I would have none of that.

"We're not using garbage," I told him.

We rested him between a row of withered tomato vines and the unpicked rhubarb that had been flattened against the ground by the weather like wet newspaper. Freeway's limbs were as stiff as chair spindles and the other dogs shied away from him. They seemed to know that something was going down because they positioned themselves at various distances away from the hole.

Even Freeway's hair had stiffened and it gave me the creeps to see his whole body move when I lifted his head and wrapped one of Mom's blue silk scarves around his neck. Silk was a little feminine, but I thought he needed some color. Freeway had lived his whole life as a black and white. Willard put his motorman's hat on Freeway at a jaunty angle, almost covering one eye. It was the same hat Willard had worn the day Dad brought him over to be my new housemate. Then he pulled a Pup-Peroni stick out of his pocket and wedged it between the toes of one of Freeway's front paws like a stogie. It was something Freeway could dream about as he raced into his new frontier.

Using the sheet as a sling, we stood on each side of the pit and lowered Freeway down, making sure his hat stayed on. I hated this part the worst. The hole made the separation so permanent. I tried to rationalize it by thinking of it as reincarnation. Freeway's nutrients would fertilize next year's rhubarb-strawberry pie and we'd all take a little bit of him in and try to become as vigilant as he was in herding the ones he loved away from trouble. But it wasn't working. The fact that Willard didn't believe in an afterlife, even for humans, made it worse. "This is the whole show," he'd told me once. There were tears leaking down both of my cheeks as I watched Freeway resting obediently at the bottom of the hole.

Neither one of us were particularly religious, but we each agreed to say a prayer out loud. Willard was doing better than could be expected, which meant he was able to stand on his own power while I said mine. The way he swayed though, I thought he was going to just keel over into the pit with his dog. Then it was his turn.

"You were a stray waiting to be found," Willard said, choking on his words, "just like the rest of us. I wish . . . I could've been better to you. So many things I promised . . . and didn't come through on, pal." Death did that, I thought, made the survivors choke on their own guilt. For some reason, even though we knew no one was going to live forever, we all held back, waiting for just the right moment to spring something nice, to let them know how much they were appreciated. Then poof and there weren't any more next times.

I let Willard drop in the first shovelful, then he handed me the shovel and fell down on his knees. Mrs. Churchill waddled over to Willard and just stood there with her big ears drooping in respect. The first few shovelfuls dusted the top of him and I could still see Freeway's shape as clearly as if he were resting on the mattress downstairs. I didn't want to hear the dirt hitting him and started shoveling faster and faster until I was hyperventilating. When his shape had disappeared, I stopped and leaned on the shovel. The only sounds were Willard's moans and Billy's chews on a bone she must have buried for a rainy day.

——10——

WE GOT THROUGH OUR first Thanksgiving without Mom. It was just Dad, Willard, and me. Dad had arranged for Marge to fix us a turkey with all the trimmings, but it just wasn't the same without one or two of Mom's *experiments*, which is what we called the cranberry cornbread, yam gravy and other recipes she'd introduce to stretch our taste buds. There was also no surprise guest. Mom couldn't stand the idea of someone eating alone on Thanksgiving and always managed to find an art student or a teacher from school to join us. Once we had a Laotian man who was in some kind of trouble with the immigration authorities. Dad didn't seem to mind sharing our table with strangers; in fact, he usually ended up asking most of the questions, but I knew he wouldn't have ever initiated it.

The tourists began flocking back to Commercial Street on weekends for their Christmas shopping, to buy the antique furniture, rusted kitchen tools, and odd-shaped, tinted bottles that Stampede was famous for. I would have lodged my usual complaint with Dirk about the commercialization of Christmas, but he wasn't around so I complained to Willard instead.

"Think of it this way," Willard told me. "The ones who come up here are the good ones. They don't like disposable." He had a point. They should have been my people. They were the ones who wanted to sit in the same kind of chairs that Virginia Woolf and D. H. Lawrence had used.

I read *The Second Sex*, searching for messages. Rozene's note was so cryptic. I identified with Simone de Beauvoir though. So many passages resonated with what I imagined Mom would have said. I loved the way she turned the supposed female disadvantages into pluses.

Rozene and I sat together at lunch a few times, but both of us acted as if nothing had changed since the ride home from Ned's. My normal penchant for candor had ebbed and, for the first time in my life, I seemed to be choosing words rather than just letting them flop out of my mouth. I would have loved to tell her what had happened with Bagmore under the grandstands, how I tried to spit out his saliva on the way to the girl's can afterward. I wanted to ask her how she would have handled it. Had I given the wrong signal? Was everyone else putting up with that kind of crap?

On the day before the Christmas Open House, when John Carlisle and the other Victorian home owners opened their doors to the public, Dad held back the front page for my normal review and edit.

"How come, Dad?"

"Trust me. This one I have to do myself."

So I saw the story for the first time on the stack at Ned's when I went in to buy my breakfast, a pack of crackers with cheese spread and a plastic knife, on the way to school. In fact, Ned had to point to the stack or I would have missed it. I'd stopped reading the *Herald* at home once I started flyspecking it at the office. Ned had a sly grin on his face.

"A lot of folks are going to be saying 'I told you so,' huh?"

There it was, in one of Dad's minimalist headlines over a story that wasn't even lead: "Local Publisher Charged."

I grabbed the paper off the stack, mistakenly taking an extra in the process, and made for the back of the store. *My God*! This wasn't driving under the influence or failing to yield. John Carlisle had been charged with rape in the third degree and sexual misconduct with a minor. I had to lean against the bread and cupcake shelves. My heart was a vibrator. *Who? When? Come on, Dad.* I raced down the column for details, but there were no names and no dates. If Dad had sanitized the story any more, we could have eaten off it, but he couldn't hide the obvious. *There was a God in heaven after all*!

I wasn't going to school until I found out the whole skinny, so I paid Ned and bolted for the office with the new issue rolled up in my hand like a billy club.

The reception desk where Pamela Palmer sat was empty and so were the offices I passed along the hallway.

Someone had left the country music station on. Without knocking, I opened the door to Dad's office and suddenly whatever was coming out of his mouth was vacuumed back in. Everyone turned to look at me. It was an office-wide meeting. Even Les Showalter, the driver who only worked delivery days, was there. It was as if they'd never seen someone with frayed cuffs and holes in the knees of her jeans that were dripping with loose threads. Or maybe it was because I hadn't polished the scuffs out of my black oxfords or tucked the pendleton into my pants. After the incident with Bagmore, I'd gone back to the clothes I was comfortable with.

Dad was leaning back against the edge of the desk, his coat off, tie loosened, and a shock of hair drooping carelessly over his right eyebrow. He looked at his watch. "Piper, can you wait outside a minute?"

I looked around at Gerry Alexander and Louise Mead, the people I'd joked with in the doghouse. Their arms were crossed. Their brows were furrowed. I was a bum on the street with a Dixie cup in my hand. They were going to walk right by me. I could feel a blush working its way up my neck. My legs were wobbly.

"Let her stay," Alexander said. "She's one of us." I could have kissed him on his split lip.

Dad rubbed hard under his chin with the edge of his index finger and changed the cross of his legs. I unfurled the paper I'd been choking in my hand. I didn't know what I was going to say exactly, maybe filibuster the assembly by reading the story frontwards and backwards until they let me in on it, but I had to know what was happening. The implications were too important. Dad must have seen the makings of an episode.

"Okay," he said, "but you're under the same constraints everyone else is. Nothing I say leaves this room."

Louise Mead scooted over to free up the left half of her folding chair. "Sit down before he knocks you down," she whispered and winked. I was in. Finally, I wasn't Tom Scanlon's daughter; I was going to be Tom Scanlon's employee and, therefore, the recipient of a whole lot more information.

"As I was saying, the state must still prove its case beyond a reasonable doubt. Meantime, the law says he's innocent."

Pamela Palmer's hand floated up. She was chewing gum and it cracked just as Dad motioned toward her. "Have you talked to him yet?"

"Yes, I have."

"Well . . .?"

"He was as shocked as the rest of us." They always said that, I thought.

"In all candor, Mr. Scanlon" — Pamela asked the question out of the side of her mouth like this was all on the QT — "what do you really think?"

Dad shot her an accusatory look. "The truth? I think it's bunk. I've known John Carlisle since he was a kid. Someone's gold digging."

Pamela nodded respectfully as if to signal her allegiance. It was obvious what was going on. This was John Carlisle's paper and these were John Carlisle's employees. Dad wasn't going to let anyone break ranks.

There were more questions about when the trial would be (he didn't know), whether he'd be held in jail (he was out on his personal recognizance — no surprise, he played dominoes for quarters with the judges), and when my dad had found out (day before yesterday). I figured he'd already told them who the kid was and the other details before I got there. I'd wait until everyone cleared out to catch up. Dad looked like a candidate for the United States Senate, deftly handling each question and pointing his finger at whomever had the next turn. He spoke with conviction, which was his nature, and he had a good radio voice, an even better television face. Not a perfect face, that would have been boring, but even the minor imperfections were heading in the right direction. The eyelids that weighed down his eyes made him look more intense. The upturn at the end of his nose was playful. The thin scar on the side of his neck suggested a man who'd overcome adversity.

Louise Mead was fidgeting and I had to brace my feet to prevent her from wiggling me off the chair. I knew there had to be a Salem long floating across her frontal lobe as she regretted for the umpteenth time that she'd quit smoking. "Tom," she said, "what's this going to do for circulation?"

"Let's not pile fear on top of speculation, Louise. I'd rather deal with facts." Of course, Louise was hardly the one to scold over exactitude. She did want ads, where exaggeration was expected. Everyone in the room knew that Dad was ducking, but they gave him as much room as he wanted.

When he'd taken the last question, he walked over behind his desk. "Come on, we've got a paper to put out."

There was a release of energy in the room. Every limb that had been cocked suddenly fired. Shoes hit the floor, nylons chafed, people jumped up to shake Dad's hand. Pamela Palmer threw her arms around him as if he'd been the one charged. Affection in front of his employees must have embarrassed Dad because rather than return the embrace he just let his arms dangle at his side. He was glaring straight over her shoulder at me and I could tell he was peeved I'd skipped school, but I was ready to throw his own words back at him. "One of my dreams was to own a business where my kid could learn to work," he'd told me. "I don't want you to be just another employee. I want to see ink in your veins."

Well, here I am, Dad, ready to drink your ink.

I waited in the back and accepted the pats on the shoulder as people filed by, shaking their heads and muttering. "Who would have thought?"

Louise Mead was the last one to leave and whatever she was saying to Dad she punctuated it with finger pokes into the space between them. *Pow. Pah. Pow.* Unrelieved nicotine anxiety. I could imagine what she was saying. *Tom, put some distance between you and that man. You're the boss here. You're the one everyone looks up to.* She had a roughness about her that let her cut through the crap. Dad had been reduced to head nodding. Louise's parting gesture was a sharp snap of her fingers. *Just say jump, Tom, and we'll ask how high.*

On the way out, she brushed close to me and whispered, "I softened him up for you, sugar."

After Louise closed the door, the only sound was the hum of the computer, interrupted by an occasional gurgle as the processor bit something off and swallowed. Sometimes I'd heard Dad turn on the portable radio on his credenza and listen to National Public Radio, but right then I wanted the country music station, something bluesy and overdone to break the suction of silence between us. He was leaning against the edge of the desk again with both his legs and arms crossed. He wasn't coming to me; I had to go to him. I let the newspaper flap across the backs of the chairs like a playing card against bike spokes as I walked slowly toward his desk. I reminded myself that in this room I was his employee, so didn't he owe me the same explanation he'd given everyone else?

"Now you know why I had to proofread the front page." His voice was kind. This was going to go better than I'd thought.

"You were in a pretty awkward spot, huh?" I rolled the paper up and slid it back and forth through the loop I'd made with my thumb and index finger.

"I couldn't not report it. Nobody's beyond the reach of the public's right to know."

I had to think about that for a moment. With my dad, I'd learned to operate in a different gear. Maybe it was his Jesuit training. *The universe isn't just a jumble of accidents, Piper. There's an order in the essence of things, even in the intangibles like fear or jealousy. It's our job to discover that order.* If you didn't get off on principles and syllogisms, you wouldn't understand my dad. That's just who he was. But, hey, this one was going in the right direction. I was part of the public so didn't I have a right to know? I was feeling giddy again, the same rush I'd had in Ned's when I first saw the headline. Dad hadn't even mentioned my truancy. I put my foot up on the closest chair and leaned on my knee so we could talk man-to-man.

"Who was the kid, Dad?"

He brushed his hand in the direction of my leg. "Don't put your shoes on the furniture."

"Oh . . . sure." I stood up and resumed reaming the finger loop with my newspaper.

"The bench-press rules don't allow us to disclose names of minors in a situation like this."

"Did you tell *them*?" I gestured to the empty couch and chairs.

"Piper, I'm not going to budge on this one."

I wanted to cuss, but instead I just crammed the end of the paper into the palm of my hand like I was snuffing out a cigarette. *The bench-press rules don't allow us*? He sounded like the Pope. "So much for the public's right to know," I said.

"Don't get cute."

I shook my head in frustration. "Dad, this affects me. It affects us. What did he do?"

"He didn't *do* anything. Didn't you hear what I said? This is an accusation . . ."

"Okay, okay, what was he *alleged* to have done?"

He stood up, uncrossed his arms, and gripped the lip of the desk. His lids tightened down over the tops of his eyes. "Okay, you asked and I'm going to tell you. This is in the charging affidavit. If you went to the courthouse, you could read this." His Adam's apple moved up, then down, as he gulped. "They say he sodomized a boy . . . you know what sodomy is?" I nodded, my mouth too dry to speak. "There are multiple counts. They're saying it was a predatory relationship. It's hard even to say it." He wiped away the start of a tear under one eye and took a deep breath. "Now you know more than they do."

"I know how you feel about the Carlisles, Dad, but . . . isn't there a silver lining in all this?"

"Hah!" He stood up and went around behind his desk. I knew he was about to kick me off to school and I had lots more to say. It might be a long time before we worked ourselves back to this same ledge together.

"The paper won't sell, will it . . . with this kind of cloud?"

He lifted things off the desk and flopped them back down. We'd never discussed the argument I'd overheard between him and Carlisle and I half-expected he'd tell me to leave it alone the way he told me to take my foot off the chair. "It was only an inquiry, but yes it could affect a sale. How'd you know about that?"

"You know, loose lips in the doghouse."

"If he goes down it's because I let him go down."

"That's crazy, Dad. You're not his guardian. Let him take the flop."

He coupled his hands together like a train hitch. "John Carlisle and this paper are like that. He needs someone in his corner."

This wasn't making sense. Even the Catholic Church had corrupt popes, but the institution lived on. Why didn't Dad let go? John Carlisle was dead weight in a leaky life raft. If Dad held on, he was going down with him. "He doesn't need *you*. He needs a psychiatrist."

The veins in the side of Dad's neck engorged and he clenched his fist like an Irishman in a pub who'd just been called a candy ass. "I've worked for the Carlisles for twenty years. The roof over our heads was paid for with Carlisle money. I'm going to investigate this thing myself! I'll find out what the truth is. And when I do, I'll print it and let the chips fall where they may!" He slapped his day calendar down on the desk so hard that a pencil jumped. He seemed crazed by the whole thing and what he was saying sickened me. I'd always thought of John Carlisle as someone Dad had put up with. The paper worked in spite of Carlisle, not because of him. In his heart, I always thought Dad must have despised him more than anyone in Stampede. The Scanlons were self-made, the Carlisles were inherited, surviving on someone else's money, someone else's sweat. Scanlon sweat. But the more Dad talked, the more he was pulling us into the same tent as the Carlisles.

"If you're going to take sides, why don't you take Mom's side?"

He spun his head around. "What's she got to do with it?"

"Why didn't you investigate her death?" I was strangling the newspaper in my hand, resisting the temptation to throw it at him and quit his damn paper. I didn't know exactly where I was going with this. It was still murky and I hadn't had the chance to figure it out yet, but there was a connection here. It was the part I'd hoped Dad would help me with. I'd visualized us on the same page, him sitting me down, marshaling his formidable deductive skills, and telling me how this exculpated Mom.

"I'm not going to stand in my own office and argue with you about John Carlisle. The truth will win out. It always does." He turned away from me and started fussing with the papers on his desk. He'd gone back into his journalist's vestments. We were back at day one of life after Mom, when my life with Dad had really begun, and he was trying to shield me with ignorance again. Why couldn't he run our relationship the same way he ran the newspaper? The truth was king for the paper, but it was a thief between us.

It was mid-morning when I left Dad's office and the repair and sales vehicles gathered for the donut break had filled the street in front of Marge's — Cascade County PUD, U.S. West, Washington Natural Gas, and the Stampede Police. Marge poured coffee for one of the booths by the window and mouthed me a greeting through the steamed up glass. I took my hand out of my jacket and waved back. She was smiling, pleased to be busy. There was a rack next to her cash register for newspapers and I guessed for once the *Herald Stampede* would outsell *USA Today*.

In the middle of Commercial Street, a truck with a tall stepladder on the flatbed was parked under one of the artificial Christmas wreaths strung across the street. A short guy in galoshes wearing one of those Russian hats with ear flaps that stuck out from his head like shelves stood two steps from the top, unscrewing one of the dead bulbs. Three people steadied the ladder. As I walked on up the street, I noticed that most of the wreaths had come undone during the windstorm we'd had a few nights ago. The storm before the storm.

I thought of Mom and wondered how she'd have taken the news of the charges against John Carlisle. She'd always looked up to him as a cultivated man. When she couldn't think of the name of an artist or a painting, I'd heard her say, "John will know." And in that appreciation they'd formed a bond of outcasts. He was too high up the ladder and she was too far left of it to be accepted. Mom wasn't vindictive like me. When I'd asked her if she didn't just hate the people of Stampede sometimes for the way they gossiped, she said, "In the right circumstance, every one of us is capable of doing just about anything. How can you hate what's only human?" I wasn't a total stranger to darkness. I'd read *Lord of the Flies*. I'd watched the heirs of the widow in *Zorba the Greek* pick her house clean before the corpse had cooled. If I'd been the starving Raskalnikov, I could have bludgeoned the old pawnbroker. That kind of survival instinct resonated with me. Put me in a dark alley with Condon Bagmore and I'd cut off his scrotum next time he tried to come on to me. Give me a shallow pond with John Carlisle and I'd hold his head under until the bubbles stopped rising for what he'd done with Mom. And when I found out who he'd diddled with, I'd push him under and drown him again.

There was only one flaw in my logic. If John Carlisle was a freak, then maybe so was I. The only difference was he'd acted on his impulses and been caught.

THE NIGHT OF THE Christmas open house it was raining, so Willard and I waited under a giant blue spruce across the street from the Carlisle house to stay dry. The roots at the base spread out above the ground like church kneelers and a white phosphorescent fungus that grew against the north side of the tree smelled like cottage cheese when I split it open under my nose. Occasionally, a gust of wind shook down a shower of giant drops through the boughs.

Willard sometimes went out without an umbrella, but he never went anywhere without one of his dogs and tonight it was Paddy, the Irish terrier with the flat skull and elongated muzzle. In seniority, Paddy had been second to Freeway. Willard brought him, he said, "Because we need a daredevil in case things get crazy." The terrier was known for its courage and carried messages across enemy lines in times of war and that's what it felt like as we hugged the trunk of the spruce and took the names of those who crossed the Carlisle threshold.

"This'll tell us whether anyone believes he's innocent until proven guilty," I told Willard.

Since Freeway's death, Willard had become quieter and harder to decipher. He'd taken to spending more time hunkered down in his room, petting the dogs. I recognized the syndrome and felt it was my job to come up with excuses for getting him out of the house. When I first told Willard what John Carlisle had been charged with, he'd gone stone cold on me and just sat on the edge of his bed, puzzling the idea. I wasn't comfortable explaining sodomy to him.

"Willard, he molested an underage kid." I wanted him to take the same perverse joy in the news I had. The emperor wore no clothes.

He just nodded and rubbed the stubble on his face, making a sound like the bristles of a whisk broom. "What's gonna happen?" he finally asked.

"They'll probably convict him."

He got real dreamy and massaged a couple of dog kibbles in the palm of his hand. "I went to jail once. They thought I stole Humphrey's jackknife. I didn't, but I know who did." I had no idea who Humphrey was, but I knew it had to be someone he worked with in the asparagus fields. The kibbles turned to sawdust and dribbled out the bottom of his hand.

Payton Miller pulled up in front of the Carlisle house in the same black four-wheeler that we'd used to put Freeway down. He got out and pushed up the canopy of his umbrella, which had broken loose from the prongs on one side, and he centered it over his head as he walked around to the other side of the vehicle and opened the door for his wife. She was short and had to slide down off her seat until her feet hit the ground. Then she took her husband's arm and marched up the steps with him to the Carlisle's Queen Anne mansion, which had every turret and cubbyhole lit for the event.

"Why did Dr. Miller have to come?" I said.

"It's his job."

And Willard was right. Dr. Miller attended to the afflicted. If John Carlisle were well, he would have stayed home. Still, I thought, it was a pretty pathetic turnout. If Dad wanted to get an early poll on where his readership was, all he had to do was stand under the spruce tree and count them. They were staying away in droves. John Carlisle was a one-man plague and nobody wanted to touch him. Of course, if I told Dad about the low turnout, he'd probably blame it on the weather.

Willard tapped me on the front of my sweatshirt with the back of his hand. "Hey, why don't you go in?"

"Have you gone loco?" I hadn't been in the house since Mom died. "You go."

Willard stroked Paddy's head, pulling the forehead skin back so hard that it made little whitecaps at the tops of his eyes. "Take *him*."

The idea of going inside the house made me itchy, but I had to admit I was curious. I'd never stood next to an accused felon and I wondered what kind of transformation the charge had accomplished in him. I'd be able to tell by looking him in the eye whether he'd done it. I'd put the question to him directly and see if he blinked. Still, my mere presence could be interpreted as a sign of support. He'd assume I was there because of Dad. "Let's just watch it from here, Willard, and say we went in."

As I was fingering Paddy's tail, a threesome of guys without umbrellas or raincoats came up the hill, laughing and cackling. One of them was wearing a muscle shirt with no sleeves. Skin exposure was something I'd never gotten into, like the girls in our class who wore cutoffs when it was snowing. The three guys were a huddle in motion, as one of them walked sideways to keep up and another one backwards. When they passed under the streetlight I could see that the only one walking frontwards was Condon Bagmore. At the gate, they turned left and started up the walk toward John Carlisle's door.

"I changed my mind, Willard. I'm going."

Willard stripped off his belt, looped it around Paddy's collar for a leash, and handed me the tapered end, which was still warm. Needless to say, the charges against Carlisle had been topic number one at school that first day. The jokes ran rampant. "If Carlisle is a ram and an ass is a donkey, how come a ram in the ass is a goose?" Someone had already painted a sign on the Carlisle Bridge: "In Stampede, you separate the men from the boys with a crowbar!" I was certain Bagmore would know who the kid was. He was a bottom feeder.

A black man with a goatee and tails answered the Carlisle door. His gaze started somewhere on the bridge of my nose and journeyed down to Paddy's paws. "Sorry, Ma'am, no animals."

My immediate reaction was to laugh nervously while I thought of what I was going to do. Willard said any establishment worth its salt allowed dogs. The doorman smiled and I hoped that meant he wasn't going to be a hardass about it. He must have been from out of town, someone

Carlisle had hired for the night. "I'm friends of the family," I said. In this house I felt no obligation to tell the truth.

The man pulled a towel from one of the hooks in the closet, bent down, and started wiping Paddy's paws. Willard had told me that dogs' feet were like their private parts. I tightened up on Willard's belt and watched the hair on the back of Paddy's neck in case he decided to bite. I was beginning to feel bad I'd lied. This is when I should have had a buck for a tip, but the only things in my pockets were the note from Rozene and a condom in an unopened foil packet that Colleen Waterston had found in the tunnel under the bleachers. The butler never actually petted Paddy — that would have been to treat him like an animal — and when he was done, he just assumed his perfect posture, adjusted the maroon cummerbund under his jacket, and watched us go inside.

There were lighted candles everywhere, on the quarter-round tables, the sideboards, the armoire, the grand piano, and even on the sitting spaces in the bay windows. The candles gave off a generic holiday scent, part fir tree and part fruitcake, that covered the mildew I remembered from the last time I was there. Several couples milled around the hors d'oeuvres that were spread like a garish truck garden the length of the multi-leafed dining room table. One lady had her five-year old in tow, dressed in a coat and tie, but I noticed she wasn't letting loose of the grip on him, just in case the state's presumption of innocence was mistaken. Her husband had stacked his China saucer with prawns from the ice mold centerpiece and he was dipping them in the cocktail sauce and rushing them to his mouth before the sauce could drip onto the oriental rug. I took a rolled slice of rare roast beef and slipped it to Paddy when no one was looking. Even though I was wearing jeans with full knees and a hooded navy blue sweatshirt with no paint marks, I was woefully underdressed.

The walls were adorned with paintings — silhouettes of contorted horses in the midst of stars and planets, a couple doing the tango in the eye of a swirling meteor, and a bloody meat cleaver slashing down toward what looked like the neck of a man in a bathing suit. Paddy was pulling on the belt, trying to take me back to the roast beef table, but I dragged him over to a picture of a nude draped across a canvas director's chair. Each of the limbs and the parts of her languid torso — I thought it was a female — had taken on different shades of violet, crimson, and burnt orange. She was arresting, on fire, a kind of asexual Joan of Arc. My eye followed the arm that drooped over the back of the chair to a point just beyond the touch of her fingertips in the right hand corner of the painting. "K. Cooper," it said, my mom's maiden name. I looked again at the figure in the painting and wondered if it wasn't a self-portrait, then I hurried back over to the dancers and the meat cleaver. They were all "K. Coopers." I'd never seen any of these and I could feel myself blushing. These must have been painted in John Carlisle's house.

Outside the half-bath next to the Jacuzzi, I ran into Bagmore and his cadre. One of them was Clete Oster, the kid who confused Pythagoras with pyromania in sophomore geometry. The Osters were reputed to be so lazy they poured milk on their kitchen floor and let their cats and dogs lick it up to clean it. Bagmore was going through the bottles of pills on the shelves in the medicine cabinet. He had rubbed charcoal under his eyes the way football players did to cut down on glare, and it was smeared where he must have tried to wipe something out of his eye.

"This one says, 'Guaranteed to make flagpole erections,'" he said, and his boys guffawed.

"Maybe it'll cure premature ejaculation," I said.

"Look what the cat dragged in." He'd undoubtedly told his minions how he got me in the supply shed. Somewhere in his bedroom, or in his cardboard memory, he probably kept a list of his targets. Since the incident in the shed, he'd left me alone. Somehow my sharing a sexual experience with him, however faulty, had given me immunity. I was off his list. Bagmore looked like his metabolism was running too fast or he was on speed the way his eyes watered and his fingers fidgeted with the tube in his hand. This wasn't the guy I'd want holding the gun to my temple. The neurons shooting off inside him might twitch his trigger finger. Then he noticed Paddy. "Hey, guys, *here's* Carlisle's lover."

"Say that again and he'll bite you where it hurts." I jerked on Paddy's belt to make it look like I was holding him back, but Paddy could no more bite Bagmore than conduct a symphony.

"I like a woman with spunk." His grin revealed the gap between his teeth that you could have slid a plastic stirrer through.

"It's a he," I said, nodding at Paddy.

He laughed. "I meant you, Scanlon." Bagmore elbowed Oster and he laughed too. They could explain it to him later.

"In your dreams," I said. I let them finish their laughter, and waited for the chance to find out what I'd come in for. With these guys, thoughts came with big spaces between them so it wasn't hard to change the subject. "Who was the kid?"

The laugh creases on Bagmore's face disappeared. "I thought *you'd* know. Through your dad." His stupid grin was blooming again, and I knew I'd just exceeded his attention span. "We're working on it though. I'm checking out assholes in gym."

I pulled on the belt. "Come on, Paddy. You'll lower your IQ if you stay around these guys."

If one of them grabbed me, I'd already envisioned myself spinning and smashing my elbow into the side of Bagmore's face like the meat cleaver in Mom's painting, but they left me alone and I could hear them giggling and farting away in the bathroom as I passed through the library. There was no one in the dining room so I grabbed some cheese sticks and a couple of beef rolls for Willard and Paddy. I'd have made it out of there too, except that Dr. Miller called my name out just as I was passing the life-sized mahogany native with the exposed genitals. I put the fistful of meat and cheese under my armpit.

"Oh, hi, Dr. Miller. Merry Christmas."

John Carlisle, who'd been talking to Dr. Miller, turned as well. We were five feet from each other. He was wearing that same gaudy red vest he wore the day I saw him in front of the emergency room at the hospital. He inspected me and the dog, all the time advancing like he was going to touch me. I was backing toward the door and I could feel the belt against my legs as Paddy twisted it around me.

"Piper Scanlon, how nice," he said, with a Peter Lorre smile.

"I gotta go." My fist was still buried in my left armpit and I could feel the cheese oozing between my fingers. He was close enough to read his eyes. *Come on, you coward, Piper, ask him the question.*

"Don't rush off," he said, and I could feel the heat of his body.

Paddy had wound the leash so tight around me that I was immobile. Only my tongue was still able to wag. "So what about the charges, are they true?"

Just when I thought I saw him flinch, Dr. Miller stooped over to pet Paddy and his affection was so stimulating that Paddy spun me around. Everyone laughed. A glob of cheese fell to the floor and Paddy lapped it up while Dr. Miller ruffled the hair on his back. I used the distraction to hide behind my back what was left of the food in my fist. My test had been contaminated. I was the one squirming.

"He's gotta pee," I said, nodding toward the dog, crab-walking sideways to the door.

John Carlisle followed me.

The butler opened the door and I stepped onto the straw welcome mat, the air instantly attacking my cheeks with its coolness.

Holding onto the door jamb with his free hand, John Carlisle leaned out and whispered. "You of all people need to believe me, Piper. Please."

The fresh air and the vast space in which to escape emboldened me. "Who was it?"

"Please. Have some compassion."

I threw the cheese ball in the general direction of the

leaded glass windows in the bow window, but it stuck to my hand on the follow-through and landed harmlessly in the hedgerow next to the walk. "Shit!" He'd won this round. I'd come as pathetically unprepared to confront him as I'd come underdressed. I'd learned nothing from my dad's plodding, tradesman-like habits as a journalist. My techniques for truth-telling were as primitive as black cats and broken mirrors.

Paddy stiffened his legs, wanting to stay with the festivities inside. His nails scraped against the cement as I dragged him toward the safety of the tree with Willard. When I looked back, Bagmore was standing on the porch pointing towards us.

The accusations against Carlisle became the buzz in the doghouse.

"It was a mistake his mother ever let him take dance," Pamela Palmer said. "Why didn't they make him wear a mitt and catch flyballs like everyone else?"

"I think it was those Frenchies at the Sorbonne," Gerry Alexander said.

Everyone swarmed in to take a piece of him. But now that I'd tasted the rush of direct confrontation, the behind-the-back stuff seemed tame, in fact, unfair.

"There's something else going on here," I told Louise Mead. "I think we put our celebrities on pedestals so we can throw turds at them." I surprised myself sometimes with my high-mindedness.

Louise had taken up chalk sticks as a substitute for her cigarettes and she pulled one out of her blouse pocket and puffed on it. "You shock me, Piper."

"Nobody can stand the idea of someone else having more than they do."

"You're saying all this talk is just envy?" There were little chalk kisses on her lips.

"No. Revenge."

I knew because the symptoms were so obvious in me.

In the weeks that followed the announcement of the charges, John Carlisle seemed to be everywhere.

On the way to the *Herald* one afternoon, the Gracio Brothers produce truck was parked in front of Marge's with the motor running. The side door was open and a crate jammed with lettuce, cucumbers, and carrots rested on the sidewalk next to the truck like someone had forgotten it. I reached the crate at the same time John Carlisle did. He was wearing a powder blue sweatsuit with a white stripe down the outside of the legs and the sleeves.

"Can you catch the door for me?" he said.

I was startled. "What door?"

He stooped down, bending at the knees, keeping his back straight, and hoisted the crate up against his middle. "Please."

As I ushered him into Marge's, everyone in the restaurant turned to watch John Carlisle hump a crate of vegetables past the stools and through the swinging doors that led to the rest rooms and the walk-in cooler. Before I could escape, Marge pulled a chocolate-covered cake donut out of the rack and handed it to me on a plate.

"It's day old," she said. Marge knew I had a weakness for cake donuts and by the time I'd slid a buttock onto the edge of the stool she had a cup of coffee and a sugar packet sitting next to the plate. "You can't work on an empty stomach."

Carlisle emerged, brushing his hands together like he'd just unloaded the entire truck. I thought he was going to join me at the bar, so I stood and took a huge bite of donut. Instead, he patted me on the arm with a thank you as he passed and returned to a booth where there was a half-eaten club sandwich and a bowl of tomato soup with the spoon in it. Jesse Little's dad followed him into the booth with his coffee cup rattling against the saucer and sat down. Smelly, bloodshot, unshaven Mr. Little dining with the town's prodigy. What an equalizer a criminal charge was.

A few days later, I saw Carlisle jogging through Kla Hah Ya Park in black tights and a pair of yellow running shoes. His legs were spindly compared to his upper body, which was bundled in double sweatshirts with a towel tucked into the neck hole. He carried small white dumbbells in each hand that he pumped up and down in rhythm with his strides. He was surprisingly light on his feet and I thought maybe he really was once a member of the *corps de ballet*. He stopped at the gazebo to stretch, bending left, then right, joining his hands over his head, rising on his toes, and then with his body perfectly straight, he balanced on one leg and stretched the other one to the side, parallel to the ground. When Mom had told me how John Carlisle used to dance, I'd always tittered to myself. *And I used to play football for the Seahawks.*

A couple of school kids on bikes wheeled by, their tires throwing off gravel and pieces of wet bark. They were riding two abreast on the path, jabbering and cussing at each other. I recognized the attitude, that I'm smarter than anyone else and even if I'm not I don't give a damn as long as I have my wheels. They skidded to a stop next to the gazebo and I watched them from under the eaves of the stone lavatory.

I couldn't hear what they were saying, but the kid with the basket strapped to the carrier on his back fender slid his middle finger up and down in the tube he'd made with his hand and the other kid bent over laughing. Carlisle stopped his stretching to talk to them. I knew I should have gone over there and broken it up. It wasn't as if I thought Carlisle was innocent. I figured they still only had him for a fraction of what he'd gotten away with. Still, I thought, those two little punks hardly represented Stampede. I wanted the public conviction.

The other kid set his bike on its side, edged closer to Carlisle, dropped the back of his pants and mooned him. It was over in an instant as he scrambled back to his bike and the two of them tore out of there whooping and hollering.

One afternoon, I edited an article for the paper announcing that John Carlisle had given fifty thousand dollars to the Lake Spigot Boys Camp scholarship fund for needy kids. Because I had no idea what the size of that contribution represented, either to the Boys Camp or to the Carlisle fortune, I didn't know whether our running a story meant it was news or simply the prerogative of the owner. When I made the mistake of questioning Dad about it, his Irish came out.

"What do you think we're running, a vanity press?"

The same day I edited the story of the scholarship contribution, I found an envelope on my desk with "Piper" hand-written on the outside. It had been sealed with a lick on the point of the flap and broke open easily. Inside, there was a long article that had been cut out of a national news magazine listing the best colleges in the United States. A yellow sticky on the front said:

Piper,
You need to be thinking of your future. Pick one and I'll help.
John Carlisle

I hurriedly ran down the column showing the cost of attending the best liberal arts colleges in the United States. Four years cost more than the boys at Lake Spigot were going to get. Then I realized that my scholarship offer was no different than the Lake Spigot donation. They were both part of Carlisle's desperate campaign to save his image and his ass. When his peers walked into that jury box, he wanted them to remember his unparalleled generosity to the community. His offer to me was probably aimed at Dad. He knew he couldn't tell Dad what to write, but he could certainly bend his head in the right direction. If that was Carlisle's strategy, however, it was flawed on two counts: he'd wildly overestimated my influence on Dad, and he'd underestimated my cynicism.

I ripped the magazine article into four ragged squares and dumped it into the recycle box next to my desk.

Dirk Thurgood had continued to be *persona non-communicata* since the poster flap, and when I asked at the vice principal's office why he wasn't coming to school, they said he'd contracted infectious mononucleosis. I didn't believe them and decided to check it out for myself. I hadn't been to Dirk's in months, probably the result of false pride. He was the one who'd cut me off after the poster thing, so I figured it was his job to paste things back together once he'd gotten over it. Besides, I knew he'd be back. We'd been friends too long. He'd sulked in his tent before.

There was a Century Real Estate "For Sale" sign in his front yard, hanging by thin silver chains from the crossbar of one of those fancy half-crucifixes that realtors used. This didn't make sense. Dirk's dad had retired to Stampede. I looked up at the naked maple trees, the branches as dead as roasting sticks. At its best, in the heat of summer, when the smell of sweet peas and heliotrope were bewitching and the sunflowers in the vacant lots gaped at you like circus clowns, Stampede was still a hard sell. It wasn't like we built 737s or mini-vans. Who would buy a house here in the wintertime?

His dad answered the door. I was always surprised how short Colonel Thurgood was compared to his reputation. He was in good shape for a man nearly sixty, partly because he played handball with old service buddies several times a week in Everett, but his face was always flushed like he'd been out in the weather or had popped his face veins from too much drinking. His sideburns were cut at an angle just above the place where his jawbones ground.

"Whadda you want?" he said, holding the door just wide enough so I could see his crewcut head and the curlicues of gun-metal gray chest hairs in the neck of his undershirt.

"I want to see Dirk."

"What for? He's sick." A drift of stale air hit me, like something trapped inside a shoe clambering to get out.

"School stuff, just take a minute." I could be as peremptory as the Colonel.

"Give it to me." He wasted no syllables and his words were clipped, as if he didn't want to waste his voice on someone so inconsequential. I couldn't imagine doing boot camp under this guy.

"It's up here," I said, pointing to my head, "something from his teachers."

He scratched his butt in a way that made his sweatpants wag with each stroke. Then he opened the door. "He's up there," he said. "Make it snappy." I was on his base, so he must have figured I was under his command.

"Yessir," I said, making a partial salute.

I turned sideways to get by him and headed straight for the stairs, glancing left into the living room as I passed. A game show was playing on the television and the floorlamp next to the Naugahyde Lazy Boy chair was lit. I took the stairs two steps at a time. The door with the "D. Thurgood, Private First Class" plate was closed. This was a promotion. When he first moved to Stampede, the sign said "Private, E-1," the lowest rank in the U.S. Army. There was another television playing inside Dirk's room. I knocked and the volume instantly muted.

"Sir?"

"It's me. Piper."

There was a shuffling inside, a book hit the floor, a hanger sprung off the rod in the closet, then he was standing in front of me in a terrycloth bathrobe that was yellowed around the collar. He cast his eyes downward and pressed one bare foot on top of the other as if to hide the toenails. His hair was greasy, unwashed, and uncombed. "Come on in."

The floor was papered with neat stacks of three-holed notebook filler. Clusters of video cassettes stood on his desk like tanks in battle formation. The monitor was frozen on a scene with doctors in surgical gowns and masks.

"They said you're sick."

He rocked his head from side to side in an expression that was maybe yes, maybe no.

I picked my way between the stacks on the floor and lifted up one of the cassettes on the desk. "M*A*S*H: #27." The next one was "M*A*S*H: #28." They were all "M*A*S*H" tapes.

"Where'd you get all this?" I said.

He mumbled. "Someone's collection."

"You what?"

He shrugged his shoulders. "I bought 'em. All two hundred fifty-one episodes."

I hung a pair of his jeans over the back of the desk chair and sat down, moving a stack of papers on the floor to find a place for my feet. The index card on top of the stack said "Corporal Radar." The notes on the first page, in Dirk's handwriting, gave Radar's weight, height, date and place of birth, grade school, high school, favorite color, religion, and other information. The minutiae went on for pages. The stack next to my other foot was labeled "Hot Lips." Next to that one was "Hawkeye." There must have been twenty-five stacks on the floor. "This is what you've been doing?"

"Pretty much." He sat cross-legged in the middle of his bed, his back rounded and his shoulders sloped. There was no spark in his voice. He sounded more like one of the geriatrics I'd seen when Mom and I visited her great uncle in the nursing home, with that same faraway look. I hated that place.

"Have you heard about Carlisle?"

He looked down and picked at his toes.

"Well, was I right or was I right?"

No answer.

I tossed one of the cassettes onto the bed and it slid next to his bare feet. "Speak to me, Buddha." The left side of his cheek buckled slightly as if someone had pushed it up with a stiff finger. "Hey, I know you polished his silverware, but come on." Still no rise out of him. He was methodically picking his toes, working from biggest to smallest. One knee was raised so I could see the inside of his thigh and his underpants. "The good news is you're no longer sick joke number one in the lavatories."

His lips were trembling. I couldn't tell if he was angry or confused. "It was me," he said.

"What?"

"I'm the one who made the charges."

My heart dropped like someone had severed the elevator cables. I'd pictured the victim as some blonde ten-year old out in the new subdivision on Horse Heaven Highway. "I'm sorry, Dirk. Jesus. You worked for him, I should've known . . ."

"Don't sweat it. It's not all bad."

"What's the good part?"

"These tapes, for one." He nodded toward the battalion on his desk.

"You bought these with Carlisle's money?"

"Hey, I made out." He sounded like a character from one of his videos and I didn't want to believe him, but there was a matter-of-factness in his voice that made it seem real.

"I can see why you're not at school."

"I'm not afraid of school!" There was a mood swing and he was suddenly defiant. "My dad won't let me go."

"He won't *let* you?"

"I'm grounded."

"He can't do that."

"The Colonel can do a lot of things" — there was hatred in his voice — "for now."

"Not if I report him."

He gave a dismissive laugh. "Leave it alone, Piper. It'll play itself out and then we'll all be better off. You too. Especially you."

I could only shake my head. I was missing it. If this was another one of his Hollywood-induced delusions, I didn't like it. He was going to be chewed up and spit out so hard once word got out that he'd wish he was dog puke, but he seemed to relish the idea. The old shame was gone.

"Sometimes there's a higher purpose served," he said. More video talk, I thought. Maybe he'd had a psychotic break. The experience with Carlisle had pushed him over the edge.

─── *12* ───

BEFORE THE CHARGES WERE filed against John Carlisle, I thought I had pretty well figured out what had happened between him and Mom. I'd composed the whole thing in my daydreams and nightmares, editing it until every scrap of truth I could get my hands on fit, and telling no one what I knew.

Mom was restless, aching for attention. The spirited tides she'd ridden as a young woman had deposited her high on the beach and receded. Although Dad wasn't the kind of man who danced nude at rock concerts in the forest or painted peace symbols on his forehead, he was attracted to her independence, to her disenchantment with the status quo. It resonated with his own thirst for the unvarnished truth of things. He brought her to Stampede, but Stampede was too vanilla for her. She hungered for self-expression, as a way to distinguish herself from the dutiful housewives and working mothers. Dad didn't understand pigments, mixing knives, brush strokes, and the clash of colors. Why would someone use a hog bristle brush and a palette of a dozen colors to express themselves when there was a printing press and the vocabulary of Shakespeare? Colors tickled the sense of sight; words engaged the full labyrinth of the brain.

Mom was drawn to the eccentric like a moth to the light-bulb's heat. Enter John Carlisle, the would-be toe-dancer amidst a mob of shufflers. He appreciated her passion. He didn't just talk the talk, he bought her pieces, I'd seen them in his living room. Neither of them held steady jobs. They had time. First, it was painting in his library or the den. Then the painting was followed by a hot tub. With bathing suits, gradually without. What man wouldn't be moved in the presence of a wet Kathryn Scanlon? Their stolen glances grew to playful touches — the arch of a foot in the water, a squeeze of the knee, a neck rub, he behind her, and then in reverse. John Carlisle probably dried her off with one of those oversize Turkish towels he stacked in the dressing room next to the Jacuzzi. Maybe they danced naked to his bed that first time, pirouetting, then waltzing, then collapsing in laughter on the bedspread, she warmed by his appreciative eyes, the same eyes that had admired her on canvas. He was her husband's boss, so who would suspect? They were on the fringe anyway, so who would care?

They must have been playing in the Jacuzzi that day. One of them dropped something. Maybe it was one of Mom's twin dolphin earrings. Giggling, they tried to pick it up between their toes, but it kept slipping out and fishtailing to the bottom. *I'll get that little devil*, Mom said, and she somersaulted head first like a duck, with her white buttocks breaking the surface. She felt along the bottom of the Jacuzzi with the flats of her hands, tickling his toes, holding her breath, trying to keep from laughing and losing her air. Her long, chestnut hair drifted toward the drain like smoke to an exhaust fan and then it caught. As more of it was sucked through the grate, the opening in the drain became smaller, and it sucked harder and harder until it had wound every strand onto its spool. Upside down in the murky water, Mom tried to find John Carlisle's bleached torso, but she couldn't move her head. She screamed and, in doing so, traded the precious air left in her mouth for warm water. She tried to kick, but she was pulled so tightly against the grate that she was not even sure her feet reached the top. The hum and gurgle of the jets camouflaged the bubbles rising from her trapped head and, desperate for air, she inhaled a sinkful of water laced with bacteria. Her body, no longer buoyant, collapsed to the bottom of the tub and her face went flush with the drain. She registered a last silent protest against the force that was threatening to pull her head through the grate like an egg slicer and it was at that moment the devil in the water plucked out her eyes.

I wasn't exactly sure what John Carlisle was doing while Mom struggled at the bottom of his Jacuzzi — that part of the story was still in gestation — but it couldn't have taken more than a minute because I'd tried a hundred times since to see how long I could hold my breath and never gotten past about fifty-five seconds.

Initially, I had entertained the idea he'd drowned her because she threatened to tell my dad about their affair, but that didn't make sense. Why would she tell on herself? Then I decided his crime wasn't homicide as much as trespass. He'd wandered into someone else's pasture, not just Dad's, but Mom's and mine as well. He'd already taken one of my parents with his newspaper; it wasn't fair that he should have both of them.

The new truth, the one that Dirk had admitted to, however, was like an icicle driven through my brain. But it offered relief from the alternative I'd imagined. The same man couldn't have done both.

On the last day of school before Christmas vacation, I headed downtown to find a present for Dad at the Star Center Mall, a cavernous red brick building that used to be the Stampede Armory. Because of the job at the paper, it was the first year in my life I had money, so I knew I had to get something nice, maybe a brimmed hat (he was developing a bald spot on the back of his head) or one of those juicers (so he could make his own V-8). A brown Corolla pulled up next to the curb. At first, I thought it had stopped for the mailbox. The horn piped lightly and I looked over to see Rozene Raymond rolling down the passenger window.

"Need a lift?"

I didn't *need* the ride anymore than my dad needed the juicer, but *want* was a different proposition. "Sure," I said, already moving toward the door she'd swung open.

She took the bridge over the river and drove out Highway 9. I didn't protest. The heater was cranked up and she had a Kate Bush tape in the cassette. She seemed so comfortable, as if we did this every Friday afternoon. I rested my left arm on the top of the seat and turned so that I could watch her drive. She'd pulled a ligament in a girls' intramural basketball game and the cast on her right foot kept the speedometer needle just over the limit. I was there when it happened and had to resist the urge to run out on the court and comfort her. Two teammates put her arms over their necks and helped her limp off the court to the nurse's station.

As she turned into the road for Harvey Field the aluminum crutches standing up in the backseat slid over and banged against the window. "Oops," she said. We took a service road past a row of galvanized metal hangars and past a fleet of single engine planes secured to the ground with guy wires. The road ran parallel to the runway until it petered out and turned to gravel. She looped over to a place about a hundred yards past the ground lights and directly under the flight path, pointed us back toward the runway, and put the car in "Park."

"How's that?" she said.

"Are we supposed to be here?"

"Nobody's ever kicked me out."

"You do this a lot?"

She laughed. "I come out here alone. Something about flying turns me on." Then she picked up her leg and started maneuvering it out of the driver's compartment. "Do you mind? This thing's a killer if I don't stretch it out." She held her leg in the air while I tried to scoot over far enough so that she could set her cast on my seat, but my legs were too long and I couldn't get out of the way.

"That's all right." The weight of her felt nice on my thigh and I cautiously touched the plaster that entombed her foot. It was hard and coarse and I could smell the gauze in the mold. She reached over to adjust her cords so the ribs of the corduroy lined up with the extension of her leg. There was a lone salutation on her cast in a language I couldn't understand, signed "Mom."

"It's Wakashan," she said. "May the river flow through your veins."

"Does your mom speak it?"

"God, no. She assimilated and that's what she wants me to do. But she can't help herself." I'd heard from Mom the story of how Rozene's father was white, a Russian fisherman who'd become a boozer and physically abused Mrs. Raymond until she became fed up and fled to Stampede. "Do you know where Condon Bagmore's brother came down?" she said.

Bagmore was on my mind too, but it wasn't just because we were at Harvey Field. In some eerie way, being confined with her in the Corolla reminded me of the supply shed with him under the grandstands. It was intimate. It was sexual. Instead of not trusting Bagmore though, I didn't trust me.

"Hey, what's the matter? You're spacing on me."

"Sorry. Bad subject, I guess."

"Okay, let's talk about the Mile High Club."

"The Mile High Club?"

A smile broke out on her face and she flopped her elbows, accidentally honking the horn. We both laughed and looked around to see if anyone had heard us.

"You know Nick Oster," she said. "Clete's dad? He runs a crop dusting business. One of his planes is supposed to have a featherbed that covers the entire tail section." She was gripping the top of the steering wheel and trying to contain herself. "People pay him to take them up while they have sex." She raised her eyebrows and waited for my response.

I was stunned, first because I prided myself on knowing what was going on in Stampede, and second, because of the way I'd always thought of Rozene. Her glee at the prospect of folks fornicating on Nick Oster's featherbed as they cruised over the homes and churches of Stampede surprised me. I didn't want her that assimilated. "Do you know anyone who's done it?"

"The Morrisons have," she said, biting her lip to keep from laughing.

"The Minister Morrisons?" I pinched one of her toes and laughed with her. Gordon Morrison was the Presbyterian minister in Stampede, a fairly young guy with a British accent, who coached the boys' select soccer team. It was his wife, Twyla, whom Mom had slapped across the face when she said something derogatory about Ashley Carlisle.

"They wanted to conceive and they'd tried everything else."

"She's so mousy." I tried to imagine this floating featherbed in the sky, with portals so you could count the church spires as you were going down on your partner. Was there a divider between the lovers and the pilot? Did Nick Oster change sheets between customers? Were there seatbelts for takeoffs and landings? Did Nick do loops to help the sperm reach Twyla's uterus? There seemed to be a growing chasm between appearance and reality. Ministers prayed to the heavens and did it in the clouds. And Rozene Raymond was sitting with the weight of her broken leg on me.

A single engine plane painted with a purple and orange Federal Express logo on its fuselage circled the field. The drone of its engine grew louder as it reached our end of the runway, then faded as it went past. If I continued to play with the toes that stuck up through the plaster boot in my lap I was afraid the hum of my own engine would drown out the plane. When I brushed the underside of her index and middle toe, she curled them around my little finger and held on. The plane had aligned itself with the runway and was returning. I could hear it cutting through the wind, idled down, as it glided over the top of the Corolla and then dropped like a falcon onto the concrete runway. I squeezed her toes as the plane bounced and finally settled on all three wheels and shrunk its way to the other end of the field.

"Wasn't that beautiful?" she asked.

My scruples were breaking down. She was making this too easy. There was none of the pushiness involved with boys, none of the differences like whiskers and sports and the aperture between the legs. "I better go home."

"Boo."

Maybe it was an excess of Catholicism, but I let her take her leg back and start the car. I knew this outing meant something different to me than it meant to her and, if I didn't let her go, that difference was going to become painfully obvious. I kept thinking she must have an ulterior motive — she wanted me to help reinstate her mom at the paper — but there'd been no such request.

The light was on in the kitchen when Rozene pulled the car up in front of my house. Willard liked to eat early with the dogs so he could digest things before bedtime. He said undigested food gave him nightmares about Freeway. There was no light in the living room, which meant Dad wasn't home yet.

"Do you want to come in a minute?"

"I better go," she said.

"I can give your book back." I sounded desperate.

"Sure."

As I walked ahead of her toward the porch, I experienced shortness of breath. Her crutches creaked and the rubber caps plucked each time she lifted them off the sidewalk. I was trying to remember what my room looked like, whether I'd managed to flop the blankets up over the pillows. It was okay to look casual, but I didn't want to seem sloppy. I glanced into the kitchen and smelled the Spam. There was a frying pan on the stove with a tired spatula resting in it and the counter had open jars of mayonnaise, horseradish, Dijon mustard, and grape jelly.

"All clear," I said, screening the doorway so she wouldn't be able to see into the kitchen.

She hesitated at the bottom of the stairs.

"Oh, God, I forgot."

"No big deal," she said.

Just in case she stumbled backwards, I let her go first and she stumped her way up: good foot, crutches, good foot, crutches. Her cords fit snugly around her buttocks and there was a flash of brown just above her belt each time she lifted the crutches to the next step. Part way up she stopped for a breath and teetered until I steadied her with my hand in the hollow of her back, which was warm.

"My room's on the main floor," she said. She didn't need any excuses; she was in better shape than I was.

"I like it upstairs." *Please, Willard, don't pick tonight to come to my room.*

At the top of the stairs, I passed her and made an advance sweep through my room, kicking shoes under the bed, gathering up the dirty underwear and socks in a wad, and pulling the bedspread over the top of the tangle of blankets and sheets. It wasn't everything, but hopefully it would put me over the sleazeball threshold. She appeared in the doorway just as I snapped on the light.

"Wow, who does your room?"

"Sorry for the mess."

"Clean room, dirty mind," she said, and we both laughed.

Like a hummingbird to honey, she went straight for my bookshelf, which I considered a good sign, and pulled out one of my Anais Nins. She tilted her head and studied the titles on the spines. I could feel myself blushing at how many I'd accumulated. She'd think I was a nymphomaniac. Maybe we should have just stayed in the living room. I could have offered her carbonated mineral water. As I looked around my room through her eyes, I realized how loaded it was with revelations — the Vaseline on the nightstand, the training bra that hung from the hook on the back of the closet door, the lump in the middle of the bed from the pillows I squeezed between my knees when I slept, and the sappy ("When your heart speaks, take good notes") and not so sappy ("A woman is a foreign land") notes I'd taped onto the wall over my desk, not to mention the button collection ("I'm a castrating bitch"). I didn't have to ask her in, I didn't have to bring her to my room. I must have wanted to run the risk of her knowing how twisted I really was.

"Weren't she and Henry Miller lovers?"

I smiled. Maybe I'd found a soulmate. My copies of *Tropic of Cancer* and *Tropic of Capricorn* were safely stored in the drawer of my nightstand, hidden from Dad the same way Mom had hidden them.

"Can I borrow her?" I liked the way she said *her*, as if the books had hearts and kidneys.

"As long as you promise to tell me what you think."

I took off my shoes and made a short stack of pillows on the bed to sit on. While Rozene studied the quotes over my desk, I put the lid on the Vaseline and crammed it and two used flossing strings into the top drawer of my nightstand. When she'd worked her way around to the bed, she balanced on one leg like a stork and set her crutches on the floor, then sat down on the bed with her back to me.

"One more week of these and I'm going to look like a linebacker," she said, rolling her shoulders.

I rested my hands on her and pushed my thumbs against the muscles between the shoulder blades. Suddenly I was aware of how stale my breath was, like each exhalation had been inside me for a month. "You're tight."

She folded her shoulders back and groaned. Her hair brushed against the tops of my hands. "I'll give you a million dollars to keep doing that."

Mom used to massage me, making me lie face down on the bed while she sat on my butt and straddled me. I loved it when she slid her hands under my shirt and pressed me into the mattress with all her weight; it was how I imagined lovemaking must be, when your partner practically joins you. The pads of my thumbs tiptoed up Rozene's vertebrae to the nape of her neck and she let herself go limp as I explored each curve and bump of her skull, rubbing in penny circles. She was taking deep breaths and with each inhalation I could feel her rise, then collapse again. I ventured over the crest of her shoulders until I could feel the ridges of her collar bones, which made little lakes that I dipped into with my thumbs and scrubbed the shorelines. With my hands under her shirt, I rubbed the smooth beach between her throat and her breasts and my face was so close to her hair that I could smell peaches. On the upstroke, my fingernails brushed under her bra straps.

"I'm melting," she said, and her words were like fingers across my nipples.

If I'd mapped it out on paper, I would have said it couldn't have happened, not this soon, not with me, but when she stretched herself out on the bed in front of me her breasts were right about where the dough would be if I were kneading bread. Extending my right arm as far as it would go, I managed to advance the switch on the three-way lamp to the lowest setting. Her eyes were closed and there was a residue of moisture on her lids which I grazed with my finger, feeling the heat of her eyeballs. Without saying anything, she unbuttoned the top of her shirt, far enough that I could see the little ribbon bow where the white satin cups of her bra connected. It was my turn to take a deep breath and the air that came out must have been hot against her skin.

With her eyes closed, she found my hands and placed them on her bosom and I was afraid to move. Then she whispered something as tender as anything I could have imagined. "I'm glad your mother will finally be vindicated, Piper."

It was in answer to nothing we'd talked about at the airport. We hadn't even mentioned my mom, but with those words my fingers moved again and I traced the soft furrow where the edge of her bra met skin. Her arms lay open, palms heavenward at her side, and she made no effort to stop me.

As I devoured her chest with my eyes, I dreamed of Rozene and me in the Mile High Club, reading Anais Nin out loud to each other as Nick soared above the clouds in swoops as long and graceful as an eagle's. We'd take turns rubbing almond oil into each other's skin, and I'd straddle her the way Mom straddled me, and as the plane climbed out of a dive I'd press against her as hard as I could until she could feel us disappearing as one into the featherbed. And when we were tired, we'd ask Nick to take the long way home while we wrapped ourselves in the comforter like two larvae in a cocoon waiting to become butterflies.

It would have been the perfect afternoon, except for the fact of Dad sticking his head in my door.

"Excuse me," he said. It was dark so I didn't know how much he saw, but I pulled my hands out of Rozene's shirt.

"He must have noticed the car," Rozene said, after he closed the door.

Later that night, Dad and I nearly collided in the hallway on my way to bed. "I haven't seen the Raymond girl for a while," he said. It was an invitation for an explanation.

I felt myself blushing and stepped back to make sure I was out of the light coming from the kitchen. "She gave me a ride home."

"The greatest human organ is free will, you know. It runs everything else." I knew I was being reproached.

"I'm not gay, Dad, if that's what you're implying. I don't even like the word."

There was a stern look on his face and I wanted to say something about seeing him necking under the Carlisle Bridge, but I wasn't sure enough of myself to force him into any comparisons.

——13——

WILLARD HAD THE BRIGHT idea of bathing the dogs in the basement shower stall to get them ready for Christmas. He didn't really ask me to help, but when I saw how hard the pug was fighting him I knew he'd have no chance with the bigger dogs. Besides, I needed something to ground me.

I was bouncing between coal-black guilt and a giddiness so light it threatened to vaporize me. I could hardly wait to see Rozene again. I was composing letters to her in my journal. I was practicing out loud what to say in the lunchroom or passing in the hall. I made a list of Christmas presents for her. I separated the clothes in my closet, shoving to the right side of the bar everything I thought she'd consider dull. An hour later, I was afraid to see her again. I was in a spiraling free-fall into the darkness Catholics recognized as original sin, unwashed man and woman. From portholes in the darkness, I caught glimpses of Mom and Dad staring aghast as I spun past them.

I held Paddy with one hand on his collar and the other one under his belly while Willard washed, the soap suds building on his forearms like sheared fleece. With my head in the stall, I could smell the musty aroma of the mold-speckled tile.

"They're like cars," Willard said. "If I don't baby them, they're going to break down on me." Willard still blamed himself for not catching the cancer or whatever it was that had eaten away Freeway's insides like battery acid.

"I don't think a bath's going to make any difference. Look at the animals living in the wild."

He stopped scrubbing and looked over at me like I was a zoological dunce. "They don't have parents."

"Of course, they have parents. You mean they don't have masters."

He ignored me and resumed his work around Paddy's hindquarters, scrubbing the inside and outside of his legs, his penis, his tail, inside his ears, and between the toes. No body part was off limits. Although Paddy looked betrayed, he made no attempt to bite or bark. He just eyeballed me, wondering if this shivering humiliation would ever end. When Willard was satisfied that he'd babied him enough, he filled the mop bucket with warm water and dumped it over Paddy. Hair filaments swirled around in the bottom of the stall and washed down the drain.

Willard let me wash Billy, the cross-breed with the lively eyes. "She's a girl," he said, "and besides her hair is shorter." In other words, easy enough even for someone unfamiliar with the ways of the canine species.

As I sudsed up her underside with long, firm strokes, I kept thinking of Rozene and it made me woozy. I'd awakened with a headache as hard as an anvil realizing that not only had I given free reign to my concupiscence, I'd betrayed Dirk.

"Keep it away from her face," Willard said.

I kept scrubbing and my thoughts drifted. "Willard, do you think Mom liked being a mother?"

He raised a shoulder to wipe some suds off his chin. "It was all brussel sprouts to her."

"What do you mean?"

"I mean she knew it was good for her, but she had to work at it." He cackled to himself. "When she was little, she had more dolls than you could shake a stick at. Long, floppy ragdolls. Little bitty stiff ones. She made 'em beds out of cereal boxes, fed 'em, sang songs to 'em, even married them off. I told Carol, 'Our Kitty's going to have a dozen kids some day.'" Then he stopped talking, at least externally; there could well have been another conversation still going on between him and Grandma Carol.

"So what happened?"

"What do you mean, what happened? Carol died."

We'd disconnected again and I looked at him to make sure he wasn't just pulling my leg. "I mean why didn't Mom have more kids?" I had always harbored the notion that life would have been easier if there were more of us in the boat. If I'd had a brother, maybe I would have learned normal responses to boys.

"Why do some folks dance?" he finally said. "Why is your dad Irish? Why did I live longer than the wife? God only knows." I knew that wasn't true. This puzzle had a solution.

"I must have been a disappointment." My guess.

He gave me another one of those unblinking stares, his eyes soap bubbles waiting to burst. "You do her ears?" Sometimes I swore his back wheels weren't following his front ones.

I lifted one of Billy's ear flaps and spoke directly into the drum. "Tell your master he didn't answer my question." The vibration of my voice must have tickled Billy because she shook, spraying soapy water all over the bathroom, and rocking Willard back on his heels laughing.

I didn't push Willard for more history. I wasn't sure exactly what I wanted him to say anyway. If I was brussels sprouts, I could live with that. I wasn't trying to make Mom and me into the Madonna and child. I was drawn to struggle, the salmon who swam upstream to spawn, the loggerhead songbird who impaled its prey on thorns, the wasp who paralyzed the attacking tarantula, laid eggs on him, and covered him with dirt. I didn't need sweet. The world gorged on sweet and regretted it afterward. A woman had to look out for herself to survive. Mustard was my built-in protection against the casual cannibal.

"Willard, were you ever attracted to someone you weren't supposed to?"

He folded his legs under himself on the floor. "You mean like Carol?"

"Some *femme fatale* you knew you should stay away from?"

"A what?"

"Someone so attractive you wanted to be owned by her."

A knowing smile broke out from under the specks of soapsuds on his face. "Someone has a boyfriend."

I played along. "What if you were different nationalities or something?"

"That's what they told me about Carol, you know." He reached over and petted Billy. "Her parents said I was the wrong kind. Shoot, even a dog knows the difference between being kicked and being stumbled over. It just made me more determined to prove 'em wrong."

With the towel, I dabbed the suds off Willard's face, wishing I really were a crazy Cooper like he was. I wanted his ability to shut out the rest of the world, to listen to the aberrant beat of my own heart.

Working at his desk, Dad had gotten into the habit of playing with his hair, twirling it around his finger until he had a wrap and then pulling on it until he had a thatch that stuck out of his noggin like a hair tit. It put him in a kind of reverie I hated to interrupt. On the other hand, I knew the best time to ask him anything important was the moment after I'd set a freshly edited page of the paper on his desk, so that's what I did.

"How's your investigation of the Carlisle charges going?" I thought this would be a way to segue into what I'd learned from Dirk.

The skin was dark around his eyes like he hadn't been sleeping. Not bothering to look up, he said, "Working on it." It was a fence without a gate.

The way he was spending so much time away from the paper during the day, I'd figured he was working on the investigation. I'd seen his car in front of stores and homes that had no connection with the stories I was editing for the paper. I saw him sitting on the porch with Mrs. Norman, the nosy lady who lived across the street from us. I saw him walking with Carmela Castillo carrying her grocery bags. I even saw him go into the Comet with Seth Armstrong, the prosecuting attorney. The employees in the doghouse had noticed it too.

"My sister-in-law saw him eating alone at the Hush of the Lark the other day," Louise Mead said. The Hush of the Lark was an upscale bed and breakfast place out on Skylar Road on the way to Machias that included a restaurant dripping with ferns and planter baskets like Hammurabi's garden. People from Seattle went there to celebrate anniversaries or job promotions. Single mothers from Stampede without high school diplomas and women like Rozene's mom changed the sheets and swished out the toilet bowls with bristle brushes and Dutch cleanser. It wasn't Dad's kind of place, not when you could get a rib steak, fries, and a green salad at Marge's for five-ninety-five plus a tip.

He made up for time lost during the day by working later at night. I'd clocked him in at twelve-forty-five, twelve-thirty, and one a.m. the last three nights. Dad had the nasty habit of letting the storm door on the side of the house clatter shut — the pressure had gone out of the door closer — but I didn't bother to mention it because it was such an easy way to keep track of him. Maybe; he wasn't investigating at all. Maybe he'd taken up with the whale woman, Nadine.

On Wednesday, I heard him tell Pamela Palmer he was going to a dinner meeting in Seattle and to lock the door when she left.

Around quarter to five, when people were starting to put their coats on and switch off the lights in their cubicles, I moseyed down the hallway to the print room, closed the door behind me, and slid under the behemoth printing press. There was no one else in the room. George Pester, the printer, always took the day off after a new issue and, unless someone went in there to cop a plug of chewing tobacco from the can he kept next to the shutoff switch, I figured I was safe. There was a patch of dust where the broom didn't reach that was a shadow as wide as the undergirding. The steel plate six inches above my nose could have been the pan of an automobile engine except the smell was electrical, ozone rather than petroleum. I listened to people wish each other good night, their voices fading like bird chatter down the hallway. On the first day after a print, nobody worked overtime other than Dad, and even he slacked off, as he did tonight in taking a meeting in Seattle.

I ran my fingers along the bottom of the printer, which

was ice cold and slightly abrasive like the metal on the strongbox Willard kept under his bed for stocks and bonds. That's also where he kept his and Grandma Carol's birth certificates — he was born in Yakima seven years before her — and when I asked him why he'd bothered to keep them he said, "To prove my eligibility." That was all he said, his *eligibility*, and I thought at his age for what else would he need to prove his eligibility.

I kept count of the voices outside, which were now down to Pamela, the receptionist, and Gerry Alexander, the photographer. The print room was growing dark. I put both hands on the underside of the printer and, for the heck of it, pushed up to see if I could make it budge. Nothing. It was like my dad, I thought, immovable, but when it spoke, accurate. Finally, there were no more voices and the elongated field of artificial light that had been projected onto the cement floor next to me disappeared. I waited a few minutes to make sure Pamela hadn't forgotten something and come back for it. Hearing nothing, I grabbed the edge of the printer pan and scooted myself out. There was dust all over the back of my pants and shirt and I did my best to spank it clean. The only way to really get it would have been to take off my clothes and shake them, which I wasn't about to do.

I tiptoed up the hallway and as soon as I entered Dad's office my heart started beating like a Geiger counter. I snapped on the desk lamp, one of those halogens on an extension arm, and pushed it down closer to the desk so that it didn't illuminate the whole room. Even though his office couldn't be seen from the street, I didn't want to take any chances. I gripped the desk, closed my eyes, and took a deep breath to settle myself. What I was doing had to be some kind of sin, but for the life of me I was unable to name it. Hadn't Dad told me you didn't have to tell a good reporter to swipe the victim's picture off the mantel? Of course, he'd also told me you had to return it when you were done.

I was still trembling as I pulled the handle on the top drawer of the file cabinet, the one that was usually open when he was working at his desk. Each file tab was labeled in typed script — Kiwanis, Sports Schedules, City Council, Bond Issues — mostly dross, except for a handwritten one that said "Project Carlisle." This must be the one for the sale of the paper, I thought. Why not find out exactly how much this little sweat shop was worth? Instead of financial statements though, I found photographs, receipts, and xerox copies of Dad's weekly calendars. The first photo triggered a gag reflex: it was Mom in a cocktail dress dancing cheek to cheek with John Carlisle. His fingers were spread across the bare skin in the saddle of her back where the dress plunged, touching as much of her as possible,. There were other people, unrecognizable, dancing in the background. On the back it was dated with an inscription that read "Party." It must have been taken at one of the staff parties at the Eagles Lodge. There were more pictures of the party, people sitting at tables with their wine glasses raised in self-conscious recognition of the camera, more shots with Mom and John Carlisle, and then a blurred one of them coming out of Marge's Cafe that had a note on the back in a hand I didn't recognize, "Tom, here's the picture I mentioned." The invoices were mostly MasterCard slips for the account of "Kathryn C. Scanlon." She'd purchased jeans and shirts at the Gap in Seattle, art supplies from Daniel Smith, and meals at various restaurants. The only restaurant I recognized was a meal for "$56.89" including tax and gratuity from the Hush of the Lark. On the xeroxed calendar pages, he'd penned in entries for such things as "Kate in Seattle," "Kate at art class," "Kate and JC at Hush." I checked the date of the "Hush" entry against the MasterCard slip and they matched. I drew a ragged breath. My God! This must be part of Dad's investigation. But why Mom?

I closed the file and slipped it back into the drawer between "Printer" and "Public Auctions" where I'd found it. I ran my fingers across the rest of the tabs in the drawers looking for anything that might bear a relationship to child molestation or sodomy or Dirk Thurgood. I found one file with letters to Dad from his brother Seamus, but decided it was none of my business the way John Carlisle and Dirk Thurgood were. I held my wristwatch under the lamp — it was six-twenty — and calculated how long it would take Dad to drive back from Seattle. Then, it hit me. The computer! Dad's investigation would be on the computer.

I swiveled my chair sideways and felt around the edges of his computer until I found the power switch. The screen crackled with shards of green light, the processor hummed, the monitor filled with a gray page full of unintelligible codes, and finally the gobbledy-gook cleared and the cursor blinked in the lower left-hand corner of the screen behind the words "User password." Damn! I sat there with my fingers on the keyboard staring at the pulsing cursor, thinking of those monkeys locked in a room with type-writers, wondering how long it would take them to type the Gettysburg Address. I typed Dad's last name, his first name, the month, day, and year of his birth, and each time the computer said, "Error." I tried "Herald" and "Pulitz," all with the same rejection. Then I went monkey and started typing in swear words. Still nothing. The computer was laughing at me.

I rested my hands in my lap, closed my eyes, and tried to transport myself into Dad's head. At first everything was blank and it was so quiet I could have heard my eardrums stretch. Then I heard his voice singing some Irish ditty in the shower about "Crazy Jane and her virginity." He had a good tenor's voice, a lot like Dennis Day's on those old seventy-eight records in the attic, but that was so long ago. I hadn't heard him laugh, much less sing, since Mom died. His singing voice always warmed me, so did his poetry voice when he'd ask us to fold our hands and close our eyes at the dinner table and he'd recite a Yeats poem instead of grace:

> She carries in the dishes,
> And lays them in a row.
> To an isle in the water
> With her would I go.

There was romance and derring-do in Tom Scanlon, but Mom's death had smothered it like a mudslide.

Dad always said don't use a long word no one understands when there's a short one they do. The password had to have something to do with Mom. I opened my eyes and typed in "Cooper," her maiden name, the name he would have courted to and recited poetry to when his love for her was fresh. The computer came alive, humming like a grasshopper quartet through tobacco leaves. *Dit, dit, dit, dit, dit, dit, dit, dit, plunk, dit, dit, plunk, dit.*

Computer Science was mandatory in second-year and I'd cribbed my way through Mrs. Oliphant's course, trying not to be so good I would predestine a career for myself as a typist or a data processor. I'd rather rake leaves or pick up litter using one of those poles with a nail on the end of it than numb my brain in front of a computer screen all day. But I found the list of files on the "C" drive. It felt like I was walking around in Dad's brain, each file another circuit to explore. I scrolled quickly to the end of the list and then returned to the beginning. There were hundreds of them, alphabetized by six-letter titles that made me guess at their contents. Many involved John Carlisle, including speeches Dad had written for him to deliver at Kiwanis and Cascade County Democrat lunches. There was no end to the slavery Dad had been subjected to in his service for the Carlisles.

"JCINVS" turned out to be the file I wanted. At the top of the first page, it said: "CONFIDENTIAL: HOLD UNTIL TRIAL!" The piece was entitled: "The Rest of the Story." My Geiger counter was racing again and I squeezed my eyes shut to do an examination of conscience, the kind Sister Graziana had taught us. "You're little house cleaners," she'd always said, in that sickly, Hansel and Gretel witch's voice. "Swish your brooms into every nook and cranny, girls." Before she paraded us across the asphalt playground and through the side door of St. Augustine's for First Friday confessions, Sister made us put our heads down on our desks for fifteen minutes of sweeping. Since then, I'd become a faster sweeper and I managed to finish this examination in seconds. I was going to read whatever Dad had written. I'd learned a long time ago it didn't take any more work to confess the big dust balls than the micrococcal.

I scrolled down until the screen was filled with text:

(STAMPEDE, WA) The rape and sexual misconduct charges against John Carlisle have shocked a county and challenged a way of life in this hidden corner of the world where people want to raise their children.

There is an ebb and flow to these revelations that has been as predictable as the tides and the fractions of the moon. First there was the denial as people insisted, "It couldn't happen here. Not in my town. Not with my children. Not by one of our most revered citizens." The denial was followed by self-doubt as each citizen explored his and her own flaws and once again became humbled by the frailty of the human condition. "Maybe it could have happened. I always wondered why he was such a loner." Now we are caught up in the third and most cynical phase of the cycle, where folks just heap it on in a desperate attempt to differentiate themselves from the accused. This is when nervous parents corner their kids and almost demand their participation. "Are you sure he didn't touch you while you were shopping? What about when you saw him at the swimming pool? How can you be sure?"

Unfortunately, such accusations are like smoke and once they are made they can't be put back in the bottle. True or not, they float among us, leaving an enduring odor of suspicion, especially when something as dear as the safety of our children is at stake. Like Salem, Stampede has become the breeding ground for unfounded accusations against a decent man.

There is something else that should be as dear to a town as the safety of its children. And that is the reputation of an innocent man.

The light in the hallway went on. *Damn, it must be Dad!* There was no time to get out of the file so I just flipped the computer off, punched the halogen lamp switch, and as quietly as I could lifted myself out of Dad's chair and placed, not walked, my feet one foot in front of the other until I was in my own cubbyhole office next to his. I could hear somebody moving in the hallway. What if he turned on the computer to work on the investigation and the file was already open, or lost? I hadn't paid close enough attention in Mrs. Oliphant's class to know what happened when you shut the computer off in the middle of something. She'd always made sure we didn't do that, with her baby-step directions, proving my point once again that you learn best by making mistakes, rather than avoiding them. What would I say I was doing down here? I never set foot in the paper after hours, unless it was to drag Dad home, which Mom made me do sometimes. I could say I was doing homework, a paper, better yet a thesis. *Sorry, Dad, I know I should have asked first, but you were gone.* Anything was okay as long as he didn't know I was into the John Carlisle article, which wasn't really an article as much as an editorial. "The good editorial captures the voice of a whole community," he'd told me.

Dad had never hit me but I knew he'd do it for breaking into his computer. Confidentiality and protection of sources were sacred to the journalist. The dust balls were beginning to roll out of reach of my broom. How would I explain why I was in the dark? I should have left the lights on. Maybe he was just down here to pick up some copy to read at home. If I turned the lights on now, it was a guaranteed confrontation. I'd have to have some excuse. *Oh, Dad, I must have passed out from the bad air. I haven't been eating well. Willard gave me some putrid meat. I'm fasting to cleanse my systems. I fell asleep and didn't realize everyone else had left.*

"Anyone home?" The ceiling light in Dad's office flashed on, but it wasn't Dad's voice. It was an older man, not someone I recognized. I was sitting on the floor in the dark, leaning into the chairs stacked against the wall of my office. The edge of a molded seat was digging into my back, but I didn't dare move for fear the whole stack would shift. Maybe it was a security officer and he'd shoot me if I surprised him. *Jesus, Mary, and Joseph, pray for us thieves and sinners now and at the hour of our death. Amen.*

Squeaky wheels entered Dad's office. There was the banging of something and whistling and I recognized the hollow sound of a wastebasket. It must be the night janitor! I was fine. I could go back and finish reading the file. I'd tell him I was working on a story. I just had to transition gracefully from hidden to visible. I'd wait until he was finished doing whatever else he was going to do, but he seemed to take forever as he lifted pictures and paper-weights off the desk and dusted and fussed. Then he dragged the vacuum into the office and did the carpet. I could hear the rubber guards on the sides of the brush hood bumping into furniture and walls. Everything had to be perfect for the editor-in-chief. Then he shut off the vacuum and punched in someone's number on the phone. I had him now. If he squealed on me, I'd squeal on him. Whoever he was calling must not have been home because he cleared his throat and left a message.

"Hey pumpkin, it's your knight in shining armor. I was thinkin' about what you said and I'm ready to take you on. So get those sugar limbs warm, huh? And don't bolt the door." So much for pleasing the boss.

He limped out of the room, singing "Hey look me over" to the accompaniment of the wheels on his cleaning cart.

He didn't close the door, so that was the first thing I did when I came out of hiding. Then I went back to the desk, found the switch to the computer in the dark and fired it up. It sounded like an overheated pot in a baking oven the way it swelled and cracked and finally advanced to the password test, which I nailed on first try. Before I could move on, however, it asked me if I knew there was another program running and I crossed my fingers and responded, "Okay."

Relief! The file was still there. I quickly scrolled "Page down" until I found the place where I'd left off. I expected details about what Dirk had told the police, how many times he'd been assaulted, where it happened, when, but the author of this piece wasn't telling that story. It assumed the reader knew all of that. This was counterpoint. "Hold until trial," it said. This was going to be Dad's *deus ex machina.*

The article went on to talk about John Carlisle's father and grandfather, material I would have deleted if I were the editor, and I skimmed it looking for the juicy stuff. Then I found it! But it wasn't about Dirk.

> Kathryn Scanlon's patron in the arts was John Carlisle. Records show that he purchased no less than fourteen of her works, pieces ranging from landscapes of the Skykomish River to interpretive and revealing self-portraits, some of which were painted in the Carlisle mansion.

My skin was beginning to crawl. This was more than an editorial. It was a confession, someone else's confession, not Dad's. What did this have to do with the charges against Carlisle?

> Like all relationships, theirs had to evolve, grow and become closer, or wither and die like the unwatered tendrils of a grapevine. On one of the very days that John Carlisle is accused of sodomizing the alleged victim, the record shows that he dined with Kathryn Scanlon at the Hush of the Lark. On that same evening, John Carlisle took the honeymoon suite. Yet there is no mention of the

Hush of the Lark in the criminal charges. It strains the credulity of a reasonable man to believe that John Carlisle, a lover of creature comforts, would abandon the Lark's finest suite to grovel on the floor of his own wine cellar with a boy on the same evening.

This was making me nauseous as well as angry. Dad was practically offering up Mom as John Carlisle's alibi. *Sorry, folks, he was sleeping my wife that night, it couldn't have been him.* What kind of masochism was he engaged in that he would print this kind of stuff, even if it was true? Especially if it was true.

The blur of tears made it hard to read the rest of it, but masochism must have run in the family because I pushed on to the end.

Let those of us who are without sin cast the first stone. But cast it for the right reason. Don't call a thief a rapist. Don't call a heterosexual a faggot. And beware of fierce winds that blow stones back against those who cast them.

His mom was right. Dad was a priest, a cold-blooded one at that, and he didn't much care who he took down with his homily. As long as it sang.

"Hey, who're you?" I almost blacked out I was so surprised. It was the janitor, with a dustpan in his hand.

"I'm . . . Piper Scanlon, his" — I pointed to the chair I was sitting on — "desk. Daughter."

He stepped into the room, his head tilted, rubbing the dustpan up and down the sides of his overalls. They were unbuttoned like he might have just come from the restroom. His face was still hard to make out because of the glare of the halogen next to me. "Prove it," he said.

"You must be new," I said. "Everyone knows me at the paper." I pulled the wallet out of my back pocket. I didn't have a driver's license, but the student body cards had pictures on them. As I opened to it, I realized the picture was last year's, when I had a full head of scraggy hair.

When he leaned over to inspect the picture, I recognized him. He was the butler who'd let me in at the Carlisle open house. He looked up at my head, which because of Rozene I'd started to let grow again, and back to the picture. Finally, he straightened up. "Nice hair. Where were you earlier?"

I was going to make it, just one more white lie. "I must have passed out. The air is so bad in here."

"Tell me about it. Hey, aren't you the one who got in the tiff over at Mr. Carlisle's?" Damn, he was going to squeal on me.

"It was a misunderstanding."

He managed a weak smile. "I liked your style."

After he left, I sat there staring at the pulsing cursor. The thought occurred to me to delete the whole file, but it wasn't the file that was the problem. It was my dad's heart.

———14———

ON CHRISTMAS EVE MORNING, there was a note from Dad propped against the green tomato salt shaker on the kitchen counter. I'd slept in and my eyes felt glued together as I rubbed them clean and read it again:

Good morning Piper/Hello Willard,
Can you make a salad or something for tonight's dinner? I'll take care of the rest of it. Maybe dress up a little. We have company.
                                    Love, Dad/Tom

It wasn't eloquent, but it was intriguing. Eating at home with Dad was a rarity, but the prospect of company was downright radical. We hadn't had any since Mom died.

I thought it might be Dad's brother, Seamus, who Dad had been trying to get out here since Mom died. Seamus was unemployed again, laid off from his grounds keeping job with the New York City Park Department, but I was sure Dad would have offered to pay his way out to Stampede. It would be just like Seamus to not say anything and just show up on our doorstep Christmas Eve.

"It's gonna be that little patootie from down at the cafe," Willard said.

"Marge?"

"The cook."

"Marge *is* the cook. No way."

We argued while eating our Cheerios on what to make for our dish. Willard wanted a potato salad, German style, with the potatoes cut in big chunks and rings of onions. I told him that was a summer salad, something to fix with hamburgers and hot dogs.

"That's what I want," he said. "Hamburgers."

"You can't have hamburgers for Christmas."

I convinced him we had to make a cranberry salad. I'd never made one and didn't particularly like them, but it was traditional and I didn't want to disappoint the company. I found a recipe in the *Good Housekeeping Cookbook* that had a cranberry thumbprint I guessed was Mom's on the same page as the recipe. She made as big a mess as Willard when she cooked. I looked at the print closely to see if the whorls bore any resemblance to my own. Even though I knew I was adopted, I'd spent my life searching for likenesses between us. If a husband and wife could *grow into each other* to the point where they ate the same foods, enjoyed the same TV shows, and laughed at the same jokes, why couldn't we? I'd seen doddering older couples who I thought could have passed as brother and sister. Given the myriad possibilities, there had to be something we shared. But the thumbprint was too blurry to tell.

"That's it?" Willard said when I had wiped the slop from the side of the copper fish mold we'd poured the salad into.

"We chill it."

"Cold salad?"

"What are you talking about? Potato salad's cold."

"But you cook the potatoes."

Each time we checked it during the day, I tipped the mold to see if it had set, but the cranberry gluck sloshed back and forth. "Damn. What's wrong with it, Willard?"

He bent over and studied it for the longest time, then dipped his finger in and licked it. "It needs corn syrup." I'd heard him recommend the same thing to stop car engines from pinging.

Corn syrup was a stupid idea, but it gave me another one which wasn't. I dragged a chair over to the cupboards and rifled through the cake mixes and puddings on the top shelf until I found a raspberry Jello. I poured a trail of Jello along the spine of the fish mold and then stirred it in with a spoon.

Willard just shook his head. "I want my name off it."

Dad came home around three o'clock with a produce carton full of champagne and snack foods that he set on the kitchen counter. Then he went into the dining room and fooled around with the radio until he found a station playing Christmas music, turning it up loud enough to be heard throughout the house. It was the first time I'd seen him since going through his files at the office, and his mood disarmed me. He hummed along to the "Drummer Boy" while he put away the groceries, spread fresh linen on the dining room table, and arranged a pine bough centerpiece with little Christmas balls and cones. His eyes were wide and lively like the dogs' were when Willard asked them if they wanted to go for a walk.

"What about candles?" I said.

There was an electromagnetic nimbus swirling around him as he hurdled the stairs two at a time and disappeared into the attic, singing "Adeste Fideles," exaggerating each measure in his Dennis Day tenor's voice until it was nearly operatic. When he came down again, he was carrying the white beeswax candles from our emergency kit, one in each hand.

He wouldn't say who the company was, but whoever it was, I knew that his mood had more to do with them than with us. Somehow, he was just better in the presence of other people. He had the ability to turn it on for total strangers, to render them defenseless in the face of his full-court Irish press. Me, I was the opposite. I shrunk. Whatever modest confidence I might generate one-on-one evaporated in the face of a crowd. That's probably why I could count my friends on the prongs of a tuning fork.

When I'd read what Dad had written about Mom, I almost took the hammer to the lyre I'd bought for him at Monkey Shines. "Rarely do we get a musical instrument in such mint condition," the woman had told me. At first I thought it was a guitar, but she straightened me out quickly. "Honey, this is what the Greeks played when they recited poetry." That did it. Dad had always bemoaned the fact he'd never learned to play an instrument. It had cost me more than I figured on spending, but if he hadn't given me the job at the paper I wouldn't have had the money anyway. Besides, I was too old to get away with something homemade, like the collection of "Famous Sayings By Irishmen" I'd penned into one of those books with blank pages last year. I made up half the quotes, trying to work in things I could imagine Dad saying, like "The difference between puffery and the Pulitzer is squeezing the ticker and feeling the story pulse in your hands" and "The poet reads what isn't written."

Dad's cheerfulness had somehow shaved the peak off my anger. Maybe his Carlisle apologia was just a diary of weird ideas he never intended to publish. Personal therapy. I could hardly condemn him for his thoughts, even though that was basically the Roman Catholic system. If I could be damned for every covetous thought I had ever entertained, I might as well put my hands over my head and surrender now. I preferred the system that made inside the head out of bounds. Hang a man for whom he stabs but not for whom he dreams of stabbing. At least, it was a good theory.

The doorbell rang at about five after six. Nobody ever rang our doorbell. The custom in Stampede was to crack the door and call out a *Yoohoo!* or *Anyone home?* as you entered. Dad floated into the room from the kitchen in a mossy green turtleneck with a pendant hanging around his neck, effervescing with a limey cologne.

"I'll get it."

I stuck a stick pretzel into the book I was reading and stood up to see who was coming for Christmas dinner. Dad disappeared out the door and I heard a man's voice. There was some shuffling and wiping of feet and Dad re-emerged carrying a shopping bag, trailed by John Carlisle. Our company wasn't a they; it was a he.

"Hello, Piper." Carlisle extended his hand and I couldn't help looking over his shoulder, hoping someone else would be joining us. Maybe his new paramour. "It's just me," he said.

I shook his hand, which was cold and smooth with lotion. His hair was plastered down with pomade and I could smell the fragrance of freshly sliced apples. Dad gave a nervous laugh and went into the kitchen with the shopping bag.

"Can I hang your coat?" I said.

He seemed taken aback and touched the wing of his bow tie to adjust it. "That would be nice, Piper." He turned and let the coat slip off the back of his shoulders. It was full length and heavy, with a fuzzy liner and a broad belt.

I took my time schlepping his coat. I knew without looking that there wouldn't be any free hangers in the closet. *Hang your coat* in our house was a euphemism for dumping it on the master bed. I tried it on for kicks, and although it was the right length I swam in it. My hands slipped into the pockets and I found one of those breath atomizers and a half-used roll of Tums.

I figured Carlisle would drift into the kitchen with Dad, but he was still in the living room studying the family pictures on the mantel when I returned. I wished Willard had come up so there'd be someone else to talk to. Carlisle was holding the picture of me and Mom on the rocket ship slide at Klah Hah Ya Park. The first time we'd slid down it together, I was four and Mom held me around the middle from behind while Dad snapped our picture. Mom liked the picture so much she'd had it blown up and framed. For fun, I dragged her over to the park the summer after my first year of high school and we duplicated the pose, with the same scaredy-cat look on my face, the same knee in the air, and the same desperate grip of Mom's arms around my middle. In both photos, which rested side by side on the mantel, Mom was looking skyward, her neck arched back, and laughing.

"She was a joy to the world, wasn't she?" he said. There was an undeniable affection in his voice. He lowered his head and with the toe of his shiny loafer ironed a pathway through the pile in the carpet alongside his other foot. I was uncomfortable talking to him about Mom and I almost asked him about his family. Kids lit cigarettes off the gas flame that burned at his dad's monument in Klah Hah Ya Park. "Piper, you never answered my note." His voice was soft, almost a whisper.

I was embarrassed. "Your note?"

"About college. I was serious. I can help."

"We have money."

"Let me say it another way. I want to help."

Dad rescued me. With the fingers of one hand balancing a cutting board, he carried three long-stemmed glasses into the room. "I see you two are getting along. How about some champagne?"

Carlisle helped himself to a glass, still studying me.

"Piper?" Dad never offered me alcohol at home. I knew of kids whose parents had given them wine with dinner since puberty, the theory being to learn moderation. Catholics binged. Forty days of Lenten fasting followed by pastry gorging. Sexual abstinence that led to nymphomania the first time a guy touched the seam of a girl's crotch.

"Are you sure, Dad?"

"It's Christmas."

Willard finally stumbled upstairs, his hair wet where he'd slicked it back, wearing a string tie with a sliding plastic cowboy boot for the knot. He was slightly stooped over as he headed toward Carlisle with a bead in his eye like he was going to knock him over. "I didn't know we was going to eat with the head cheese." He stuck his hand out and shook Carlisle vigorously, like they were bosom buddies.

Everyone was caught off guard by Willard's irreverence. "Maybe Willard would like a glass of champagne," I said.

"The bottle's in the kitchen," Dad said, pointing.

Willard followed me into the kitchen, where there was a beautifully tossed Caesar salad in a serving bowl on the counter. I found the cupboard with the stemware and handed Willard a glass. "Here, you old patootie."

In the refrigerator there were two bottles on their sides where we usually kept the leftovers and a third one, open, standing next to the milk cartons. The more I poured into Willard's glass, the more his hand shook. There was only a little bit left in the bottle, so I tipped it up and drank it myself.

"I'm glad I dressed up," Willard said, stroking his tie with his free hand.

"You're overdressed. It's just Carlisle."

"I've never eaten with the Carlisles."

As I was putting the empty into the recycle bin, I noticed a plastic tub with dressing and pieces of lettuce stuck to the insides that had been crushed down into the garbage can. I fished it out, springing back the sides so I could read the label.

"Hey, Willard, look at this."

Willard finished sipping his champagne and looked down at the tub in my hand.

"He *bought* it. At the QFC."

Nothing seemed to register as he continued to lick his lips.

"Don't you get it? We busted our hump to make a cranberry salad and he bought a carry-out in Seattle."

"Your mom used to do that."

"Buy plastic salads? No way. Not on Christmas." We did eat a lot of TV dinners though.

The dining room table was ablaze with the emergency beeswax candles when we sat down for dinner. I asked Dad to do a poem instead of racing through "Blessus ohLord andthese thygifts whichweareabout toreceive fromthybounty throughChristOurLord Amen." He shook me off and I thought we were going with the standard grace, until Carlisle leaned over and rested two fingers on his forearm.

"That would be nice, Tom."

"If you insist. Close your eyes. This is for all the members of our families, living and dead, who couldn't join us this day." Then he recited by heart "Stopping By Woods On A Snowy Evening." It wasn't Irish but it seemed perfect for a cold day in December. He spoke slowly enough that I could imagine the sleigh and a frozen lake in the woods on the darkest evening of the year. Then he dropped to a whisper as he gave the closing refrain, which hit home despite its familiarity.

But I have promises to keep,

And miles to go before I sleep,
And miles to go before I sleep.

"Bravo, Tom!" Carlisle said.

I knew it was small of me, but I made sure Willard and I each took larger helpings of the cranberry salad than the Caesar. There had to be some reward for creativity or else what kind of plastic world were we living in? Were we going to abdicate to the fast food chains? Furnish our kitchens with pneumatic tubes connected to Burger King? I didn't say any of these things out loud, of course. I didn't have to. Thanks to the champagne, I had a raging good conversation going on right inside of me. Dad, on the other hand, took a heaping serving of the Caesar salad that spilled over onto his turkey. *Come on, Dad. You scraped it out of a plastic bucket.*

The dinner conversation bubbled along pretty much without me, thanks primarily to Willard, who was fearless.

"Are you as rich as everyone says you are?"

"Willard!" Dad said.

"That's all right," Carlisle said, seeming to enjoy it. "How rich is that?"

Willard looked over at me for guidance, then back at Dad who was busy spreading peanut butter on his Parker House roll. "Do you like dogs, Mr. Carlisle?"

Carlisle laughed. "My sister and I used to have one."

"So?"

"She died."

"Your sister?"

"Willard!" Dad said, irritated again.

Carlisle put his napkin to his lips. "I meant our dog."

"Oh." For Willard, nothing more needed to be said.

If I had a fraction of Willard's abandon, I would have waded in at that point and pressed Carlisle with my own list of particulars. I didn't care how rich he was. I wanted to ask him how he could come into our house and sit in Mom's chair, how he could set a finger on the forearm of the man he'd cheated. I wanted him to tell me he'd pressured Mom to do the Jacuzzi that day. I wanted an apology for what he'd done to her. I wanted him to break down, fall on his knees, and tell us he was sorry he'd ever cast a covetous glance at her.

The sound of a fork scraping across a plate, which I realized was mine, brought me out of it. I was clenching the handle in my fist like I was going to stab someone. There was a piece of gravy-laden turkey on the tablecloth where I'd bulldozed it off my plate, and everyone was looking at me. Champagne was supposed to make you giddy and amorous, but I was fighting wars inside my head I didn't have to fight.

I cleaned up everything on my plate except for the cranberry salad, which was horrible. Willard, on the other hand, cleaned up all of his, although I'd noticed him mixing it with his other food groups. I was a monogamous eater, one food at a time. I didn't like to cover up the faults of one group with the virtues of another. Carlisle was the last to finish, principally because he cut everything into such tiny bites. I wondered if it was for dietary reasons. Willard had told me about one of his bowling buddies who used to chew up steak meat for his Jack Russell terrier because it wasn't secreting enough saliva.

Dad made a grand entrance with the third bottle of champagne, ricocheting the cork off the ceiling and into the remains of the purplish goulash Willard and I had put together. I was past caring. I imagined putting my hand over the top of my glass when Dad came around, but somehow the bubbly must have poured right through the knuckles because when I looked again my glass was full.

Carlisle excused himself and came back with a gift, nicely wrapped with a gauzy red bow that rose off the top of the package like a poinsettia, and handed it to me.

I looked around. "Nobody else gets one?"

The package was the size of a shoe box and heavy. Lead heavy, not water heavy. I shook it, thinking it might be coins, Carlisle's down payment on my college tuition. There was nothing this man had that I wanted and I couldn't imagine that anything he'd pick out would bear the least resemblance to my own tastes. As a courtesy, I thought he could have given something to Willard, who was reaching over, trying to help me undo the ribbon. I was thinking of a way to refuse his gift, unopened, to make a statement right there in front of Dad, to make it clear there was someone in the family whom Carlisle couldn't buy off. The contents were rolled in flimsy tissue paper that I uncoiled into my lap until there was nothing left but a rough-hewn brass hand. A lady's hand. The fingers were cradling empty space that could have been a plum.

"It's your mother's," Carlisle said. "Her art and her hand."

I pulled it against my stomach and gulped. I knew she'd fooled around with clay. Some of her crumbling, mostly unrecognizable, pieces were still in our attic. But I'd never seen anything metal and nothing so personal. I knew this was Mom's hand. I'd watched her paint with it, smooth my eyebrows down with it when she tucked me in at night. It was better than any bag of school money. Yet, rather than just thank him, I couldn't help but smolder. What else did he have of hers that we didn't know about?

"Let me make a toast," Dad said.

I sat up from my slouch, rested Mom's hand in the trough between my legs, and reached for the stem of my glass. In my mind, I quickly counted out the time that had elapsed since her drowning, something I'd calculated with regularity. Every day since her death I'd engaged in that pitiless game of asking myself what she and I were doing a year ago that same date. Last Christmas Eve, we were eating honey-glazed ham and croissants that had turned out more like scones. Willard was with us, as a guest not a boarder then, as well as Louise Mead from the paper and her daughter, who had Downs Syndrome.

Dad tipped his glass toward Carlisle, with a tear in his eye. "Here's to vindicating John Carlisle."

"No!" I blurted, without thinking.

Dad glared at me. When he tried to set his glass on the

table, it caught on the edge of his plate and spilled onto the tablecloth. "Take that back."

I looked over at Willard, who was perspiring, to see if he was following this. There was a vacuous look on his face, but I couldn't tell if it was shock or champagne. I shut my eyes. I was mad that Dad had plied us with champagne. What was I supposed to do, say I was hoping Carlisle would skate free of his criminal charges on the back of Mom's good name? It had been two days short of four months since her death. *My God, Dad, where's the poetry in this man? Are you so spooked by life that you have to settle for this?*

"Piper?" Dad said.

I couldn't look at him. It was the darkest evening of the year and the woods were filling up with snow. I gritted my teeth, knowing that if I said anything, it would be pure bile. I set the brass hand on the table, but when I grabbed the arms of my chair to scoot back, I must have caught the edge of the tablecloth because the hand thudded to the floor.

"You can't just walk out! You're being rude . . ." Dad's voice was fading as I passed the rack with the Collier Encyclopedias and headed up the stairs.

I slammed the door to my room and flopped stomach down on the bed. A tidal wave was washing over me, and I knew I had to take strokes against the current to get back on top. I was losing Dad and I was angry because I'd been so damned inarticulate. I hated it when it took me two days to think of the right thing to say. Then it was too late. Our family dinner had turned out to be a parody. There was no family. This was a house inhabited by transients. Wherever we were heading, it wasn't going to be together.

Then I heard Dad's footsteps coming up the stairs, in that strong-footed, this-is-my-castle way he used when I'd sassed Mom or melted one of his long-play records on the radiator. I thought of hiding in the closet, then I considered facing him down on the threshold of my room, and then I thought of the roof.

It was freezing outside and the shingles were slick from the frost. I closed the window behind me, leaving a crack just wide enough to get my fingers back under, and perched on my haunches like an owl as close to the gable as I could manage. A fog was visible in the flood of the streetlight at the corner. I could see the lights blinking on the Normans' Christmas tree in the house across the street. There were two extra cars parked in front, probably their sons' families home for Christmas. Mrs. Norman still canned fruit in the summer and brought us Mason jars with peaches and pears. It was a little old-fashioned; after all, fresh fruit was available practically year round. But at least their family was still together. Same father, same mother, same old Norman boys.

Then Dad's magnified shadow appeared on the shingles next to me, his elbows up and his hands shading his eyes against the window pane. I scrunched up closer to the wall so he wouldn't see me. What more was there to say? He'd said his piece and I'd said mine. Some things you couldn't legislate. The window scraped in the sash and I tightened myself into a cannonball.

"Piper! I want to talk to you." I played possum, the same way I used to do in hide-and-seek, thinking if I didn't move they wouldn't be sure it was me and couldn't call off my name. "Let's not leave it like this."

I mumbled into my knees. "What do you want me to do?"

He was bracing his palms on the weatherboard and leaning out the window. "John feels terrible."

I didn't know if he meant it as a provocation to make me jump off the roof, but that's how it hit me and I felt the same rage I'd experienced reading Dad's pithy little redemption piece in the computer files. "Fuck John!"

"What did you say?"

"Why are you going around town trying to pick up dirt on Mom? She's dead. Leave her alone."

"You're acting hysterical."

"What's wrong with hysterical? Why aren't you a little hysterical?"

"Piper . . ."

"You've spent so much time stuffing all that journalism in there's nothing left but a pinhole for any feelings. Your greatest organ isn't your free will, it's your sphincter."

He slammed the window down and I could hear the counterweights bumping around inside the casing. His shadow disappeared from the frame of light on the shingles. The door banged shut. He was cranked. Good, maybe he'd wake up and come to his senses.

My heart was still racing and perspiration had broken out on my face despite the temperature. As usual, I'd exaggerated my case. It wasn't true he had no feelings. He was crushed that Seamus had promised to come out for Christmas and then never showed. He was scavenging on the side for a little intimacy the same as I was. I'd severed something and the thought of drifting in space unattached to my tether frightened me. I wasn't sure how or if I'd ever get back to the comfort of the shuttle that was my ride home. For sure, I was on the wrong side of the moon.

When I looked up into the ether, searching for a single star, there were none. I knew Mom was up there somewhere laughing her head off. She thrived on confusion. "Your Dad has to be shaken up like old paint sometimes," she'd told me. Well, I'd done that all right. I'd dumped open the whole can.

I stayed outside until it started to snow. As each flake landed on my knee, I just let it rest there. They lit catty-corner and cock-eyed, each one having trouble fitting against the others, leaving space. More space than body. Yet from a distance they formed a monolith. Like the Normans across the street. Like the Scanlons might have if Mom hadn't died.

I sat there motionless, offering no resistance to the elements, warmed by a single thought. I was keeping the promise I'd made to Mom.

———15———

THE GROUND STAYED FROZEN throughout Christmas vacation. The ridges formed by the tire tracks on the dirt roads were so hard I could walk the tops of them like train rails and, as each ridge petered out, I found another one to jump to. The Parks Department filled the children's wading pool at Kla Hah Ya Park for ice skating, rimming the edges with two-by-fours to act as expansion joints so the force of the ice wouldn't break the concrete. There was always a community bonfire going there at night between the restrooms and the swings. Toddlers with wobbly ankles warmed their backsides, as teenagers lit cigarettes off the ends of smoldering sticks and slunk back into the night to talk. I couldn't have been more than eleven the time Jesse Little tried to feel me up with his mittens on while I was tightening my two-bladed skates next to the cement tortoise where the water comes in. Of course, I didn't realize that's what he was trying to do until several years later when he tried the same thing in the school auditorium during lights out for a film documentary on *The Red Menace*. Like I said, there wasn't that much to feel, but Jesse didn't have a lot of choices.

When I came home from school, I heard the faucet running and looked out back to see Willard watering the garden. The excess water was draining toward the garage and pooling up in the low spots. It couldn't have been more than twenty-five degrees out and the stalks and vines in the garden looked like bent coat hangers, but he was rocking the hose up and down like a fishing rod, letting the water lap at the base of each vine. He didn't seem to notice me when I came out the back door and stood next to him.

"What are you doing, Willard?"

When he turned, the hose turned with him, and I had to jump out of the way to avoid getting soaked. "Carol sent you?"

"No, Carol didn't send me."

"Gotta' get the root zone, she says. I never get the root zone." He wore no gloves and his hands were shaking.

He's dying inside, I thought. *Don't do this, Willard.*

I wrapped my hands around his. He was humming and bouncing the hose up and down, but I tightened my grip until he stopped fighting me and the humming stopped.

"I think you've drenched 'em pretty good." I said. The truth was any water that reached the root balls would just freeze and choke them to death.

I walked him downstairs and helped him change out of his wet clothes and into a pair of moth-bitten suntans I found in his drawer. I slipped a dry pair of socks over his feet. As he warmed up, his sense of place seemed to return.

"Is the boss coming tonight?"

"You mean Carlisle? I don't understand why you treat him like such a VIP after what he did with Mom."

He stopped lacing his shoes and looked up at me. "Kitty?"

"He's a cheater, Willard. He cheated on Dad."

"You mean . . ."

"He . . . slept with her." It made me nauseous to say it.

"Kitty and Mr. Carlisle?" His voice was thin, like the idea had never entered his mind, and I was sorry I was the one who'd burst his bubble.

"I'll burn the paper down before I'll let Dad save Carlisle's ass."

Willard's eyes grew big. "Burn the newspaper?"

He'd missed one set of eyelets in his right shoe and I bent over to restring it. "To get back at what he did to Mom. You bet."

He rubbed his pants thoughtfully, but I had no idea how much of this was sticking.

About a week before Carlisle's trial, Rozene was peeling an orange in the cafeteria, trying to take it off as a single, contiguous skin when Bagmore came by. I'd never seen him pay any attention to her.

"You want to go for a walk?" He was standing over her, and I knew he was trying to see down her blouse. I was sitting kitty-corner across the table from them, finishing a chili dog I'd bought from the snack bar. Sauce was dripping down my chin.

"I have to work on a history assignment with Piper," she told him, which was news to me, but I played along and mumbled my assent through a mouthful of warm frankfurter. One thing I could say in Bagmore's favor: his radar was good. He'd picked up on something between me and Rozene and he seemed determined to jam it. Maybe I was flattering myself, but the way he went about it made me think he was doing it to spite me for dissing him in the storage locker.

The fantasy in my diary that night took off from Rozene's orange peel, which I had saved and reshaped into a perfect ball that carried the indentations of her fingernails. When I put it against my nose, I could smell her. When I cupped it in my palms, I imagined that it was one of her breasts. On the blanket I created in the privacy of my diary, we laughed about the orange and I pulled her hands against my cheeks and smelled the sweetness of pulp in the tips of her fingers and, in this way, anchored my fantasy with one shred of reality.

I was interrupted by Dirk's phone call. I'd tried several times to get past Colonel Thurgood, but he'd tightened security, saying nobody was supposed to talk to him because of the trial. Dirk wanted to meet at the billboard, which, compared to my fantasy, wasn't particularly attractive at that moment. He was practically whispering.

"I wouldn't ask you if it wasn't important."

"Is your dad trying to screw you over again?"

"You've got part of it right."

I was the first one to arrive and worked my way up the braces, sniffing like a dog to see if anyone else had used it since we were there last. The thin frost that had formed on the planks soaked through my jeans when I sat down. I pulled the collar of my jacket up around my neck and wished I'd grabbed one of the knit pullover hats from the top shelf in our closet on the way out the door. Even though I'd stopped shaving my head since the day Rozene and I sat in her car under the flight path at Harvey Field, growth was slow and it still felt cold. Dad told me that a person lost a third of their body heat through the head and a third through the feet, conjuring in my mind the picture of someone lost in the woods trying to stave off hypothermia with nothing on but a hat and a pair of wool socks. His theory strained credulity, the way a lot of things he'd been saying lately did.

Sitting in the billboards was such a throwback to the days when Dirk and I had to make up problems to solve. Now they were coming at us like a meteor shower. I was glad I had a few minutes to switch gears. I'd let my fight with Dad blot out everyone else's problems. Dirk had never given me any details, except to say that Carlisle used to sometimes insist he "take a tub" with him when he'd finished mowing the lawn or cleaning leaves out of the rain gutters. I'd wondered if they wore swimsuits. Maybe he'd gotten him in the shower next to the Jacuzzi while they were rinsing off the chlorine. Maybe he hadn't entered him at all, and it was all fingers and fondling. *Ugh.* I gathered up the saliva off the inside walls of my cheeks and spit, watching it disperse into a scattershot that rained down between the supports.

"What're you doing?" Dirk was on the crossbars below me.

"Sorry, I forgot you were coming."

He moved easily up the incline with his tennis shoes, balancing himself with hand-over-hand action along the supports over his head. When he stood on the platform in front of me, his Chicago Bulls jacket seemed baggy. He looked twenty pounds lighter than when I'd seen him last. I'd always imagined Dirk as someone who would become obese when he got out of school and lived a regular life. In his cutoffs, I could see definition in the silhouette of his calves. The field stubble on his face had become a scraggly chin beard. "You're wasting away," I said.

He held up his arms and puffed his chest. Where the

jacket lifted, his stomach was a memory of its former self. "I'm fasting."

"Fasting?"

"Ramadan." It wasn't Ramadan, I thought, it was the thrill of impersonation. Anything was better than being Colonel Thurgood's son. Dirk could be Bogart one week, Hawkeye the next. Why not a follower of Muhammad?

I waited while he fished a pack of cigarettes out of his pocket and lit up. What the match illuminated was an oval of tension: squinty eyes, cheeks hollowed like a giraffe's, and rapid blinking. He tilted his head back and held onto the first inhalation, sucking it dry of nicotine, then released it out the side of his mouth like so much exhaust. "God, it's been too long," he said, rubbing his hands quickly down the outsides of my arms.

His touch was sweet and softened me instantly. I reached out my hand, but couldn't manage to do anything better than a swat on the sleeve of his jacket. "We should've kept better track of each other."

"Tell me about it." He squatted down on the platform, sideways to me, and took another drag.

This was Dirk's meeting so I had no intention of going into all of the crap that was happening at my house. I just wanted to prime the pump, show him that whatever it was he had to say wouldn't shock me. In my experience, people told you as much as you told them. Once when I lied to a woman on the Greyhound bus saying that I was going to Seattle for an abortion, she told me how she had to shoot bullets into the floor the last time her ex-husband came around drunk, looking for a warm place to stick his dick. "I hope you cream Carlisle's ass."

He slapped the cross-piece so hard in front of him that the fire broke off the end of his cigarette and he threw the rest of it down in disgust. "Pisser!"

"What's the matter?"

He straightened up so he could get his hand inside his pocket for another cigarette, lit up, and then held the first drag with his teeth bit into his upper lip. "You remember that picture Bagmore taped to the blackboard?"

"Of course."

"My dad went apeshit when he found out."

"I know."

"He kept calling me a homo, and I didn't know how to answer him, so I just blurted it out. I said he was right." Dirk was trembling, his body heat exiting with the words he was spitting out. "I thought if me being a faggot was the worst thing that could happen to him, I wanted to be a faggot. I told him Carlisle and I had been sucking each other's dicks for months. 'How do you like that, Colonel?' I told him. He slapped me around and called me a liar. That's why I decided to go to the police with it. To shame him." Dirk pushed his palms into his eye sockets, with a cigarette still caught in the fingers of one hand. "But it's a lie, Piper. I made it up."

I stood up on my knees and wrapped my arms around him. He started sobbing, nuzzling his head against my chest. I was in six states of shock. I'd believed Dirk. Except for Dad, the whole town had believed it happened. I could feel the wetness through my shirt. Dirk was always such a softie, scared at the sight of his own blood, spooked by spiders, queasy in confined spaces, but I'd never seen him cry. He was the doughboy you could tease and poke and he'd just sag and give and rise again. But what he was doing to his dad was the stuff of young Shiite boys who strapped bombs around their rib cages and rode busses with the Israelis knowing that in their moment of glory they'd be as dead as their enemies.

"It's all right," I said, patting him awkwardly on the back. "Nothing's irreversible." Except suicide, I thought, because that's what was going through my head. I could almost imagine the headlines in the *Herald*. Dirk would be revealed as a public liar. What further jiggling would it take to detonate the bomb?

"I wanna go through with it," he mumbled into my shirt.

"What are you talking about? You can't."

"I'm not going to let *you* down."

"Me?"

"It'll clear your mother." His hands were locked onto the back of my jacket like the pinchers of a lobster. "If he was doing me, nobody would believe he had anything going with her."

"That's stupid." The going-nowhere circles I was making on his back replicated the thought processes in my head.

"I can't not do it now. It's not like the guy's a saint."

I cradled him until the sobbing stopped and then he curled into a fetal ball between my legs and I stretched out my shirt and wiped the tears away from his eyes. It was as if Dirk had put a power in my hands I didn't deserve. Like with the woman on the Greyhound, it was my turn to tell him something. Rozene Raymond would have been a good place to start. I could have told him about the aching I felt for her, the touches that had become milestones, how I was the Jezebel stalking his Rozene. As I looked down on this lump of a man in front of me, I couldn't help but feel a profound welling of affection.

He fell asleep with his face against the jeans on the inside of my thigh, his mouth and nose contorted so that it made him snore. I moved my legs in closer to cover his bare knees and calves. There was nothing to lean back against so I alternated between leaning forward and sheltering him like the hood of a car and then sitting up and supporting myself with my palms stiff-armed against the plank behind me. Dirk's revelation had pushed me back to a precipice I thought I'd already navigated. If Dirk was lying, that meant Dad was right and something was happening between Mom and Carlisle.

Dirk woke up and rubbed his eyes when a semi coming down Horse Heaven Highway pumped its air brakes and shuddered to a stop at the intersection.

"Hey, cowboy," I said, "we've never slept together."

He managed a smile. "How was it for you?"

On the way home, we took the shortcut through the asphalt playfield next to St. Augustine's, which was pitch dark. He kept putting his arm around me and squeezing me.

"I don't know what I'd do without you, Piper." As if somehow I'd put a dent in his problem.

He kicked a stick, sending it shuffling across the hopscotch courts painted on the pavement. "Does Rozene ever ask about me?"

His question startled me and I almost walked into the pole that tethered the girls' volleyball, even though I would have sworn I could find that pole blindfolded under a minus moon. My first instinct was to lie, but I couldn't lie after I'd just begged him to come clean about the Carlisle thing, so I equivocated. "Everyone's worried about you."

He probably knew it was a crock, but he didn't say anything more until we were at Commercial Street. "I guess we better go our own way, huh?"

I was feeling pretty low-down and decided to make one last try at being a friend. I bunched his sweatshirt into my fists. "Look, Dirk. Nobody's ever risked their ass for me like you're doing, but life's not that long and I don't want you to spend the next twenty years of it in jail for perjury."

He put his stubby hands over mine. "Don't take this one away from me, Piper. Okay?" His voice was firm. The trembling was over.

"You can drop the whole thing and come clean."

"Don't squeal on me, okay?"

I let go, leaving the protrusion of little tents where I'd twisted his sweatshirt. "Only if I have to."

He shook me playfully by the shoulders, which were limp. "I know you won't. You're one of us." As if we were a whole gang. But I knew what he meant, even if I still didn't know what I was going to do with what he'd told me.

He headed east and I headed west, but after about twenty uncertain steps I turned around to watch him cut across the street toward the Comet Tavern. Before his dad went into seclusion and put the house up for sale, he might have been there with his handball buddies. The streetlight cast a shadow in front of Dirk that he was walking into. His shoulders were stooped like he was carrying a cross on each of them and his scarecrow arms drooped lifeless at his side.

I was editing a story about the Payton Miller family reunion when someone knocked on my door.

It was John Carlisle, in his loafers and tights with leg warmers bunched around the ankles and a teal-colored silk ascot looped under his chin and tucked into the V of his shirt. A week ago I would have told him I didn't want to talk to him, but Dirk's revelation had undercut me. "How're you doing?" he asked.

When I made a nervous exhalation, a little snot shot onto my upper lip. I wiped a sleeve under my nose and fluffed up the pages on my desk, wishing I'd come to work earlier and avoided this little tête-à-tête. "Fine, I guess. My dad would probably be a better judge of that."

"He's a good teacher, isn't he?" He smiled and rested one buttock on the two-drawer filing cabinet. "Do you mind?"

"No, fine."

"I think it's special when a father and daughter work together."

"Beats mowing lawns, I guess."

"I always thought my sister Ashley and I would end up working together." He reached down and evened up his leg-warmers.

"That's nice."

"When Dad didn't come home from Vietnam, Mother started drinking. Then she developed Parkinson's. That was on top of the neurosis." He laughed to himself and I evened up the papers on my desk, wondering why he was telling me this. "It got so bad she was ashamed to go out of the house. Of course, I would have been ashamed if she had."

"The house where you live now?" I could at least comment on the logistics.

"She made my sister do all the cooking and cleaning and blew up at her if she caught me helping. At night, Mother would get buzzed on her sherry and lecture Ashley about how she was too sloppy and too bitchy to find a husband." I wanted to ask him why they didn't just cut off her liquor supply if she never left the house, but then it occurred to me how easy it would have been for a Carlisle to phone out for deliveries. Gray Cab still worked the territory between Stampede and Machias. "Mother was the sloppy one. We had to put a bib on her. One night, Ashley became fed up and dumped a Tapioca pudding in her lap and Mother started throwing dishes at us. She banished Ashley to the attic and made me take away the ladder."

"That's child abuse."

"Not in those days, not here. I snuck her bread and Velveeta cheese and bottles of 7-Up, then crawled up there and slept on the floor with her at night." I had trouble picturing anyone named Carlisle eating Velveeta and drinking soda pop. The rest of what he was saying totally eluded me. "We told each other stories, how Dad would come back and storm into the house and break all her bottles in the fireplace and make her wait on Ashley."

"What ever happened to Ashley?"

"I hired an investigator to comb the east coast for her. She probably thought it was Mother looking for her. Anyway, she never surfaced." He rubbed his thumb along the front edge of the filing cabinet, then turned the corner and rubbed it down the other side. "My fear is she got as addicted and pathetic as Mother."

"I wouldn't give up."

He lowered his head. "No, she's gone. Mother chased her away." I turned and fidgeted with the hard copy on my desk. "You know you remind me of Ashley. The last time I saw her she wasn't much older than you are." He crossed his ankles and braced his palm under his chin as if he were trying to keep his head from flopping. "Sorry to run on like this."

"Don't be sorry."

"There was one important difference."

"Between me and your sister?"

He stroked the ascot under his throat. "Ashley *wanted* her mother dead."

He was on the verge of weeping and turned to leave. My eyes followed the back of his green leggings. The legs that used to pirouette on hardwood floors in a New York dance studio quivered.

I was immobilized and unable to manage a goodbye. I didn't understand why he'd told me this any more than I understood why he would dress like a danseur in the middle of a town where boots and Levis were the standard. I was still angry at Dad for trying to save him, and astonished at Dirk for setting him up.

But, for the first time in my life, I'd seen something from inside his skin.

16

THE NEXT DAY AFTER school, Mr. Wendall asked me to stop by and see him, probably about my mid-term grades, which except for American Lit. had gone into the toilet. In fact, I was pretty sure Dad had already called school to ask what was going on. A call from Tom Scanlon would be taken seriously. It wouldn't have surprised me if Dad was in Mr. Wendall's office when I got there, maybe Willard too, and Marge, and the people from the paper, in one of those interventions they do for alcoholics. *Come on, Piper, you're only hurting yourself. We love you, but you've got to pull a three-point-O.*

When I entered his office, Mr. Wendall was alone, chewing gum, his sleeves rolled up, working on a stack of folders with clear plastic covers. The one in his hand was entitled "Mick Jagger and Richard Nixon," by Jesse Little. The assignment was to compare two personalities in Modern American history. Mr. Wendall looked at his watch the way teachers always looked at their watches, moved a jacket off the chair next to his desk, and angled the chair so I'd be facing him. I sat down and crossed my legs, noticing the mud on my cuffs where the boots had rubbed. He put his pen into the trough of Jesse Little's paper and closed it, as if the contents were confidential. Every idea in there had probably been cribbed from some book in the library. At the high school level, accurate plagiarism was what the teachers wanted.

"Piper, you seem distracted lately." He looked deeply into my eyes. "Do you want to talk about it?"

"Not really."

"Do you mean you don't think you're distracted or you don't want to tell me about it?"

"Both."

"I didn't go into teaching just to talk about the American Revolution and the Civil War." He paused to let it sink in. "We're your confidants. Whether it's trouble at home or personal growth issues, we're here for you." He was speaking in code. Personal growth issues meant my sex life, which I wasn't going to talk about with any teacher, but I wondered if I'd been that obvious. "I know how hard it must have been losing your mom."

"I thought this was about school."

"Well, it is. Indirectly."

"Do I have to stay?"

"You don't have to, but . . ."

"Then I gotta meet someone. Thanks for your time, Mr. Wendall. I'll pick up the pace."

I got up and scooted the chair back to where it belonged. I didn't know if this was supposed to be a coming on chat or a coming out one, but I wasn't going to stick around to find out. It would probably cost me on the grade for my paper, but "FDR and Eleanor: Who Wore the Pants?" was hardly destined for publication anyway.

My face was still hot as I walked toward the parking lot on my way to the paper. It was Two DTP ("Days To Publication" in Dad's lexicon), which meant that we'd be finishing the galleys for the back pages today. Dad always saved page one until the last minute in case something big broke, which in Stampede was not often, unless you counted the School Board's decision to cut band and drill team expenses or the City Council's directive expanding recycling to cover plastics. I knew there would be hot copy waiting on my desk when I arrived.

There was a big huddle in the second aisle of the parking lot, which usually meant a fight. This was where the grudges that developed in the hallways or lunchroom were settled, as in, *Meet me in the parking lot after school, you chickenshit.* This one wasn't a fight or at least not yet. Rozene Raymond was in the middle of the circle in her brown Corolla, with the engine idling. Condon Bagmore was sitting on the hood, leaning back against the wind-shield. The car was trapped in a web of restless high-schoolers, mostly guys, but also some girls, punkers with rainbow hair and tattoos on their ankles.

"I'll move when you tell me I can sit inside," Bagmore said. The heels of his boots were braced against the top of the hood and I was sure he was going to scratch the paint.

Every time Bagmore issued a challenge, people in the crowd whispered "Oohs" and "Hey mans" in support. Someone yelled, "Scalp her pussy!"

The window on the driver's side was rolled down and Rozene was hugging the outside of the door with her arm. "Honestly, Condon. I'm going to ask you one more time and then I'm going to leave it to centrifugal force."

"Did you say cunnilingus?"

People laughed.

I cut my way through to the front. "She told you to get your butt off her car, Bagmore. What part of that don't you understand?"

"The harlot's daughter," he said.

If I had a bat I would have swung it at him. If I carried a switchblade I would have pulled it. All I had was my rage. I ran at him and jumped, thrusting my shoulder, but my legs banged into the fender, sapping the energy from my charge, so that instead of cold cocking him all I delivered was a spank. The windshield wiper came off in Bagmore's hand and he speared it into the air, laughing.

"Ole!"

As I was rubbing my kneecaps, Martin Miller, the veterinarian's colossal son whom everyone called Lenny because of his resemblance to the Steinbeck character, stepped out of the crowd. "You okay, Piper?" he said, ignoring Bagmore.

"Yeah, fine." God, was I glad to see him. I didn't have a follow-up to my futile charge.

Lenny stooped over to speak to Rozene. "Did I hear you say you want to go?"

Rozene nodded her head and put both hands on the top of the steering wheel.

"You guys in front clear out," Lenny said. He didn't yell. He said it about the same as if he'd asked what time the bus was coming, but people started backing away.

Bagmore hugged the broken wiper against his chest. He didn't have a good record against Lenny. Bagmore had once challenged him to fisticuffs because Lenny had the audacity to ask Bagmore to lighten up when he had a red-headed freshman kid named Ed Mooney cornered in the phone booth next to the bookstore. The fight was a non-event. Lenny palmed Bagmore's head with one hand like it was a basketball and held him far enough away so that Bagmore's swings landed harmlessly against his arm.

"You just drive out of here," Lenny said.

Rozene was trembling and seemed uncertain.

"Do what he says," I told her.

"Come with me."

"I've got to work."

"Please, I need to talk. I'll drop you off."

As I walked around the car under Lenny's protective gaze, people cleared an aisle for me. Rozene leaned over and unlocked the door. Bagmore glared at me through the windshield like a monkey from his cage. I thought his face was going to break out in zits as I took the seat he'd been vying for. Rozene patted me on the leg. "Thanks."

Lenny leaned into the window again. "Just drive normally, okay?"

She returned her hands to the wheel and I watched the tendons flex in her forearms. "What's normal?" she whispered.

"Burn rubber," I said, and we both had to bite our lips to keep from laughing.

I couldn't hear what Lenny was saying, but Bagmore handed him the wiper blade, which Lenny gave to Rozene, who handed it to me. Then he grabbed Bagmore by the front of his zip-up windbreaker, lifted his butt up off the hood, and held him in the air. Bagmore grimaced like Lenny had gotten some skin twisted up with the jacket.

"Go ahead, Rozene," Lenny said, with the unflappable tone of a man whose lot in life was to lift overturned cars off pinned drivers and carry children down the ladders of burning buildings.

As the Corolla moved forward, Bagmore's butt, then his heels dragged across the windshield and out of sight only to reappear momentarily in the rear window. I stuck my head out the window and watched Lenny lowering Bagmore to the asphalt. Bagmore stumbled backwards a few steps, but Lenny steadied him and smoothed out the wrinkles in his jacket. I'd always thought I wanted Lenny's power, but now I wished I had his restraint.

When Rozene was about to pull up in front of the *Herald*, I ducked down in the seat and waved her on. "Let's go to the airport."

I stayed down while she motored along the storefronts on Commercial in case Dad had gone over to the drugstore or struck up a conversation with someone on the boardwalk. While we were stopped at the only light in Stampede, Rozene rolled down her window. "Hey, Dirk! Where you been hiding?"

Oh, Jesus, Rozene, not now. From his voice I guessed he must have been in the crosswalk, and he was coming closer. I scrunched down further with my head against the floor and my butt up like an ostrich.

"Hi, where you going?" Dirk said. "Nice wheels." Now he was standing next to the car and I could tell from the drop in his voice that he'd seen me. Why hadn't I said something about Rozene when I was with him last night? "Is that you, Piper?"

Dammit.

"We're going for a drive," Rozene added, cheerily.

I uncoiled myself and crawled back onto the seat like a slug. My face was warm, probably red. "Hi, Dirk."

He seemed disappointed, confused. Maybe he thought if I hadn't been there he could have gotten a ride with Rozene. There was an awkward silence while he probably wondered whether we were going to invite him along and make it a threesome.

"Green light," Rozene said. And she pulled away, leaving him standing in the middle of the street.

I leaned my head back on the seat and closed my eyes, feeling very much a traitor. After all my preaching at Dirk to come clean, I was the orthodontist with crooked teeth.

We took Highway 2 to Monroe, then Sultan and Startup. Rozene's cast was off and she was acting giddy again. "We need elevation," she said. The defroster couldn't keep up with the heat I was throwing off from the twin engines of anxiety and arousal, and every time the windshield fogged up she'd open her window and let the wind flutter her hair. We were heading toward Stevens Pass. The Jimminy Cricket on my shoulder that Catholics called conscience was shrinking. On the way back from the billboards last night he was as mammoth as Lenny Miller and I'd vowed to have a heart-to-heart talk with Dad about the pickle Dirk was in. Dad knew the law and, better yet, he knew the people in the Prosecutor's Office. If anyone could lead Dirk out of this morass, it was Dad. I was in way over my head and right now I wished Dirk hadn't even told me. Knowledge always carried power in its frontseat and pain in the backseat.

Rozene put her *Evita* tape in. Madonna was singing "Don't Cry for Me, Argentina," and snow was beginning to dust the discarded cigarette butts, beer cans and other man-made detritus on the shoulder of the road. My conscience had shrunk to a midget and if we didn't turn around soon it was going to fit comfortably under my thumb. She turned off on a spur road that had been plowed wide enough for one lane.

"Do we have chains?"

"I won't go in that far," she said. Rozene wasn't just pastry and sweetmeat. Behind the wheel of her car, she was a bulldog. She set her jaw and her nose flared as she glared through the windshield. If her ancestors could make it through the Bering Strait in canoes, she could do this.

Although the road was still fairly flat, the snow must have been two or three feet deep and the boughs of the pine trees were lazy with it. I couldn't help but think what could happen to us. Worst case, we'd run out of gas and freeze to death while trying to combine our body heat in the backseat. There were worse ways to go. On a wide turn that had a lookout down to the Skykomish River, she left the friendly troughs of the spur road and headed for the vista. The Corolla rocked and bumped, then slowed until the tires finally lost their grip and whined like tomcats on the make.

"Well, how's this?" she said, pointing toward the river.

"It'll have to do. We're stuck."

I had two cigarettes left in a pack I'd rolled up and stuck into the breast pocket of my jeans jacket for emergencies, and I offered one of them to Rozene. I didn't know about her, but I needed something to calm my nerves. She hesitated, then took the cigarette and punched in the lighter. I pulled out the ashtray and noticed it was clean except for a layer of quarters.

"Mom saves 'em for the laundromat."

She lit her cigarette off the lighter, but when she offered the lighter to me I directed it back into the well. "*You* light me," I said.

She put the cigarette back in her lips, and drew on it until there was a hot coal that I leaned into, nose to nose, and lit mine.

The foot vents were blowing warm air on my legs and the tape deck was turned down low. It was already getting dark and I could only see the river where it frothed over the boulders. The windows steamed up and she cracked hers, letting in the breathy sound of the river. Once again I relished the opportunity to have her so close, and I wondered if the reason she wanted to talk bore any resemblance to the reason I wanted to see her.

"Did you notice my leg?" she said, lifting it onto the seat between us. She'd kicked off her shoe and the arch of her foot rested against my thigh. I could feel my motor starting to run. "It's skinnier than the other one. See?" She put her other foot against me, pulled her pant leg up, and pushed the top of her sock down under the ankle bone. "Feel it." I had practically creamed my jeans the first time she'd put her leg on me at Harvey Field when she still had a cast on and the only live part I could touch was her toes. Now I reached over and put my hand around the narrowest part of her ankle, and rubbed my middle finger up and down one side of her Achilles tendon. "That part hasn't changed," she said, "but check out the muscle."

When I cupped my hand and let it slide up the soft fuzz on the back of her leg, it was like rubbing dry sticks together and I thought something was going to ignite. I kneaded the soft part of her calf with my thumb.

"Now, try the good leg," she said. In this tactile paradise, it was easy to forget the purpose of my mission. Which good leg? Was there a better one? I didn't want to let go of the first one, so I assigned a hand to each ankle and moved slowly up and down both calves trying to memorize every slope and curve. "That one is skinnier."

"It's like comparing satin and silk."

She curled her toes against my leg. "Oh, Piper, honestly. Let me see yours."

I let go of her instantly. "It wasn't me who broke a leg!" We weren't in the same ballpark when it came to calves; mine were as skinny and unyielding as a broomstick. She'd get slivers if she rubbed too hard.

"I just want to see." She put her feet back on the floor and leaned over into my compartment, trying to reach my ankles. I stretched my feet against the firewall to put them as far away from her hands as I could. Her chest was pressed against the top of my legs and her hair cascaded over the top of her upside-down head. I could feel her fingers working under the cuffs of my pants. "Come, on, Piper, I showed you mine."

We were both laughing, mine as much terror as delight. Sloppy clothes hid a lot of imperfections, but I knew that if she ever discovered that the circumference of my calves was comparable to most people's wrists, I was history. Finally, she stopped struggling and went limp in my lap with her arms draped over my legs. Except for the tiny green light on the tape deck, it was pitch dark and we were operating strictly by touch. I meant to just slide my hands under her jacket, but they slid under her shirt. She was warm and each vertebra I dallied on felt like a precious stone sewn into the fabric of her skin.

"That feels nice," she said, as I worked my way back up, stretching her bra strap far enough to let me reach her neck.

She rubbed my legs through the pants, which felt safe, and I let go of the tension I'd been holding like a cocked bow in the lower half of my body. I pulled one hand off her back and followed the mound of her buttocks to the thigh. If I were a kitten, I would have been purring.

When *Evita* started over for the second time, Rozene sat up. Her face was inches from mine and I could feel the warmth of her breath. There were lots of places where she could have placed her hands, but she'd put one of them on my crotch. So many times when I reconstructed this moment later, it seemed as if I was intoxicated, operating under the influence of something I wasn't very good at: intimacy. So maybe I didn't have all my wits about me, but I knew if you'd put me back in that same position a thousand times I would have done the same foolish thing. I kissed her. At first, it was just the cheek, but that was only because it was dark and I'd missed. I suctioned my lips to the corner of her mouth, then to the center, and I pressed and prayed it would last forever. However long we held it, I would have sworn it was voluntary on both our parts. It was long enough that our tongues found each other somewhere in the middle of the wineskin we'd made of our mouths and that's when she broke.

"Oh, God, Piper! We can't do this." I remembered the *we* part later, which I took to be an admission of complicity, testament to the fact I hadn't just dreamed all this up and remodeled it to fit my preconceived fantasies. "I'm not like that," she said, wiping her lips with the sleeve of her jacket. "I want to have a house and kids and get married. Don't you?"

At that moment, I knew I'd lost her. I'd been caught, with the blood in my groin, but throw me out of a plane and I knew how to land on my feet. I had to. "Me too. I was just . . ."

"Experimenting," she said.

"Yeah."

"It was my fault. I'm not even supposed to be seeing you. It was dumb to come out here like this. We're probably stuck."

I had answers to everything she'd said, because I'd already thought of the same questions. We could move away from Stampede and be anonymous, just two nine-to-fivers in a high-rise apartment in Seattle. And when we'd saved up enough for a down payment, we could get a fixer-upper on Capitol Hill, with a picket fence and a patio with evergreens planted around it for privacy, and a dog. As far as kids were concerned, we could adopt them, two, three, as many as she wanted, as long as there were more than just one. *I was stupid. I rushed you, Rozene. But don't throw out the laundry with the wash.*

She patted my hand, but her mind had already shifted gears. It was over. She turned on the headlights and they cast double-barreled beams that grazed the bank in front of us and then joined before shooting out into the void over the North Fork of the Skykomish River. When she revved the gas pedal, the tires just spun.

"Goll dang it," she said.

I got out and traipsed to the front of the car, figuring it would be easier to backtrack than make a new path forward. I'd done this before with Dad when we were cutting a Christmas tree on the Weyerhaeuser tree farm and had to help the people in front of us. Rozene kept trying to gun it.

"Rock it," I told her. I didn't know why I was being helpful, because I didn't really want to go home.

She rolled the car up onto the wheel wells we'd spun and then rocked back. Front, back, front, back. Each time it started back, I put my shoulder against the grill and pushed. The vessels in my neck bulged and I could smell the exhaust and feel the heat of the engine on my face. Finally, in one perfect combination, the wheels broke over the back of the snow wells and the car kept going. I churned my feet, trying to keep pressure against the car, but as we reached the troughs in the spur road it picked up speed and I fell down face first in the snow. The blurry headlights bounced away from me, and I realized I was crying. *God, tell me it didn't happen this way, it's not over, this is just a matter of calibrating our timing, this isn't the last time we'll ride in the little brown Corolla together.*

"Piper! You okay?" Rozene was yelling at me from behind the glare of the headlights.

I stood up and cleared my throat. Snowmelt had worked into my shoes and soaked the arches of my socks. My face was as wet as the front of my pants, but she would assume it was from falling down. It didn't really matter anyway; I could have stripped off my pants and let her see my skinny legs. We had so many other hurdles to clear. "I'm coming!"

Rozene backed the car up for what seemed like a mile until we found a wide place in the road to turn around. Then she turned the tape deck off. Everything was eyes ahead and straight again.

I tried to get back on task once we were on Highway 2 and in the relative safety of wet asphalt. I had to prepare an excuse for missing work and decide if I still had the courage to talk to Dad about Dirk. Each time we met an oncoming car, I watched Rozene's sculptured face to guess what she might be feeling. Her face was so wise, the lips succulent, her cheekbones pillows for the eyes. Rather than soothe me as it had just hours before though, her beauty tore into me like a whiff of Purex straight out of the jug. I was foolish to have thought she'd share it with me, but I wasn't sure I could stop the wishing.

17

WILLARD WAS WAITING ON the front porch when Rozene dropped me off, just sitting there in the glow of the yellow bug light, chewing on a red plastic stirrer, and petting the Irish terrier who'd curled down next to him, arching its chin up onto his leg. In the summer I used to sit in that same spot reading when the house was too hot and the whitewash would come off onto the back of my shirt like chalk. I wasn't particularly in the mood to see anyone, but better Willard than Dad. Willard knew about hiding the things you loved.

"Where in blazes you been?" This wasn't the greeting I wanted.

"Where's Dad?"

"Been here and gone," he said, jutting out his jaw. I assumed Willard's hard-heartedness was simply an imitation of Dad's mood when he stormed through the house earlier looking for me.

"We go to print day after tomorrow. It's no wonder he's upset."

Willard took the plastic stirrer out of his mouth. "I thought you wanted to burn the paper."

My socks and pants had dried out from the heater in the Corolla, I was starving, and Dad was peeved. Adding it all up, I knew what I had to do. In one of her diary entries, Anais Nin said, *Life shrinks or expands in proportion to one's courage.* He couldn't do anything worse than Rozene had already done.

I never went to the paper at night. Like school, it was a daytime thing. I peered into Marge's on the way, which was full of people I didn't recognize. Marge was talking to a man with an Afro and a Channel 7 emblem on the back of his jacket. The men in the booths had loosened their ties, a sure sign they weren't from Stampede, not because they'd loosened them, but because they wore them at all. They must have been here for the John Carlisle trial, which started tomorrow.

The front door was locked so I rang the after-hours buzzer, which echoed like a tin can walkie-talkie down the hallway. Dad usually walked to work so there was no way of knowing if he was in by virtue of spotting his car. He only drove when he had to go out of town or he wanted to gas up at Carlisle's private pump at the back of the *Herald*. I didn't want to ring again and jangle his nerves any more than they'd already been jangled. *Hello, Dad, it's me, your diligent little copy editor.* Maybe I'd catch him with a woman and he'd be the one that had to do the explaining. *You have to be the captain of your passions, Dad.* Then there were footsteps, the bolt slid back into its hatch, and the door cracked. Dad's sleeves were rolled up and he had a pen in his hand. In order to avoid further shrinkage, I kept my eyes open.

"About time I checked in, huh?" I expected him to look at his watch and unload on me, but he just stood there staring, which forced me to go on. "Something came up at school. I had to do something with . . . with Dirk." I crossed my fingers hoping Dirk hadn't come around looking for me at the paper. It was working. Dad's grip on the edge of the door relaxed. "I'm sorry I screwed up. Can I still help?" I did everything but kneel down.

He opened the door and I followed him down the unlighted hallway towards our offices. Except for the crackle of the linoleum where our feet stepped on places that had bubbled up, it was dead quiet, sans the usual buzz of fluorescent lights, word processors, and staff chatter. If I had to work down there alone, I'd at least crank up some background music, a little Enya or one of the other New Age artists Mom had listened to while she painted. Dad had lost his music. The tap, tap, tapping on his computer had drummed it right out of him, truth in lieu of rhythm, the hardbound declaratory sentence instead of the jazz riff.

I marched right through his office, which was warm with his smell, and flipped the wall switch as I entered my cubicle, the "annex" Dad called it, expecting to find copy on my desk, but it was bare. Of course, I thought. Dad had probably done it himself, as he had a thousand editions before I ever came along. It wasn't as if he needed my edits. They were make-work. Maybe it was my Catholicism showing through, but I was disappointed. I needed work.

"I already finished the back section," he said, startling me from behind. "How would you like to start on the front page? We're coming out a day early."

"Early?" He never varied from the schedule. The employees in the doghouse joked reverentially that when Tom Scanlon was called by his creator he'd look at the calendar on his watch first to see how many days it was until the next issue.

"We've got something hot." He was holding a sheet of hard copy by the edges, curled over on itself so I couldn't see what it said.

This was weird. I'd screwed up and for my consequence he was going to let me in on something hot. Dad kept a saying on his desk, a little wooden plaque in a brass stand, that read: "Transgressions require consequences, not punishment." I would have more readily understood it if he'd asked me to clean the dirty wax out of the seams between the molding and the linoleum with my toothbrush. He was the prodigal, taking joy in the return of his wayward daughter.

"Except for John, nobody else has seen this." He choked up as he said it and I thought this must be the issue announcing the sale of the paper. "Treat it with the respect it deserves." He sucked in through his nostrils. "I haven't had as much difficulty writing something since your mom died."

Oh, God, I'd misjudged the whole situation. He wasn't letting me off at all. He was going to rub my nose in it. He was going to have the last word after all. "It's about Mom, isn't it?"

His voice was on the verge of breaking. "Here . . . read it." He set the copy on the crooked stack of cardboard boxes against the wall and left the room.

With the copy stretched between my hands, I backed my way over to the chair without even looking where I was going. When I glanced at the headlines, it was as if a big stone had been lifted off my chest and I was taking in new air so fast I was hyperventilating. Or maybe I wasn't taking in any air at all. The buzzards were overhead, but it wasn't Mom they were circling.

MORE CHARGES FILED AGAINST CITY LEADER. Cascade County Prosecutor Seth Armstrong announced today that John Carlisle is being charged with thirteen counts of child molestation in the first degree. The charges, involving children under the age of twelve, arise out of complaints made by parents of boys who have resided at the Lake Spigot Summer Camp, a facility endowed with funds donated by the Carlisle family.

These charges are in addition to the rape and sexual misconduct charges for which Carlisle is scheduled to go on trial tomorrow. "I see no reason to delay the first trial," says Armstrong.

John Carlisle chose to make no statement in response to the new allegations, which represent potent aftershocks to the quake that rocked the county less than three months ago.

The Prosecutor's statement alleges that Carlisle engaged in illicit "touching and fondling," including incidents with boys he led on overnight "survival campouts" in the Mt. Pilchuck foothills. The campouts are part of a Lake Spigot manhood ritual.

One of the parents said, "I became suspicious when the first charges were brought." Another one said, "It's despicable what this man has gotten away with in the name of charity."

My hands were shaking by the time I finished the article, which also included the obligatory mention of Renfred Carlisle, John Carlisle's great grandfather and the first mayor of Stampede at the turn of the century. Renfred must have been turning over in his grave. I was past disbelief and into the garden of make-believe with goblins and harpies. What happened to Dad's counteroffensive, the information he had on Carlisle and Mom? Was he saving it for another aftershock? I tried to study the piece again for grammatical errors, punctuation, and syntax, but my critical powers were mush. In a vague way, I felt a responsibility to tell Dad that Dirk's charges had been made up, but in the face of so much corroboration I wasn't sure whether I believed Dirk's disavowal anymore.

I stumbled toward Dad's office, steadying myself against the stack of Xerox boxes and the door jamb, and plopped into the nearest armchair, the article drooping from the pinch of my fingertips like a soiled flag. I wanted to show the respect for the situation I felt. "What did *he* say?"

Dad nodded his head, took a hard swallow, and whispered. "He's comatose."

They suspected the fire started at the gas pump, which was in the breezeway just outside the print room, then spread to the inks and solvents, and the rolls of paper on deck ready to be fed into the press for the morning run of the *Herald*. I heard the phone ringing at home, the door slamming, and sirens wailing in the distance while I was trying to go to sleep. I knew it had to be more than the Stampede station because there were two different siren pitches and one of them was coming from the north, which meant they'd called in help from Machias. From my window I could see the glow over the downtown like the aurora borealis.

There was a crowd in the street when I arrived and a young policeman was pushing people back to the sidewalk opposite the entrance to the *Herald*. I could feel the heat from the flames that had broken through the roof and blown out the windows. Payton Miller, the veterinarian, stood next to me.

"The tar in that roof is like corn to a hog," he said in a husky voice.

"Have you seen my dad?" The thought had occurred to me once I got there that I'd only imagined the phone ringing and the door slamming.

"Sure haven't."

There was a fireman standing by the tailgate of the pumper truck parked askew in the middle of the street, and I made a dash for him. I could hear the policeman yelling at me as I grabbed the fireman by the front of his rubbery yellow jacket.

"Is anyone inside?" I yelled over the noise of the pumps. He put his gloved hand to his ear. "Have you checked for people?"

He nodded his head and put a heavy hand on my shoulder. His badge read "Machias Volunteer Fire Department."

"My dad's the editor," I said.

He shrugged, like so what.

Judging from the fire licking the sides of the building, I tried to figure where it was in relation to Dad's office. I looked up to see if the Machias fireman was watching, but he was scratching himself under the brim of his helmet and staring off in the direction of the breezeway that separated the *Herald* from the Horse and Cowboy next door.

I snuck around to the front of the truck, running my fingertips along the polished metal sheathing, then with my hands in my pockets made a slow, deliberate walk toward the front door of the newspaper, which was open. Willard had always told me that you could walk into the nicest hotel in the world and use their swimming pool and towels if you just kept reminding yourself that you belonged there. Well, I belonged. I knew the floor layout better than any fireman from Machias did. As I stepped over the bulging canvas fire hose that snaked through the front door, somebody grabbed me from behind.

"What're you doing?"

"Oh, God," I said, wrapping my arms around Dad and squeezing him.

He walked me across the street and into the portico of The Stamp Box. We just stood there gawking back at the flames erupting from the bowels of the building. Dad stroked the outside of my arm in a distracted way. The pumper truck was deluging the roof with an arc of water that oscillated between the parapets, and several fighters worked on foot from the breezeway, directing water through the blown windows. I felt as if we were losing a member of our family and I didn't even particularly like the place. I could only imagine how devastated Dad must have been.

"Can you rebuild it?"

"That's John Carlisle's call."

"Can't you start your own?"

"Hah! You must be mixing us up with the Kennedys. We're the shanty Irish, remember?" I knew he didn't really believe that. He was just discouraged.

"Nobody knows more about newspapers than you do." I wasn't fishing for affection, but it sure felt good when he pulled me real tight against him. "What about the John Carlisle story?"

"The dailies in Seattle will probably pick it up in a few days, run their usual two column inches. But bad news carries well here by word of mouth."

"It wasn't something you really wanted to publish anyway, was it?"

"Not much choice was there?"

Louise Mead came by in a rumpled pea jacket and threw her arms around Dad, dropping ashes from her cigarette down the back of his coat. All she probably wanted was the same thing everyone else at the paper wanted: for Dad to tell her it wasn't really happening. Then a man in black slacks and a pocket protector in his shirt came by and introduced himself as the fire inspector. Dad shooed us off with his eyes and Louise transferred her grief to me, slipping her hand inside my arm.

The owner of Monkeyshines was hosing down the front of his store, making sure an errant spark didn't catch in the folds of his awning and burn up his inventory of old furniture, and we walked out into the street to avoid his spray. The crowd in front of Marge's had swelled — more people from the paper, other Commercial Street shopkeepers, kids from school. I looked for Rozene, but she wasn't there, neither was her mom. The light was on in Marge's and I noticed she'd set out a stack of cups, cream and sugar, and day-old donuts and cookies on a table by the coffee urn. Colonel Thurgood walked by with a baseball cap pulled down over his face, his hands in the pockets of Dirk's Chicago Bulls jacket, and I wondered what Dirk was doing the night before a trial he knew he wasn't supposed to be in.

When Louise had snubbed out her last butt on the sidewalk, she left me to find some OPs. "Other people's," she said. I didn't feel particularly sociable anyway, which was normal for me, and I remembered how encouraged I was when I read that despite Albert Einstein's passionate sense of social justice he shunned contact with other human beings. They were great if you didn't have to deal with them.

As I leaned against the brick, I realized this wasn't just John Carlisle's paper or even my dad's. The *Herald* was the eyes, ears and larynx of Stampede and, the way Dad ran it, its conscience. Things could be said between customers at Marge's, or by the checker at Ned's, or from the pulpit at St. Augustine's, but until it showed up in the *Herald* it hadn't really happened. The paper validated a story's importance to the larger community. God only knew how few people would run for a city council position paying twenty-five dollars per meeting if there wasn't the reward of getting their name in the paper. How could a town survive its inferiority complex without a newspaper?

Somebody bumped my shoulder, knocking me off balance, and when I turned, Condon Bagmore was standing there with a cigarette stub stuck to the mucous on his lower lip.

"Hey, if it isn't skinny Scanlon?"

I elbowed him back, eying his cronies, Jesse Little and Clete Oster. "Who let you guys out of your cage?"

He ignored my comment. "Hey, doesn't your grandpa live with you? Stubby little fart wears one of them construction vests?"

"So?"

"He's a flaming pyromaniac." Bagmore's boys chortled at their leader's adroitness with redundancies.

"What are you talking about?"

He reached out to put his hand on top of my shoulder and I squirmed away. "We saw him with a smoking gun, if you know what I mean." Another chortle from his boys. "Right over there" — he pointed to the breezeway between the *Herald* and the Horse and Cowboy — "I saw him running outta there 'bout two hours ago. Looked like he'd seen a ghost."

"You're full of shit, Bagmore." That's what I said at least.

"Ask Clit." That's what he called Clete Oster, who'd take any abuse to be one of Bagmore's allies. "He was with me, weren't you Clit?"

"Had a dog with 'em," Clete said. "Fucking red-haired dawg." Clete wasn't smart enough to have made this up. What you saw with Bagmore's boys was what you got.

"He sometimes does the janitor work," I lied.

"So you're saying he was burning garbage, huh?"

"I'm not saying anything, asswipe."

"Ooh!"

I wanted to make a deal with him to keep his mouth shut, but I couldn't think of anything I had that he wanted. All I could do was devalue his information. "My dad already knows about Willard being here." As dry as my mouth was, I managed to roll a goober and spit it onto the sidewalk between Clete's and Jesse's feet. "See you boys in church."

I was probably as transparent as Saran wrap, but I had to have a strong exit.

I went straight home, but Willard wasn't in his room. Billy, Churchill, and Diller rose to be petted, but Willard and the terrier were AWOL. *Dammit, Willard! What the hell have you done?*

I went up to my room and tried to read the Eva Peron biography I'd picked up at the library, listening all the time for Willard to clatter the basement door shut. The glow over the downtown had faded and it was an ordinary starless night in Stampede again. My mind kept wandering over my conversations with Willard. What had I said, *Kill the newspaper*? Sometimes I wondered if I had the brains to *be* in Bagmore's gang.

I'd totally misjudged Willard. He wasn't the Simple Simon met a pieman I'd built up in my mind. After all, he'd grown up where justice meant field justice, executed in the language of machetes that could sever an asparagus stalk with the flick of the wrist. Maybe Willard was more like me than I thought. The ends justified the means.

Dad came home about three a.m. and I cracked my door to listen. I was sure he thought I was asleep, which was just as well because I didn't want to talk to him until I knew for sure what had happened with Willard. Dad had enough to worry about without Willard right now. The liquor cupboard over the refrigerator popped open. Then I heard ice clinking into a drinking glass. He was probably having a Jamison, the whiskey he drank when his brother Seamus stayed with us. I heard the chair at his roll-top desk squeak, followed by silence. The living room lights were off, which meant he was sitting there in the dark. The thought flashed through my head that it wasn't Jamison in his glass but the bug poison he kept in the same cupboard.

I crawled out to the top of the stairs and lay on my belly so I could hear what was going on through the banisters. He was talking on the phone. All I could make out were snippets of the conversation. Then he said, "I love you, Seamus," and I heard the receiver nestle into its cradle. My God, he was talking to his brother. He never talked to his brothers. I felt a cavernous pang of inadequacy, realizing how much Dad missed an adult companion. The chair creaked again as he changed positions and I put my hands on the steps to push myself back up. That's when I heard a groan of the kind I imagined death would be like. I went rigid, every cell of my body just listening. There were three short, strangled releases of breath like the shots from an air gun, followed by a deep, convulsive sob. I'd never heard my dad cry like that, and it was a melancholy sound. I knew I should have gone down there, but I was chicken to see him that way.

When I finally heard him blowing his nose in the bathroom, I snuck down to the basement to see if Willard had come back. He wasn't there so I lay down on his bed in the dark, flat on my back, and stared up at the ceiling. There was a chill in the room, so I pulled a crumpled sheet and blanket from out of the pile at the foot of the bed and spread them over me, shoes and all.

And that's how I slept, like a corpse, until the coarse tongue of a dog on my face woke me the next morning.

─────18─────

THREE OF THE DOGS had climbed up on the bed and were standing over me, probably wondering what I'd done with their master. I lifted the pillow next to me, leaned over and checked the floor, but there was just me. I could understand Willard fleeing; I couldn't understanding him doing it without his dogs. He must have been hit by a car or stumbled and broken his leg. Then it occurred to me the dogs weren't as interested in Willard's whereabouts as they were with breakfast, so I gathered up their rubber dishes and scooped a fistful of dry dog chow into each of them. I had no idea how much they were used to, but the sound of kibbles hitting the rubber put them on their best behavior.

While they were eating, I looked in Willard's drawers for a note or some clue as to what he'd done and where he'd gone. The dirty shirts had been wadded up and stuffed back next to the clean ones, none of the socks had been paired, and there were underpants in every drawer. At the bottom of a drawer full of sweaters and knotted neckties I found a rubber-banded stash of photos. One of them was a black-and-white, matte finish of Willard and Grandma Carol that must have been done by a professional because the background was all wispy and ethereal. Carol was pretty in a technical sort of way, but the irritation at having to hold the pose for so long showed. In Willard's easy grin, on the other hand, I could see Mom. There was no question whose daughter she was. The picture underneath was a little girl sitting on a pinto Shetland pony with one hand on the saddle horn and the other waving limp-wristed to the camera. She was in a ruffled taffeta dress that exposed her bare knees and the patent leather mary janes didn't even reach the stirrups. On the back of the photo it said in a woman's hand, "Kathryn, Easter, 5 years."

Dad was already gone when I went upstairs, but I knew where he'd be. It didn't matter the place had burned; it was habit. He was like the expectant dog who waits by the front door for his master.

The fire was still smoldering when I arrived, emitting an odor akin to old tires burning. A fireman was hosing down the building in what appeared to be a case of overkill because there wasn't much left to burn except for the blistered panel sign on the brick facade: *Home of the Herald Stampede.* Firemen with gas masks, axes and flashlights wandered in and out of the front door while a small crowd huddled in the middle of the street behind a yellow tape strung from blocker to blocker around the building. I counted thirteen *Herald* employees, including Les Showalter, the smokeless tobacco-chewing driver of the doorless hearse I'd thrown bundles out of for the paper carriers. This would have been his delivery day.

As I got closer, I realized the crowd was watching Dad, who was being positioned in front of the rubble by a KZIT television reporter with a pink bow around her ponytail and a microphone in her hand. They must have come for the Carlisle trial and caught the fire as a bonus. I knew Dad didn't suffer TV journalists gladly. "They're ambulance chasers," he'd told me. "They leave the heavy lifting for the print media." He was as unyielding as a kid getting his face washed as the reporter turned him at different angles in response to the hand signals of her cameraman, but once the camera was rolling he seemed at ease with his words.

"With God's help, we'll have the *Herald* up and printing by the fourth of July." He looked over at the gaggle of employees in the street. "If I have anything to say about it, nobody's going to miss a paycheck or send their kids to school without new cords and tennis shoes." I had no idea where a shanty Irishman was going to get the lucre to back that promise up, but it didn't surprise me he'd said it. Last night he was bawling like the world had ended and this morning he was promising everyone safe passage. Listening to him talk like that gave me goose bumps and reminded me of the Yeats poem he used to recite for us:

> I made my song a coat
> Covered with embroideries

Out of old mythologies.

Of course, in the poem, fools stole the coat and paraded it around as if it were their own and Yeats said let them take it:

> For there's more enterprise
> In walking naked.

Well, that's about where we were. Naked.

When Dad was done, everyone congratulated him and patted him on the back. His reservoir still had something left because his eyes watered as he moved through the staff trying to shake everyone's hand or give them a hug. Seeing him this way helped me realize what the sadness in his phone call to Seamus meant. His job had become his life, so had these people, and poof, it was gone. We were either a gaggle of fools or charter members of Tom Scanlon's Optimist Club for wanting to believe it was all going to be as easy as he said it would be, but if I let myself just focus on his steady blue eyes and the easy wave of his inky black hair as he walked through his people I was transported too. Some folks blabbered, showing you everything inside of them, and it was easy to tell that the pieces spewing out were nothing but trinkets and costume jewelry. Dad shuttered his innermost thoughts and, like the sand working inside the oyster, added value to them, so that when he finally shared them you knew you had experienced something precious.

When he reached the edge of the crowd, he saw me and winked. I thought we were going to have a chance to talk, but Louise Mead was clinging to his arm. "Did you hear what he said, Piper?"

"Yeah, that's great news."

Because Louise pretty much controlled his whole right side, there was no way Dad could give me a hug so he stuck out his arm and brushed me around the back and shoulders like we were in-laws that didn't care that much for each other. Somebody else cut in and hugged him, leaving just me and Louise standing there.

"Have you seen your grandpa?" she whispered.

"This morning?"

"This morning, last night. They're looking for him."

I felt panicky and looked up at Dad to make sure he wasn't listening. "Maybe he went fishing or something with one of his buddies." I knew I was way off on this one — his buddies were dead, it wasn't fishing season, and he'd left without his dogs — but it was the first thing that flashed into my head. "He'll show up. You know how he likes to wander." Worrying about Willard had always been Mom's job.

There was a commotion over by the entryway. Two firemen emerged from the building carrying a stretcher. The heavyset one with a helmet pushed up on his forehead signaled to Dad. "Scanlon! Come here."

Dad disentangled himself from the crowd and stepped over the yellow tape. I followed. He'd said *Scanlon*, hadn't he?

The two firemen were kneeling down next to the lump in the middle of the stretcher, picking at it, and shining their lights on it. "I guess we weren't as lucky as I told you last night, Tom."

Dad tried to push me around behind him, but I could see everything. The body was in a fetal position with the fists in front of its face, the skin shriveled onto its emaciated frame, and no hair. Around the waist I could make out a leather belt that had been grafted onto the torso like a strip of pepperoni. I didn't want to look, but at the same time I couldn't not look. Something in the back of my mind registered the thought that I was glad Mom had died by water and not by fire. The feet were crossed and I noticed a blackened metal medallion embedded into the shoe leather. I recognized the medallion. I'd seen it on a pair of Frye boots with stacked heels.

"Lookit here," one of the firemen said, holding a string of shells he'd pulled away from the neck.

Dad knelt down next to the stretcher, practically touching the corpse, his shoulders caved and his back rounded. He put his hands over his face and I could see from the rocking of his body that he was weeping for the second time in less than twelve hours.

"Who is it?" the fireman asked.

The first time I'd seen those boots and the pukka shell necklace was in the hallway of the hospital just outside the emergency room where they had Mom. They belonged to someone I thought I hated, someone it was clear I'd never understood. Staring at those sunken, browless eye sockets, a whole new and equally gruesome picture was starting to form and my heart sank. Willard hadn't just killed the town's newspaper, he'd killed its nobility.

"He's the owner of the paper," I said glumly. "John Carlisle."

I only half-assimilated what Dad was saying to the employees after we crossed back over the yellow tape because my head was buzzing with fear of what was going to happen to Willard. This wasn't just the nursing home; this was hard time. Without his dogs, he'd die. Maybe we could prove he was insane or temporarily deranged. I could testify as to his memory lapses and the time warps. My God, he was the gentlest man I knew, he crossed streets to help people carry their groceries home. Didn't there have to be malice aforethought to convict someone of murder? Whatever malice Willard might have once possessed had spilled onto the asparagus fields a long time ago.

The women on the staff were bawling on each other's shoulders, dabbing their eyes, buckling at the knees, and stealing glances at the ambulance that had come to take away the remains of John Carlisle. Even the TV people seemed hesitant to aim their cameras directly at the corpse. I was feeling weak too, both out of shock for John Carlisle and fear for what his death was going to do to my family. He'd already taken Mom. Now, by being in the wrong place at the wrong time, he was going to take out Mom's father as well. I couldn't let it happen. The axe was still in mid-swing. There was time to pull Willard's neck off the block. If only I could find him.

The staff followed Dad in a ragged formation across the street to Marge's while I peeled off in the general direction of school, where I was supposed to be for a second period trigonometry exam on the properties of cosines and arccosines. Nobody at the paper would miss me; they weren't used to seeing me until after school.

A familiar black four-wheeler, with a coat of splattered mud like a waterline across the lower portion of the side panels and wheel covers, was parked in front of our house. I peered in at the seats as I went by.

Dr. Miller was sitting at the kitchen table with Willard, who had a blanket draped over his shoulders and a cup of hot cocoa and a plate with a short stack of toast in front of him. His shoes and pants cuffs were as muddy as Dr. Miller's four-wheeler.

"Where you been?" I yelled. "I've been scared to death for you."

Willard blinked, bowed his head, and sort of pointed with a clump of fingers toward Dr. Miller.

"What's the matter? Why won't he talk to me?"

"Sit down," Dr. Miller said. I scooted out the chair at the end of the table, keeping an eye on Willard, who was nibbling on his toast but leaving the crust, something I'd never seem him do before. "I found him out on Horse Heaven Highway sitting under a tree with his dog. I gave the dog some chow and put him downstairs with the others." Dr. Miller's voice was strong and slow and forced me to put the brakes on my panic. "Think he's had a little exposure. His temperature was down a bit. Right now, he needs blood sugar."

This was going too slow for me. "What were you doing, Willard?"

Again, Willard just fidgeted with his toast and muttered something.

I looked over at Dr. Miller.

"He's gonna be okay after some food and rest," he said,

blanketing Willard's forearm with his hand. "Told me he was going to Bonnie Holliday's, didn't you big guy?" Willard rubbed a spot on his chin real hard and nodded in agreement. Not again. This was nuts. "Going there for Kitty's birthday," he told me. That was a new one. Usually, it was to fix the Studebaker.

"Did he say anything else?"

Dr. Miller stretched his long arms toward the ceiling and clasped his hands together for a yawn. "'Scuse me." Then he put his hands behind his neck and bent his elbows back. "He didn't say much else really. Didn't have to. I could see he'd had a rough night."

It sounded as if Willard had kept his mouth shut. Maybe the confusion was cover. He always seemed to snap out of his little spells when it was time for supper. I'd even wondered if it wasn't sometimes a way for him to give his mind a recess. "He's done this before."

"His wanderings are legend."

I made a counterfeit chuckle. "I guess they are."

Willard had passed the first test. Dr. Miller was at the fire and even he hadn't put two and two together. There weren't very many people in Stampede as smart as Payton Miller, although Dad was certainly one of them. If Dr. Miller was fooled, maybe everyone else would be too, at least until Bagmore's testimony received official sanction.

I'd already decided on the walk home what I had to do, worked out the itinerary in my head. The only unknown was when I'd be able to put the plan into action, but now that Dr. Miller had brought him back, it could start as soon as Willard finished his cocoa and toast. It had to; we didn't have that much time. While Willard blew on his cocoa, Dr. Miller made small talk about the dogs, which seemed to draw Willard out of his daze as he interjected simple but disconnected comments in response. Dr. Miller and I nodded intently each time Willard chimed in as if he were explaining the laws of thermodynamics. I asked Dr. Miller if there was any special medicine Willard needed and he excused himself to go out to his four-wheeler and brought back a brown plastic bottle with pills.

"I use 'em for animals that are going to be shipped," he said. "Give him half a one tonight after dinner. It'll help him sleep."

"These are okay for humans?"

He laughed. "You think I'd poison your gramps?"

Willard and the dogs snuggled on the bed while I searched through the closet and drawers for everyday clothes and stuffed them into his hard-shell Samsonite with the broken hinges. There was room for a few luxuries too, like the Burlington Northern brakeman's hat one of his bowling buddies had given him with Willard's name stenciled on the side, a pack of Roi Tan cigars, and the cache of family pictures. I made him write the combination to the safe on a page in a magazine and, on the third try, I was able to pull out the brown paper sack with his stock certificates and bonds. I threw a clean pair of khaki pants onto the bed together with dry socks and a pair of shorts turned blue from laundering them with the darks. Willard saw no need for separate loads, told me it was wasted water. "Put these on," I said.

While he changed into his clothes, I rifled through Dad's room until I found the keys to the Skylark, which had been stored in the spare garage over at the Socket Street house since the fender bender with Buzz Little. Dad had naively hung them on a high nail in his closet, probably assuming they'd be out of reach for a five-foot three geriatric delinquent, but this time Willard had a taller accomplice. I packed my own stuff into a duffel bag, favoring the more expensive things like sweaters over T-shirts that had been given to me as souvenirs from Sodality Retreats and Antique Car Festivals. I also threw in my diary, three Anais Nins, *Portrait of an Artist,* half a box of Tampons, and *The Second Sex*, which I'd purposely never given back to Rozene so I'd have an excuse for her to call me. I didn't know when, if ever, I'd be back so these humble possessions would have to suffice as the contents of my time capsule. When I went back down to the basement, Willard was sitting on the oval rug next to the bed, surrounded by his dogs, still pantsless.

"Come on, Willard! You gotta get dressed."

He looked down at his hairless, milky legs. "I forgot."

"I'll be back in fifteen minutes. Don't leave this room. And do the pants."

The garage doors sagged on their hinges and I had to lift them over the dead weeds in the crown between the wheel troughs to open them. Somebody must have used the car since Dad put it in storage because the blue tarp was in a heap on the floor. The smashed fender had been pried away from the tire. The whole place smelled like a litter box. A spider web the size of a continent had been spun from the outside mirror and antenna to the wall of the garage. I looked around on the dirt floor and found a brick with mortar stuck to one edge, held it above the spider web, and dropped it. The strands crackled like static electricity as the brick ripped through, hit the wheel of the hand mower, and bounced against my ankle. "Ouch!" This was beginning to feel like how I imagined Purgatory, nothing ever working right.

The garage was so narrow I had to turn sideways to slip myself through the door and into the front seat, where I was greeted with the smell of cigar ash. The key with the square shoulders slipped easily into the ignition and the lights on the instrument panel came on as I turned it clockwise. Although I'd never taken driver's ed, Mom had let me drive on her sketching trips into the countryside, apparently more fearful of missing a good landscape than of me missing a turn in the road. The engine labored, coughed, sputtered, and despite my pumping on the gas pedal, settled into a steady rhythm of futility. *Err . . . err . . . err . . . err . . . err . . . err.*

I turned the key back to center and just sat there in case it was flooded, trying to imagine what Dad and the staff were doing and how much time I had. Marge had probably fixed them her iceberg lettuce and tomato salad, maybe spaghetti and meatballs, and toast sprinkled with Parmesan and garlic salt. When I tried again, the engine sounded like it was pulling old taffy the way it bogged down and quit. "Come on, you sack a shit!" I yelled, slapping the dashboard, making the little plastic hula girl swish and sway her hips. I hadn't figured on the damage inactivity could inflict on the spirit of the internal combustion engine.

I finally put it in neutral, climbed out, and braced myself between the back bumper and the garage to get it moving. The troughs in the driveway guided the wheels like the gutters of a bowling alley. To get over the hump in the "Y" where the driveway intersected the alley, I had to dig in and lift on the bumper. Then the car suddenly became lighter and I had to run to catch up. I jumped in and steered the car across a compost pile and through a couple of plastic garbage cans that tumbled out of the way like tenpins before I popped the clutch and the engine shuddered into being. Dirk had taught me how to start a car by compression, something he'd seen in *American Graffiti*.

Willard didn't make a very good fugitive. Contrary to my instructions, he was out in the back yard with one of the dogs when I pulled up in the Skylark. I left the car running and ran inside for our belongings. My duffel bag was heavier than Willard's suitcase, probably because of all the books. We'd already loaded the four dogs into the car when Willard reminded me of their food, so I ran back to the basement, nested the rubber food dishes, and shoved them into the top of an open bag of Purina Chow. Willard had left the brakeman's cap on the apple crate nightstand and I put it on. It was a little tight, but it fit.

I thought of letting Willard drive until we were out of town, but he was still so dreamy and absent-minded I feared he would space out and get us into another wreck. Anyway, he wanted to ride in the backseat with the dogs, who were panting and gawking around as I counted them again through the rearview mirror. When I put my hand on the gearshift to put us in drive, I had a pang of conscience like a bone caught sideways in the throat. I remembered how often I'd regretted that Mom hadn't left a note. It would have helped so much to have that connection.

"Willard, stay here, I forgot something. And I mean *in* the car."

In the kitchen I found a flyer for the St. Augustine's Bazaar, turned it over, and wrote on the back:

> Dear Dad,
> I don't want you to get all freaked out by this, but Willard and I are going away. Please don't come searching for us. I'm almost of legal age and certainly will be by the time anyone finds us. I'm sorry I didn't turn out as planned, but you and Mom have given me a good start and for that I will always be thankful. My timing is either the worst it can be or the best it can be. But I thought better to get all the crap out of the way at once. Even though you seldom show it, I can only guess at how much agony you're in. I can't tell you every-thing right now, but someday I hope I can, at least by letter. And don't worry about Willard, he has his dogs, four of them (one died). Sorry to keep this from you too. I'll be thinking of you always.
> Love,
> Piper
> PS. You're a whale of a journalist and I've been proud to touch the raw material that you chiseled into statuary.

I put the note in his bathroom sink in case he didn't go into the kitchen for a while, and took a deep breath that caught at the edges going down. The note to Dad must have reminded me of something else I was leaving behind, because I went upstairs to retrieve Mom's brass hand from my nightstand before heading out the front door.

It was just bad luck that Mrs. Norman was out on her parking strip jockeying a recycle bin into place as we pulled out and I turned my head the other way as we went by.

"Duck, Willard!" With the brakeman's hat, maybe she wouldn't recognize me. The escape would have worked better at night, but we didn't have that luxury. The gathering at Marge's wasn't going to last all day. The Bagmore story would spread and, without the newspaper, Dad had no place to go but home. I watched out the rearview mirror to see if Mrs. Norman was writing down the license plate number, but she just stared after us and I hoped she didn't have a good head for numbers.

I made one sentimental detour, a drive-by of the trailer park. I wasn't going to see Rozene again either. By the time I did she'd have a husband who was an insurance broker and be living in the suburbs of Seattle with a triple garage larger than our house, and a nanny for the kids so she'd be free to do her aerobics and volunteer work during the day. Down the middle row, I saw the brown Corolla, with its hood under the canvas awning at the side of her trailer. She must have left the car home for her mom. The cafe curtains had been pulled open but the windows were as dim as the insides of an empty packing carton.

We took the back roads, staying off Horse Heaven Highway until we got farther out of town, and headed east where there was more open space and nobody who'd ever heard of the *Herald Stampede* or Scanlon. Pretty soon we were passing three-wire fences instead of pickets, hen houses instead of garages, silos instead of neon signs. The setting sun shone like track lighting through a slot between the horizon and a ceiling of dark clouds. Even though there was a breeze blowing through the car from the window Willard had opened for the dogs to stick their heads out, my hands were sweating and I had to keep wiping them off on my pants.

"Where we going?" Willard yelled over the wind.

"Surprise." The only destination I'd thought of was Seamus's place in Manhattan, if the car would make it that far. I knew he'd take us in. Seamus was another bent arrow, someone who'd bummed around and fought off the responsibilities of the world, and he knew how impatient Dad could be with screwoffs like me and Willard. Trouble was, he might feel obligated to call Dad. As unreliable as he'd been, I didn't want to test Seamus's brotherly infidelity with Willard's freedom.

Willard grinned at me and a wisp of hair danced on the top of his head. I thought he'd be nervous about going away, old people were supposed to be such creatures of habit, but he seemed grateful, the way a dog was when you took a thorn out of its paw. As far as stealing the car, I figured it was Willard's anyway and Dad and Mom had even talked about buying it for me when I graduated. Besides, the car was small potatoes compared to our reasons for leaving.

Passing through the small towns — Frylands, Duvall, Novelty, Stillwater, Pleasant Hill — triggered recollections from Willard's middle and deep memory. He talked about places where he'd bucked hay, played pool, square-danced, gone to church, played cards, hunted pheasant, fished, fixed cars, built barns, even worked on highway crews. I was relieved he was able to put aside the memories of his traumatic night. We could deal with all of that later. Right now, we were unrestricted as to time and geography. As long as there was gasoline left to be pumped in the free world, we could stay on the move.

The dogs had to pee once we reached I-90, so we pulled off onto Denny Creek Road and I let Willard and the dogs empty their bladders beside the car. My waste water must have evaporated because I just stayed at the wheel. I needed to import water, not export it.

At Snoqualmie Pass, the peaks of the Cascades had lanced the undersides of the clouds and they were dripping with rain. It was dark and I was glad we were on a separated highway because from a distance every car coming from the opposite direction looked like it was in my lane. Passing under an arc light I glanced into the backseat. Willard had his knees on the floor and his torso nestled in between Paddy's butt and Mrs. Churchill's flaccid muzzle. When we passed Cle Elum, at the toe of the eastern slope of the Cascades, we were officially in Eastern Washington, territory reputed to be inhabited by rednecks, militia, and just plain hicks if you believed the people from our side of the mountains. They voted Republican, worshiped Protestant, and named streets after John Wayne.

We pulled off for a boughten meal at Martha's Cafe in George, which I chose based on the number of semis idling out front. I made Willard wear the brakeman's hat inside out so nobody would be able to read his name on the front and I pulled a knit cap down to my eyebrows. A gum-snapping girl with red hair and tattoos on her biceps showed us to a booth with disposable placemats illustrated with events from George Washington's life. "Three Times a Lady" was playing on the juke box. The counter must have been the smoking section because plumes of blue smoke rose from the heads of the guys in logger boots with belt buckles as big as cement trowels, who sat there working down their dinners and sipping coffee. Willard took off his hat and set it on the seat.

"Keep it on," I said. "It makes us look like regulars."

"Regulars?"

"Truckers."

When I asked the waitress in my deepest voice which was better, the bacon burger or the cube steak, she said, "Beats me. I'm vegetarian." Her name tag said "Starbuck" and I asked her what nationality that was.

She laughed. "That's my communal name. We choose our own. My boyfriend's Ishmael." She cracked her gum as she spoke, with her pencil poised to write down our order in case we ever gave it. "You know . . . the great white whale and all that." I looked over at Willard to see if he was getting any of this, but he was busy following his finger down the laminated menu, probably looking for something that would make good leftovers for the dogs.

"What grade are you in?" I asked.

She laughed again and I studied her very full, kissable lips. "You mean in the affairs of man or school?"

"Both."

She looked up at the greasy ceiling register. "I turned

tricks to earn my way through community college. But that was before Ishmael. I'm clean now, except for a little dope."

So much for John Wayne.

We drove another fifty miles or so after dinner, but I had a splitting headache so I pulled into a rest area and parked as far away from the restrooms as I could get. "That's enough for the first day," I said.

"Suits me."

Willard turned the overhead light on, gave the dogs the rest of his pancakes, and divided a single little pig sausage between them. I retrieved the snow emergency blankets out of the trunk, threw one in the back for Willard, and kept one for myself. They smelled like a combination of welcome mat and motor oil, but they represented heat. Willard tried to make room for his disciples in the back and finally gave up. The coonhound was too heavy to lift over the seat so Willard had to lead her out the back door and into the front one. While he was doing that, the other dogs broke out of the car for more sniffs and pees.

Once everyone was back in, Mrs. Churchill kept putting a paw on my seat, begging to get up, and I quietly pushed it back down so Willard wouldn't know I was being so selfish. I sat up with my back against the door and shared a Hershey with Willard. He had a big sweet tooth, which was one of the reasons he wore dentures, but now that he'd crossed that hurdle the incentive to save his teeth was gone. Occasionally, the headlights of a vehicle entering or leaving the rest area illuminated the upper part of the car, then it was dark again, the freeway a dull hum in the distance. I tried to picture Dad finding my note and wondered whether he'd be sad or relieved I was gone. I'd been nothing but a pain in the butt for him since Mom. He'd think of calling my friends and then discover he didn't know who they were. Couldn't blame him; I had trouble with that list myself. Certainly he'd call Dirk.

Crap, Dirk! I'd forgotten all about the trial. He must have been relieved to find out there was no longer a defendant he had to testify against. He wouldn't have to manufacture the big lie. On the other hand, there was no longer anyone alive who could deny what Dirk had sworn happened between the two of them.

"I used to read bedtime stories to your mother," Willard said out of the blue. "*Huckleberry Finn.*" He sat cross-legged in the middle of the seat, the blanket wrapped around him like an Indian squaw, with a dog on each side. "I loved the trip down the river on the raft. Old Jim would get scared and Huck had to settle him down." Willard chuckled to himself. "*I 'uz hungry, but I warn't afeard, Huck.*"

"Jim was the wise one, you know."

"No, he warn't." Now Willard was even talking like Jim. "He was a slave."

"It's irony, Willard."

"Well, Kitty and me liked 'im anyway." He pulled the blanket up around his ears and I thought he might be mad at me for being so uppity, but then he started talking again in a voice that drifted slow like a wide river. "She promised me we'd go on one them steamboat paddle wheelers . . . float down the Mississippi clear to the Gulf of Mexico." I thought I'd heard all their stories, but this one was new.

I felt a lump in my throat thinking of him and mom together on that steamboat. "How old was she when she promised you this?"

"Couldn't have been any bigger'n a border collie. Tried to get the wife to go, but she didn't like the idea of sleeping someplace she had to share a toilet."

"Maybe you and I can take that trip, Willard."

"Don't pull my chain." It was an expression he must have picked up at one of the construction sites.

"I'm serious."

"What language you speaking?"

"I mean that's where we're going." It came to me just then. There was no other place that made sense. Mom had promised it; I was going to do it. "To the Mississippi River."

He slapped the upholstery and bounced up and down on the seat. "You hear that guys? We're going down the big one!"

We talked about it some more and I tried to recall my grade school geography so I could tell him exactly where we'd be heading. Then I tried to settle him down so we could get some sleep, but he kept breaking into dialect and making wisecracks about whatever came into his head and laughing. I remembered the pills Dr. Miller had given me. Willard was supposed to have one the first night. Now I could see why; he was going manic on me. We didn't have any water in the car so I explained how he had to get it down by making a big goober. Old people were supposed to be skeptical of new ideas, but not Willard. He squeezed out so much saliva that he was drooling like Diller by the time I slipped the pill between his lips.

I was still awake, with my eyes wide open and looking up at the seams in the ceiling upholstery when I heard him snoring. I kept thinking how proud Mom would be at the way I'd taken charge, how I was going to keep Willard out of the nursing home in Mount Vernon, and jail. But for the first time since we'd left, I felt alone and I was scared. I was scared because Willard trusted me and I was afraid I was going to let him down.

19

FOR THE SECOND DAY in a row, I was awakened by the dogs. This time they were barking and the air was heavy with the sourness of their breath. For a moment, I didn't know where I was. My feet were cold where they'd stuck out the end of the blanket and my eyes were crusted over. When I raised up, my shoulder hit something hard that knocked me back down. I felt around, then grabbed what turned out to be the steering wheel. There was a second noise behind the dog noise, a tapping sound, metal against glass. Someone was tapping on the driver's window with a coin. Mrs. Churchill, normally as placid as warm milk, had crawled over to the driver's side of the car and was barking in my ear.

"Shut up, all of you! I hear it."

The windows were glazed with hoarfrost, but I could see the shadow of someone's head next to the glass, with knuckles in the foreground moving in a circle. Whoever it was wanted me to roll the window down. I looked into the backseat; Willard was sound asleep. Through the glaze on the rear window I saw a blue light blinking on top of the car behind us and my heart started racing again, the same gallop it did when Bagmore told me he'd seen Willard running from the fire two nights ago.

As I rolled down the window, I could see a man in a wide-brimmed hat and at first I thought he was Royal Canadian Mounted Police and we'd inadvertently crossed the border, but his name badge said, "W. Rasmussen, Washington State Patrol."

"Good morning." He had a friendly smile, pink in his cheeks, and bright, eager eyes that had already started casing the interior of the car from the moment I cracked the window. Even though it was daylight, he leaned over and shined a flashlight into the frontseat. Mrs. Churchill was wagging her tail now, anxious to make up for the poor first impression she'd made. Paddy stretched his head forward between the window and the headrest, desperate to be recognized. "These yours?"

"His really," I said, pointing over my shoulder, not wanting to use names.

The officer leaned his head in behind mine and shone the light into the back. I could smell baby powder deodorant. He must have just come on shift. "Is he okay?"

I was relieved I'd given Willard the pill. Hopefully, he'd sleep through this little interrogation. "He's a heavy sleeper. A little old, you know." I gave a chuckle, making sure my teeth didn't chatter. This was just like walking into one of those fancy hotels Willard talked about. I just had to act like I belonged here.

The trooper stood up straight and I could see he was on the lanky side, in excellent physical condition, not a wrinkle in his creased pants except for the sitting marks across the lap, which was at eye level. "Let me see your license."

I looked down at the dash. The key was still in the ignition. I wondered if I turned it whether the car would start or sputter the way it had in the garage. *Come on, Piper, you belong here. You belong here as much as he does.* "Actually, he was driving . . . we traded seats . . . he's shorter."

"Give me his then."

This was like one of those mazes in a children's magazine; every pathway led to Officer Rasmussen. I got up on my knees and leaned over the seat. Willard was sleeping with his butt against the back of the seat. Diller licked my wrist as I pulled Willard towards me and dug into his back pocket for the billfold. It was just as likely his wallet would be filled with coins and bottlecaps from one of his treasure hunts as a license. The leather was weathered like he'd left it outside and so worn at the corners that the plastic credit cards stuck through. I flipped open one of the plastic windows to a picture of Mom with her Jackie Kennedy bouffant hairdo, a miniature of the high school graduation picture she'd shown me once from what she called her virginity chest. The rest of the windows, cracked and opaque, contained pictures but no license. The bill compartment was crammed with membership cards from the Humane Society, PAWS, Greenpeace, and Doctors Without

Borders. Finally, I found the driver's license, with Willard's leprechaun likeness sealed beneath the lamination, and pinched it over to Officer Rasmussen's waiting fingers.

"Car registration?"

I flipped the visor down and the clip-on case with the registration fell off and into my lap. *Bingo.*

"Be right back," he said, and I watched his buns recede in the rearview mirror. There wasn't an iota of hula in those tightass, military hips.

He left the door to the patrol car open and I watched him make a call on his radio. If we were going to run for it, this was the time to do it. Instead of using the car, I wondered if we'd have better odds going cross-country, like *The Defiant Ones*, shackled convicts running for their lives through swamps in the deep South. Of course, that would require Willard's cooperation and he was still in a drug-induced coma.

"Willard! Time for breakfast." I practically yelled, "Breakfast!" He shifted position and wrapped his hand around Diller's hind hock like it was an overhead handrail.

We weren't going to be the defiant ones.

It seemed like the longest wait and I wondered if the trooper had called for reinforcements. Maybe they were blockading the freeway. The morning sun had defrosted the windows on the passenger side, which meant that was the direction of the Mississippi River. Hopefully Officer Rasmussen would be satisfied with the documentation and be on his way before Willard woke up. I was still afraid that if Willard as much as saw the uniform he'd spill his guts.

I puffed out the window and my breath rolled into a churning fog. Maybe it was because that's the way I'd last seen her, in a fog, but I thought of Rozene and wondered what she'd think when she found out I'd taken off. Would there be an enormous ache of regret? A tingle? There was already a yawning hunger in me I knew would never be satisfied. I couldn't imagine ever taking the chance again with someone else that I'd taken with her. From here on in I had to reconcile myself to the fact I'd live my life out in the company of misfits like Willard, and if he ever left me I'd sleep with his dogs, and when they were gone, I'd find more strays like Willard had done.

"Overnight camping here is against the law, Ma'am." I hadn't heard him sneak up.

"We weren't camping, sir," I answered out of reflex.

He scratched an "X" with his fingernail into the softening frost on the outside of Willard's window. "Looks to me like you've been here all night."

"Yeah, but . . ." I wanted to explain how we hadn't used the restrooms, how we'd hardly gotten out of the car. Could that be camping?

"This isn't his car," he said, "and the driver's license has expired."

"Maybe he's got a new one in his bag . . ."

"I checked. He hasn't had a valid license in nine years."

"He's forgetful, officer . . ."

"That's not the bad news." Officer Rasmussen had suddenly become pushy, the cherub smile had disappeared. He wanted to run over the top of us with his information. "He's wanted for questioning back home."

How stupid I'd been! I should have at least tried to get away when we had the chance. Against my better judgment, I'd sat there and done whatever Fuhrer Rasmussen asked me to do. I'd gone soft. "He's an old man," I said. "You can't do this to an old man. He's practically senile. How could he break the law if he's senile?"

"Step out of the car, please."

"Nazi," I mumbled.

When I reached for the keys, he thrust his arm through the window and glommed his hand onto my wrist like a manacle. "I wouldn't do that if I were you," he said, as he managed to open the door while pulling me out onto the pavement by the wrist at the same time. The dogs spilled out the door and scattered like somebody had thrown a handful of marbles across the parking lot. "Call 'em back," he said.

"Run, you guys!"

"I don't want 'em to get hurt."

"You're melting me with your compassion, sir." I knew I was blowing any chance for a change of heart, but I couldn't help it. I was pissed at myself for letting Willard get caught.

"You haven't even asked me why they want him for questioning," he said, twisting his grip on my wrist a little tighter. "Why not?"

Mistake number thirty-nine! I'd forgotten to act like we were paid guests in the hotel. "You didn't give me a chance . . . I figured it was routine . . . why *are* you questioning him?"

He smiled that roadside grin he'd probably learned in trooper school. "Say, you're a tall one, aren't you?"

"Doesn't he have a right to know what you want to ask him?" I tried to shake the trooper loose, but he would have none of it and dragged me back to the passenger side of the patrol car. "Isn't there a Constitution? You can't just push innocent people around. We're on a trip. He's my grandpa."

The heat was on full blast in the patrol car, and there was an unmistakable man's smell. Everything was masculine, the upright rifle attached to the grip on the dash, the dented aluminum thermos bottle tossed onto the seat, the two-way radio that buzzed and crackled with cryptic messages. Rasmussen walked around the front, eye balling me all the way, and dropped into the seat behind the steering wheel with his legs spread, one heel on the door sill, and wrote more on his clipboard. I leaned back to see if I could read what he was writing in large block print, but he tilted the board away from me. The dogs sniffed around the picnic tables, looking for the scraps of fried chicken and burgers they could undoubtedly smell even though the crows had long ago picked the area clean. Still there was no sign of Willard stirring and I thought how rich it would be if he'd already awakened, saw the police car, and slithered out the side door on his belly like a snake into the "Pet Area." Judging from the effect they were having on Willard, Dr. Miller must have given us horse pills.

Then the trooper picked the mike up off its hook. "Hey, Steve, this is one-seventy-nine again." He held the mike away from his mouth and waited for a response while staring over to my side like he owned me. There was a subdued hum of the kind you get in between radio stations.

"Yeah, one-seventy-nine, I read you."

Rasmussen held the mike against the corner of his mouth like a fist. "I'm gonna tag the car."

"Roger, trooper."

"Can you also send Animal Control?"

"Oh, no," I broke in, "you're not taking the dogs!"

"Justa minute, Steve." He gestured toward me like the mike was a stone he was going to cuff me upside the head with. "You're interfering with police business, Ma'am. One more outburst and I'm going to arrest you for obstructing justice." He paused. "You got that?"

"I was just suggesting the dogs ride with us." I said it in a very calm, unobstructive voice, quietly enough so that the dispatcher on the other end wouldn't hear me. "Otherwise, the guy you want to question's going to have a heart attack on you. That's all."

Steve spoke up. "You need assistance out there, trooper?"

Rasmussen punched the button down. "Negative. It's just a dame with a loose tongue. Don't insult me."

"Roger. Tow truck and dog catcher on the way."

We were getting farther and farther away from the paddle wheeler; it was more like we were drifting toward Niagara Falls in a barrel. How was I going to explain to Willard what lay ahead? He'd go along with anything but losing the dogs. They'd have to shoot him before he'd let go of them. I didn't know what the worst morning of his life had been, but this was probably going to offer some stiff competition unless I could think of something real fast. I'd heard of women getting out of speeding tickets by flirting with the trooper. There was a policeman from Machias who used to park himself across the street from the high school and pull over coeds who made illegal U-turns on the street in front of the school, until one day a teacher caught him in his patrol car with one, his pants pulled down to his knees. If I wasn't feeling so sexless, I might have been tempted to try something.

The trooper was becoming impatient and asked me to wake up Willard. "We can't question a man who's unconscious," he said.

I whispered in Willard's ear, rocked him, petted the side of his face, but he just readjusted himself and kept on sleeping. The trooper poked him in the ribs and Paddy growled under his breath like he was going to tear a patch out of Rasmussen's ass.

"Sir, I wouldn't do that if I were you."

We went back to the patrol car and I tried to make small talk, asking him where he was born, where he went to college, whether he was married (he didn't have a ring). He said he was Scandinavian and grew up in Ballard, where his parents still lived in a cracker box bungalow walking distance from Market Street. His older brother had gone to law school and would have become a lawyer except that he gave up on the bar exam after three tries and became a shoe salesman at Nordstroms.

"I guess I like the respect the badge gives me," he said. "People give me a wide berth."

"Isn't it a little fruitless writing up speeding tickets? Everyone speeds anyway."

"You said your dad writes a newspaper. Does everyone read it?"

He had me on that one.

Just when I thought I was starting to get somewhere, Willard woke up and stumbled like a zombie from the Skylark back to the patrol car. He was in stocking feet and his hair stood up in spikes on his head like some new age Svengali who disdained material possessions and routine toiletry. The dogs were following him.

"Go easy," I said. "Don't hit him yet with the part about the questions. Let me tell him that."

The dogs were so proud to see Willard awake that they wagged and rubbed against the trooper's legs when he stepped out of the car to greet their leader, even Paddy, who'd almost lost it earlier. "Good morning, Mr. Cooper."

Willard looked over at me, flattered but confused. "Do I know him?"

"I know your granddaughter."

"How 'bout that?" Willard said, relieved. There was a red crease down one cheek where he'd slept on the upholstery cord. Willard squinted into the radiance of the haze the morning sun was trying to burn through. "Nice day, wouldn't you say?"

The trooper agreed we could feed the dogs before we did anything else and so we set their dishes out on the pavement between the cars. When Rasmussen bent down and petted them while they were eating, I could tell he'd already had his heart pickpocketed. There were no speeders in that group. Then he put Willard in the backseat and when the dogs scrambled in around him Rasmussen made a half-hearted effort to get them out, but the dogs just panted like he was speaking a language they'd never encountered.

"See? They're fine," I said.

I was so dejected it made my ribs hurt when I had to take the bags out of the trunk of the Skylark and load them into the patrol car. We hadn't even dirtied our first set of underwear. I hadn't cracked a book or made a single entry in the diary. I'd imagined writing our own version of the *Canterbury Tales* before I ever saw Stampede again.

While the trooper was painting a pink fluorescent number on the back window of the Skylark, I finally had a chance to talk to Willard. "I thought you said the car was yours?"

"Tom made me sign it over."

"You should have told me."

Willard looked away, staring into the frontseat, defeated.

I didn't know why I'd said it so sharply. Dad was the one who'd pirated the car. If it was registered to Willard's son-in-law, wasn't that close enough? How could he steal his own car? The car didn't matter anyway. They had us for sleeping in a no camping zone, driving without a valid license, and suspicion of arson. "I'm sorry, Willard. I shouldn't have pulled over here in the first place. It's my fault. We're still going to the river though." He turned to look at me and a sheepish grin broke out on his face. "They want to ask some questions when we get back there, but just let me do the talking, okay?"

"Back where?"

He still hadn't gotten it. And I hadn't even told him about Animal Control. I was trying to steer a course between truth and Willard's sanity and so far I'd favored sanity. "He wants us to go back to Stampede and start the trip over."

When the trooper came back to the car, Diller was sitting in the driver's seat. The trooper smiled, picked up the pug with one hand under his belly and set him on the passenger side. "Not so fast, partner," he said. Diller licked his hand and looked up at the trooper with those deep forehead furrows that were black in the bottom like someone had dug them in with a burnt stick. Diller's inscrutable stare must have been the straw that broke the camel's back because Rasmussen picked up the mike and called the dispatcher.

"Cancel Animal Control. I'll take care of the dogs."

It was the first good news of the day and, I hoped, an omen of what was to come.

I reminded the trooper we hadn't eaten breakfast and he pulled off the freeway and took us to a McDonald's. To save having to cuff us, he used the drive-thru and I ordered a Sausage McMuffin, orange juice, and coffee. Willard insisted on pancakes again, with extra syrup, and the trooper ordered a large coffee and another Sausage McMuffin to split among the dogs. I tried to pay for Rasmussen's but he insisted on kicking in a couple of bucks. "Regulations," he said. I counted sixty-nine dollars in my billfold, which would have been enough to last us past Montana before I had to wire for the money I'd put in savings from my work at the *Herald* or cash in any of Willard's stock.

Back on the road, Willard dozed off again with his plastic fork floating on the pool of syrup in the Styrofoam plate on his lap. The dogs slept too, leaving just me and Rasmussen, but I'd run out of chitchat. As we climbed the backside of Snoqualmie Pass, my ears plugged and I started to tighten, not just my muscles, but my heart. It was humiliating to be dragged back home after making such a belligerent exit, but that was just vanity. What was about to happen to Willard was life and death. I looked over at his slack jaws and wished Dr. Miller had given me pills to prevent him from admitting to what he'd done. False serums. Then it would be Willard's word against Condon Bagmore and Willard would win hands down in that one. Willard could lie to my dad about the dogs, but I couldn't count on it with a uniformed officer. He was too shot through with traditional values to lie to the police. That was up there with divorcing a woman just because she was a cold fish. You lived with the choices you made, come hell or high water. Pain built character. A man was only as good as his word.

Coming into Stampede, the trooper took the turnoff at Horse Heaven Highway, drove past the airport at Harvey Field, and stopped at the four-way intersection next to the double billboards where Dirk and I had smoked dope and talked sex. My stomach churned, threatening to surrender the McMuffin. I tried to look up Avenue "D" to the high school, but my eyes were bleary with anxiety. We turned on Commercial and drove past the rotten tooth in the block that used to be the *Herald*. The smoke had stopped, but I thought I could still smell the decay of burnt flesh.

The trooper drove into the alley and parked behind the police station, where there was a loading dock not unlike the one where George Pester used to stack the newspaper bundles for delivery, except this dock was for prisoners. Rasmussen cracked the windows, opened the door for Willard and me, and made sure the dogs stayed in the car.

On the way into the police station, I slipped Willard another pill.

"Dr. Miller said you have to take another one."

There was a little booth just inside the back door and a city policeman stepped out and patted us down. He skimmed the obvious places like my waist and hips and avoided the erogenous zones altogether. I didn't recognize the policeman.

"That's all right, Sergeant," Rasmussen said. "I think they just want to ask the old man some questions about the fire."

Willard flinched. *Damn.* We still hadn't worked out a story.

This must not have been the trooper's first visit to the Stampede Police Department because he seemed to know his way around, unless all small town police stations had the same floor plan. He led us down the hallway and I stopped Willard next to the drinking fountain and pointed to the pill in his pocket. While Willard was taking his pill, a plain-clothesman in a tweed sport jacket greeted us.

"If it ain't Bonnie and Clyde," he said, revealing a set of tobacco-stained teeth. This man I knew. He used to pass the collection basket at St. Augustine's and I could remember as a kid how his chin bulged out under his lower lip from the wad he kept down there. The first time I saw him spit a line of juice onto the tulips in front of church I almost puked. He must have been dying for a spit now because he took a sallow hanky out of an inside coat pocket, pressed it against his mouth, and studied me with his baggy eyes. Then he motioned us to go ahead of him and I pinched Willard's sleeve to slow him down. He was being led to slaughter.

Then the plainclothesman stepped between us like a cowpoke cutting a calf from the herd. "End of the line, Highpockets." He stuck his tongue down in front of his teeth and tamped his chew. His tongue was dark when he spoke. "Put her in the other room."

My face got real hot like it was going to burst. Willard turned as if to ask me with his eyes if this was all right, the same way he always did. In the story he remembered, the slave didn't get caught because his resourceful partner knew how to stay one step ahead of the law. Willard was shuffling sideways, still looking back at me. He had that same pitiful look the day Dr. Miller carried Freeway up from the basement and out to the four-wheeler. I didn't have to explain. This corridor was one way.

I expected bars, but my cell, if that's what it was, reminded me of my cubbyhole at the *Herald*, walls without windows. It figured that Stampede wouldn't have the real thing. We'd learned to live with facsimiles: a movie theater that was an aerobics club on weekdays, a mayor who was really the undertaker, and a city father who was a philanderer. There was a single door with a gap at the bottom that allowed me to hear mumbles of conversation out in the office. I wondered if Rasmussen had stuck around and what he'd done with the dogs. Compared to the plainclothesman, he'd turned out to be a prince. I twisted the knob, expecting it to be locked, and it opened, which meant I could escape, but that would leave them alone with Willard.

I kept expecting to see Dad come charging through the door, and dreading it. By now, someone must have told him they'd found us. Although I couldn't remember the detective's name, I knew he knew Dad. Who didn't? Maybe Dad was meeting with the insurance adjusters, or Carlisle's lawyers. Whatever consequence the law had devised for this, I knew it would have an end point when they'd unlock my cell, hand me back my billfold, and tell me to be on my way. Dad's disappointment would last a lifetime.

At five o'clock in the afternoon, they still hadn't bothered to ask about lunch, probably part of their modus operandi to make people talk. I hoped Willard's pill had kicked in. I opened the door and called out. "Can someone come here a minute?"

A new officer showed up, a beefy man with kind eyes. "What do you need?"

"My grandpa's diabetic and I have to give him his shot."

I stuck a hand in my pocket and bulged it out with my finger like that's where I was carrying the needle.

He had to think about it for a while. "You a nurse?"

"No, but I'm the one, you know, I give him shots."

He said he had to ask someone and closed the door. This was like grammar school, where nobody did anything without asking permission. I got down on my knees and held my ear next to the crack under the door, but I couldn't make out what they were saying. Then there were footsteps and the doorknob bumped the side of my head as I was straightening up.

"Sorry," he said. "You can see him they said, but just for the shot."

The policeman led me down a long hall and through a steel doorway that looked like it was controlled electronically. Now we were in the real part of the jail, I thought, where they kept the men, but Willard's wasn't a cell either, at least not one with steel bars. It was some kind of holding room with a nicked-up table that had initials and names penned into the top of it and several straight-back wooden chairs. The plainclothesman was in one of the chairs and Willard was slouched over the table.

"If it isn't Florence Nightingale," the plainclothesman said, not bothering to stand up. "Your grandpa acts like he has dropsy. What's the matter with him?"

"I told you. He needs his shot."

"Well, go ahead and shoot him," he said, erupting in a wheezy laugh that made his plug slip up onto his lip.

"Can we have a little privacy?"

"Is this a blow job or a shot?" he said, laughing again at his own joke.

"Have a little respect. I've got to lower his drawers."

"Shit," he said, pushing himself up out of the chair. "Come on, Wally. Give 'em two minutes." The detective wasn't only crude, he was stupid. What did I know about diabetes? He hadn't even asked to see the needle.

I waited for them to close the door and then turned to Willard, straightening him up by the shoulders. His head bobbed like a floating apple. "What have you told them? Huh?"

His eyelids were heavy and he slurred his words like a common drunk. "I hadda take a pee . . ."

I looked down at his crotch. "You have to take a pee?"

He shook me off. "At the paper." We were running out of time and he was just babbling.

I shook him by the shoulders. "Don't say squat or you're never going to see your dogs again. Do you understand?"

His eyes kept rolling up under his lids like mice hiding from the light. I could only hope my words were sticking in there somewhere in that fractured zone between the subconscious and the unconscious.

20

MY DAD SHOWED UP before a meal did. The beefy policeman who ushered him in belabored the obvious. "There she is, Mr. Scanlon." Dad looked glum and older than when I'd seen him last. There was a bruised darkness under his eyes and his hair was mussed, not just like he'd been running his hands through it, but like he had Vaseline on his fingers. He moved closer and just stood over me for the longest time, his frame shading me with his shame and cooling my insides.

"I'm disappointed in you, Piper." His voice was controlled. "The one thing I thought I could count on was your intelligence, but running away with Willard was just plain stupid." He stopped like he was expecting me to look up at him, but I couldn't give him that satisfaction. He not only wanted me to hear his condemnation but to see it in his weary eyes. I trained my gaze on his oxblood dress shoes, still streaked with ash from walking around the fire. "You know how much I detest duplicity. It's lowdown, it's cowardly, it's wrong. I thought you were tough-minded. A Scanlon doesn't run and hide."

I was warming up fast. I was a furnace and Dad was at the control panel, pushing buttons. "Don't say that, Dad."

"You've done your grandpa no favors. Fleeing has only compounded his problems. Before this one is over, he'll wish we'd *put* him in that nursing home."

I tried counting to myself, I might even have raced through a quick prayer, which in the temper I was in would have constituted blasphemy. I must have been tasting a nip of what Dirk had when his dad stood over him with the video camera, and I wanted to fight back with everything at my disposal. I stood up and faced him. "You've got it all wrong, Dad. Dead wrong. Get your facts straight before you blast away. Willard didn't set that fire." I looked at him when I said it and with every duplicitous nerve in my body, I stabbed him with my eyes. "I did." It was cold-blooded and he must have wondered what kind of a monster he'd raised that I could say this without blubbering and saying I was sorry.

"I don't believe you." That's what he said, but he stumbled back from me like I was the devil incarnate. "The Bagmore kid saw him. You couldn't have . . ."

I grabbed the back of the steel chair and pushed it as hard as I could straight at him. He dodged and the chair clattered to the floor between us. "Why do you say that? You don't even know me. I'm *not* a Scanlon. *That's* the lie." My arms were flailing, searching for more things to fling. "I don't look like you. I don't think like you. I'm a freak in more ways than you'll ever know. I hated John Carlisle for what he did to Mom and I hated him for the monster he made out of you. Burning his newspaper was the smartest thing I've ever done. And I don't care if he *was* in there." I wasn't thinking any more, I was vomiting. A year's worth of bile.

"You don't mean that."

"You don't know what I mean."

"You're covering up. They saw him. There are witnesses."

"If you're so cocksure I couldn't do it, how can you be so cocksure Mom was sleeping with Carlisle?"

"Quit it!"

"I'll tell you one thing. If Willard *had* set that fire, I'd cover him up till hell froze over. Course you wouldn't understand that. . ."

He reached over and put his hands on my shoulders. "Don't say something you'll regret."

I shook him off. "Jesus, Dad! You're worse than I thought. You could use a little coverup. Isn't anyone worth that much to you?"

"What are you talking about?"

"Mom! I'm talking about Mom. You were ready to throw her to the masses. 'There she is folks. My wife was banging the boss!' If that's what you call truth, I'll take the slimiest lie in hell any day."

"You're flipping out. I was exploring the story."

"You were her husband. Isn't there a shred of compassion in you? Were all those pretty poems you recited for us just bullshit? How could you even think of trading her for Carlisle?" I was yelling.

The jailer stuck his head in the door. "Everything all right in here?"

Dad waved him off and waited for the door to close. Then he came over and tried to put his arms around me. As much as I craved his allegiance, I didn't want to be lulled out of this one and I kicked him in the shins. My skinny, breastless, body had never felt stronger, nor a lie more succulent. If I let him hug me, I was afraid I might succumb to his resignation.

His eyes were enlarged and they told what he couldn't admit to. He was scared too. Scared of me. Scared of our whole life. "Stay in here then. Rot with your stupidness."

He turned for the door and for a moment I considered throwing myself around his ankles, reminding him how Mom would have felt to see her father in jail, but I was too afraid he'd boot me away. I'd gone way over the bright line we'd painted between ourselves. It was hopeless. If he was willing to crucify his wife in public, how could I expect him to save a foolish old man and a daughter that wasn't even his?

If he could have just admitted he was on the wrong side, I probably would have melted and burst out with the truth, how Dirk had lied about John Carlisle, how I understood as well as he did the sorry situation Mom had gotten herself into, but as long as he was going to keep his distance, I was going to hold onto the drop of truth I had and hug it like it was the last jug of water on earth. Dad was the one who'd taught me that. Truth was power and as long as I had a molecule of it that he didn't, I still had something to bargain with. Give it up and Willard was dead meat. *I know what I'm doing, Dad. Some things are more important than high-mindedness.*

They moved me to a room with a thin bed that resembled a doctor's examination table. As I lay there, I began to feel panicky and rehearsed in my mind what I was going to say when they questioned me, manufacturing details for my story to make it more credible. Maybe I could get Dirk to back me up. He'd lied about John Carlisle, why wouldn't he lie about me? But nobody read me my rights and nobody arrested me. Why didn't they just bring in a stenographer or a tape recorder and ask me to spill my guts? I was beginning to suspect Dad's hand in this. Maybe he was going to try and protect me even if I was hell bent on getting myself convicted.

On reflection, I decided that my confession, though possibly rash, wasn't foolish. I knew kids at school who'd stolen cars or broken into houses and gotten off with a month for a first offense. Whatever they did to me, there was no way they were going to be as hard on a juvenile as an adult. Besides, I was stronger than Willard and without dependents.

I tried the door knob again. This time it was locked. *Come on, somebody talk to me. Either throw the book at me or let me out of here, but don't just leave me in limbo.*

Maybe because this was beginning to feel like my last night of freedom, I had a powerful urge to pleasure myself. I lay down on the little bed and pulled the sheet up over me. Maybe I just wanted some reassurance that part of me was still functioning properly. I unzipped my jeans and pushed my pants down so I had room to work, to transport myself the way I had so many times, to experience the intimacy from afar I couldn't seem to accomplish up close. My fingers were cold and I rubbed them down the insides of my pantlegs. The fingers had to be warm.

I tried to think of Rozene, her sweetly curved mouth, the patches of tan skin I'd touched on her neck, the insides of her arms, the fleshy part of her calves. But I was dry, flaccid, pathetic. I was sick, maniacal. I was the killer whale who'd ostracized myself from the pod. I thought of the stories I'd read about arsonists who sat across the street from the fires they'd set, masturbating towards the heat. *Well, who was I kidding? I was no better than they were.*

I was still sleeping the next morning when the policeman who'd checked us in brought me a tray with orange juice, cocoa (they said I had to be eighteen to have coffee), and biscuits I recognized as Marge's. She must have had the contract for the jail, not exactly something a person would advertise, but her food had never tasted better.

About eleven-thirty, the same officer opened the door to let Dad in and my nervous system shifted to red alert. I didn't have the strength to go over this again. I had nothing more to say. He was wearing his camel sport jacket, something he often wore to work, and there was a puzzled expression on his face, a mixture of fatigue, relief, and deep concern.

"How was your night?" It was an improvement over the start of yesterday's conversation, but I could tell by the way his eyes were drilling me that he knew something I didn't know. Who didn't?

"Fine. Stiff." The same as my demeanor.

"I know who set the fire." He said it calmly, devoid of any sense of victory, and I decided I should just keep my mouth shut and listen for a change. "I received a letter today from John Carlisle. It's postmarked the day he died." He took a deep breath and crossed his arms over his rib cage like he was trying to provide support for his lungs. "John set the *Herald* on fire. It was self-immolation."

"Oh, God."

"He had to stop the hemorrhaging. It was a matter of honor."

I'd never gotten past the notion Willard had set the fire, so I'd never even entertained the idea it could be John Carlisle. He was the victim, not the perpetrator. But I wondered why, if it was a matter of honor, he hadn't done himself in when Mom died in his Jacuzzi? If it was family reputation at stake, why hadn't he fallen on his sword when Dirk made his accusations? "That means he was guilty of the molesting stuff?" I said.

He shook his head. "I don't know."

"But, Dad, he killed himself. Doesn't that speak for itself?"

"I'm not comfortable judging other people. Not without all the evidence."

"Course that will never happen now, will it?"

"The law doesn't try dead people," he said. "At this point, it's pretty much between him and his creator." His answer seemed like a cop-out.

"Don't the survivors have a right to know the truth?"

"What's truth? Something a newspaper reporter and his editor happen to agree to?"

This was starting to sound a lot unlike the Tom Scanlon who'd been nominated for a Pulitzer prize. "I can't believe you're talking this way. You've always been . . . well, it sounds like you don't care."

"Oh, I care." His facial expression had lost its ambiguity. He was melancholy again, the same melancholy I'd heard in his weeping after the phone call to Seamus that night. He reached into a breast pocket and pulled out an envelope that was ragged on one side where he'd probably opened it hurriedly with his finger. "He talks about your mom too. Here." He offered me the envelope.

I recoiled my hands, unsure if I was ready for John Carlisle's version of the truth. "What does it say?"

"Don't let some newspaper hack put his spin on it. Read it yourself."

Wasn't this what I'd been hungering for since Mom's death, a confession by someone who had nothing to lose, someone who knew that in a matter of hours no meaningful retaliation could be launched against him? Wouldn't the utterances of a dying man be truth? I knew I should take the ragged envelope Dad was holding out to me, but I couldn't lift my arm. If I didn't like what he said, I could never undo his words, never cross-examine him, beat on him, or scream in his face. "Why do you want me to read it? You didn't even want me to see what *you* were writing about Mom."

"Maybe it's because I'm running out of answers."

I let my chin drop to my chest and reached up for the letter. Knowing that the man who had stuffed it and licked it shut was dead made the flesh on my fingers tingle when Dad slipped it into my hand. The return address was for his yellow, turreted Queen Anne on top of the hill, the family home, the last house on earth Mom had walked into. His cursive was delicate, formal, and perfectly even. There was a respectful "Esq." after Dad's name. "I hope I don't regret this," I mumbled as I pulled the pages out of the envelope and unfolded them in my lap. Dad came over to the padded bed and sat down next to me.

Dear Tom,

When you get this letter, I'll be gone, free of this mortal coil as they say. I thought you, of all people, deserved an explanation. I couldn't have asked for a better colleague. You not only brought a professionalism to the paper I could only pretend to, but you were a friend, a man I could count on to stand up to my detractors, of which there were many, I know.

So why am I doing this? I think you know why and if I don't do it everyone else will know too. It's strange. For a person who always prided himself on not giving a whit what everyone else thought of him, I didn't think this would be necessary, but it is. There are some things worse than death and one of them is living in the shame of your own waste because that's what I've let myself become, a wastrel. I've wasted my relationships, of which there were precious few, and I've wasted the family name and the little talent I once possessed. No matter what happened in any trial, I would always be known as the village pervert. So this really isn't an act of self-destruction. It's too late for that.

There is much you could despise me for, including this, but there is one overarching offense I tried but could not forgive myself for. That's, of course, Kathryn. I wasted her too. Never in all the places I traveled or lived have I met someone who so unabashedly celebrated life. She had the ability to suspend her disbelief of the people and things that swirled around her. That's why she was such a marvelous artist and that's why she could befriend me. I would have left Stampede years ago if it weren't for the pleasure of watching her. But rest assured, Tom, it wasn't the way you must have suspected, even though you never accused me. She was faithful to you. That was a given. We both knew I wasn't worth her risking that. For me, sadly, she was cover. If I could attract an angel like her, how could anyone know me for what I really was? I was a fish out of water, but Kathryn quenched me with her kindness and her craziness. Frankly, without her, the value of my life plummeted to rubbish and it's time to just set a match to it.

I wasn't finished, but I had to put it down and wipe my eyes. My hands were trembling and the pressure in my head was building to the point I thought something ugly was going to just gush out. "This is so bleak," I said, looking over at Dad. He must have been reading it again over my shoulder because he was crying. "I'm not sure I'm getting it all." He reached his arm over and rubbed me in the center of my back, and I pushed in against him like a cat leans into someone's pet.

"When truth is buried," he said, "it smolders until it finally explodes."

The day she drowned was the bottom of the abyss. I wasn't even in the tub with her when it happened. I was having a smoke and we were just chatting when she went under to retrieve her wedding ring. It was all so typical of my ineptitude. When I couldn't pull her up, I tried to shut it off, but I didn't know where the switch was. I screamed for my yard boy, but by the time he turned it off it was too late. Before the police came, we put one of my spare bathing suits on her and I swore him to never tell what he'd seen. I paid him not to tell. People didn't need any more ideas than they already had. Of course, their fantasies, which I allowed to exist, were nonsense because I've never had carnal knowledge of a woman.

I stopped again. The words in the letter were like turpentine pouring through a funnel, but the opening in my brain was too small to let it all in at once. I had to let it back up and pass at its own speed. *The yard boy? Did that mean Dirk was there? Mom being wrestled around naked like a piece of sod. He'd never told me any of this. Why hadn't he told me?* I looked over at Dad and he gave me a look that perfectly reflected what I was feeling. Flattened. There was one more page.

About the newspaper, Tom, it's yours. I'm going to use enough gasoline to get rid of me as well as the galleys for tomorrow's print, but the fire department will put it out before much else is damaged. Don't worry, there will be no cans or blow torches to show how this started. It's an old building. They'll assume it was an electrical fire. I've had your name on my life insurance policies since Kathryn's death. You'll have enough to repair the damage, as long as you destroy this letter. They don't pay on suicides.

Unlike me, you have everything to live for — a flair for your trade, normal human appetites, and a precocious but untamed daughter. My watch of her has ended. She's all yours now. Seize the day, as they say. Win a Pulitzer. Remarry and rejoice.

I will be eternally in remorse for the pain I have caused you and Piper.

A friend still, I hope,

John J. Carlisle

I sucked in some air, reordered the pages of the onion skin stationary, and stuck them back into the envelope. My backbone was bent over like a willow shoot and I wanted to collapse onto the jail bed and digest what I'd read. There were voices murmuring at the other end of the hallway and laughter, probably more precinct humor. Odd man out, that part of his letter I had understood. As much as this was the Carlisles' town, it wasn't a town for John Carlisle. So why hadn't he gone back to New York or Paris or San Francisco? Was the territorial imperative so overpowering that someone as miscast as him insisted on staying? Accept me or die?

Dad patted me on the shoulder and I became aware of his presence again. He was giving me the respect of silence, the way he did that Christmas he gave me the Rubik's Cube and let me figure it out on my own.

"Do you believe him?" I said.

"Which part? As far as the Spigot Lake kids are concerned, I'm satisfied from my own investigation it was a case of parental hysteria. But I'm not sure he could have convinced a local jury of that. Not once they'd pegged him as the man he pretended not to be."

"What about him and Mom?"

He winced. "That's harder. I tend to be agnostic in my own affairs."

"He said he'd never known a woman. Why would he go to this much trouble to tell a lie?"

"Pride, shame, anger? I don't know."

"Why can't we just accept it? There's nothing more you can do about it anyway."

We were sitting side by side, staring at the floor. With the edge of his loafer, he was probing the seam where the linoleum buckled up. "I don't know what your mom did with him, but whatever happened I had it coming. I'd confused my job with my life."

"You're being too Catholic, Dad." Somewhere between the day Mom had drowned and me finishing the letter, he and I had traded places. I used to lament the fact he was able to get on with the rest of his life after her death, but once again I'd underestimated the ability of the human heart to harbor pain. "Why can't you just let the newspaper editor in you put a good spin on it?"

"Is that what you're going to do?"

I'd walked into another Tom Scanlon logic trap. He'd told me once that a fair deal was one in which you were willing to sit on either side. *You have to be willing to sell to your partner for the same price you'd buy him out.* If Dad had to accept John Carlisle's word, so did I. "I'm working on it," I said. "Give me a few days. You were his partner for umpteen years. Reading this letter I feel like I've just met him."

"He was dead right about one thing," Dad said.

"What?" I expected him to explain what the letter meant about Carlisle's watch ending.

"You're untamed."

"I hoped you'd say precocious."

He rested his hand on my leg. "I didn't want to give you a big head."

"You're going to destroy the letter, aren't you?"

"What would you do?"

"It seems like he owes you something."

"Nobody owes anybody. We each got what we bargained for."

I'd have to think about that one. In any event, I knew I was determined not to be saddled with the same compulsions of guilt Dad was. He'd dwelled too long on the scriptural side of the culture, while I'd already converted to the skepticism of Joyce's Stephen Dedalus, the fabulous artificer Dad had introduced me to. Dedalus would help me adjust and revise this thing in my own mind until I could live with it.

"Are you ready to get out of jail?"

"Not if it means Willard has to stay in my place."

"Who's being stubborn now? I think you should talk to him yourself." He was still going to let me work the Rubik's Cube on my own. "I gotta go."

"Can you do one thing?"

"What's that?"

"Make sure the dogs are okay."

"I've taken care of the dogs." The way he said it, so abruptly, made me think he'd called the pound.

"They take a cup of dry each with some wet mixed in."

He waved me off. "I used to have a dog."

"I didn't know that."

"There's lots you don't know."

I wondered if I should apologize for what I'd said last night. I'd obviously been guilty of the same thing I'd accused him of, making Mom Carlisle's lover. The only difference was he was willing to be honest about it and I was going to deny it to my grave. Maybe it was my peculiar vantage point, but I believed what Carlisle had said about him and Mom. Carlisle had proven Dad and me both infidels. There was something, however, I had to say. I made sure our eyes met. "I'm sorry about what happened to John Carlisle."

He didn't say anything, and I realized it wasn't clear whether I was talking about Carlisle's life or his death, but it didn't matter because I knew Dad was suffering for both.

They gave Willard a lie detector test, which he passed, and released him, but I was still skeptical. I'd seen him walk through land mines of exploding truths and emerge unscathed.

He came by in the early afternoon, at Dad's request, wearing his fluorescent orange construction bib with yellow Velcro straps, seemingly oblivious to the fact that he'd just been here a few hours ago. "Say, these are nice rooms," he said. "Plenty of privacy."

He admitted he was at the paper that night, in the breezeway where the gas pump for the delivery truck was located. "I always go in there if I have to go to the bathroom."

"You go in there to pee?"

"It's family property."

"No, it's not. Dad just works there."

"I thought he owned it." He stuck his thumbs inside his vest. "Paddy was with me. He'll back me up."

"What did the police say to your story?"

"They said I'm gonna have to find a new place to pee." He laughed his wheezy laugh. "Course they never asked me about my cigar."

"What cigar?"

"Set it down, took a leak, then I couldn't find it."

"You set your cigar down by the gas pump?"

"Couldn't stick it in my pocket. Then someone came out of the paper and Paddy and I high-tailed it outta there."

That someone had to have been Carlisle coming outside to fill his can with gasoline. Maybe Willard thought he *had* set the fire. Of course, if he had it would have been an accident, a careless old man's accident instead of the gruesome, premeditated finale that John Carlisle had insisted on.

Somewhere in this there was logic, maybe justice, something I should understand.

21

ON THE FIRST SATURDAY in May, Willard and I took the dogs on a hike out to Harvey Field to watch the Stampede Air Show. It was supposed to include Nick Oster doing stunts in his crop duster, and a landing by a replica of the *Gossamer Albatross*, the human-powered craft that crossed the English Channel.

"Who's peddling it?" Willard wanted to know.

"Icarus," I said, and he jerked his head around, throwing me a distrustful look. "You know, the guy who flew too close to the sun."

"Never heard of him," he said, straight-faced.

Willard wore his brakeman's cap to keep the sun out of his eyes and a pair of mechanic's coveralls. This time he looked like he really was stepping off to Bonnie Holliday's to work on her Studebaker. His gait, short abbreviated steps not always going in the same direction, reminded me of Charlie Chaplin. I carried a day pack full of tuna sandwiches, carrot sticks, and enough plastic bottles of water for us as well as the dogs. It was a perfect day for flying upside down and doing the loop: blue sky padded with gauzy clouds.

By the time we passed under the Carlisle Bridge, the sweat between my shoulder blades where the pack rested had made a washcloth out of my T-shirt and we stopped in the shade to give the dogs their first drink of water. I'd forgotten to bring a dish, so Willard cupped his hands and I poured water into them as the dogs fought like kindergartners at a fountain to get their turn. "The hand is still the best tool ever made," he said. The only dog to act like a gentleman was Paddy and I petted him on the head to assure him we'd break open a fire hydrant if we ran out.

It turned out Dad had known about Willard's dogs all the time, which made me wonder what else he knew. "I got suspicious," he said, "every time Willard came by the paper courting a different dog." When I asked him why he didn't say something, he said, "I thought the secrecy would give you a reason to keep an eye on him."

The heat rising in the distance off Highway Nine turned the asphalt into a shimmering stream. We walked on the shoulder and Willard tried to get the dogs to stay alongside us in the ditch. "This is where we need Freeway," he said, one of the few times he'd mentioned Freeway since the day we buried him in the backyard. Maybe the fact he could mention him out loud meant he was getting over it.

In the galaxy of town events, the Air Show was right up there with the Antique Car Festival. Cars whizzed by us on the highway. Spectators were also arriving by air because I could see single engine planes circling Harvey Field like buzzards, then swooping down and disappearing.

"It ain't a paddle wheeler," Willard said, pausing to catch his breath, "but isn't this going to be dandy?"

Our hike reminded me of the times I used to traipse through meadows next to the river with Mom, when we took off our shoes and skipped across the flower fields, letting stalks of heather, dogwood, and Indian paintbrushes weary our legs until we toppled over and lay there on our backs giggling, sucking in the sugary scent of the petals. Today, instead of the buzz of grasshoppers, we had the drone of airplanes. Instead of watching Mom replicate the landscape of an Alpine lake, we were going to watch someone replicate the flight of a bird against the skyscape. And instead of Mom, I had her father, but they both had that same childlike sense of awe that made them Coopers. Willard and I had never talked about the fact I was adopted and I wondered if he might have actually forgotten it somewhere along the way. I couldn't bring myself to say anything for fear it would break the bond between us.

When Father Tombari, the pastor at St. Augustine's, stopped to offer us a ride, I thought at least there would be someone to administer last rites if Nick Oster missed a loop. Willard came up to the car, pressed his face against the window glass, and stared into the backseat.

"Is that you, Bonnie Holliday?"

"Willard, come on." I tugged at his sleeve. Maybe he'd dehydrated from the heat.

There was a whir as the rear window lowered and a woman in an Easter bonnet with plump, rosy cheeks leaned across the lap of the other passenger in the back and stuck her head out. She clutched a charcoal kitten against the cleavage of her ample breasts. "I'm Edda, Bonnie's little sister."

Willard just stood there limp, confounded, staring back at this apparent bubbling likeness of his old flame. The dogs gathered around the car, eyeing the kitten who'd spread her claws like crow's feet against Edda's flowery pink sundress. Edda filled the frame of the window as she leaned out, the upside-down kitten clinging frantically to avoid the pack of dogs below her. Then Edda wrapped one arm around Willard's neck, drew him to her bosom and planted a wet kiss on him.

"I remember you," she said. "You're the little fixer."

Over Willard's protest, I turned down the ride, but when Father Tombari maneuvered his car back into the driving lane Edda's head was still sticking out the rear window, blowing kisses back at him.

"Why'd you tell 'em no?"

"We couldn't put the dogs in there with the cat."

"She looks just like Bonnie."

"She's with the pastor. That means she's probably Catholic."

There was a pair of scarlet lips tattooed to his forehead. "I can be Catholic."

We resumed our trek, with the dogs working the ditches for jackrabbits. There was a controversy swirling in Cascade County over their burgeoning numbers. The farmers said they were destroying the seed crops, threatening their economic survival. On the other hand, groups like Doctors Without Borders, of whom Payton Miller and Willard Cooper were the only local members, opposed the slaughtering of the rabbits.

"It's too much like what we did to the Indians," Willard said.

I wasn't really surprised when Dad turned John Carlisle's letter over to the insurance company. But there wasn't going to be any newspaper story.

"Where's the news in what your mother and John Carlisle did with their afternoons? They were private citizens." I had assumed his investigative records were consumed by the fire, but it turned out he had all of it on a disk at home. I should have known he'd have a backup. "There was no third-party corroboration anyway," he said. This last statement I suspected was for his own benefit, to cast doubt on what might have happened, to make it easier for him to manipulate the whole thing around in his stomach to a more digestible state. Of course, Dad's honesty in turning over Carlisle's letter also robbed him of the money to rebuild the newspaper.

"What about the promises you made to the employees?" I asked him.

"I'm sick about it."

"You should have taken the money."

He just looked at me, disappointed at what little I'd learned.

I was sitting out on the front lawn with Willard and the dogs counting grass blades when a glossy white BMW with a personalized license plate that said "TRUT" pulled up in front of our house. A soft-bellied man in a pair of cords and scuffed Rockports stepped out, extended his arm toward the hood of his car, and zapped the alarm on. He looked at me and Willard like we were part of the Crips, waiting until he turned his back to hotwire his car.

"Is this the Scanlon residence?" Dad was home, so we just pointed him toward the door and went on about our business.

After a while, Dad called me inside and as soon as I walked into the living room I could smell the lemon in the hot tea he'd fixed for them. The man in Rockports was squatting on the green bean bag chair with papers spread out on the coffee table in front of him. This man who'd pretty much ignored me on the lawn struggled to extricate himself from the bean bag, stood, and shook my hand, all the time studying me up and down. *Go ahead and say it,* I thought, *you sure are a long drink of water.*

"Piper, this is Richard Millstone from Seattle." Stampede people always mentioned the fact that someone was from Seattle, as if it was an institution of higher learning. "He's the attorney for the Carlisle estate." Based upon his dress, I wouldn't have guessed he was an attorney, but as I noticed how the skin under his eyes had greyed and crabbed it was obvious he'd read a lot of fine print. I must have been introduced in my absence because I noticed that Dad didn't bother to say who I was.

We sat down and I could feel the dampness from the grass on the butt of my pants. Dad asked him if he wanted more hot water, which he politely refused. "What about you, Piper?" Mainly because I didn't want Dad to go out of the room and leave me alone with him, I also declined. "Richard, why don't you go ahead and explain the terms of the bequest?"

He cleared his throat and scooted forward on the chair, the beans rustling under him. "Ahem, yes. Mr. Carlisle bequeathed his house to your mother." I couldn't help but gulp. Frankly, despite whatever good intentions John Carlisle might have had, I was getting a little tired of all these niceties between him and Mom. Every one of them made it harder to accept the truth of what he'd said in his letter. I would have been just as happy if I didn't have to deal with another Carlisle legacy. "In the event your mother predeceases him, the Will provides that the house goes to you." He held out his hand to congratulate me.

"Me? I don't want his house." I wasn't even sure I wanted to live in Stampede.

"Well, the law says it's yours." He looked over at Dad. "I think she'll change her mind when she thinks about it."

"I wouldn't count on it," he said.

"Why doesn't it go to Willard?" I said. "He's her father."

The beans rustled again as he smiled politely and ignored my question. "It will take several months before I can close the estate and make distribution. By that time, you'll be eighteen and I can deed the place over to you directly rather than set up a guardianship." As he blathered on about the responsibilities of ownership, I decided Millstone was an apt title for what this man did for a living.

"Richard, can you excuse us for a minute?" Dad said, snapping me out of my stupor.

I watched the attorney stand, hitch up his cords, and pad out to the kitchen. When I looked back at Dad, he was tugging on his hair the way he did at work when he had a difficult story. "What's the matter?" I said.

"There's more."

I shrugged my shoulders, playing dumb, not wanting there to be anything more to anything. From upside down, I could read the title of the document in the blue folder Dad was picking up: "*THE LAST WILL AND TESTAMENT OF JOHN J. CARLISLE.*" What more could there be?

"I wish Kathryn were here. I never imagined it would be me telling you this."

"What?"

He turned to the first page of text and all I could make out was the word "*PREAMBLE.*" He spoke slowly. "The house wasn't meant as something to placate you. You're entitled to it, if not more." He wiped his eye with the back of one hand. "Let me read what it says." He traced his finger down the page. "*I declare that I am unmarried and have no children, living or deceased. I have one sister, Ashley Marie Carlisle, who is presumed deceased, and one niece, my sister's daughter, Piper Scanlon, who was given over at birth for adoption.*"

It was like Mom had died all over again. "Why didn't someone tell me?"

I could feel the wrap of his arms, trying to rock me. "Kathryn and John thought it would mark you."

"What do you mean, mark me?"

"Make you feel illegitimate. Bind you to Ashley's fate.

Look, Kathryn raised you from infancy. She did everything but nurse you. This doesn't take any of that away."

I felt woozy. I reached over to the table and picked up the blue folder. Through the blur, I tried to read the words myself, to see if there wasn't a footnote to cast doubt on what Dad had read. I'd spent my life disparaging the Carlisles and now this document told me I was one. It was as if I were a slave who'd been traded. My new keepers were the Carlisles, and the boozy recluse who'd raised John Carlisle and banished Ashley to the attic was my grandmother. But there was going to be no family reunion because, at the moment of being bound over, all known Carlisles in the world were either dead or presumed to be.

The prospect of my own death began to haunt me, and I didn't want to leave behind booby traps to maim the survivors. The first thing that had to go was the diary, which was chock full of rantings written in the heat of the moment, indictments of Dad, pathetic spewings about Rozene. I took the diaries with me early to school one day and snuck into the furnace room to burn them, but it was Spring and the furnace had been shut down, so I borrowed a pair of scissors from the office, took the diaries into the girl's can, cut the pages into strips, and flushed them down the toilet, discarding the covers into the waste bin. I missed first period.

I also had a dream one night where Willard and I were walking to the Air Show and a jackrabbit popped up on the opposite side of the road. Paddy made a reckless dash for it and a car sent him tumbling like a gunnysack of potatoes across the pavement. Then Willard ran after Paddy and a hollow thud sent Willard airborne until he landed facedown in the shoulder gravel at my feet. I bent over him but the only movement that registered was my own trembling and the dust particles floating around us in a cloud like we'd already passed into the next world. Dog muzzles pushed in around us, trying to see his eyes. The eyes would tell us what we had to know. One arm was caught under his belly and his stubby legs were askew. I could hear the exhaust of an idling car and voices gasping above me, but I couldn't take my eyes off the little man in the dirty coveralls. I straightened his legs, and when I slid my hands under his head and rotated it, I almost retched. His face was a piece of raw steak that had mopped up the shoulder gravel. I stretched out on the ground, the length of my body touching his, whispering, begging him to live. I petted down the quills of gray hair standing out from his head, fingering the hole in the shoulder of his coveralls. As they were closing the door to the ambulance, a woman in short pants and thongs handed me a crumpled brakeman's cap and a dusty set of dentures. They took us to the same emergency room where they'd taken Mom, with the same result. Willard Cooper, my would-be grandfather and sidekick, died on the operating table before the *Gossamer Albatross* ever landed. As if it offered comfort, the doctor said if he'd survived he wouldn't have been capable of coherent speech and his cognitive capabilities would have been severely impaired anyway, which was really no consolation at all because Willard's best parts were non-verbal, always had been. That's why he got along so well with four-footed creatures.

While I was looking through my closet for other time bombs, I came across Dirk's poster behind a pile of outgrown clothes. I unfurled it, and there was Dirk in all his glory in the boy's head. Even though he'd returned to school after John Carlisle died, it wasn't the same between us. I finally told him how I felt about Rozene, and he was mad at first, then just confused, which made two of us. I didn't have a job so there was time for Dirk and me to hang out, but we didn't, partly because he had to stay after for tutoring, and partly, I thought, because of all the omissions that had become lies between us. I decided to return the poster as an excuse to talk. I was feeling about as old as the house I'd inherited, certainly too old to climb the double billboard, so I asked him to meet me by the swings at Klah Hah Ya Park. Besides, the billboards represented a kind of intimacy I wasn't feeling toward Dirk just then.

I cut across the dewy grass and stuck the poster through the buckle connecting the swingseat to its chain and took the swing next to it, one of those strap seats. The moon was so bright I could see my shadow in the sand as I pushed gently back and forth. I wanted this to be a reconciliation meeting to bridge over everything that had happened. In truth, Dirk was still the only friend I had. I hoped the fact I was bringing back the poster would be a reminder of how I'd tried at least once to stick up for him.

He was wearing a pair of baggy jeans with a low crotch that came down almost as far as his knees, and he was clean-shaven with energy in his face like he'd had a makeover. But we were two Dobermans on leashes meeting for the first time. When I gave him the poster, he snarled. "Bet you and Rozene enjoyed studying this."

"Don't flatter yourself. I forgot I even had it."

"What took so long to give it back then?"

"What took you so long to tell me you were at Carlisle's that day?" I planted my feet in the trough and twisted my swingseat to face him. "Huh, why didn't you say something?"

He tried to scratch his crotch, but there was so much material in the way he had to settle for grabbing a handful of jeans and tugging it up and down. "You're hardly in a place to talk about honesty. Who told you?"

"None of your business."

"Jesus, you didn't want her found naked, did you?"

"She was dead. How bad could naked be?"

He flung his swing clanking against the poles. "Don't you understand? I was the one who shut the damned thing off. It took me so long I thought I'd screwed up." He grabbed my chains and shook them as he shouted at me. "I was embarrassed for her. And for you!"

I reached up and put my hand on his fist, which was as cold as the cast steel chain it was clenched around. It occurred to me his hiding what had happened to Mom was no different than me ripping the poster off the blackboard. We were trying to protect each other from the ridicule and the pain, but we'd both failed. The pain had found its own seams to seep through. "I'm sorry to jump on you, Dirk. I probably would have done the same thing."

He kicked some sand. "I'm so fucked up I couldn't blame you for hating me. How many people have a friend who's killed someone?"

"You didn't kill him."

"I'm not stupid. It was the day before the trial. I was going to lie my face off about him. I know something about shame and he had a lot farther to fall than I ever did."

This business of protecting someone else's privacy was getting complicated, and as I looked at the tears in his eyes I could see that Dirk had aged too. He was no longer just the kid who loved Cagney and Bogart flicks. He'd made an investment in my life and he'd paid big-time for it. "It wasn't *your* charges that made him do it."

"Bullshit."

"Carlisle wrote a letter to my dad. Mailed it the day of the fire." Dirk licked the depression under his nose. "It was suicide, but it was because of new charges against him, not yours. Dad had already written up the story. They said he molested some kids at Lake Spigot."

"Jesus, do you think he really did?"

I let my hands slide down the chain links that might have been worn smooth by the same kids John Carlisle was accused of molesting. "I don't think so. Dad says it was hysteria, people piling on."

He spun my swing seat around. "All that dough and he ends up this way."

Neither one of us spoke and Dirk continued to play with my swing chains. It felt good to be flopped around aimlessly. I was usually so hysterical if I wasn't in control. I knew this would have been a good time to tell him I was a Carlisle too, but I wasn't ready to go that far, not until I could say it without bitterness, not until I could see it the way Mom must have seen it.

Deliveries started arriving on our doorstep — boxes of chocolate samplers, smoked salmon, salami and cheese displays, soup bones and dog biscuits — some with perfumed letters, all from Edda Holliday. Some nights, Willard asked me to look after the dogs.

"Give 'em their walk and feed 'em breakfast."

"Breakfast?"

"You know. In case I get tied up."

Each time he'd go calling, he'd shave with his straight edge, buff up his shoes, and wear matching socks. His diet even changed. I caught him eating leafy salads and cottage cheese on canned pears with paprika sprinkled on top. She came by and took him to church on Sundays, alternating between St. Augustine's, St. John's Episcopal, and Zion Lutheran. She gave him reading assignments, juicy romances with bodice-ripping pictures on the jackets.

"You've got to help me, Piper. I can't keep up." He was both frightened and giddy.

"This is trash."

I read *In the Grip of the Night*, *Amber Love*, and *Lullaby of the Heart*, and gave him book reports in sufficient detail so that he could fake a conversation with her. In truth, they were page-turners and I began to wonder if the critics hadn't overrated the classics. But I worried how Willard was ever going to satisfy a woman with such inflamed expectations.

On the fourth of July weekend, Willard moved in with her. It wasn't the Holliday he'd had the crush on since putting a hose in her parents' car at the Phillips 66 station. That would have been Bonnie, who was Willard's age and now deceased. But Willard didn't seem to mind the switch and I knew he was going to have his hands full keeping up with a woman seven years his junior. The secret ingredient was going to be their dependents. It turned out that while Willard was vacuuming up the stray dogs in Stampede, Edda was doing the cats. She was also pro-life and refused to have them spayed, which had proven to be a dangerous combination because she now had twenty-six of them.

The courtship was rapid. Edda, who'd been widowed twice, once by an overturned combine and then by prostate cancer, knew what she liked and disliked. Willard's tastes, on the other hand, had been sanded smooth by Grandma Carol's unrelenting strictness. As long as he could have his dogs though, Willard could have fallen in love with just about anyone who wouldn't ignore him. The day he told me she'd asked him to move in with her I was washing the mud off his basement windows where the drips from the eaves splattered.

"She's got pillows for the cats on her bookshelves," he said. "And the spare beds are swarming with 'em."

"You can't just shack up with someone, Willard." It was hard to admit the real reason for my reticence, especially after all the fuss I'd made about him coming to stay with us in the first place. "The cats'll scratch the dogs' eyes out."

"She wants to set up a half-way house for strays."

Half-way to what, I thought, as I swished the squeegee around in the mop bucket, stirring up the ammonia fumes until my eyes watered. For a dog, living with Willard would already be heaven. "She sounds like your kind of woman." I looked up and his eyes were watering too.

"I don't want to move away."

That's what I wanted him to say, but I knew it was wrong to hold him back. Reagan was still President the last time he'd slept with a woman and that was Grandma Carol, who'd made him choose between her and the animals. "I don't want you to move either."

"I can't sponge off you and Tom forever."

I wished I had the words to explain how far from *sponge* he really was. For as long as he'd been here, he'd left far more than he'd ever taken. "Tell me one thing, Willard. Do you love her?"

"Like a found dog."

"Then you have to do it."

22

IT WAS HARD TO let go of Willard, mainly because I didn't want to. Father Tombari came by the house to see Dad, who was gone, so he talked to me and the subject got onto Willard.

"I didn't realize how much I'd gotten used to him being here," I told Father.

"You're going through a kind of grieving process."

I only half paid attention as he ran through the seven stages or whatever. It was difficult to trust anything he said about the subject, given that his first question had been whether or not Willard and Edda were living in a state of sin. As if Willard were some covetous Beelzebub. Anyone who knew him knew a man who always found room on the path for fellow travelers, who always had enough in his lunch box to split with whomever he sat. The pittance of sin Willard had to confess would make the priest blush. God would scold the priest and let Willard pass.

The truth was Willard had become a presence in me. When I looked in his room, I could hear him conversing with his dogs as if they were chums from his old unit. When I scrambled an egg, I could smell the grease from his Spam burning. Every time I passed under the Carlisle Bridge, I could look up and see him in one of his dumb hats with a cheap cigar clenched in his teeth, aiming a pebble at my noggin just for a joke.

Rozene came by one afternoon in her brown Toyota. I was out front weeding the flower beds for the first time since Mom had done it the summer before. We sat on the front porch steps and I stared out at the empty passenger seat that used to be mine. I almost wished she'd been with a guy, so I wouldn't have to think it was just me.

A column of sunshine bathed her like a waterfall, and I realized once again what a special class of beauty she was in, the kind that made you feel like a mechanic in coveralls when you were next to her. More than her beauty though, I admired her sense of who she was. Unlike me, she didn't obsess about her isolation. In the ten years she'd been in Stampede, she'd never let anyone blow her off course with their cold shoulders and their taunts.

"That's nice about Edda and your grandpa," she said.

"I miss having him here."

"Anything I can do?"

For a moment I let my mind run wild with the possibilities, but I knew begging wasn't becoming. "Thanks for asking."

"Piper, I'm sorry for giving you the ditch like that."

I harrumphed like no big deal from my side.

"I don't have your guts," she said. "When things get sticky, I revert to type."

"I don't believe that for a second."

She put her hand on the dirty knee of my jeans. "Give me time to get past myself, okay?"

And then she left.

Unknowingly, Dirk had probably given me the best advice on how to deal with Rozene when he came by a few days later on his way to California. A cousin on his mom's side knew a stuntman who'd promised him a grunt job with one of the movie studios.

"I gotta make something of myself first," he said. "Then the dames'll fall all over me."

"What's your dad say about you going down there?"

He shifted his weight from one foot to the other. "He wanted me to enlist in the Army, just to make sure it's all out of me."

"If that's his problem, why would he throw you in with a bunch of guys?" It was a chance for Dirk to pile on, but he just chuckled, which made my remark seem vindictive and uncalled for. "Hey, are you still moving?"

"They are." Dirk moved his mouth around like he was adjusting an imaginary toothpick between his lips. "'Fraid I'm gonna miss roll call that day."

"Don't forget who your main woman is."

He raised his arms like he was going to wrap them around me, but then he just patted me on the outsides of my arms, and I wondered if it was because he'd remembered. "Don't worry," he said. "I'll be back. Riding into town in a black Cadillac."

"Look at you," Willard said, when Edda dropped him and a couple of the dogs off for a visit while she went to the beauty parlor. "You're moping." He'd caught me curled up on the couch reading. If he'd come forty-five minutes earlier, he'd have seen me painting the back porch. For some reason, I was getting into home improvements lately, little chores that didn't talk back or let you down.

"There's nobody to do anything with."

"Darn you, girl. What about your dad?" Willard was wearing a powder blue dress shirt with a starched collar and a brown vest with an adjustable waist tab, Edda's work. "You bellyached he worked too much at the paper and now he's home."

"I think he's still sore about me running away and lying to him."

"Pooh. What's that between a girl and her dad?"

"We don't have that much in common."

"What's wrong with pretending? He says bowling, you say when." The romance with Edda had turned Willard into a matchmaker. He wanted everyone to be hopelessly in love.

"Would you come with us?"

He straightened himself up, tucked in his shirt, and stuck his thumbs into his vest while he thought it over. "Well . . . sure, maybe. Edda. I'd have to check with Edda." Then a light went on inside that bobbing head of his. "Say, didn't we have a deal? What about that trip to the Mississippi?"

"I thought you'd forgotten."

"Maybe I had and maybe I hadn't, but I want to cash in. Under one condition."

"Edda goes?"

"No. Your dad."

"You're crazy. He'd never do that."

"Ask him."

The idea grew on me. I checked into the train, thinking that's how Willard and Mom might have done it if they'd taken the trip when she was young. Flying would have been too pretentious and, besides, how could you count telephone poles and spot license plates from thirty-thousand feet? Willard was a hands-on kind of man, someone who had to step out and stretch his legs on solid ground once in a while. No pre-heated dinners from stacks of aluminum trays with cold silverware packaged in plastic. But Amtrak didn't go through Hannibal. I thought of hitchhiking, and kept imagining being picked up by goons from Hood River or Pocatello with tomahawk haircuts, rifle racks across the back windows of their pickups, and the inside door handles removed. Condon Bagmores gone bad.

When I broached the idea with Dad, I made it sound as if Willard and I were already going, and it was just a matter of adding a third.

"What about that summer job you were going to get for your college money?" he said. So far, college wasn't a big issue with me and I'd missed all the deadlines for applications. Like Dirk had said, "In college, they teach you the theories. Why be satisfied with theories?"

"No Tom, no trip," Willard said, when I told him about the cold water Dad had poured on the idea. The trip was down for the count. Kaput. I went back to summer and my home improvements, waiting for Rozene to get past herself.

Then one night while I was writing a letter to Dirk I hoped I'd send, telling him the truth about my adoption, Dad interrupted me with a knock on the door. I turned the tablet over and covered it with a book before inviting him in.

"I've been thinking over what you said the other day about that trip," he said. He was in his stocking feet, his hair was mussed, and he seemed rootless. There wasn't that divided look on his face of needing to be someplace else. He shuffled one hand in and out of his pocket like he was going to show me something but his hand came up empty. "Is there still room?"

"What about your job search?" Dad had been circling items in the classifieds from the newspapers that were still being delivered to our house from all over the country.

"Before I go to work for someone else, I need to retool. I'm stale."

"What are you talking about? You could write a story with the dirt under your fingernails."

Dad wasn't one to let accolades be mumbled over him. "You haven't answered my question. Can I come?"

This was a nice twist. I had something he wanted and he was asking for it rather than presuming he could have it. "It wouldn't be any picnic," I said. "We'd have to do it Willard's way, you know. In the Skylark. Making bologna sandwiches in our laps on the fly, staying at places that'll take dogs. I'm talking low down on the food chain."

"Sounds like rich material."

"Oh, no," I said. "You can't do this as an assignment."

He ruffled his hand through his hair and his eyes brightened, as if this kind of hand-to-mouth existence was just what he'd been seeking. "For a budding socialist, you're sure a taskmaster," he said. "I promise, cross my heart, I won't talk shop. I won't even take my laptop. Unless there's room."

I wasn't sure if he was serious or joking, until he laughed that warm Irish Tom Scanlon laugh that was as much chagrin as grin.

Dad made a last minute plea to rent a Winnebago, but desperately needing to finish something I'd started I said it had to be the Skylark. At Willard's urging, I did agree to a full lube and tune up, and I made one more concession. I stood for the Washington State driver's license exam and passed, despite hitting the windshield wiper instead of the turn signal for a lane change on the way back to the licensing office. Willard declined Dad's suggestion that he renew his license.

"I'll goof up drivin' and Tom'll yell at me," he said. "Besides, this trip's for you and your dad. Me and the dogs are just baggage."

We picked up Willard at Edda's place, a little farmhouse just outside of town surrounded by a picket fence, with moss on the shakes, a porch roof that swayed like the back of a workhorse, and hanging baskets full of geraniums and black-eyed Susans. The cats were perched on railings and window sills, watching the dogs bound off the porch and run circles around Willard and Edda as they walked arm-in-arm toward the car. Instead of the broken suitcase held together with bungee cord, Edda had lent Willard a soft navy blue Pullman case with leather trim. When they embraced at the gate, Willard seemed slight next to Edda, but he closed his eyes hard and finished with a grab of her behind.

"You all take care of my Willard now," she giggled as I shooed him and the dogs into the backseat.

Once we were on the road, things became a little tense when Willard asked to stop at the first three rest areas.

"Again?" Dad said, looking at his watch, and I thought Willard must be regretting his insistence on Dad coming along.

"It's for the dogs," Willard said, but I noticed that each time they reached the pet area, he unzipped and peed right next to them.

"Willard, how is it you could keep those dogs in the basement for a year without me seeing you and now you have to run them in and out of the car like a hockey squad?"

Willard couldn't see the smile on Dad's face. "Sorry 'bout that, Tom. We'll reorganize back here."

There was always at least one rear window cracked open and the dogs took turns sticking their noses out. The noise from the wind had the effect of cutting the frontseat off from the back. Dad and I could converse fairly normally, but we had to yell to be heard by Willard. When we passed an exit sign for a rest area, Dad automatically put on his blinker and looked into the back..

Each time, Willard waved us on with a zip of his lip. I leaned over and looked behind the seat to see if they were peeing into a milkshake carton. Willard had a smug look on his face. He and Dad were in a duel.

Finally, at the La Grande exit, Dad blinked. "Okay, Willard. Uncle! I'm going to burst if we don't pull off."

Willard whistled through his teeth and everyone laughed.

By the time we reached Boise, I figured Dad and I had spent about as much time one-on-one as we had the whole previous year, and we were running out of things to say. I was grateful, therefore, when we slipped into a rhythm of next driver sleeping. It was especially hard to talk about anything important in the broad daylight, strapped next to each other in the frontseat like a cosmonaut and an astronaut who'd rendezvoused in orbit, neither speaking the other's language except for basic survival phrases.

Each night we found a battered motel, usually with buzzing neon signs that said "Hot water" and "Color TV." Anything qualified as long as they took dogs. The place south of Provo, called the Motel Utah, consisted of twelve dilapidated white cottages in green trim, set in a U-shape around what used to be a swimming pool but was now a children's play area half full of garden bark and cluttered with rusty sand buckets, one-pedaled tricycles, and candy wrappers. Instead of packaged soap bars in our room, there were slivers and ovals in greens, golds, and ivory that had been used by previous guests. The hot water warmer for coffee had a chunk of plastic missing at the base that exposed the coils. The toilet paper ran down to the cardboard on my first pull and I had to use a piece of newspaper from the wastebasket.

After we washed our plates and cups in the sink, Dad and Willard poured themselves a glass of Chablis from the jug we were carrying and things loosened up. Dad proposed a slam poetry contest, where each of us had five minutes to write a poem and recite it out loud. My nutty ideas fell onto the paper like acorns, randomly and with long pauses in between. By the time I was done, there were more words crossed out than not, and I figured it didn't really matter which ones I read because random selection would probably improve it. Dad's poem was flowing and melodic.

"I plagiarized Yeats," he confessed.

Willard's, which he didn't bother to write down, we called doggerel:

> A prince of toads named Willard
> Fell head over heels for Edda.
> The dogs ate the cats,
> And the cow jumped over the moon.

"Bravo, Willard," Dad said, clapping for him. "There's no such thing as a bad poem."

By the fourth day, Dad and Willard seemed to be warming up to each other. I attributed it to the state patrol pulling Dad over for speeding near Rifle, Colorado.

"Who's Willard Cooper?" the patrolman asked after he'd examined the registration.

Dad pointed sheepishly to the backseat. "He is." Willard had been emancipated. Dad had signed the Skylark back over to him.

Willard and Dad started acting like kids who'd never been out of Stampede. They wanted to climb Pike's Peak, buy souvenirs in Kit Carson, and stop in Russell, Kansas to find Bob Dole. Willard, of course, had to mail postcards to Edda from every town. We'd sit in front of post offices with the engine idling, helping him spell words like *fervent* and *voluptuous*. We were his thesaurus. Dad even lent him lines from Yeats.

"She wants to mark our trip on the globe," Willard said.

At rest stops, Dad and Willard started racing the dogs to the pet area and worked on their retrieving skills with a ragged tennis ball Dad had found. I was the one who had to coax them back into the car. Just as you could tell by the way someone held a baby whether or not they'd raised kids, you could tell Dad had grown up with dogs the way he knew how to rub them so they'd roll over on their backs and beg him to keep doing it. But he could also be firm and he scolded them if they jumped out of the car before he said okay. They seemed to love him for that too. I'd catch him palming pieces of his sandwich, slipping it to them in the backseat, and letting them lick off his fingers.

At Topeka, we left the interstate and headed north to take the path less traveled. "We've got to get in the mood for the river," Dad said, "and away from those little reflectors that shoot at your tires when you veer across the lane." While Dad drove and Willard slept, I read passages from *A Portrait of the Artist* out loud and asked Dad to explain them to me. It was better than talking to his brother Seamus. I learned about his affection for the Jesuits, how they'd encouraged him to become a priest just like his mother had. "You just grip the bedpost at night if you have impure thoughts, they told me." But I was relieved to hear of his reservations. "I kept imagining doing some horribly scandalous thing and being drummed out of the order. I felt dirty next to their aspirations for me." Of Dad, I was beginning to think the same thing that Samuel Clemens's mom had said about her son. *He's a well of truth, but you can't bring it up in one bucket.*

Crossing through Cameron, Chillecoth, Meadville, Wheeling, and other small towns in Missouri that didn't look that different from Stampede, we did word associations, which I liked because there were no wrong answers and no commentary. Each word was the trigger for the next one.

Dad: "Sign of the cross."
Me: "Guilt."
Him: "Sweat."
Me: "Crotch."
Him: "Humm, athletic supporter."
Me: "Penis."
Him: "Pig."

Me: "Chauvinist."
Him: "Chaucer."
Me: "Tales."
Him: "Pony."
Me: "Sunset."
Him: "Romance."
Me: "Impossible."

I tried to figure out why the chemistry was different, why I wasn't feeling overwhelmed by him, and decided it was because we were meeting on neutral space. Not the interstate highway or the cab of the Skylark, but an imaginary space out there that neither one of us was used to visiting called childhood.

At Shelbine, Missouri, Dad splurged and pulled into the full service pumps at a Texaco. We sat there while Willard walked and watered the dogs. A high school girl scrubbed the bugs off our windshield, and I popped the question that had been bugging me since reading John Carlisle's will. "Whose idea was the adoption, Dad?"

He raised his eyebrows and puffed his cheeks and I wondered if he was going to sanitize his answer so as not to offend me. "It wasn't that simple." He studied the remains of a yellowish-green bug on the windshield. "Of course, your mom was intrigued by the idea and, well, it seemed like the right thing to do."

"You were skeptical."

I knew I'd stumbled into a room where I didn't belong because his face tightened and he put his hands on the top of the steering wheel and pushed himself back against the seat. I noticed he'd started wearing his wedding ring again on this trip, a simple gold band. "I just wanted to make sure it was best for everyone. Especially you." I tried to imagine the debate that must have transpired between them eighteen years ago. I remembered Seamus telling me how Mom was such a Bohemian. When I had asked him what that meant, he said, "She didn't give a whit about china patterns." "So? Neither does my dad," I answered, and he said, "Yeah, but your dad respects people who do," and I kind of understood.

I waited until the girl had finished squeegeeing the soap off my side of the window. "Why couldn't Mom have a baby on her own?"

"We tried," he said. "Fertility drugs, sperm tests, the works. It wasn't meant to be. Then the situation with Ashley presented itself."

"What did Ashley think about it?"

"The family had already decided she had to give up the baby. We met her in Minneapolis, just before you were born. It felt very awkward, like we were window shopping. Everything was hush-hush. The Carlisles didn't want anyone to know she'd conceived a child out of wedlock. She was sixteen."

"That's younger than me."

"She was gifted, smart as a whip. That's why the family sent her away to a prep school for girls in St. Cloud. That was the Carlisle way." The way he said it I knew Dad didn't agree, and I wondered whether he knew what kind of abuse Ashley had been subjected to by her mother. "But things didn't go well. She had the baby, dropped out of high school, and then bummed around until she finally fell through a crack somewhere."

"Who was the father?"

"Ashley would never tell."

"He must have been tall and skinny."

Dad cupped his hand on my bony knee. "Oh, come on, you've got a model's build."

"Do you think losing her child set her off somehow?"

Dad took a deep breath and gripped the steering wheel again. "I didn't think so then, but maybe it did."

My paranoia over the adoption seemed a pittance in comparison to Ashley's plight. She didn't have any more choice in the matter than I did. If I was the result of a pinhole in a condom or no condom at all, at least someone had stepped forward to claim the mistake. Ashley didn't have a savior. "I guess I had no business prying into all this."

"The hell. We probably had no business keeping it a secret."

It was late when we arrived in Hannibal, but Willard insisted we find Mark Twain's boyhood home, which wasn't hard because of all the signs. We parked in front of the home, on Hill Street, and Willard and the dogs burst out of the car. I was beginning to realize there was a method to Willard's exuberance. Every chance, he'd made sure Dad and I were alone.

The Mark Twain home was a rather small, two-story frame house and, even though it was closed, Dad and I walked over to it. I leaned against a tall wood fence that connected to a corner of the house and looked heavenward. They said that Halley's Comet flashed across the world the night Samuel Clemens was born, scattering stardust through the skies, and it didn't come back again until the night he died, seventy-five years later. I kept looking for a signal in the air, something particularly evocative, something that would have inspired a man to write his brains out, but everything looked so normal. Even allowing for the fact that the sidewalks and asphalt were probably added later, I was still struck with how much it was *like* every other town I'd ever seen.

"Are you disappointed?" Dad said.

"A little bit. Maybe Willard shouldn't have seen this."

"It teaches you something about the power of imagination," he said. As we'd gotten closer to Hannibal, Dad had explained how Mark Twain was a newspaper man before he ever turned literary. He worked for his brother Orion on the *Hannibal Journal*, a weekly they had to move into their house to keep alive. It finally went dead broke when cows wandered into the house and ate the type rollers.

There was a streetlight almost directly overhead that buzzed, reminding me of the crickets in the field next to the double billboards. I kept thinking of Mom and how she was supposed to have ended up here with Willard and that made me flash for the umpteenth time on the Jacuzzi and then I thought of something worse than dying and that was the prospect of living short. In all the ordinary days when Mom and Willard had lived in the same town they could have said anything to each other, gone anywhere together, come to Hannibal, but they'd busied themselves in their lives and let the sand run out of the hourglass. I was feeling the pain of distance, from the biological parents I never knew, from Mom, and even from the dad who was standing by the fence with me.

We gawked around, staring at the stars, neither one of us able to crown the moment with the right words and I wondered if that's the way it was between him and Mom. One of the reasons marriage had never appealed to me was the prospect of being stuck in the same room night after night with the same person and having nothing to say to each other for the rest of your lives.

"You're being kind of quiet," he said.

"Dealing with my demons, I guess."

"Anyone I know?"

"I was missing Mom."

"Me too."

"Really?"

"Why do you believe me when I tell you the Jesuits made me grip the brass bedpost at night, but you don't believe a word of what I say about your mother and me?"

"I guess it's because I didn't see you gripping the bedpost the way I saw you and Mom avoiding each other."

His voice was rigid. "I gave her freedom. That's what I thought she wanted. Our marriage was a series of compromises like everyone else's. I wanted to go to Chicago or New York and work with one of the big newspapers, and she wanted to be near her parents. And she wanted you to grow up some place wholesome. Without weirdos. I figured I'd just work harder to be noticed in a place like Stampede, find something amongst the family reunions, wedding anniversaries, and spelling bees that could be elevated to a story I could be proud of. That was my beat, but it's funny. Your mom didn't want to have anything to do with everyday truth. She wanted to imagine a more fascinating place than the one we lived in. She wouldn't move out of

Stampede, but she wanted to paint the world from there. Jungian archetypes. Screech owls. Pileated woodpeckers that looked like Roman Catholic cardinals. Samuel Clemens with a paint brush."

Like so many things, I'd had this one wrong too. I'd thought it was Dad who'd made us stay there and forced his purgatory onto Mom, making her the caged bird. I'd never appreciated or even much noticed her nesting instincts. "Was it different before I came along?"

"None of it was your fault, if that's what you mean."

"Really, I want to know."

He picked at the slivers in the fence boards. "You mean were we passionate as lovers? I thought she was the sexiest creature alive. The earth moved when we made love. Is that what you wanted to know?"

"I wish I could have felt it."

"But it changed. That's when you separate the pretenders from the real players, when your wife becomes more fascinated with your boss than you."

I looked around to make sure Willard and the dogs weren't about to pounce on us, but they were nowhere to be seen. "Were you ever unfaithful to her?"

"Wow. Why am I surprised you'd ask?"

"I'm sorry. You don't have to answer."

"I don't have to, but I'm *going* to," he said. Mark Twain's home was twenty feet beyond us and Dad's head was framed against the light reflecting off the whitewashed siding. I could have tossed a stone through one of the paned windows and maybe that's what I should have done to stop him from answering me. "I was never unfaithful to her with another woman. It wasn't purity of heart, believe me. But I was unfaithful in one very unforgivable way." He bowed his head and pawed his shoe along the ground. "I stopped being as curious about her life as I was about my own. I stopped wondering who she was and where she was heading."

"She didn't make it easy for you."

"You mean her relationship with John Carlisle?"

"Yeah."

"I was obsessed with it, but I figured, worst case, she'd cheated on me and I still loved her."

"Were you really going to print the story about her and Carlisle?"

He pushed his back against the fence and spread his arms in a crucifixion. "Only if I had the guts to print the rest of the story."

"What do you mean?"

"I was there too."

"At Carlisle's?"

"We'd gone to his place to celebrate the nine-hundredth issue of the *Herald* or some foolish thing. John wanted to have champagne and make a big deal of it and we'd all had too much to drink." Dad was scraping the arch of his shoe against one of the planks in the fence. "We'd had a terrible argument that day. I told her people were talking. I wanted her to come home, but she took off her clothes and climbed into the tub. She begged me to join her. 'Stay, Tom, have some fun,' she said."

"Did you stay?"

His voice dropped and I could hear the air go out of him. "I left . . . I just left."

His words hung in the air like a big spider. He was probably waiting for me to call him a coward, but I couldn't. Then I felt the fence moving, like someone had a hold of the posts and was shaking them, but it was Dad, sobbing into the jacket he'd pulled up over his face.

I pushed myself against him. "You didn't know."

"I should have stayed . . ."

I put my arm around him and the weight of his back trapped my hand flat against the fence. He kept the coat over his face. The misery of no second chances. "Dad, stop beating yourself up. Don't you see what happened? Nothing was going on with Mom and John Carlisle. He was gay. He was also my uncle. But he was abandoned. You know what a sucker Mom was for orphans. That's why she picked me." I could feel his arms moving against my back. "Her last words to you were beautiful. It's what I would have imagined her saying when she fell in love with you in Chicago and you were nursing her back to health. She wanted you. It never went away. You were still her Irish poet." He was definitely squeezing me now and the corner of my mouth was pressed against his jacket so hard that I wasn't even sure he could hear me. "I know I'm not making sense. You need a Tom Scanlon in your corner, someone to see the truth in this, and all you've got is me." I'd never been held onto like that and I realized that's what he must have felt like to Mom.

Our conversation had knocked the wind out of him, and he was gradually coming out of it, regaining his bearings. He took a couple of deep breaths and let go of me. I stepped to the side and he pulled out a handkerchief and blew his nose. I knew he was probably embarrassed at having lost it. That wasn't his natural state.

We walked along the white plank fence toward the house, and then started around the house. Neither one of us said anything. I would have welcomed the chaos of Willard and the dogs just then, but they'd probably disappeared into the neighborhood, looking for garbage cans and pee spots from other dogs. I knew we weren't done. It was my turn and if I'd had a piece of paper and a pen, I would have just scratched something out and handed it to him. His first bad poem.

"Dad?"

"Yeah." His voice was normal again.

"This comes under the category of confessions, I guess. Maybe letdowns." I half expected him to say there were no bad confessions, to tell me we'd had enough for one night, but he just kept treading the perimeter of the house like a sentry listening for suspicious noises. "I know I didn't turn out the way you and Mom had hoped. She was so beautiful and womanly and I'm so clunky and genderless."

"Genderless?"

"You know. Sexually ambiguous."

He let out an exasperated breath. "Sexually what?"

I must have been mumbling. Maybe he thought I'd said *sexually ambitious*, and he was going to launch into his sermon on free will, and I'd have to stop him and tell him it was worse than that. "Mom always wanted me to find a nice man, but . . . I'm not going to. I can't."

"Oh, come on. You're still young."

"Dad. I don't *want* to find a man. I'm not that way." There, I'd said it. I kicked a piece of paper in the dewy grass and it stuck to my shoe. "It wasn't like I didn't try. All my life I wanted something in me to be like her. The sexiness, the artistry, but there was nothing." I wasn't crying, but my insides were heaving and I was feeling chilled along my front where I was still sweaty from being against him. "She'd be so disappointed in me."

I watched his shoes stop in the grass. "You're wrong about that part," he said.

"You can't say that, Dad. You didn't hear some of the things she said to me."

"She proved it, didn't she? You just said so. Through John Carlisle. She wasn't disappointed in *him*."

Something broke open in me when he said that, but I knew what it was. Mom had said I'd be bathed in light like Aphrodite. That had turned out to be hyperbole. Mine was more like the glimmer from a faraway comet, a happening that I had no control over and still only dimly understood.

I looked over at Dad. He was rubbing his face hard with the insides of his hands. I waited until he stopped. "What about you, Dad? Are you disappointed?"

He hesitated, maybe he was letting his eyes readjust. "How can I be disappointed? That's who you are. It's just going to take me a while to get used to the idea. My Irish didn't prepare me for girls like you and your mother."

The next morning, after celebrating our arrival with a sit-down meal of hotcakes and country sausages at a cafe in downtown Hannibal, we went upriver until we found a low bank where we could walk right next to the Mississippi. We were well off the highway so we just let the dogs go free and, like rainwater, they drained down the slope until they hit the river, and waded out. It was a working river, muddy and powerful like a tugboat, and I thought I could detect a faint smell of diesel. I threw a stick in to make sure it was moving, and it sure was, flowing toward New Orleans like geologic time. Across from where we stood, there was an island in the middle of the river and I wondered if it was Jackson Island.

"Hey, Willard," I said, "there's where Huck and Jim boarded the floating house and found the naked dead man."

He put his hand over his eyes and squinted. "He was naked?"

We could have gone to Bemidji, Minnesota and tried to run the whole two thousand miles of the river, cruising past Minneapolis, but I wasn't sure the paddle wheelers went up that far. Besides, I knew Willard would enjoy the business end of the river more, for the same reason he respected the business end of a socket wrench.

Willard found a dilapidated raft along the shore, sun-bleached planks hammered onto three slimy logs by bent-over spikes. "Piper, here's what we've been looking for." I knew what he meant. The makeshift raft represented the romance of the river, an amalgam of dream and practicality. "Let's put something on it and send it down."

I sat on the ground next to the raft and watched the subtle patterns of current form in the water like the creases in newsprint. Willard soon lost interest in the raft and moved along the shore exploring for more treasures. I watched him and Dad throw sticks for the dogs and make them sit for pictures on the bank. Grown men with boyish hearts. I'd never thought of Dad as a caretaker, but there he was, with his pack. That's also why John Carlisle had stayed around Stampede, to watch over me, to make sure I didn't fall between the cracks like his sister had. Willard had said it. *We're all just strays waiting to be found.*

I was also thinking about the phone call to the Prosecutor's office that Dad told me about after breakfast. The Spigot Lake kids had recanted their statements. It was small town hysteria just the way he'd figured it all along. I told him that Dirk's accusations were false too, something else Dad had always known. He'd written it up that way in his own investigation of the charges, the story that never ran. I was relieved to know that John Carlisle was innocent of the heinous acts he'd been accused of, but now I was deeply saddened at the way I'd treated him, how I'd missed the opportunity to share in his grief over Mom's death. I'd mistaken an ally for an adversary.

Although I hadn't told Dad yet, I'd also decided what to do with the Carlisle house. It was so obvious I didn't know why I hadn't seen it immediately — maybe it was because I kept thinking of it as a place I had to live — but I was going to sell the house and give the money to Dad so he could rebuild the newspaper. He and Seamus could run it like the Clemens brothers had run the *Hannibal Journal*. If that didn't suit him, he could use it as traveling money and knock on the doors of some of the big dailies. After all, he was the one who'd earned it, covering for John Carlisle all those years. All I wanted out of the house were Mom's paintings. If Dad refused the money, I was going to give it to Willard and Edda for their halfway house for cats and dogs.

I pulled a crumpled paper sack out of my jacket, opened it, and stuck my hand inside. It was something I'd saved for no particular reason and dragged along on the trip: a sack of hair, the hair I'd shaved off after Mom died. It was weighing me down. When I pulled a fistful of it out the mouth of the sack, the breeze caught a few tufts and they wafted downstream like dandelion seed. It was soft and compressed easily when I stuffed it back inside and rolled the sack into a package the size of a leftover half-sandwich. I had to let go of something.

I wedged the sack between two of the cross-pieces on the raft, kicked off my shoes and waded into the river. The silt on the bottom squished between my toes and my hair had grown back far enough that I could feel it tickling my forehead. I dislodged the raft from the tangle of brush and pulled it out next to me. I thought of how Rozene had helped open something powerful in me and I could hear

Mom's voice in the back of my head. *Well, honey, it's not what I had in mind, but at least you've managed to save your confidence as long as your virginity.*

When I told Dad I didn't know how I'd ever get used to the idea of being a Carlisle, he said, "You'll never plow a field by turning it over in your mind." And I knew he was right.

The water clapped against the undersides of the planks. I pushed the end of the raft under water and it popped right back up, the water beading off the dry membrane of the boards. Everything was working. I shoved it as hard as I could toward the center of the channel where it rocked and bobbed and finally settled into the drift of the river. Knee-high in the water, the current flowed between my legs as I watched until the raft disappeared on the river's horizon.